The Unforgetting Heart: AN ANTHOLOGY OF SHORT STORIES BY AFRICAN AMERICAN WOMEN (1859-1993)

EDITED BY ASHA KANWAR

aunt lute books

SAN FRANCISCO

First Edition
10-9-8-7-6-5-4-3-2-1

Aunt Lute Books
P.O. Box 410687
San Francisco, CA 94141

Cover and Text Design: Pamela Wilson Design Studio

Cover Art: Ann Grifalconi
From *Flyaway Girl* by Ann Grifalconi. Copyright © 1992 by Ann Grifalconi.
By permission of Little, Brown and Company.

Text Art: Bridget Goodman

Typesetting: Debra DeBondt

Production: Jayna Brown
Vita Iskandar
Chris Lymbertos
María Luisa Márquez
Moire Martin
Renée E. Stephens
Kathleen Wilkinson

Production Support:
Lisa Kahaleole Chang Hall
Melissa Levin
Fabienne McPhail Grant

Printed in the U.S.A. on acid-free paper

Library of Congress Cataloging-in-Publication Data

The Unforgetting heart : an anthology of short stories by African American women,
1859–1992 / edited by Asha Kanwar. — 1st ed.
    p.   cm.
    ISBN 1-879960-31-1 (alk. paper) : $19.95. — ISBN 1-879960-30-3
(pbk. : alk. paper) : $9.95
    1. Short stories, American—Afro-American authors. 2. Short stories,
American—Women authors. 3. Women—United States—Fiction.
4. Afro-American women—Fiction. 5. Afro-Americans—Fiction.
I. Kanwar, Asha.
PS647.A35U53   1993
813'.01089287—dc20   93-3240
                                                              CIP

We would like to thank the following for permission to reprint copyrighted materials:

The Lesson ©1972 by Toni Cade Bambara. From *Gorilla, My Love and Other Stories.* Reprinted with permission from the author.

Johnnieruth ©1987 by Becky Birtha. From *Lover's Choice*, Seal Press, Seattle. Reprinted with permission from Seal Press.

In The Laundry Room ©1984 by Alice Childress. reprinted with permission from Flora Roberts Inc.

Croon ©1993 by Wanda Coleman. From work in progress, *Jazz & Twelve O'Clock Tales*, to be published by Black Sparrow Press.

The Life You Live (May Not Be Your Own) ©1987 by J. California Cooper. Reprinted with permission from St. Martin's Press.

Fifth Sunday ©1985 by Rita Dove. From *Fifth Sunday* by Rita Dove, Callaloo Fiction Series, Lexington, KY 1985 & University Press of Virginia, Charlottesville, VA 1990. Reprinted with permission from the author.

The Library ©1970 by Nikki Giovanni. Reprinted with permission from the author.

Mom Luby and the Social Worker ©1968 by Kristin Hunter. Reprinted with permission from Don Congdon Associates, Inc.

Isis ©1924 by Zora Neale Hurston. Reprinted with permission from Lucy Hurston.

Brooklyn ©1961 by Paule Marshall. Reprinted with permission from Feminist Press.

A Happening in Barbados ©1968 by Louise Meriwether. Reprinted with permission from Louise Meriwether.

Ma'Dear ©1987 by Terry McMillan. From *Breaking Ice: An Anthology of Contemporary African American Fiction*. Reprinted by permission of the author.

Kiswana Browne ©1980 by Gloria Naylor. Reprinted with permission from Viking, Penguin.

Doby's Gone ©1972 by Ann Petry. From *Miss Muriel and Other Stories*. Reprinted with permission from Russell & Volkening, agents.

After Saturday Night Comes Sunday ©1971 by Sonia Sanchez. Reprinted with permission from the author.

Emerald City: Third & Pike ©1992 by Charlotte Watson Sherman. First published in *Killing Color*, Calyx Books. Reprinted with permission of Calyx Books.

The Funeral ©1967 by Ann Allen Shockley. Reprinted with permission from the author.

Nineteen Fifty-Five ©1971 by Alice Walker. Reprinted with permission from Harcourt Brace & Co.

Publisher's Foreword

Aunt Lute undertook this project with Asha Kanwar because we think the collection, as a whole, fills an important niche in fiction by African-American women. Because of our commitment to both developing and rediscovering women's writing, we are especially excited to reprint historical works that have previously been obtainable only in limited editions.

Of the early stories in this book, published before 1940, most reside in the public domain. We have tried to reprint them here in the forms in which they were originally published. In this spirit, all errata have been retained. This is in an effort to accurately reflect their historical context and reduce the level of modern interference and interpretation.

Acknowledgements

My appreciation and gratitude are due to the wonderful people (in alphabetical order) whose generosity and support made this book possible:

Mary Barratt, Jayna Brown, Dick Hernstadt, Kathy Hickok, Anjana Kanwar, Susan Koppelman, Vandana Kothari, Diana Lachatanere, Chris Lymbertos, Frank Moorer, Dick and Dianne Mumm, Joan Pinkvoss, Dale Ross, Sonia Sanchez, Ann Allen Shockley, Carlie and Gary Tartakov, Nancy Tepper and Verda Williams.

Arti, Nova and Anne
Sisters Under the Skin

Rosanne G. Potter, my Sister and support
and
Bill McCarthy, friend and guru.

Table of Contents

The Unforgetting Heart

The Context

> I write about some of the things
> I love. But have no civilized
> articulation for the things I
> hate. I proudly love being a
> Negro woman—it's so involved
> and interesting.
>
> *Anne Spencer*

The publication in the early 1970's of major books such as Alice Walker's *The Third Life of Grange Copeland* (1970), Toni Cade Bambara's anthology *The Black Woman* (1970), Maya Angelou's *I Know Why the Caged Bird Sings* (1970), Louise Meriwether's *Daddy Was A Number Runner* (1971) and Toni Morrison's *The Bluest Eye* (1972), inaugurated the New Black Renaissance of which the chief protagonists were women. The revolutionary character of this Renaissance was in contradistinction to the bourgeois nature of the Harlem Renaissance (1917-30) dominated by the stellar figures of Alain Locke, Langston Hughes, Claude McKay, James Weldon Johnson, and Jean Toomer, among others. While Zora Neale Hurston, Nella Larsen, Jessie Fauset and Pauline Hopkins wrote during this period, their work did not receive the attention given to the Black male writers. It is only in the seventies that the trickle of women's writing spread into a formidable stream in the 'mighty river of our race literature.'[1]

The roots of this literary outpouring lie in the Civil Rights, Black Power and Women's Liberation movements of the sixties, the teachings of Martin Luther King, Jr. and the revolutionary rhetoric of Malcolm X.

However, Black women's relationship to these movements was highly problematic, caught as it was between the sexism of the Black Power movement and the rampant racism of the predominantly white Women's Liberation struggle. That the feminist movement is divided along the color line is clear from the fact that the issues of racism identified in the 1981 National Women's Studies Association Conference[2] were still alive and unresolved eleven years later at the 1992 NWSA Conference. Similarly, Black women's subordination and marginalization by Black men in the Civil Rights, Black Power and Black Panther movements made them reassess their political position. As the Black feminists of the Combahee River Collective stated:

> It was our experience and disillusionment within these liberation movements, as well as experience on the periphery of the white male left, that led to the need to develop a politics that was anti-racist, unlike those of white women, and anti-sexist, unlike those of Black and white men.[3]

This dual dispossession has given Black women a special perspective, one that is ably articulated by June Jordan.

> As a Black woman I exist as part of the powerless and as part of the majority peoples of the world. I am powerless compared to any man because women are kept powerless by men. I am powerless compared to anyone white because Black and Third World peoples are kept powerless by whites. And because I am Black and a woman I am the most victimized of the powerless. Yet I am the majority because women constitute the majority gender. I am the majority because Black and Third World peoples constitute the majority of human beings. In short, I am a member of the most powerless majority on the planet.[4]

Being 'a member of the most powerless majority on the planet' subjects the woman of color to a variety of oppressions on the basis of sex, race, class, caste and sexual preference. All these factors conspire in subtle ways to keep the woman in her place, as 'de mule uh de world.'[5]

And it has been a more acceptable role for the oppressor that a Black woman wield a hoe rather than a pen. Traditionally assigned service positions—social workers, teachers, nurses—Black women writers have had to struggle far in excess of 'having a room of one's own and five hundred guineas a year.' In a recent interview, Sonia Sanchez recounted that in the 1950's, when she told her counsellor at Hunter College that she wanted to be a writer, the response was a curt, 'You people don't write.'[6]

How then did Black women, writing in the late nineteenth century, negotiate the ideological and the material barriers that enforced the hierarchies within their social system? Let us consider the case of Alice Moore Dunbar. Reviewing *The Goodness of St. Rogue and other Stories,* 'M.B.B.' praises the "attractive volume" and adds: 'For the reader of Paul Laurence Dunbar—and who among our own readers is not one?—there is a special interest in the dedication of his wife's book: "To my best Comrade, my husband".'[7] Instead of focusing on the writer's achievement, 'M.B.B.' seizes upon her relationship to Paul Lawrence Dunbar and implicitly reduces her work to the level of an interesting curiosity. Or let us take the example of Nella Larsen who was effectively silenced after being charged with plagiarism when her story 'Sanctuary' was published in the January 1930 issue of *Forum*.[8]

That Black women writers faced pernicious social and economic pressures is further supported by Zora Neale Hurston's suppliant letter to her white benefactress: 'I really need a pair of shoes....My big toe is about to burst out of my right shoe so I must do something.'[9] For an established writer to beg for a pair of shoes, or to face the ignominious accusations of having "abused" a ten-year old boy, or to die penniless and destitute is a sad comment on the cruelty of an unjust society in which a Black woman's status is, at best, tenuous.

And yet these intrepid women continued to write. What sustained them through all their humiliations? According to Angela Davis: 'Their awareness of their endless capacity for hard work imported to them a confidence in their ability to struggle for themselves, their families and their people.'[10]

Writing in itself was and is, for them, a political act, an act of transgression, a "talking back" in their own voices, of their own experiences, informed by a special consciousness forged out of four hundred years of oppression. As such, there are certain features common in the writing of Black women. For one thing, and most critics agree, 'If there is a single distinguishing feature of the literature of Black women...it is this, their literature is about Black women.'[11]

Another distinctive feature of Black women's writing is that while 'most older Black male writers deny any Black influence at all—or eagerly claim white paternity—Black female authors often claim descent from other Black women literary ancestors, such as Zora Neale Hurston and Ann Petry.'[12] Alice Walker's resurrection of Zora Neale Hurston exemplifies this sense of 'connectedness' with one's tradition. Toni Morrison's support and encouragement, as Editor at Random House, of younger writers like Gloria Naylor, Angela Davis and others is again specific to a nurturing tradition and sense of sisterhood found among Black women writers. Critics and academics such as Barbara Christian, Hazel V. Carby, Deborah McDowell and Mari Evans, among others, have not only directed critical attention to the works of contemporary Black writers but have also resurrected long-forgotten foremothers.

In fact this nurturing extends beyond a community of gender to the community at large. It is a love that underlies all social revolutions. As Sonia Sanchez puts it:

When we're trying to effect change, we must always maintain a sense of humanity and a sense of love, because when we get to what we want and we are incapable of love...we would be just like the people we're trying to displace or replace. So the idea of love is always important, the idea of humanity is always important, even when we're studying ideology.[13]

The Form and Content

> Stories are important. They keep us alive....
> How it was; how it be. Passing it along in the relay....
>
> *Toni Cade Bambara*

Stories are important, and yet critical attention, along with the corporate sectors of publishing and academia, has always favored the novel as *the* literary genre, relegating the short story to the status of a 'cinderella of Black fiction.'[14] Has this marginalization something to do with the fact that 'the short story has offered itself to...women, blacks—writers who for one reason or another have not been part of the ruling "narrative" or epistemological/experiential framework of their society'?[15] Or does this ghettoization result from the short story being seen as a 'popular,' as opposed to 'highbrow' form?

The development of the short story genre is closely tied to the industry of magazine publication. The fact that the first short story ever to be published by an African-American woman appeared in the Black *Anglo-African Magazine* (1859) indicates the limited venues that Black women writers had for publishing their short stories. And though there were a few outlets in late nineteenth century magazines,[16] it was not until the advent of the magazines *Crisis* and *Opportunity,* with their short story contests, that the form began to gain some visibility and prominence.

And yet, given the limited access for publication, many Black women continued to write short stories. Why is this? Is it that, as suggested earlier, the short story has always attracted 'submerged population groups'?[17] Especially because economic pressures on writers reduce time and opportunity for writing? Or could it be that since it is a relatively new genre, it does not have an intimidating tradition of 'great masters'? It may be that this newness and disconnectedness is exactly what appeals to some Black women writers—'the open-ended qualities of the short story may offer a transforming potential, an ability to ask the unspoken question, to raise a new subject matter.'[18]

Furthermore, could it be that this propensity for Black women writers to 'ask the unspoken question' or raise 'a new subject matter' accounts for the inadequate representation of their short stories in anthologies? In Alain Locke's classic *The New Negro* (1925) Zora Neale Hurston's 'Spunk' is the single story by a woman. And in *Best Short Stories by Afro American Writers 1925-1950* (1950), edited by Nick Aaron Ford and H.L. Faggett, of the forty stories featured, only three are by women. In Langston Hughes' *The Best Short Stories by Negro Writers* (1967), the number increases to nine out of the forty-seven stories in the collection. And in *By and About Women* (1973), edited by Beth Kline Scheiderman, there is token representation of two Black women in a tally of nineteen stories.

It is not that Black women did not write enough stories; it is simply that not until we are well into the New Black Renaissance did their works begin to attract the attention they deserved. Mary Helen Washington's anthologies, *Black-Eyed Susans* (1975), *Midnight Birds* (1980) and *Invented Lives* (1987), brought Black women's fiction to a wide and eager readership. Constructed thematically, these excellent anthologies include short stories and excerpts from novels. Under the editorship of Henry Louis Gates, Jr., Oxford University Press brought out the invaluable Schomburg Library of Nineteenth Century Black Women Writers. The Black Periodical Literature Project directed by Henry Louis Gates, Jr. has catalogued its research in *Black Literature 1827-1940* (Chadwyck-Healy, 1990), thus opening up a whole treasure of short stories, originally published in magazines, that would otherwise have been banished to obscurity.

In compiling *The Unforgetting Heart*, I decided to restrict myself to short stories, rather than taking up excerpts from novels. While excerpts from novels allow the editor to include the best fictional sample by a writer, taking a piece out of context often leaves the reader dissatisfied. 'Brooklyn' from Paule Marshall's collection *Soul Clap Hands and Sing*, though termed a novella by the author, works as a short story, whereas Octavia Butler's excellent science fiction does not. On the other hand, 'Kiswana Browne,' though integral to Gloria Naylor's *The Women of Brewster Place: A Novel in Seven Stories*, also succeeds as a separate piece.

Another consideration was to include a wide range of writers, familiar names such as Alice Walker, Toni Cade Bambara and Terry McMillan as well as lesser-known writers like Ruth D. Todd or Adeline F. Ries. Moreover, not all the writers included here are known primarily as writers of short stories. Writers like Alice Walker and Zora Neale Hurston will be better remembered for their novels. Frances Harper's novel *Iola Leroy* has earned her a lasting name in the field of letters. Sonia Sanchez and Nikki Giovanni are poet-revolutionaries first, having written only the occasional short story. Yet each writer included here has made a tranformational contribution with her story.

The stories were also selected on the basis of their social, historical and cultural relevance so that the reader can get a synoptic view of the diverse and complex dimensions of the African-American experience. While individualism is the organizing force of Western culture, African-American culture forms a basis in collective destiny, bound by historical experience. This solidarity and support between members of the community is a hallmark of African-American life. And in the center of this community is the Black woman, intensely humane, an ordinary and multi-faceted human being with the courage to look her failings and sufferings in the eye.

The chronological sequence of the stories does not simply introduce the writers over the years but gives an overview of the development and change in the concerns of these writers which reflect the changing culture of a society. Frances Harper's protagonist in 'The Two Offers' is a white middle-class woman and the story is aracial. However, it is a feminist critique of the role of woman vis-à-vis marriage and the family. Independence is better than 'an ill-assorted marriage' and the destiny of a woman exceeds society's restrictive roles of wife and mother. Harper believed that 'the true aim of female education should be not a development of one or two, but all the faculties of the human soul, because no perfect womanhood is developed by imperfect culture,' an idea that goes back to eighteenth century feminist Mary Wollstonecraft.

This feminist concern is also found in 'Tony's Wife,' a poignant story of sexual oppression and material and emotional exploitation. As bell hooks has said, 'Nineteenth century Black women were more aware of sexist oppression than any other female group in American society.'[19]

This awareness was mediated within the restrictive framework of literary and social conventions. The heroine could either be white or a beautiful mulatta with magnolia skin, violet eyes and raven black hair. The octoroon in 'A Dash for Liberty' has 'long black ringlets, finely-chiselled mouth and well-rounded chin, upon the marbled skin veined by her master's blood,—representative of two races,—to which did she belong'? 'The Octoroon's Revenge' features 'a beautiful girl....with masses of silken hair of a raven blackness, and with eyes large and dreamy, of a deep violet blue.' Fannie Barrier Williams creates a similar creature in 'After Many Days,' whom she describes as having 'a complexion of dazzling fairness with the tint of the rose in her cheeks, and the whole face lighted by deeply glowing violet eyes.' These descriptions give us an idea of the commonly valorized image of beauty within a romantic tradition. Black was still not considered beautiful and white readers 'could identify human feeling, humanness, only if it came in a white or nearwhite body.…"Fairness" was and is the standard of Euro-American femininity.'[20]

As we move into the Harlem Renaissance the images of women begin to change. Mary Elizabeth in Jessie Fauset's story of the same name is a 'small, weazened woman, very dark, somewhat wrinkled, and a model of self-possession.' This family resemblance is traceable in Larsen's 'Sanctuary' where Annie Poole is described as 'a tiny, withered woman…with a wrinkled face the color of old copper, framed by a crinkly mass of white hair.' By the 1960's there is a positive celebration of Blackness: in Louise Meriwether's 'A Happening in Barbados,' where we are told that 'our Black bodies on the white sand added to the munificence of colors'; and in Toni Cade Bambara's matter-of-fact description of Miss Moore in 'The Lesson': '…with nappy hair.…Black as hell.'

This change in image is closely related to the overall change in images of women in fiction from stereotype to character.[21] Aunt Lindy is a mammy-like figure who lives with her Uncle Tom husband in idyllic Arcadian surroundings reminiscent of the happy plantation myth. On the other hand, published twenty-four years later, Adeline F. Ries' powerful story 'Mammy' subverts the stereotype of the fat contented nurturing mammy, showing her resistance and pain.

A confidence in one's ethnicity is reflected in the use of language. The earlier stories are written in standard English occasionally ornamented with rural dialect. In the later stories, the language mirrors Black migrations to the North, evolving into the rapping/syncopated style of the inner city. These speech rhythms and innovative uses of language infuse a vitality and creativity to the writing of Black women. 'It was the wite/dude eyes she had once called em, half in jest, half seriously. They wuz begging now, along wid his mouth.…' This description from 'After Saturday Night Comes Sunday' captures the oral cadences of 'ebonics' or what linguists term Black English. As Frantz Fanon said in *Black Skins White Masks*, 'To speak means.…to assume a culture.…Every colonized people finds itself face to face with the language of the civilizing nation.…in every country of the world there are climbers, "the ones who forget who they are," and, in contrast to them, "the ones who remember where they came from."' [22] These Black women writers certainly remember their roots as their language is derived from the rich tradition of African cultures.

Of the thirty-two stories featured here, eleven are in first person narration. According to Henry Louis Gates, Jr., 'The impulse to testify, to chart the peculiar contours of the individual protagonist on the road to becoming, clearly undergirds even the fictional tradition of Black letters.…'[23]

The development of the short story genre indicates how the writers come to terms with their own identity, celebrating their Blackness, thus subverting the insidious thrust of racism. The earlier stories, rooted as they are in a "genteel tradition," often capitulate to mainstream perspectives on Black life and letters. This denial evolves into a feeling of nationalism, then protest, the militancy of the 1960's and then, in the 1970's, a coming to terms with their own identity as Black women.

As we move towards the twenty-first century, we notice yet another shift in the concerns of Black women writers. They take on the complexity of being a Black person in a racist society. Their focus now includes Black men and other women of color, as exemplified in the last selection of this anthology, Wanda Coleman's 'Croon.' While the stories in this anthology deal with different themes and cover a variety of forms, they help us to understand 'the complex interplay of ethnicity and gender, of racism and sexism—of how race becomes gendered and how gender becomes racialized—in American society.'[24]

The progression of these stories, then, is an oral history of Black women struggling to take what is rightfully theirs, even if it means wrenching it from those who would deny it. And for this struggle to bear fruit, it becomes imperative to forge coalitions with other women of color, not simply on the basis of identity but on the basis of shared concern.

The Struggle

> The thing I would like to impress upon every Afro-American leader
> is that no kind of action is ever going to bear fruit unless that action
> is tied with the overall international struggle.
>
> *Malcolm X*

The struggle of the African-American people has historically been closely related to the struggle of other oppressed people of the world. They have aligned themselves with the struggles of people in South Africa, India and elsewhere. The Indian struggle for independence, and particularly the nonviolence of Mahatma Gandhi, are well known to African Americans, especially during the Civil Rights movement and through the practices of Dr. Martin Luther King, Jr.

My major motivation in compiling these stories is to be able to translate them into Hindi so that readers in India will have access to the expressive culture of the African-American community in the United States, for though the contexts may differ, the concerns are similar.

There is even earlier historical evidence of the connection between the African-American and Indian struggles in W.E.B. DuBois' novel *The Dark Princess*

(Harcourt Brace, 1927) which tells the story of the love and solidarity between an African American and an Indian princess and how 'together they search a way of rebuilding the world across the color line.' (It is interesting to note that DuBois sent parts of the manuscript to the Indian freedom fighter Lala Lajpat Rai, asking him for comments and criticism, to which the latter responded in a letter from Calcutta, dated December 21, 1927.) But contemporary African Americans may be less familiar with an aspect of Indian life and culture that bears close comparison with their own situation in the United States: the Dalit community.

The word 'dalit' literally means the 'oppressed' and is a name that politically-aware 'untouchables' prefer to give themselves. 'Untouchable' was a name given to them by their masters for centuries—a denial of identity that is a familiar strategy of apartheid. The lowest in the caste hierarchy, the untouchables lived in segregation, had no access to education and were socially and economically exploited. The term 'Dalit' deals with social, political, economic and religious forms of oppression and includes 'Members of the Scheduled Castes and Tribes, neo-Buddhists, the working people, the landless and poor peasants, women....'[25] The very adaptation of the word is connected to African-American struggle. 'The word was coined out of the aspirations and struggles of our Black sisters and brothers in America.'[26]

One seventh of India's population are untouchables. Most of them, despite government efforts, still remain on the fringes of society—poor, homeless, exploited, unemployed, oppressed, illiterate. It was Gandhi who first brought the cause of 'untouchability' to international attention. However, the Dalit community was skeptical of his contribution as he had a reformist approach and wanted to uplift the untouchables within the framework of the caste system. The Dalit community's leader, Dr. B.R. Ambedkar, felt that only a destruction of the caste system could emancipate the outcastes. In 1956, in an attempt to opt out of this debilitating caste system, Ambedkar, along with 500,000 other untouchables, embraced the more egalitarian religion of Buddhism.

Frustration with ineffective government policies led to the formation of the Dalit Panthers in April 1972. Following the example of Huey Newton and Bobby Seale in America (1968), Raja Dhale and Namdeo Dhasal launched the party, acknowledging in their manifesto, 'Even in America, a handful of reactionary whites are exploiting the Negroes [sic]. To meet the force of reaction and remove this exploitation, the Black Panther movement grew....we claim a close relationship with this struggle.'[27]

At the root of this radical consciousness was the emergence of a new Dalit voice. Up to this point, other writers (Munshi Premchand, Mulk Raj Anand, etc.) had articulated the condition of India's oppressed. Now it was the oppressed themselves who were beginning to write. Short stories began to appear in the 1950's, but greater creativity was witnessed in the late 1960's moving quickly 'from protest to revolt to rebellion and revolution.'[28]

> These twisted fists won't loosen now
> The coming revolution won't wait for you
> We've endured enough
> Once the horizon is red
> What's wrong with keeping the door open?[29]

It is the struggle to live with dignity and honour that informs the themes of this poetry. Like African-American women, Dalit women are victims of a double oppression—gender and caste. Hira Bansode—in a touching poem that illustrates the overall amnesia in relation to women's contribution to society—highlights the oft-neglected role of Yashodhara, the wife of Prince Siddhartha:

> I am ashamed of the injustice
> You are not to be found
> In a single Buddhist vihara
> Were you really of no account?
> But wait—don't suffer so,
> I have seen your beautiful face,
> You are just between the closed eyelids of Siddhartha
> Yashu, just you.[30]

While there are contemporary Dalit women writers such as Kumud Pawade, Jyoti Langewar, Aruna Lokhande, Surekha Bhagat, Sugandha Shende and Asha Thorat, among others, the search for their 'mothers' gardens' is still to begin. The foremother of Dalit women writers is Muktabai who, as a young girl, read an essay on the problems and sufferings of untouchables in 1852. While the African-American house slave could still have access to literacy in liberal homes, the untouchables were denied entry into the homes of upper-caste Hindus. Access to education was the prerogative of caste Hindus, and 'If a Shudra [low caste person] listens to a recitation of the vedas [Hindu religious texts] his ears shall be filled with molten tin or lac. If he recites Vedic texts his tongue shall be cut out....'[31]

Like their African-American counterparts, Dalit writers are in search of their cultural identity. As Dr. J.M. Waghmare, a well-known Dalit literary critic, has pointed out: 'The experience of both is based on social and cultural inequality. Both write out of social commitment. The language of both is a language of cultural revolution.'[32] Dalit writing also has its roots in oral culture: folk songs, lullabies, wedding and work songs. In addition, writers from both cultures make use of non-standard language and autobiographical modes of expression.

Poet Jayne Cortez has shared a platform with Dalit poets in New York. J. California Cooper has dedicated her collection of short stories, entitled *The Matter is Life,* to 'Especially all the people of India who suffer under the word "Untouchable." You are not Untouchable. Consider the source.'[33] Baburao Bagul dedicated his book[34] to Martin Luther King, Jr. '…your war was for the liberation of humanity, to enhance the status of the human in this world.'

It is clear then that the Dalit movement has drawn support from its African-American brothers and sisters. By translating this anthology into Hindi, for an Indian readership, I hope to foreground our common concerns in the interests of greater collaboration between students of literature and culture. This anthology, in its Indian incarnation, has this additional charge and challenge.

The Title

Kings and Queens may have *their* crowns and welcome. What's there to *them?*—But the kind Aunt Phoebe wears—that different. She earned hers, Vic, earned them through many years and long of sorrow, and heartbreak and bitter, bitter tears. She bears with her the unforgetting heart.—And though they could take husband and children and sell them South, though she lost them in the body— Never a word of them, since—she keeps them always in her heart.— I knew, Vic, I know—and God who is good and God who is just touched her eyes, both of them and gave her blue crowns, beautiful ones, a crown for each. Don't you *see* she is of God's Elect?

The title for this collection was inspired by the ninety-year-old Aunt Phoebe from Angelina Weld Grimké's story 'Goldie.' She is the ancestor figure, the grandmother of African-American communities, the wise woman of the neighborhood whom people come to for direction. She holds the wisdom of and connection with the past, with which she sees into the future. She is the embodiment of African-American collective memory. Aunt Phoebe could be many of the fictional sisters of this book; she could well be Oya of 'Emerald City: Third and Pike' whose 'unforgetting heart' could 'feel all the broken dreams of my mama and my grandmama and her mama swell up and start pulsin in my blood memory….'

Finally, one has to wonder about the consequences of sending *The Unforgetting Heart* out into the world. Will this anthology empower Black women? Will it help white men and women become less racist, men less sexist? Will these stories help us think about the *causes* of racism and sexism? As for my own experience, the stories have spoken directly to me. For someone brought up on a staple diet of English literature where one is confronted not only with an alien tongue but also descriptions of an alien culture—where blue eyes and golden hair are celebrated—the Pecolas and Celies of African-American literature seem like kindred souls, reflecting my own identity, and crisis of identity, as a brown woman in a neo-colonial patriarchal society. The 'womanist' concerns in these stories are my concerns, and in the complex interplay of the aesthetic and the political, as well as the dynamics of race and gender, I come away with a feeling of affirmation that accompanies a powerful literary experience.

NOTES

1. Gertrude Mossell, qtd. in *The Works of Katherine Davis Chapman Tillman*, ed. Claudia Tate (New York: OUP, 1991), p. 32.

2. Chela Sandoval, "Feminism and Racism: A Report on the 1981 National Women's Studies Association Conference," in *Making Face, Making Soul*, ed. Gloria Anzaldúa (San Francisco: Aunt Lute Books, 1990), pp. 55–71.

3. "A Black Feminist Statement," in *This Bridge Called My Back*, ed. Cherrie Moraga and Gloria Anzaldúa (New York: Kitchen Table, 1983), p. 211.

4. "Where is the Love?" by June Jordan in *Making Face, Making Soul*, p. 174.

5. Zora Neale Hurston, *Their Eyes Were Watching God.* (New York: Negro University Press, 1969) p. 29.

6. Unpublished interview, December 8, 1992, Philadelphia.

7. *Southern Workman*, 1900: p. 187.

8. Marion Boyd in "Our Rostrum," *Forum*, April 1930.

9. Letter to Mrs. Mason dated April 27, 1937. Qtd. in introduction by Mary Helen Washington. *I Love Myself When I Am Laughing*, ed. Alice Walker (New York: Feminist Press, 1979), p. 13.

10. "The Black Woman's Role in the Community of Slaves," *Black Scholar*, December 1971: p. 11.

11. Mary Helen Washington, ed. *Invented Lives* (New York: Anchor, 1987), xxi.

12. Henry Louis Gates, Jr. *Reading Black, Reading Feminist.* (New York: Meridian, 1991), pp. 3–4.

13. Unpublished interview.

14. Peter Bruck, ed. *The Black American Short Story in The Twentieth Century* (Amsterdam: B.R. Gruner, 1977), p. 15.

15. Clare Hanson, ed. *Re-reading the Short Story* (London: Macmillan, 1989), p. 2.

16. Some of the black publications in which short stories were published were: *The A.M.E. Church Review, The Voice of the Negro, Colored Home Journal, Howard's Negro Magazine* and *The Black American Prose*. (Dubuque: William C. Brown Co., 1971), xv.

17. Frank O'Connor, *The Lonely Voice*. (New York: The World Publishing Co., 1963), p. 18.

18. Mary Eagleton, "Gender and Genre," in *Re-reading the Short Story*, p. 65.

19. Qtd. in *Afro-American Women Writers 1746–1933*, ed. Ann Allen Shockley (New York: Meridian, 1988), p. 110.

20. Alice Walker. *In Search of our Mother's Gardens*. (New York: Harcourt, 1983), p. 301.

21. For a detailed discussion of the change in images of women from stereotype to character see Barbara Christian, *Black Women Novelists: The Development of a Tradition*. (Westport: Greenwood Press, 1980); Carole McAlpine Watson Prologue; *The Novels of Black American Women, 1891–1965*. (Westport: Greenwood Press, 1985) and Hazel V. Carby, *Reconstructing Womanhood, the Emergence of the Afro-American Woman Novelist* (New York: OUP, 1987).

22. In Geneva Smitherman *Black Language and Culture: Sounds of Soul* (New York: Harper & Row, 1975), pp. 4–5.

23. *Bearing Witness: Selections from African-American Autobiography in the Twentieth Century* (New York: Pantheon, 1991), p. 4.

24. Henry Louis Gates, Jr., foreword in *The Collected Works of Effie Waller Smith* (New York: OUP, 1991), xii.

25. "Dalit Panthers Manifesto," in *Untouchable! Voices of the Dalit Liberation Movement*, ed. Barbara Joshi (London: Zed Books, 1986), p. 145.

26. "Dalit Self-determination means Separate Electorate, Separate Settlement, Religious Separation," *Dalit Voice*, Jan. 16–31, 1992, p. 3.

27. "Dalit Panthers Manifesto," trans. from the Marathi, in *Untouchable! Voices of the Dalit Liberation Movement*, p. 145.

28. Dileep Padgaonkar, *Times Weekly*, Nov. 25, 1973, Vol. 4, No. 17.

29. J.V. Powar, "Its Reddening on the Horizon," ibid.

30. "Yashodhara," trans. Jayant Karve and Philip Engblom. ibid.

31. Dharam Sutra: an ancient Indian religious text qtd. in *Untouchable! Voices of the Dalit Liberation Movement*, p. 1.

32. Dr. Gangadhar Pantawane, "The Enemy Within" ibid., p. 86.

33. New York: Bantam Doubleday, 1991.

34. *Maran Swasta Hot Ahe* (literally: "Death comes cheap").

Frances Ellen Watkins Harper

The Two Offers

"What is the matter with you, Laura, this morning? I have been watching you this hour, and in that time you have commenced a half-dozen letters and torn them all up. What matter of such grave moment is puzzling your dear little head, that you do not know how to decide?"

"Well, it is an important matter; I have two offers for marriage, and I do not know which to choose.

"I should accept neither, or to say the least, not at present."

"Why not?"

"Because I think a woman who is undecided between two offers has not love enough for either to make a choice; and in that very hesitation, indecision, she has a reason to pause and seriously reflect, lest her marriage, instead of being an affinity of souls or a union of hearts, should only be a mere matter of bargain and sale, or an affair of convenience and selfish interest."

"But I consider them both very good offers, just such as many a girl would gladly receive. But to tell you the truth, I do not think that I regard either as a woman should the man she chooses for her husband. But then if I refuse, there is the risk of being an old maid, and that is not to be thought of."

"Well, suppose there is? Is that the most dreadful fate that can befall a woman? Is there not more intense wretchedness in an ill-assorted marriage,

First published in *Anglo-African Magazine* 9 (Vol. 1, No. 9: Sept. 1859–Vol. 1, No. 10: Oct. 1859)

more utter loneliness in a loveless home, than in the lot of the old maid who accepts her earthly mission as a gift from God and strives to walk the path of life with earnest and unfaltering steps?"

"Oh! what a little preacher you are. I really believe that you were cut out for an old maid—that when nature formed you she put in a double portion of intellect to make up for a deficiency of love; and yet you are kind and affectionate. But I do not think that you know anything of the grand, overmastering passion, or the deep necessity of woman's heart for loving."

"Do you think so?" resumed the first speaker, and bending over her work she quietly applied herself to the knitting that had lain neglected by her side during this brief conversation. But as she did so, a shadow flitted over her pale and intellectual brow, a mist gathered in her eyes, and a slight quivering of the lips revealed a depth of feeling to which her companion was a stranger.

But before I proceed with my story, let me give you a slight history of the speakers. They were cousins who had met life under different auspices. Laura Lagrange was the only daughter of rich and indulgent parents who had spared no pains to make her an accomplished lady. Her cousin, Janette Alston, was the child of parents rich only in goodness and affection. Her father had been unfortunate in business and, dying before he could retrieve his fortunes, left his business in an embarrassed state. His widow was unacquainted with his business affairs, and when the estate was settled, hungry creditors had brought their claims and the lawyers had received their fees, she found herself homeless and almost penniless, and she, who had been sheltered in the warm clasp of loving arms found them too powerless to shield her from the pitiless pelting storms of adversity. Year after year she struggled with poverty and wrestled with want, till her toilworn hands became too feeble to hold the shattered chords of existence, and her tear-dimmed eyes grew heavy with the slumber of death.

Her daughter had watched over her with untiring devotion, had closed her eyes in death and gone out into the busy, restless world, missing a precious tone from the voices of earth, a beloved step from the paths of life. Too self-reliant to depend on the charity of relations, she endeavored to support herself by her own exertions, and she had succeeded. Her path for a while was marked with struggle and trial, but instead of uselessly repining she met them bravely, and her life became not a thing of ease and indulgence, but of conquest, victory and accomplishments.

At the time when this conversation took place, the deep trials of her life had passed away. The achievements of her genius had won her a position in the literary world, where she shone as one of its bright particular stars. And with her fame came a competence of worldly means, which gave her leisure for improvement and the riper development of her rare talents. And she, that pale intellectual woman, whose genius gave life and vivacity to the social circle and whose presence threw a halo of beauty and grace around the charmed atmosphere in which she moved, had at one period of her life known the mystic and solemn strength of an all-absorbing love. Years faded into the misty past had seen the kindling of her eye, the quick flushing of her cheek and the wild throbbing of her heart at tones of a voice long since hushed to the stillness of death. Deeply, wildly, passionately, she had loved....This love quickened her talents, inspired her genius and threw over her life a tender and spiritual earnestness.

And then came a fearful shock, a mournful waking from that "dream of beauty and delight." A shadow fell around her path; it came between her and the object of her heart's worship. First a few cold words, estrangement, and then a painful separation: the old story of woman's pride....And thus faded out from that young heart her bright, brief and saddened dream of life. Faint and spirit-broken, she turned from the scenes associated with the memory of the loved and lost. She tried to break the chain of sad associations that bound her to the mournful past; and so...her genius gathered strength from suffering, and wondrous power and brilliancy from the agony she hid within the desolate chambers of her soul...and turning, with an earnest and shattered spirit to life's duties and trials, she found a calmness and strength that she had only imagined in her dreams of poetry and song.

We will now pass over a period of ten years, and the cousins have met again. In that calm and lovely woman, in whose eyes is a depth of tenderness tempering the flashes of her genius, whose looks and tones are full of sympathy and love, we recognize the once smitten and stricken Janette Alston. The bloom of her girlhood had given way to a higher type of spiritual beauty, as if some unseen hand had been polishing and refining the temple in which her lovely spirit found its habitation....

Never in the early flush of womanhood, when an absorbing love had lit up her eyes and glowed in her life, had she appeared so interesting as when, with a countenance which seemed overshadowed with a spiritual light, she bent over the deathbed of a young woman just lingering at the shadowy gates of the unseen land.

"Has he come?" faintly but eagerly exclaimed the dying woman. "Oh! how I have longed for his coming, and even in death he forgets me."

"Oh, do not say so, dear Laura. Some accident may have detained him," said Janette to her cousin; for on that bed, from whence she will never rise, lies the once beautiful and lighthearted Laura Lagrange, the brightness of whose eyes had long since been dimmed with tears, and whose voice had become like a harp whose every chord is tuned to sadness—whose faintest thrill and loudest vibrations are but the variations of agony. A heavy hand was laid upon her once warm and bounding heart, and a voice came whispering through her soul that she must die. But to her the tidings was a message of deliverance—a voice hushing her wild sorrows to the calmness of resignation and hope.

Life had grown so weary upon her head—the future looked so hopeless—she had no wish to tread again the track where thorns had pierced her feet and clouds overcast her sky, and she hailed the coming of death's angel as the footsteps of a welcome friend. and yet, earth had one object so very dear to her weary heart. It was her absent and recreant husband; for, since that conversation [ten years earlier], she had accepted one of her offers and become a wife. But before she married she learned that great lesson of human experience and woman's life—to love the man who bowed at her shrine, a willing worshipper.

He had a pleasing address, raven hair, flashing eyes, a voice of thrilling sweetness and lips of persuasive eloquence; and being well versed in the ways of the world, he won his way to her heart and she became his bride, and he was proud of his prize. Vain and superficial in his character, he looked upon marriage not as a divine sacrament for the soul's development and human progression, but as the title deed that gave him possession of the woman he thought he loved. But alas for her, the laxity of his principles had rendered him unworthy of the deep and undying devotion of a pure-hearted woman. But, for a while, he hid from her his true character, and she blindly loved him, and for a short period was happy in the consciousness of being beloved. Though sometimes a vague unrest would fill her soul, when, overflowing with a sense of the good, the beautiful and the true, she would turn to him but find no response to the deep yearnings of her soul—no appreciation of life's highest realities, its solemn grandeur and significant importance. Their souls never met, and soon she found a void in her bosom that his earthborn love could not fill. He did not satisfy the wants of her mental and moral nature: between him and her there was no affinity of minds, no intercommunion of souls.

Talk as you will of woman's deep capacity for loving—of the strength of her affectional nature. I do not deny it. But will the mere possession of any human love fully satisfy all the demands of her whole being? You may paint her in poetry or fiction as a frail vine, clinging to her brother man for support and dying when deprived of it, and all this may sound well enough to please the imaginations of schoolgirls, or lovelorn maidens. But woman—the true woman—if you would render her happy, it needs more than the mere development of her affectional nature. Her conscience should be enlightened, her faith in the true and right established, and scope given to her heaven-endowed and God-given faculties. The true aim of female education should be, not a development of one or two, but all the faculties of the human soul, because no perfect womanhood is developed by imperfect culture. Intense love is often akin to intense suffering, and to trust the whole wealth of woman's nature on the frail bark of human love may often be like trusting a cargo of gold and precious gems to a bark that has never battled with the storm or buffeted the waves. Is it any wonder, then, that so many life-barks...are stranded on the shoals of existence, mournful beacons and solemn warnings for the thoughtless, to whom marriage is a careless and hasty rushing together of the affections? Alas, that an institution so fraught with good for humanity should be so perverted, and that state of life which should be filled with happiness become so replete with misery. And this was the fate of Laura Lagrange.

For a brief period after her marriage her life seemed like a bright and beautiful dream, full of hope and radiant with joy. And then there came a change: he found other attractions that lay beyond the pale of home influences. The gambling saloon had power to win him from her side; he had lived in an element of unhealthy and unhallowed excitements, and the society of a loving wife, the pleasures of a well-regulated home, were enjoyments too tame for one who had avitiated his tastes by the pleasures of sin. There were charmed houses of vice, built upon dead men's loves, where, amid a flow of song, laughter, wine and careless mirth, he would spend hour after hour, forgetting the cheek that was paling through his neglect, heedless of the tear-dimmed eyes peering anxiously into the darkness, waiting or watching his return.

The influence of old associations was upon him. In early life, home had been to him a place of ceilings and walls, not a true home built upon goodness, love and truth. It was a place where velvet carpets hushed his tread, where images of loveliness and beauty, invoked into being by painter's art and sculptor's skill, pleased the eye and gratified the taste, where magnificence surrounded his way and costly clothing adorned his person; but it was not the place for the true culture and right development of his soul. His father had been too much engrossed in making money and his mother in spending it, in striving to maintain a fashionable position in society and shining in the eyes of the world, to give the proper direction to the character of their wayward and impulsive son. His mother put beautiful robes upon his body but left ugly scars upon his soul; she pampered his appetite but starved his spirit....

That parental authority which should have been preserved as a string of precious pearls, unbroken and unscattered, was simply the administration of chance. At one time obedience was enforced by authority, at another time by flattery and promises, and just as often it was not enforced....His early associations were formed as chance directed, and from his want of home training, his character received a bias, his life a shade, which ran through every avenue of his existence and darkened all his future hours....

Before a year of his married life had waned, his young wife had learned to wait and mourn his frequent and uncalled-for absence. More than once had she seen him come home from his midnight haunts, the bright intelligence of his eye displaced by the drunkard's stare, and his manly gait changed to the inebriate's stagger; and she was beginning to know the bitter agony that is compressed in the mournful words

"drunkard's wife."

And then there came a bright but brief episode in her experience. The angel of life gave to her existence a deeper meaning and loftier significance: she sheltered in the warm clasp of her loving arms a dear babe, a precious child whose love filled every chamber of her heart....How many lonely hours were beguiled by its winsome ways, its answering smiles and fond caresses! How exquisite and solemn was the feeling that thrilled her heart when she clasped the tiny hands together and taught her dear child to call God "Our Father"!

What a blessing was that child! The father paused in his headlong career, awed by the strange beauty and precocious intellect of his child; and the mother's life had a better expression through her ministrations of love. And then there came hours of bitter anguish, shading the sunlight of her home and hushing the music of her heart. The angel of death bent over the couch of her child and beckoned it away. Closer and closer the mother strained her child to her wildly heaving breast and struggled with the heavy hand that lay upon its heart. Love and agony contended with death....

But death was stronger than love and mightier than agony, and won the child for the land of crystal founts and deathless flowers, and the poor stricken mother sat down beneath the shadow of her mighty grief, feeling as if a great light had gone out from her soul and that the sunshine had suddenly faded around her path. She turned in her deep anguish to the father of her child, the loved and cherished dead. For a while his words were kind and tender, his heart seemed subdued and his tenderness fell upon her worn and weary heart like rain on perishing flowers, or cooling waters to lips all parched with thirst and scorched with fever. But the change was evanescent; the influence of unhallowed associations and evil habits had vitiated and poisoned the springs of his existence. They had bound him in their meshes, and he lacked the moral strength to break his fetters and stand erect in all the strength and dignity of a true manhood, making life's highest excellence his ideal and striving to gain it.

And yet moments of deep contrition would sweep over him, when he would resolve to abandon the wine cup forever, when he was ready to forswear the handling of another card, and he would try to break away from the associations that he felt were working his ruin. But when the hour of temptation came his strength was weakness, his earnest purposes were cobwebs, his well-meant resolutions ropes of sand—and thus passed year after year of the married life of Laura Lagrange. She tried to hide her agony from the public gaze, to smile when her heart was almost breaking. But year after year her voice grew fainter and sadder, her once light and bounding step grew slower and faltering.

Year after year she wrestled with agony and strove with despair, till the quick eyes of her brother read, in the paling of her cheek and the dimming eye, the secret anguish of her worn and weary spirit. On that wan, sad face he saw the death tokens, and he knew the dark wing of the mystic angel swept coldly around her path.

"Laura," said her brother to her one day, "you are not well, and I think you need our mother's tender care and nursing. You are daily losing strength, and if you will go I will accompany you."

At first she hesitated; she shrank almost instinctively from presenting that pale, sad face to the loved ones at home....But then a deep yearning for home sympathy woke within her a passionate longing for love's kind words, for tenderness and heart support, and she resolved to seek the home of her childhood and lay her weary head upon her mother's bosom, to be folded again in her loving arms, to lay that poor, bruised and aching heart where it might beat and throb closely to the loved ones at home.

A kind welcome awaited her. All that love and tenderness could devise was done to bring the bloom to her cheek and the light to her eye. But it was all in vain; hers was a disease that no medicine could cure, no earthly balm would heal. It was a slow wasting of the vital forces, the sickness of the soul. The unkindness and neglect of her husband lay like a leaden weight upon her heart....

And where was he that had won her love and then cast it aside as a useless thing, who rifled her heart of its wealth and spread bitter ashes upon its broken altars? He was lingering away from her when the death damps were gathering on her brow, when his name was trembling on her lips! Lingering away! when she was watching his coming, though the death films were gathering before her eyes and earthly things were fading from her vision.

"I think I hear him now," said the dying woman, "surely that is his step," but the sound died away in the distance.

Again she started from an uneasy slumber: "That is his voice! I am so glad he has come."

Tears gathered in the eyes of the sad watchers by that dying bed, for they knew that she was deceived. He had not returned. For her sake they wished his coming. Slowly the hours waned away, and then came the sad, soul-sickening thought that she was forgotten, forgotten in the last hour of human need, forgotten when the spirit, about to be dissolved, paused for the last time on the threshold of existence, a weary watcher at the gates of death.

"He has forgotten me," again she faintly murmured, and the last tears she would ever shed on earth sprung to her mournful eyes, and…a few broken sentences issued from her pale and quivering lips. They were prayers for strength, and earnest pleading for him who had desolated her young life by turning its sunshine to shadows, its smiles to tears.

"He has forgotten me," she murmured again, "but I can bear it; the bitterness of death is passed, and soon I hope to exchange the shadows of death for the brightness of eternity, the rugged paths of life for the golden streets of glory, and the care and turmoils of earth for the peace and rest of heaven."

Her voice grew fainter and fainter; they saw the shadows that never deceive flit over her pale and faded face and knew that the death angel waited to soothe their weary one to rest, to calm the throbbing of her bosom and cool the fever of her brain. And amid the silent hush of their grief the freed spirit, refined through suffering and brought into divine harmony through the spirit of the living Christ, passed over the dark waters of death as on a bridge of light, over whose radiant arches hovering angels bent. They parted the dark locks from her marble brow, closed the waxen lids over the once bright and laughing eye and left her to the dreamless slumber of the grave.

Her cousin turned from that deathbed a sadder and wiser woman. She resolved more earnestly than ever to make the world better by her example, gladder by her presence, and to kindle the fires of her genius on the altars of universal love and truth. She had a higher and better object in all her writings than the mere acquistion of gold or acquirement of fame. She felt that she had a high and holy mission on the battlefield of existence—that life was not given her to be frittered away in nonsense or wasted away in trifling pursuits. She would willingly espouse an unpopular cause, but not an unrighteous one.

In her the downtrodden slave found an earnest advocate; the flying fugitive remembered her kindness as he stepped cautiously through our Republic to gain his freedom in a monarchial land, having broken the chains on which the rust of centuries had gathered. Little children learned to name her with affection; the poor called her blessed as she broke her bread to the pale lips of hunger.

Her life was like a beautiful story, only it was clothed with the dignity of reality and invested with the sublimity of truth. True, she was an old maid; no husband brightened her life with his love or shaded it with his neglect. No children nestling lovingly in her arms called her mother. No one appended Mrs. to her name.

She was indeed an old maid, not vainly striving to keep up an appearance of girlishness when "departed" was written on her youth, not vainly pining at her loneliness and isolation. The world was full of warm, loving hearts, and her own beat in unison with them. Neither was she always sentimentally sighing for something to love; objects of affection were all around her, and the world was not so wealthy in love that it had no use for hers. In blessing others she made a life and benediction, and as old age descended peacefully and gently upon her, she had learned one of life's most precious lessons: that true happiness consists not so much in the fruition of our wishes as in the regulation of desires and the full development and right culture of our whole natures.

Victoria Earle Matthews

Aunt Lindy: A Story Founded on Real Life

I n the annals of Fort Valley, Georgia, few events will last longer in the minds of her slow, easy-going dwellers than the memory of a great conflagration that left more than half the town a complete waste. 'Twas generally conceded to be the most disastrous fire that even her oldest residents had ever witnessed. It was caused, as far as could be ascertained, by some one who, while passing through the sampling room of the Cotton Exchange, had thoughtlessly tossed aside a burning match; this, embedding itself in the soft fleecy cotton, burned its way silently, without smoke, through the heart of a great bale to the flooring beneath, before it was discovered.

Although the watchman made his regular rounds an hour or so after the building closed for the night, yet he saw nothing to indicate the treacherous flame which was then, like a serpent, stealing its way through the soft snowy cotton. But now a red glare, a terrified cry of "Fire! Fire!" echoing on the still night air, had aroused the unconscious sleepers, and summoned quickly, strong, brave-hearted men from every direction, who, as though with one accord, fell to fighting the fire-fiend (modern invention was unknown in this out-of-the-

First published in *Aunt Lindy: A Story Founded on Real Life* by Victoria Earle. New York: J.J. Little and Co., 1893

way settlement); even the women flocked to the scene, not knowing how soon a helping hand would be needed.

Great volumes of black smoke arose from the fated building, blinding and choking the stout fellows who had arranged themselves in small squads on the roofs of adjacent dwellings to check, if possible, the progress of the fire, while others in line passed water to them.

As the night wore on, a rising wind fanned the fiery tongue into a fateful blaze; and, as higher rose the wind, fiercer grew the flame; from every window and doorway poured great tongues of fire, casting a lurid glare all over the valley, with its shuddering groups of mute, frightened white faces, and its shrieking, prayerful, terror-stricken negroes, whose religion, being of a highly emotional character, was easily rendered devotional by any unusual excitement: their agonized "'Mi'ty Gawd! he'p us pore sinners," chanted in doleful tones, as only the emotional Southern negro can chant or moan, but added to the weird, wild scene. Men and women with blanched faces looked anxiously at each other; piercing screams rent the air, as some child, relative, or loved one was missed, for, like a curse, the consuming fire passed from house to house, leaving nothing in its track but the blackened and charred remains of what had been, but a few short hours before, "home."

All through the night the fire raged, wasting its force as the early morning light gradually penetrated the smoky haze, revealing to the wellnigh frantic people a sad, sad scene of desolation. When home has been devastated, hearts only may feel and know the extent of the void; no pen or phrase can estimate it.

As the day advanced, sickening details of the night's horror were brought to light. Magruder's Tavern, the only hotel the quaint little town could boast of, served as a death trap; several perished in the flames; many were hurt by falling beams; some jumped from windows and lay maimed for life; others stood in shuddering groups, homeless, but thankful withal that their lives had been spared: as the distressed were found, neighbors who had escaped the scourge threw wide their doors and bestirred themselves to give relief to the sufferers, and temporary shelter to those who had lost all. Ah! let unbelievers cavil and contend, yet such a time as this proves that there is a mystic vein running through humanity that is not deduced from the mechanical laws of nature.

A silver-haired man, a stranger in the town, had been taken to a humble cot where many children in innocent forgetfulness passed noisily to and fro, unconscious that quiet meant life to the aged sufferer. Old Dr. Bronson, with his great heart and gentle, childlike manner, stood doubly thoughtful as he numbered the throbbing pulse. "His brain won't—can't bear it unless he's nursed and has perfect quiet," he murmured as he quitted the house. Acting upon a sudden thought, he sprang into his buggy and quickly drove through the shady lanes, by the redolent orchards, to a lone cabin on the outskirts of the town, situated at the entrance to the great sighing pine-woods.

Seeing a man weeding a small garden plot, he called, without alighting, "Hi there, Joel: where's Aunt Lindy?"

"Right dar, in de cabin, doctor; jes wait a minnit," as he disappeared through the doorway.

"Good day, Aunt Lindy," as a tall, ancient-looking negro dame hurried from the cabin to the gate. Well accustomed was she to these sudden calls of Dr. Bronson, for her fame as a nurse was known far beyond the limits of Fort Valley.

"Mawning, doctor; Miss Martha and de chil'en was not teched by de fi'er?" she inquired anxiously.

"Oh, no; the fire was not our way. Lindy, I have a bad case, and nowhere to take him. Mrs. Bronson has her hands full of distressed, suffering children. No one to nurse him, so I want to bring him here—a victim of the great fire."

"De Lawd, doctor, yo kin, yo kno' yo kin; de cabin is pore, but Joel ner me ain't heathins; fetch him right along, my han's ain't afeered of wuk when trubble comes."

Tenderly they lifted him, and bore him from the cottage resounding with childish prattle and glee, to the quiet, cleanly cabin of the lonely couple, Lindy and Joel, who years before had seen babes torn from their breasts and sold— powerless to utter a complaint or appeal, whipped for the tears they shed, knowing their children would return to them not again till the graves gave up their dead. But in the busy life that freedom gave them, oft, when work was done and the night of life threw its waning shadows around them, their tears would fall for the scattered voices—they would mourn o'er their past opression. Yet they hid their grief from an unsympathizing generation, and the memory of their oppressors awoke but to the call of fitful retrospection.

"Joel, does yo 'member what de 'scriptur' ses about de stranger widin dy gates?" asked Aunt Lindy, as she hurriedly made ready for the "victim of the great fire."

"Ole 'oman, I gits mo'forgitful each day I lib, but it 'pears to me dat it says su'thin 'bout 'Heal de sick an' lead the blind,'" the old man said, as he stood with a look of deep concern settling on his aged face; "yes, ole 'oman," brightening up, "yes, dat's hit, kase I 'member de words de bressed Marster say to dem lis'ning souls geddered 'roun him, 'If yo hab dun it to de least ob dese my brudderin, yo hab dun it onto me.'"

"Yas, yas, I 'members now," Aunt Lindy murmured, as she moved the bed that the stranger was to rest upon out in the middle of the small room, the headboard near the window almost covered with climbing honeysuckle, all in sweet bloom.

"It am won'erful," she continued, meditatively, "how de Marster 'ranges t'ings to suit His work and will. I'se kep dis bed fixed fur yeahs, 'maginin' dat somehow, in de prov'dence ob Gawd, one ob de chil'en mou't chance dis away wid no place to lay his hed—de law me! Joel, mak' hast' an' fetch in dat shuck bed, de sun hab made it as sweet as de flowers, 'fore de dew falls offen dem, an' reckolec I wants a hole passel of mullen leaves; dey's powerful good fur laying fever, an' as yo's gwine dat way yo mou't jes as well get er han'ful ob mounting mint, sweet balsam—an' cam'ile," she called after him, "ef yo pass enny."

About candle-light Dr. Bronson arrived with his patient, while his two assistants placed him on the bed prepared for him; the doctor explained the critical condition of the sick man to the trusty old nurse, and directed as to the medicine. "Do not disturb him for an hour at least, Aunt Lindy; let him sleep, for he needs all the strength he can rally—he has but one slim chance out of ten."

"Pore sole, I'll look arter him same's ef he war my own chile."

"I know that, Aunt Lindy; I will stop in on my way back from the ridge in about a couple of hours."

"All rite, sah."

Uncle Joel, with the desired herbs, returned shortly afterward. "Is he cum yit, old 'oman?"

"Shsh! sure nuff,"she whispered, with a warning motion of her head toward the partitioned room where the sick man lay. Heeding the warning, Uncle Joel whispered back:

"If dar's nuffin I kin do jes now to he'p yo, I'll jes step ober to Brer An'erson's; I heah dere's a new brudder who's gwine to lead de meetin', as Brer Wilson is ailin'."

"Go 'long, Joel, dere's nuffin yo kin do jes now."

"Well den, s'long, ole 'oman, " the old man said, as he stepped noiselessly out into the sweet perfume-laden air.

For a long time Aunt Lindy sat dozing by the smothered fire; so lightly, though, that almost the rustling of the wind through the leaves would have awakened her.

The moonlight streamed in the doorway; now and then sounds issuing from the "pra'r meetin'," a few doors away, could be heard on the still evening air. After a while the nurse rose, lighted a candle, and went to make sure the sick man was comfortable. Entering softly, she stepped to the bedside and looked at the face of the sleeper; suddenly she grew dizzy, breathless, amazed, as though her eyes had deceived her; she placed the candle close by his face and peered wildly at this bruised, bandaged, silver-haired stranger in a fascinated sort of way, as though she were powerless to speak. At last:

"Great Gawd! it's Marse Jeems!"

The quick, vengeful flame leaped in her eyes, as her mind, made keen by years of secret suffering and toil, travelled through time and space; she saw wrongs which no tongue can enumerate; demoniac gleams of exultation and bitter hatred settled upon her now grim features; a pitiless smile wreathed her set lips, as she gazed with glaring eyeballs at this helpless, homeless "victim of the great fire," as though surrounded by demons; a dozen wicked impulses rushed through her mind—a life for a life—no mortal eye was near, an intercepted breath, a gasp, and——

"Lindy, Lindy, don't tell Miss Cynthia," the sick man weakly murmured: in the confused state of his brain it required but this familiar black face to conduct his disordered thoughts to the palmiest period of his existence. He again revelled in opulence, saw again the cotton fields—a waving tract of bursting snowballs—the magnolia, the oleander——

"Whar's my chil'en?" Nurse Lindy fairly shrieked in his face. "To de fo' win's ob de ear'fh, yo ole debbil, yo." He heard her not now, for white and unconscious he lay, while the long pent-up passion found vent. Her blood was afire, her tall form swayed, her long, bony hands trembled like an animal at bay; she stepped back as if to spring upon him, with clutching fingers extended; breathless she paused; the shouts of the worshippers broke upon the evening air—the oldentime melody seemed to pervade the cabin; she listened, turned, and fled—out through the open doorway,—out into the white moonlight, down the shadowed lane, as if impelled by unseen force. She unconsciously approached the prayer-meeting door. "Vengeance is mine, ses de Lawd," came from within; her anger died away; quickly her steps she retraced. "Mi'ty Gawd, stren'fin my arm, and pur'fy my heart," was all she said.

Soon from the portals of death she brought him, for untiringly she labored, unceasingly she prayed in her poor broken way; nor was it in vain, for before the frost fell the crisis passed, the light of reason beamed upon the silver-haired stranger, and revealed in mystic characters the service rendered by a former slave—Aunt Lindy. He marvelled at the patient faithfulness of these people. He saw but the gold—did not dream of the dross burned away by the great Refiner's fire. From that time Aunt Lindy and Uncle Joel never knew a sorrow, secret or otherwise; for not only was the roof above their heads secured to them, but the new "brudder" who came to "lead de meetin'; in Brer Wilson's place," was proved beyond a doubt, through the efforts of the silver-haired stranger, to be their first-born. The rest were "sleeping until the morning," and not to the 'fo' win's ob de ear'fh,'" as was so greatly feared by Aunt Lindy.

Alice Dunbar

Tony's Wife

"Gimme fi' cents worth o' candy, please." It was the little Jew girl who spoke, and Tony's wife roused herself from her knitting to rise and count out the multi-hued candy which should go in exchange for the dingy nickel grasped in warm, damp fingers. Three long sticks, carefully wrapped in crispest brown paper, and a half dozen or more of pink candy fish for lagniappe, and the little Jew girl sped away in blissful contentment. Tony's wife resumed her knitting with a stifled sigh until the next customer should come.

A low growl caused her to look up apprehensively. Tony himself stood beetle-browed and huge in the small doorway.

"Get up from there," he muttered, "and open two dozen oysters right away; the Eliots want 'em." His English was unaccented. It was long since he had seen Italy.

She moved meekly behind the counter, and began work on the thick shells. Tony stretched his long neck up the street.

"Mr. Tony, mama wants some charcoal." The very small voice at his feet must have pleased him, for his black brows relaxed into a smile, and he poked the little one's chin with a hard, dirty finger, as he emptied the ridiculously small bucket of charcoal into the child's bucket, and gave a banana for lagniappe.

First published in *The Goodness of St. Rogue and Other Stories* by Alice Dunbar. New York: Dodd Mead and Co., 1899

The crackling of shells went on behind, and a stifled sob arose as a bit of sharp edge cut into the thin, worn fingers that clasped the knife.

"Hurry up there, will you?" growled the black brows; "the Eliots are sending for the oysters."

She deftly strained and counted them, and, after wiping her fingers, resumed her seat, and took up the endless crochet work, with her usual stifled sigh.

Tony and his wife had always been in this same little queer old shop on Prytania Street, at least to the memory of the oldest inhabitant in the neighbourhood. When or how they came, or how they stayed, no one knew; it was enough that they were there, like a sort of ancestral fixture to the street. The neighbourhood was fine enough to look down upon these two tumble-down shops at the corner, kept by Tony and Mrs. Murphy, the grocer. It was a semi-fashionable locality, far up-town, away from the old-time French quarter. It was the sort of neighbourhood where millionaires live before their fortunes are made and fashionable, high-priced private schools flourish, where the small cottages are occupied by aspiring school-teachers and choir-singers. Such was this locality, and you must admit that it was indeed a condescension to tolerate Tony and Mrs. Murphy.

He was a great, black-bearded, hoarse-voiced, six-foot specimen of Italian humanity, who looked in his little shop and on the prosaic pavement of Prytania Street somewhat as Hercules might seem in a modern drawing-room. You instinctively thought of wild mountain-passes, and the gleaming dirks of bandid contadini in looking at him. What his last name was, no one knew. Someone had maintained once that he had been christened Antonio Malatesta, but that was unauthentic, and as little to be believed as that other wild theory that her name was Mary.

She was meek, pale, little, ugly, and German. Altogether part of his arms and legs would have very decently made another larger than she. Her hair was pale and drawn in sleek, thin tightness away from a pinched, pitiful face, whose dull cold eyes hurt you, because you knew they were trying to mirror sorrow, and could not because of their expressionless quality. No matter what the weather or what her other toilet, she always wore a thin little shawl of dingy brick-dust hue about her shoulders. No matter what the occasion or what the day, she always carried her knitting with her, and seldom ceased the incessant twist, twist of the shining steel among the white cotton meshes. She might put down the needles and lace into the spool-box long enough to open oysters, or wrap up fruit and candy, or count out wood and coal into infinitesimal portions, or do her housework; but the knitting was snatched with avidity at the first spare moment, and the worn, white, blue-marked fingers, half enclosed in kid-glove stalls for protection, would writhe and twist in and out again. Little girls just learning to crochet borrowed their patterns from Tony's wife, and it was considered quite a mark of advancement to have her inspect a bit of lace done by eager, chubby fingers. The ladies in larger houses, whose husbands would be millionaires some day, bought her lace, and gave it to their servants for Christmas presents.

As for Tony, when she was slow in opening his oysters or in cooking his red beans and spaghetti, he roared at her, and prefixed picturesque adjectives to her lace, which made her hide it under her apron with a fearsome look in her dull eyes.

He hated her in a lusty, roaring fashion, as a healthy beefy boy hates a sick cat and torments it to madness. When she displeased him, he beat her, and knocked her frail form on the floor. The children could tell when this had happened. Her eyes would be red, and there would be blue marks on her face and neck. "Poor Mrs. Tony," they would say, and nestle close to her. Tony did not roar at her for petting them, perhaps, because they spent money on the multi-hued candy in glass jars on the shelves.

Her mother appeared upon the scene once, and stayed a short time; but Tony got drunk one day and beat her because she ate too much, and she disappeared soon after. Whence she came and where she departed, no one could tell, not even Mrs. Murphy, the Pauline Pry and Gazette of the block.

Tony had gout, and suffered for many days in roaring helplessness, the while his foot, bound and swathed in many folds of red flannel, lay on the chair before him. In proportion as his gout increased and he bawled from pure physical discomfort, she became light-hearted, and moved about the shop with real, brisk cheeriness. He could not hit her then without such pain that after one or two trials he gave up in disgust.

So the dull years had passed, and life had gone on pretty much the same for Tony and the German wife and the shop. The children came on Sunday evenings to buy the stick candy, and on week-days for coal and wood. The servants came to buy oysters for the larger houses, and to gossip over the counter about their employers. The little dry woman knitted, and the big man moved lazily in and out in his red flannel shirt, exchanged politics with the tailor next door through the window, or lounged into Mrs. Murphy's bar and drank fiercely. Some of the children grew up and moved away, and other little girls came to buy candy and eat pink lagniappe fishes, and the shop still thrived.

One day Tony was ill, more than the mummied foot of gout, or the wheeze of asthma; he must keep his bed and send for the doctor.

She clutched his arm when he came, and pulled him into the tiny room.

"Is it—is it anything much, doctor?" she gasped.

Æsculapius shook his head as wisely as the occasion would permit. She followed him out of the room into the shop.

"Do you—will he get well, doctor?"

Æsculapius buttoned up his frock coat, smoothed his shining hat, cleared his throat, then replied oracularly,

"Madam, he is completely burned out inside. Empty as a shell, madam, empty as a shell. He cannot live, for he has nothing to live on."

As the cobblestones rattled under the doctor's equipage rolling leisurely up Prytania Street, Tony's wife sat in her chair and laughed,—laughed with a hearty joyousness that lifted the film from the dull eyes and disclosed a sparkle beneath.

The drear days went by, and Tony lay like a veritable Samson shorn of his strength, for his voice was sunken to a hoarse, sibilant whisper, and his black eyes gazed fiercely from the shock of hair and beard about a white face. Life went on pretty much as before in the shop; the children paused to ask how Mr. Tony was, and even hushed the jingles on their bell hoops as they passed the door. Red-headed Jimmie, Mrs. Murphy's nephew, did the hard jobs, such as splitting wood and lifting coal from the bin; and in the intervals between tending the fallen giant and waiting on the customers, Tony's wife sat in her accustomed chair, knitting fiercely, with an inscrutable smile about her purple compressed mouth.

Then John came, introducing himself, serpent-wise, into the Eden of her bosom.

John was Tony's brother, huge and bluff too, but fair and blond, with the beauty of Northern Italy. With the same lack of race pride which Tony had displayed in selecting his German spouse, John had taken unto himself Betty, a daughter of Erin, aggressive, powerful, and cross-eyed. He turned up now, having heard of this illness, and assumed an air of remarkable authority at once.

A hunted look stole into the dull eyes, and after John had departed with blustering directions as to Tony's welfare, she crept to his bedside timidly.

"Tony," she said—"Tony, you are very sick."

An inarticulate growl was the only response.

"Tony, you ought to see the priest; you must n't go any longer without taking the sacrament."

The growl deepened into words.

"Don't want any priest; you're always after some snivelling old woman's fuss. You and Mrs. Murphy go on with your church; it won't make *you* any better."

She shivered under this parting shot, and crept back into the shop. Still the priest came next day.

She followed him in to the bedside and knelt timidly.

"Tony," she whispered, "here's Father Leblanc."

Tony was too languid to curse out loud; he only expressed his hate in a toss of the black beard and shaggy mane.

"Tony," she said nervously, "won't you do it now? It won't take long, and it will be better for you when you go— Oh, Tony, don't—don't laugh. Please, Tony, here's the priest."

But the Titan roared aloud: "No; get out. Think I'm a-going to give you a chance to grab my money now? Let me die and go to hell in peace."

Father Leblanc knelt meekly and prayed, and the woman's weak pleadings continued,—

"Tony, I've been true and good and faithful to you. Don't die and leave me no better than before. Tony, I do want to be a good woman once, a real-for-true married woman. Tony, here's the priest; say yes." And she wrung her ringless hands.

"You want my money," said Tony, slowly, "and you sha'n't have it, not a cent; John shall have it."

Father Leblanc shrank away like a fading spectre. He came next day and next day, only to see re-enacted the same piteous scene,—the woman pleading to be made a wife ere death hushed Tony's blasphemies, the man chuckling in pain-racked glee at the prospect of her bereaved misery. Not all the prayers of Father Leblanc nor the wailings of Mrs. Murphy could alter the determination of the will beneath the shock of hair; he gloated in his physical weakness at the tenacious grasp on his mentality.

"Tony," she wailed on the last day, her voice rising to a shriek in its eagerness, "tell them I'm your wife; it'll be the same. Only say it, Tony, before you die!"

He raised his head, and turned stiff eyes and gibbering mouth on her; then, with one chill finger pointing at John, fell back dully and heavily.

They buried him with many honours by the Society of Italia's Sons. John took possession of the shop when they returned home, and found the money hidden in the chimney corner.

As for Tony's wife, since she was not his wife after all, they sent her forth in the world penniless, her worn fingers clutching her bundle of clothes in nervous agitation, as though they regretted the time lost from knitting.

Pauline E. Hopkins

A Dash For Liberty

*Founded on an article written by Col. T.W.
Higginson, for the Atlantic Monthly, June 1861*

"So, Madison, you are bound to try it?"

"Yes, sir," was the respectful reply.

There was silence between the two men for a space, and Mr. Dickson drove his horse to the end of the furrow he was making and returned slowly to the starting point, and the sombre figure awaiting him.

"Do I not pay you enough, and treat you well?" asked the farmer as he halted.

"Yes, sir."

"Then why not stay here and let well enough alone?"

"Liberty is worth nothing to me while my wife is a slave."

"We will manage to get her to you in a year or two."

The man smiled and sadly shook his head. "A year or two would mean forever, situated as we are, Mr. Dickson. It is hard for you to understand; you white men are all alike where you are called upon to judge a Negro's heart," he continued bitterly. "Imagine yourself in my place; how would you feel? The relentless heel of oppression in the States will have ground my rights as a husband into the dust, and have driven Susan to despair in that time. A white man may take

First Published in *Colored American Magazine* 3 (Aug. 1901): 243–47

up arms to defend a bit of property; but a black man has no right to his wife, his liberty or his life against his master! This makes me low-spirited, Mr. Dickson, and I have determined to return to Virginia for my wife. My feelings are centred in the idea of liberty," and as he spoke he stretched his arms toward the deep blue of the Canadian sky in a magnificent gesture. Then with a deep-drawn breath that inflated his mighty chest, he repeated the word: "Liberty! I think of it by day and dream of it by night; and I shall only taste it in all its sweetness when Susan shares it with me."

Madison was an unmixed African, of grand physique, and one of the handsomest of his race. His dignified, calm and unaffected bearing marked him as a leader among his fellows. His features bore the stamp of genius. His firm step and piercing eye attracted the attention of all who met him. He had arrived in Canada along with many other fugitives during the year 1840, and being a strong, able-bodied man, and a willing worker, had sought and obtained employment on Mr. Dickson's farm.

After Madison's words, Mr. Dickson stood for some time in meditative silence.

"Madison," he said at length, "there's desperate blood in your veins, and if you get back there and are captured, you'll do desperate deeds."

"Well, put yourself in my place: I shall be there single-handed. I have a wife whom I love, and whom I will protect. I hate slavery, I hate the laws that make my country a nursery for it. Must I be denied the right of aggressive defense against those who would overpower and crush me by superior force?"

"I understand you fully, Madison; it is not your defense but your rashness that I fear. Promise me that you will be discreet, and not begin an attack." Madison hesitated. Such a promise seemed to him like surrendering a part of those individual rights for which he panted. Mr. Dickson waited. Presently the Negro said significantly: "I promise not to be indiscreet."

There were tears in the eyes of the kind-hearted farmer as he pressed Madison's hand.

"God speed and keep you and the wife you love; may she prove worthy."

In a few days Madison received the wages due him, and armed with tiny saws and files to cut a way to liberty, if captured, turned his face toward the South.

* * * * *

It was late in the fall of 1840 when Madison found himself again at home in the fair Virginia State. The land was blossoming into ripe maturity, and the smiling fields lay waiting for the harvester.

The fugitive, unable to travel in the open day, had hidden himself for three weeks in the shadow of the friendly forest near his old home, filled with hope and fear, unable to obtain any information about the wife he hoped to rescue from slavery. After weary days and nights, he had reached the most perilous part of his mission. Tonight there would be no moon and the clouds threatened a storm; to his listening ears the rising wind bore the sound of laughter and singing. He drew back into the deepest shadow. The words came distinctly to his ears as the singers neared his hiding place.

> "All dem purty gals will be dar,
>   Shuck dat corn before you eat.
> Dey will fix it fer us rare,
>   Shuck dat corn before you eat.
> I know dat supper will be big,
>   Shuck that corn before you eat.
> I think I smell a fine roast pig,
>   Shuck that corn before you eat.
> Stuff dat coon an' bake him down,
> I spec some niggers dar from town.
>   Shuck dat corn before you eat.
> Please cook dat turkey nice an' brown.
> By de side of dat turkey I'll be foun',
>   Shuck dat corn before you eat."

"Don't talk about dat turkey; he'll be gone before we git dar."

"He's talkin', ain't he?"

"Las' time I shucked corn, turkey was de toughes' meat I eat fer many a day; you's got to have teef sharp lak a saw to eat it."

"S'pose you ain't got no teef, den what you gwine ter do?"

"Why ef you ain't got no teef you muss gum it!"

"Ha, ha, ha!"

Madison glided in and out among the trees, listening until he was sure that it was a gang going to a corn-shucking, and he resolved to join it, and get, if possible some news of Susan. He came out upon the highway, and as the company reached his hiding place, he fell into the ranks and joined in the singing. The darkness hid his identity from the company while he learned from their conversation the important events of the day.

On they marched by the light of weird, flaring pine knots, singing their merry cadences, in which the noble minor strains habitual to Negro music, sounded the depths of sadness, glancing off in majestic harmony, that touched the very gates of paradise in suppliant prayer.

It was close to midnight; the stars had disappeared and a steady rain was falling when, by a circuitous route, Madison reached the mansion where he had learned that his wife was still living. There were lights in the windows. Mirth at the great house kept company with mirth at the quarters.

The fugitive stole noiselessly under the fragrant magnolia trees and paused, asking himself what he should do next. As he stood there he heard the hoof-beats of the mounted patrol, far in the distance, die into silence. Cautiously he drew near the house and crept around to the rear of the building directly beneath the window of his wife's sleeping closet. He swung himself up and tried it; it yielded to his touch. Softly he raised the sash, and softly he crept into the room. His foot struck against an object and swept it to the floor. It fell with a loud crash. In an instant the door opened. There was a rush of feet, and Madison stood at bay. The house was aroused; lights were brought.

"I knowed 'twas him!" cried the overseer in triumph. "I heern him a-gettin' in the window, but I kept dark till he knocked my gun down; then I grabbed him! I knowed this room'd trap him ef we was patient about it."

Madison shook his captor off and backed against the wall. His grasp tightened on the club in his hand; his nerves were like steel, his eyes flashed fire.

"Don't kill him," shouted Judge Johnson, as the overseer's pistol gleamed in the light. "Five hundred dollars for him alive!"

With a crash, Madison's club descended on the head of the nearest man; again, and yet again, he whirled it around, doing frightful execution each time it fell. Three of the men who had responded to the overseer's cry for help were on the ground, and he himself was sore from many wounds before, weakened by loss of blood, Madison finally succumbed.

*　*　*　*　*

The brig "Creole" lay at the Richmond dock taking on her cargo of tobacco, hemp, flax and slaves. The sky was cloudless, and the blue waters rippled but slightly under the faint breeze. There was on board the confusion incident to departure. In the hold and on deck men were hurrying to and fro, busy and excited, making the final preparations for the voyage. The slaves came aboard in two gangs: first the men, chained like cattle, were marched to their quarters in the hold; then came the women to whom more freedom was allowed.

In spite of the blue sky and the bright sunlight that silvered the water the scene was indescribably depressing and sad. The procession of gloomy-faced men and weeping women seemed to be descending into a living grave.

The captain and the first mate were standing together at the head of the gangway as the women stepped aboard. Most were very plain and bore the marks of servitude, a few were neat and attractive in appearances; but one was a woman whose great beauty immediately attracted attention; she was an octoroon. It was a tradition that her grandfather had served in the Revolutionary War, as well as in both Houses of Congress. That was nothing, however, at a time when the blood of the proudest F.F.V.'s was freely mingled with that of the African slaves on their plantations. Who wonders that Virginia has produced great men of color from among the exbondmen, or, that illustrious black men proudly point to Virginia as a birthplace? Posterity rises to the plane that their ancestors bequeath, and the most refined, the wealthiest and the most intellectual whites of that proud State have not hesitated to amalgamate with the Negro.

"What a beauty!" exclaimed the captain as the line of women paused a moment opposite him.

"Yes," said the overseer in charge of the gang. "She's as fine a piece of flesh as I have had in trade for many a day."

"What's the price?" demanded the captain.

"Oh, way up. Two or three thousand. She's a lady's maid, well-educated, and can sing and dance. We'll get it in New Orleans. Like to buy?"

"You don't suit my pile," was the reply, as his eyes followed the retreating form of the handsome octoroon. "Give her a cabin to herself; she ought not to herd with the rest," he continued, turning to the mate.

He turned with a meaning laugh to execute the order.

The "Creole" proceeded slowly on her way towards New Orleans. In the men's cabin, Madison Monroe lay chained to the floor and heavily ironed. But from the first moment on board ship he had been busily engaged in selecting men who could be trusted in the dash for liberty that he was determined to make. The miniature files and saws which he still wore concealed in his clothing were faithfully used in the darkness of night. The man was at peace, although he had caught no glimpse of the dearly loved Susan. When the body suffers greatly, the strain upon the heart becomes less tense, and a welcome calmness had stolen over the prisoner's soul.

On the ninth day out the brig encountered a rough sea, and most of the slaves were sick, and therefore not watched with very great vigilance. This was the time for action, and it was planned that they should rise that night. Night came on; the first watch was summoned; the wind was blowing high. Along the narrow passageway that separated the men's quarters from the women's, a man was creeping.

The octoroon lay upon the floor of her cabin, apparently sleeping, when a shadow darkened the door, and the captain stepped into the room, casting bold glances at the reclining figure. Profound silence reigned. One might have fancied one's self on a deserted vessel, but for the sound of an occasional foot-step on the deck above, and the murmur of voices in the opposite hold.

She lay stretched at full length with her head resting upon her arm, a po-sition that displayed to the best advantage the perfect symmetry of her superb figure; the dim light of a lantern played upon the long black ringlets, finely-chiselled mouth and well-rounded chin, upon the marbled skin veined by her master's blood,—representative of two races, to which did she belong?

For a moment the man gazed at her in silence; then casting a glance around him, he dropped upon one knee and kissed the sleeping woman full upon the mouth.

With a shriek the startled sleeper sprang to her feet. The woman's heart stood still with horror; she recognized the intruder as she dashed his face aside with both hands.

"None of that, my beauty," growled the man, as he reeled back with an oath, and then flung himself forward and threw his arm about her slender waist. "Why did you think you had a private cabin, and all the delicacies of the season? Not to behave like a young catamount, I warrant you."

The passion of terror and desperation lent the girl such strength that the man was forced to relax his hold slightly. Quick as a flash, she struck him a sting-ing blow across the eyes, and as he staggered back, she sprang out of the door-way, making for the deck with the evident intention of going overboard.

"God have mercy!" broke from her lips as she passed the men's cabin, closely followed by the captain.

"Hold on, girl; we'll protect you!" shouted Madison, and he stooped, seized the heavy padlock which fastened the iron ring that encircled his ankle to the iron bar, and stiffening the muscles, wrenched the fastening apart, and hurled it with all his force straight at the captain's head.

His aim was correct. The padlock hit the captain not far from the left tem-ple. The blow stunned him. In a moment Madison was upon him and had seized his weapons, another moment served to handcuff the unconscious man.

"If the fire of Heaven were in my hands, I would throw it at these cow-ardly whites. Follow me: it is liberty or death!" he shouted as he rushed for the quarter-deck. Eighteen others followed him, all of whom seized whatever they could wield as weapons.

The crew were all on deck; the three passengers were seated on the com-panion smoking. The appearance of the slaves all at once completely surprised the whites.

So swift were Madison's movements that at first the officers made no at-tempt to use their weapons; but this was only for an instant. One of the passen-gers drew his pistol, fired, and killed one of the blacks. The next moment he lay dead upon the deck from a blow with a piece of a capstan bar in Madison's hand. The fight then became general, passengers and crew taking part.

The first and second mates were stretched out upon the deck with a single blow each. The sailors ran up the rigging for safety, and in short time Madison was master of the "Creole."

After his accomplices had covered the slaver's deck, the intrepid leader forbade the shedding of more blood. The sailors came down to the deck, and their wounds were dressed. All the prisoners were heavily ironed and well guarded except the mate, who was to navigate the vessel; with a musket doubly charged pointed at his breast, he was made to swear to take the brig into a British port.

By one splendid and heroic stroke, the daring Madison had not only gained his own liberty, but that of one hundred and thirty-four others.

The next morning all the slaves who were still fettered, were released, and the cook was ordered to prepare the best breakfast that the stores would permit; this was to be a fête in honor of the success of the revolt and as a surprise to the females, whom the men had not yet seen.

As the women filed into the captain's cabin, where the meal was served, weeping, singing and shouting over their deliverance, the beautiful octoroon with one wild, half-frantic cry of joy sprang towards the gallant leader.

"Madison!"

"My God! Susan! My wife!"

She was locked to his breast; she clung to him convulsively. Unnerved at last by the revulsion to more than relief and ecstacy, she broke into wild sobs, while the astonished company closed around them with loud hurrahs.

Madison's cup of joy was filled to the brim. He clasped her to him in silence, and humbly thanked Heaven for its blessing and mercy.

* * * * *

The next morning the "Creole" landed at Nassau, New Providence, where the slaves were offered protection and hospitality.

Every act of oppression is a weapon for the oppressed. Right is a dangerous instrument; woe to us if our enemy wields it.

Ruth D. Todd

The Octoroon's Revenge

He was a tall young fellow, with the figure of an athlete, extremely handsome, with short, black curls and dark eyes.

His companion was a beautiful girl, tall and slight, though exceedingly graceful, with masses of silken hair of a raven blackness, and with eyes large and dreamy, of a deep violet blue.

But while she was the daughter of one of Virginia's royal blue bloods, he was simply a young mulatto coachman in her father's employ.

The young girl was sitting on a mossy bank by the side of a shady brook while the young man lay at her feet. A carriage with a pair of fine horses stood just at the edge of the wood, across the roadway.

At last the young man spoke, looking up at the girl as he did so, and there was a world of anguish in his sad, dark eyes.

"Lillian, dearest, I am afraid that this must be our last day alone with each other."

"Oh, Harry dear, why so, what has happened? Does any one suspect us?" exclaimed the young girl as she moved swiftly from her seat and knelt by his

First published in *Colored American Magazine* 4 (March 1902): 291–95 side. He caught both her hands in his and covered them with kisses before he replied.

"No, dearest, nothing has happened as yet, but something may at any moment, Lillian darling." And the young man raised himself up and clasped the girl passionately to his heart. "It almost drives me mad to tell you, but I must go away."

"Oh, no! no! no! Harry, dear Harry, surely you do not mean what you are saying."

"Yes, darling, I must go! For your sake; for both of our sakes. Think dear one, it is quite possible that we may be found out some day, and then think of the shame and disgrace it will bring to you. Think what a blow it would give your father; what a blight it would cast upon an old and honored name. Shunned and despised by your most intimate friends, you would be a social outcast. They would lynch me, of course, but for myself I care not. It is of you that I must think, and of your father who has been so very kind to me. Dear heart, I would gladly lay down my life to save your pure and spotless name."

"Harry, dearest, although a few drops of Negro blood flows through your veins, your heart is as noble and your soul as pure as that of any one of my race. I would fain take you by the hand as my own, defying friends, father—defying the world, Harry, for I love you; and if you leave me I shall surely go mad! It would break my heart; it would kill me!" cried the girl, with frantic sobs.

"Oh, God! why was I ever born to wreck so pure and beautiful a heart as this? Why, oh, why is it such a crime for one of Negro lineage to dare to love the woman of his choice?"

"Darling, I wish that we had never met—that I had died before seeing your beautiful face—and then dear one you would be free to love and honor one of your own class; one who would be more worthy of you; at least, worthier than I, a Negro."

"To me, Harry, you are the noblest man on earth, and Negro that you are, I would not have you changed. I only wish, dear, that I also was possessed of Negro lineage, so that you would not think me so far above you. As it is dear—perhaps it is but the teaching of Mammie Nell—but I feel something as though I belonged to your race, at any rate I shall very soon, for whither you go, there too I shall be."

"My darling—what strange words—what do you mean?" he asked anxiously.

"Simply this, that we can elope!"

"Oh, Lillian, dear one, you forget that you are the daughter of one of Virginia's oldest aristocrats!"

"Do not reproach me for that Harry. Have I not thought, and wept, and prayed over it until my eyes were dim and my heart ached? I tell you there is no other way. We could go to Europe. I have always longed to visit Italy and France. Oh, Harry! we could be so happy together!"

"Lillian! Lillian! oh, my dearest!" he cried as he drew her closer within his embrace and pressed passionate kisses on her upturned face. Then he as suddenly put her from him.

"No! No! I am but mortal; do not tempt me. It would be worse than cowardly to do this. I cannot! Oh God! I cannot!"

But the girl wound her beautiful arms around his neck and asked tenderly: "Not even for my sake, Harry? Not even if it was the only thing on earth that would make me happy?"

The soft arms clinging about his neck, the pleading eyes gazing into his, completely stole his senses. He could not draw her closer to him, but his voice shook with emotion as he answered:

"Lillian, I have said that I would die for you, if it would but make you happy. And the thought of taking you away—of making you my wife—drives me wild with joy. Will you trust yourself with me?"

"I am yours—take me to your heart," was her reply.

And he kissed her again passionately, almost madly; he called her sweetheart, wife, and many other endearing names.

* * * * *

A week later the country for miles around was ringing with the news of Lillian Westland's elopement with her father's Negro coachman.

A posse of men and women scoured the country for miles around hoping to find the young people established in some dainty cottage. Cries of "lynch the Nigger, lynch the Nigger!" rang through the woods, and many were the comments, innuendoes and slighting words bestowed upon the young girl, who had been such a pet, but who had now outraged society so grossly.

It was a terrible shock to Lillian's white-haired aristocratic father. He had loved and worshipped his beautiful daughter and only child. But this madness, this ignominious conduct that his well beloved and petted darling had shown, crushed and dazed him, and placed him in a stupor from which it was impossible to arouse him. He shut himself up and refused to see even his most intimate friends.

The short, imploring, pitiful letter he received from Lillian, confessing all, and begging that in time her father would look upon her conduct a little less harshly, failed to animate him.

A month later, the news of the Hon. Jack Westland's death from suicide was announced by the entire press of that section. A deep mystery was connected with the suicide, of which vague hints were published in the daily papers. But nothing definite being known, the Westland mystery was soon forgotten by the world in general.

By only one person was the key of the mystery held, and she was a servant, who had been in the Westland's employ for many years.

This servant was an octoroon woman of about thirty-five years of age. Her eyes were the most remarkable feature about her. They were large and dark: at times wild and flashing, and again gentle and appealing, which fact conveyed to one the idea of a most romantic history. Her straight nose, well cut mouth and graceful poise of her head and neck showed that she was once a very beautiful creature, as well as an ill-used one, to judge from her story which was as follows:

It was twenty years ago that I first took the position as chambermaid at Westland Towers; I was just sixteen years of age that day—June the 17th, 1875. My mother I never knew, but I was told by an aunt, an only relative of mine, that my mother had been a beautiful quadroon woman, and my father a member of one of Virginia's best families. My aunt having died while I was as yet but ten years old, the hardships and misery I experienced during my wretched existence between ten and sixteen, can better be imagined than described.

The filth and degradation of the low-class Negroes among whom, for lack of means, I was forced to live, disgusted me so that I grew to despise them. I held myself aloof from them and refused to take part in the vulgar frivolities which they indulged in, and occupied my spare moments in study, thereby evoking a torrent of anger and abuse upon my head, from the lowest Negroes. It was therefore with great relief that I accepted a position as chambermaid at Westland Towers, preferring to live as a servant with white people than to be the most honored guest of the Negroes among whom I had lived. I was young then, and the blood of my father who was a great artist, was stronger in me than that of my mother. Naturally I hated all things dark, loathsome and disagreeable, and my soul thirsted and hungered for the bright sunshine, and the brilliancy and splendor of all things beautiful, which I found at the Westland Towers. It was one of the most magnificently beautiful places in Virginia.

The Westland family were of old and proud descent, and consisted of a father, son and a wizened old housekeeper. The son was a handsome man. In fact I will describe him as I saw him for the first time in my life. I was in the act of dusting his private sitting room, when I turned and saw this handsome young man standing in the doorway. The expression on his face was one of ardent admiration. His violet blue eyes, as they gazed into mine seeming to read my very soul, had a charm about them which drew me to him in spite of myself. His short curls, which lay about his high aristocratic forehead shone like bright gold, and a soft, light mustache hid a mouth which was better acquainted with a smile than a sneer. His figure was tall and stalwart, though as graceful as a woman's, and altogether, he impressed me as being by far the most handsome man I had ever seen.

He spoke to me pleasantly, kindly, and with a gentleness which seemed to thrill my very soul. I was young and foolish, unused to the ways of the world and of men, and when his blue eyes looked into mine, so appealingly, and his gentle, musical voice spoke to me so tenderly, telling me that I was the most beautiful girl in all the world, and that he loved me passionately, nay madly, adding that if I would only be his, he would place me in a beautiful house with servants, horses and carriages; telling me that I should have beautiful dresses and jewelry and that all within the household should worship me, I laid my head upon his breast and told him I would be his.

But when I asked him if we could not marry he replied that it was impossible. That if he ever married one of colored blood, his father's anger would be so great as to cause his disinheritance, and that then he could not place his darling in a high position, adding that being born a gentleman, it would go hard with him to try to earn his own livelihood, all of which seemed to me a very fitting excuse. He also told me that it was not a marriage certificate or the words of a ceremony which made us man and wife. That marriages were made in Heaven, and if we loved each other and lived together, God would look down on us and bless our union, adding that he would always love me and never leave me. Oh, God! that was a bitter trial! I had no mother to advise me; no friend to go to for assistance, and the very thought of giving him up for the filth and degradation from which I came, tortured me for days, during which time my great love for him overcame all obstacles, and on the 4th of July, I found myself living in a luxury of love.

We lived together for eighteen months, during which time no sorrow came to me, save the death of a baby boy. Oh, they were happy days! I was assuredly the happiest girl in all Virginia. But there came evil times. His father died, and of course he had to leave me for a time to attend to important duties.

I was sorry for his father's death and I was also glad, thinking that now no obstacle being in the way, he would surely marry me. But in this I was doomed to bitter disappointment.

A young and beautiful lady, a distant cousin of his, stole his heart from me, and when I received a letter from him telling me that grave duties confronted him, and though it broke his heart to say it, he must part from me, offering me an annuity of five hundred dollars, a great lump rose in my throat which seemed to choke me. I felt my heart breaking. The things before my eyes began to dance and gloat at me in my anguish. Then everything grew dark and I knew no more for several weeks. When I regained consciousness, my first impulse was to kill myself, but remembering that in a few months I would become a mother for the second time, I stayed my hand. I also accepted the annuity of five hundred dollars, thinking that if my little one lived, it would amount to a small fortune when of age. My love died, and in its stead lived hatred and thirst for vengence. I thought constantly of the words:

"Hell hath no fury like a woman scorned."

And likened them unto myself. I was young: I could be patient for years, but an opportunity presented itself sooner than I expected. Eight months before the birth of my child, which was a girl, Jack Westland married, and one year after his marriage, his beautiful young wife was called away by death, the cause of which was a tiny baby girl. The death of his young wife caused him such anguish that he shut himself up and would see no one. He would not even look upon the face of the poor motherless babe. He bade the housekeeper to procure a wet nurse for the infant, which was a delicate little thing, and as there were no other to be obtained, they sought me out and begged me to take the position as nurse.

I obstinately refused at first, but on learning that Jack would soon go abroad to try and divert his mind, I accepted; for an idea that would suit my purpose exactly, flashed through my brain. The two babies were almost exactly alike, both having violet blue eyes and dark hair. Indeed the only difference between them was that my baby was four months older. Supposing that the young heiress should die? Could I not deftly change the babies? I would try at all events.

Accordingly it was arranged that I should, as a competent nurse go to some watering place on account of the young heiress' health.

All things went as I had hoped. The young heiress as I expected died, and I mourned her death as that of my own, and when I returned to Westland Towers, no one noticed any change, but that the sea air had improved the baby's health wonderfully.

When Jack returned home two years later, he saw a beautiful, blue eyed baby girl, with jet black curls about her little neck. He greeted me kindly, but there was no touch of passion in his voice. In fact he treated me as an exalted servant which made me hate him all the more.

"He was glad," he said "that I took such an interest in the welfare of little Lillian," and he asked me if there was any special thing that he could do to repay me. There was one thing I desired above all others, and that was the education of a mulatto lad of ten years of age, who worked about the stables. I asked him if he would send the lad to some industrial institution, which request he readily granted. There is but little more to tell. My little girl grew to be a beautiful young lady, the pet and leader among Virginia's most exclusive circle. But the teachings of her old mammie Nellie, she never forgot.

Her sympathy was always for the poor and lowly, and though there were scores of young men of aristocratic blood seeking her heart and hand, she preferred, as I intended she should, the colored youth, Harry Stanly.

"It was the result of this little episode of the change in the babies, which I related to Jack Westwood, after the elopement, that caused him to commit suicide, and as he leaves everything to his daughter Lillian, I hope we shall live happily hereafter," said Mammie Nellie, as she arose and rung for lights.

"My poor abused mother!" exclaimed both Harry and Lillian simultaneously, who had just joined her in New York City, as both threw a loving arm tenderly around her neck. "And now," said Lillian, "your revenge is complete. Let us close up the house, and go abroad. We can remain away several years, traveling and enjoying the beauties of the Old World. What do you say to this?"

"A capital idea," said Harry.

"As well as a practical one, for even here in New York race feeling sometimes runs very high!" exclaimed the octoroon avenger, with a curl of scorn about her mouth, and a triumphant light flashing from her beautiful dark eyes.

After Many Days

A Christmas Story

C hristmas on the Edwards plantation, as it was still called, was a great event to old and young, master and slave comprising the Edwards household. Although freedom had long ago been declared, many of the older slaves could not be induced to leave the plantation, chiefly because the Edwards family had been able to maintain their appearance of opulence through the vicissitudes of war, and the subsequent disasters, which had impoverished so many of their neighbors. It is one of the peculiar characteristics of the American Negro, that he is never to be found in large numbers in any community where the white people are as poor as himself. It is, therefore, not surprising that the Edwards plantation had no difficulty in retaining nearly all of their former slaves as servants under the new regime.

The stately Edwards mansion, with its massive pillars, and spreading por-ticoes, gleaming white in its setting of noble pines and cedars, is still the pride of a certain section of old Virginia.

One balmy afternoon a few days before the great Christmas festival, Doris Edwards, the youngest granddaughter of this historic southern home, was has-tening along a well-trodden path leading down to an old white-washed cabin, one of the picturesque survivals of plantation life before the war. The pathway

First published in *Colored American Magazine* 5 (Dec. 1902): 140–53

was bordered on either side with old-fashioned flowers, some of them still lift-ing a belated blossom, caught in the lingering balm of Autumn, while faded stalks of hollyhock and sunflower, like silent sentinels, guarded the door of this humble cabin.

Through the open vine-latticed window, Doris sniffed with keen delight the mingled odor of pies, cakes and various other dainties temptingly spread out on the snowy kitchen table waiting to be conveyed to the "big house" to con-tribute to the coming Christmas cheer.

Peering into the gloomy cabin, Doris discovered old Aunt Linda, with whom she had always been a great favorite, sitting in a low chair before the old brick oven, her apron thrown over her head, swaying back and forth to the dole-ful measure of a familiar plantation melody, to which the words, "Lambs of the Upper Fold," were being paraphrased in a most ludicrous way. As far back as Doris could remember, it had been an unwritten law on the plantation that when Aunt Linda's "blues chile" reached the "Lambs Of The Upper Fold" stage, she was in a mood not to be trifled with.

Aunt Linda had lived on the plantation so long she had become quite a privileged character. It had never been known just how she had learned to read and write, but this fact had made her a kind of a leader among the other ser-vants, and had earned for herself greater respect even from the Edwards family. Having been a house servant for many years, her language was also better than the other servants, and her spirits were very low indeed, when she lapsed into the language of the "quarters." There was also a tradition in the family that Aunt Linda's coming to the plantation had from the first been shrouded in mys-tery. In appearance she was a tall yellow woman, straight as an Indian, with piercing black eyes, and bearing herself with a certain dignity of manner, un-usual in a slave. Visitors to the Edwards place would at once single her out from among the other servants, sometimes asking some very uncomfortable ques-tions concerning her. Doris, however, was the one member of the household who refused to take Aunt Linda's moods seriously, so taking in the situation at a glance, she determined to put an end to this "mood" at least. Stealing softly upon the old woman, she drew the apron from her head, exclaiming, "O, Aunt Linda, just leave your 'lambs' alone for to-day, won't you? why this is Christmas time, and I have left all kinds of nice things going on up at the house to bring you the latest news, and now, but what is the matter anyway?" The old woman slowly raised her head, saying, "I might of knowd it was you, you certainly is gettin' might saccy, chile, chile, how you did fright me sure. My min was way back in ole Carlina, jest befoh another Christmas, when de Lord done lay one hand on my pore heart, and wid de other press down de white lids over de blue eyes of my sweet Alice, O, my chile, can I evah ferget date day?" Doris, fearing another outburst, interrupted the moans of the old woman by playfully placing her hand over her mouth, saying: "Wait a minute, auntie, I want to tell you something. There are so many delightful people up to the house, but I want to tell you about two of them especially. Sister May has just come and has brought with her her friend, Pauline Sommers, who sings beautifully, and she is going to sing our Christmas carol for us on Christmas eve. With them is the loveliest girl I ever saw, her name is Gladys Winne. I wish I could describe her, but I can't. I can only remember her violet eyes; think of it, auntie, not blue, but violet, just like the pansies in your garden last summer." At the mention of the last name, Aunt Linda rose, leaning on the table for support. It seemed to her as if some cruel hand had reached out of a pitiless past and clutched her heart. Doris gazed in startled awe at the storm of anguish that seemed to sweep across the old woman's face, exclaiming, "Why, auntie, are you sick?" In a hoarse voice, she answered: "Yes, chile, yes, I's sick." This poor old slave woman's life was rimmed by just two events, a birth and a death, and even these memories were hers and not hers, yet the mention of a single name has for a moment blotted out all the intervening years and in another lowly cabin, the name of 'Gladys' is whispered by dying lips to breaking hearts. Aunt Linda gave a swift glance at the startled Doris, while making a desperate effort to recall her wandering thoughts, lest unwittingly she betray her loved ones to this little chatterer. Forcing a ghastly smile, she said, as if to herself, "As if there was only one Gladys in all dis worl, yes and heaps of Winnes, too, I reckon. Go on chile, go on, ole Aunt Linda is sure getting ole and silly." Doris left the cabin bristling with curiosity, but fortunately for Aunt Linda, she would not allow it to worry her pretty head very long.

The lovely Gladys Winne, as she was generally called, was indeed the most winsome and charming of all the guests that composed the Christmas party in the Edwards mansion. Slightly above medium height, with a beautifully rounded form, delicately poised head crowned with rippling chestnut hair, curling in soft tendrils about neck and brow, a complexion of dazzling fairness with the tint of the rose in her cheeks, and the whole face lighted by deeply glowing violet eyes. Thus liberally endowed by nature, there was further added the charm of a fine education, the advantage of foreign travel, contact with brilliant minds, and a social prestige through her foster parents, that fitted her for the most exclusive social life.

She had recently been betrothed to Paul Westlake, a handsome, wealthy and gifted young lawyer of New York. He had been among the latest arrivals, and Gladys' happiness glowed in her expressive eyes, and fairly scintillated from every curve of her exquisite form. Beautifully gowned in delicate blue of soft and clinging texture draped with creamy lace, she was indeed as rare a picture of radiant youth and beauty as one could wish to see.

But, strange to say, Gladys' happiness was not without alloy. She had one real or fancied annoyance, which she could not shake off, though she tried not to think about it. But as she walked with Paul, through the rambling rooms of this historic mansion, she determined to call his attention to it. They had just passed an angle near a stairway, when Gladys nervously pressed his arm, saying, "Look, Paul, do you see that tall yellow woman; she follows me everywhere, and actually haunts me like a shadow. If I turn suddenly, I can just see her gliding out of sight. Sometimes she becomes bolder, and coming closer to me, she peers into my face as if she would look me through. Really there seems to be something uncanny about it all to me; it makes me shiver. Look, Paul, there she is now, even your presence does not daunt her." Paul, after satisfying himself that she was really serious and annoyed, ceased laughing, saying, "My darling, I cannot consistently blame any one for looking at you. It may be due to an inborn curiosity; she probably is attracted by other lovely things in the same way, only you may not have noticed it." "Nonsense," said Gladys, blushing, "that is a very sweet explanation, but it doesn't explain in this case. It annoys me so much that I think I must speak to Mrs. Edwards about it." Here Paul quickly interrupted. "No, my dear, I would not do that; she is evidently a privileged servant, judging from the rightaway she seems to have all over the house. Mrs. Edwards is very kind and gracious to us, yet she might resent any criticism of her servants. Try to dismiss it from your mind, my love. I have always heard that these old 'mammies' are very superstitious, and she may fancy that she has seen you in some vision or dream, but it ought not to cause you any concern at all. Just fix your mind on something pleasant; on me, for instance." Thus lovingly rebuked and comforted, Gladys did succeed in forgetting for a time her silent watcher. But the thing that annoyed her almost more than anything else was the fact that she had a sense of being irresistibly drawn towards this old servant, by a chord of sympathy and interest, for which she could not in any way account.

But the fatal curiosity of her sex, despite the advice of Paul, whom she so loved and trusted, finally wrought her own undoing. The next afternoon, at a time when she was sure she would not be missed, Gladys stole down to Aunt Linda's cabin determined to probe this mystery for herself. Finding the cabin door ajar, she slipped lightly into the room.

Aunt Linda was so absorbed by what she was doing that she heard no sound. Gladys paused upon the threshold of the cabin, fascinated by the old woman's strange occupation. She was bending over the contents of an old hair chest, tenderly shaking out one little garment after another of a baby's wardrobe, filling the room with the pungent odor of camphor and lavender.

The tears were falling and she would hold the little garments to her bosom, crooning some quaint cradle song, tenderly murmuring, "O, my lam, my poor lil' lam," and then, as if speaking to some one unseen, she would say: "No, my darlin, no, your ole mother will shorely nevah break her promise to young master, but O, if you could only see how lovely your little Gladys has growed to be! Sweet innocent Gladys, and her pore ole granma must not speak to or tech her, mus not tell her how her own ma loved her and dat dese ole hans was de fust to hold her, and mine de fust kiss she ever knew; but O, my darlin, I will nevah tray you, she shall nevah know." Then the old woman's sobs would break out afresh, as she frantically clasped the tiny garments, yellow with age, but dainty enough for a princess, to her aching heart.

For a moment Gladys, fresh and sweet as a flower, felt only the tender sympathy of a casual observer, for what possible connection could there be between her and this old colored woman in her sordid surroundings. Unconsciously she drew her skirts about her in scorn of the bare suggestion, but the next moment found her transfixed with horror, a sense of approaching doom enveloping her as in a mist. Clutching at her throat, and with dilated unseeing eyes, she groped her way toward the old woman, violently shaking her, while in a terror-stricken voice she cried, "O Aunt Linda, what is it?" With a cry like the last despairing groan of a wounded animal, Aunt Linda dropped upon her knees, scattering a shower of filmy lace and dainty flannels about her. Through every fibre of her being, Gladys felt the absurdity of her fears, yet in spite of herself, the words welled up from her heart to her lips, "O Aunt Linda, what is it, what have I to do with your dead?" with an hysterical laugh, she added, "do I look like someone you have loved and lost in other days?" Then the simple-hearted old woman, deceived by the kindly note in Gladys' voice, and not seeing the unspeakable horror growing in her eyes, stretched out imploring hands as to a little child, the tears streaming from her eyes, saying, "O, Gladys," not Miss Gladys now, as the stricken girl quickly notes, "you is my own sweet Alice's little chile, O, honey I's your own dear gran-ma. You's beautiful, Gladys, but not more so den you own sweet ma, who loved you so."

The old woman was so happy to be relieved of the secret burden she had borne for so many years, that she had almost forgotten Gladys' presence, until she saw her lost darling fainting before her very eyes. Quickly she caught her in her arms, tenderly pillowing her head upon her ample bosom, where as a little babe she had so often lain.

For several minutes the gloomy cabin was wrapped in solemn silence. Finally Gladys raised her head, and turning toward Aunt Linda her face, from which every trace of youth and happiness had fled, in a hoarse and almost breathless whisper, said: "If you are my own grandmother, who then was my father?" Before this searching question these two widely contrasted types of southern conditions, stood dumb and helpless. The shadow of the departed crime of slavery still remained to haunt the generations of freedom.

Though Aunt Linda had known for many years that she was free, the generous kindness of the Edwards family had made the Emancipation proclamation almost meaningless to her.

When she now realized that the fatal admission, which had brought such gladness to her heart, had only deepened the horror in Gladys' heart, a new light broke upon her darkened mind. Carefully placing Gladys in a chair, the old woman raised herself to her full height, her right hand uplifted like some bronze goddess of liberty. For the first time and for one brief moment she felt the inspiring thrill and meaning of the term freedom. Ignorant of almost everything as compared with the knowledge and experience of the stricken girl before her, yet a revelation of the sacred relationships of parenthood, childhood and home, the common heritage of all humanity swept aside all differences of complexion or position.

For one moment, despite her lowly surroundings and dusky skin, an equality of blood, nay superiority of blood, tingled in old Aunt Linda's veins, straightened her body, and flashed in her eye. But the crushing process over two centuries could not sustain in her more than a moment of asserted womanhood. Slowly she lowered her arm, and, with bending body, she was again but an old slave woman with haunting memories and a bleeding heart. Then with tears and broken words, she poured out the whole pitiful story to the sobbing Gladys.

"It was this way, honey, it all happened jus before the wah, way down in ole Carolina. My lil Alice, my one chile had growed up to be so beautiful. Even when she was a tiny lil chile, I used to look at her and wonder how de good Lord evah 'lowed her to slip over my door sill, but nevah min dat chile, dat is not you alls concern. When she was near 'bout seventeen years old, she was dat prutty that the white folks was always askin' of me if she was my own chile, the ide, as if her own ma, but den that was all right for dem, it was jest case she was so white, I knowd.

"Tho' I lived wid my lil Alice in de cabin, I was de housemaid in de 'big house,' but I'd nevah let Alice be up thar wid me when there was company, case, well I jest had to be keerful, nevah mind why. But one day, young Master Harry Winne was home from school, and they was a celebratin', an' I was in a hurry; so I set Alice to bringin' some roses fron de garden to trim de table, and there young master saw her, an' came after me to know who she was; he say he thought he knowed all his ma's company, den I guess I was too proud, an' I up an' tells him dat she was my Alice, my own lil' gel, an' I was right away scared dat I had tole him, but he had seen huh; dat was enough, O my pore lam!" Here the old woman paused, giving herself up for a moment to unrestrained weeping. Suddenly she dried her eyes and said: "Gladys, chile, does you know what love is?" Gladys' cheeks made eloquent response, and with one swift glance, the old woman continued, "den you knows how they loved each other. One day Master Harry went to ole Master and he say: 'Father, I know you'll be auful angered at me, but I will marry Alice or no woman'; den his father say—but nevah min' what it was, only it was enough to make young master say dat he'd nevah forgive his pa, for what he say about my lil' gurl.

"Some time after that my Alice began to droop an' pine away like; so one day I say to her: 'Alice, does you an' young master love each other?' Den she tole me as how youn master had married her, and that she was afeard to tell even her ma, case they mite sen him away from her forever. When young master came again he tole me all about it; jest lak my gurl had tole me. He say he could not lib withou' her. After dat he would steal down to see her when he could, bringing huh all dese pritty laces and things, and she would sit all day and sew an' cry lak her heart would break.

"He would bribe ole Sam not to tell ole Master, saying date he was soon goin' to take huh away where no men or laws could tech them. Well, after you was bohn, she began to fade away from me, gettin' weaker every day. Den when you was only a few months ole, O, how she worshipped you! I saw dat my pore unhappy lil gurl was goin' on dat long journey away from her pore heart-broke ma, to dat home not made with hans, den I sent for young master, your pa. O, how he begged her not to go, saying dat he had a home all ready for her an you up Norf. Gently she laid you in his arms, shore de mos' beautiful chile dat evah were, wid your great big violet eyes looking up into his, tho' he could not see dem for the tears dat would fall on yo sweet face. Your ma tried to smile, reaching out her weak arms for you, she said: 'Gladys,' an' with choking sobs she made us bofe promise, she say, 'promise that she shall never know that her ma was a slave or dat she has a drop of my blood, make it all yours, Harry, nevah let her know.' We bofe promised, and that night young master tore you from my breaking heart, case it was best. After I had laid away my poor unhappy chile, I begged ole Master to sell me, so as to sen me way off to Virginia, where I could nevah trace you nor look fer you, an' I nevah have." Then the old woman threw herself upon her knees, wringing her hands and saying: "O my God, why did you let her fin me?" She had quite forgotten Gladys' presence in the extremity of her distress at having broken her vow to the dead and perhaps wrought sorrow for the living.

Throughout the entire recital, told between heart-breaking sobs and moans, Gladys sat as if carved in marble, never removing her eyes from the old woman's face. Slowly she aroused herself, allowing her dull eyes to wander about the room at the patch-work covered bed in the corner; then through the open casement, from which she could catch a glimpse of a group of young Negroes, noting their coarse features and boisterous play; then back again to the crouching, sobbing old woman. With a shiver running through her entire form, she found her voice, which seemed to come from a great distance, "And I am part of all this! O, my God, how can I live; above all, how can I tell Paul, but I must and will; I will not deceive him though it kill me."

At the sound of Gladys' voice Aunt Linda's faculties awoke, and she began to realize the awful possibilities of her divulged secrets. Aunt Linda had felt and known the horrors of slavery, but could she have known that after twenty years of freedom, nothing in the whole range of social disgraces could work such terrible disinheritance to man or woman as the presence of Negro blood, seen or unseen, she would have given almost life itself rather than to have condemned this darling of her love and prayers to so dire a fate.

The name of Paul, breathed by Gladys in accents of such tenderness and despair, aroused Aunt Linda to action. She implored her not to tell Paul or any one else. "No one need ever know, no one ever can or shall know," she pleaded. "How could any fin' out, honey, if you did not tell them?" Then seizing one of Gladys' little hands, pink and white and delicate as a rose leaf, and placing it beside her own old and yellow one, she cried: "Look chile, look, could any one ever fin' the same blood in dese two hans by jest looking at em? No, honey, I has done kep dis secret all dese years, and now I pass it on to you an you mus' keep it for yourself for the res' of de time, deed you mus', no one need evah know."

To her dying day Aunt Linda never forgot the despairing voice of this stricken girl, as she said: "Ah, but I know, my God, what have I done to deserve this?"

With no word of pity for the suffering old woman, she again clutched her arm, saying in a stifled whisper: "Again I ask you, who was, or is my father, and where is he?" Aunt Linda cowered before this angry goddess, though she was of her own flesh and blood, and softly said: "He is dead; died when you were about five years old. He lef you heaps of money, and in the care of a childless couple, who reared you as they own; he made 'em let you keep his name, I can't see why." With the utmost contempt Gladys cried, "Gold, gold, what is gold to such a heritage as this? an ocean of gold cannot wash away this stain."

Poor Gladys never knew how she reached her room. She turned to lock the door, resolved to fight this battle out for herself; then she thought of kind Mrs. Edwards. She would never need a mother's love so much as now. Of her own mother, she dared not even think. Then, too, why had she not thought of it before, this horrible story might not be true. Aunt Linda was probably out of her mind, and Mrs. Edwards would surely know.

By a striking coincidence Mrs. Edwards had noticed Linda's manner toward her fair guest, and knowing the old woman's connection with the Winne family, she had just resolved to send for her and question her as to her suspicions, if she had any, and at least caution her as to her manner.

Hearing a light tap upon her door, she hastily opened it. She needed but one glance at Gladys' unhappy countenance to tell her that it was too late; the mischief had already been done. With a cry of pity and dismay, Mrs. Edwards opened her arms and Gladys swooned upon her breast. Tenderly she laid her down and when she had regained consciousness, she sprang up, crying, "O Mrs. Edwards, say that it is not true, that it is some horrible dream from which I shall soon awaken?" How gladly would this good woman have sacrificed almost anything to spare this lovely girl, the innocent victim of an outrageous and blighting system, but Gladys was now a woman and must be answered. "Gladys, my dear," said Mrs. Edwards, "I wish I might save you further distress, by telling you that what I fear you have heard, perhaps from Aunt Linda herself, is not true. I am afraid it is all too true. But fortunately in your case no one need know. It will be safe with us and I will see that Aunt Linda does not mention it again, she ought not to have admitted it to you."

Very gently Mrs. Edwards confirmed Aunt Linda's story, bitterly inveighing against a system which mocked at marriage vows, even allowing a man to sell his own flesh and blood for gain. She told this chaste and delicate girl how poor slave girls, many of them most beautiful in form and feature, were not allowed to be modest, not allowed to follow the instincts of moral rectitude, that they might be held at the mercy of their masters. Poor Gladys writhed as if under the lash. She little knew what painful reasons Mrs. Edwards had for hating the entire system of debasement to both master and slave. Her kind heart, southern born and bred as she was yearned to give protection and home to two beautiful girls, who had been shut out from her own hearthstone, which by right of justice and honor was theirs to share also. "Tell me, Gladys," she exclaimed, "which race is the more to be despised? Forgive me, dear, for telling you these things, but my mind was stirred by very bitter memories. Though great injustice has been done, and is still being done, I say to you, my child, that from selfish interest and the peace of my household, I could not allow such a disgrace to attach to one of my most honored guests. Do you not then see, dear, the unwisdom of revealing your identity here and now? Unrevealed, we are all your friends—" the covert threat lurking in the unfinished sentence was not lost upon Gladys. She arose, making an effort to be calm, but nervously seizing Mrs. Edwards' hand, she asked: "Have I no living white relatives?" Mrs. Edwards hesitated a moment, then said: "Yes, a few, but they are very wealthy and influential, and now living in the north; so that I am very much afraid that they are not concerned as to whether you are living or not. They knew, of course, of your birth; but since the death of your father, whom they all loved very much, I have heard, though it may be only gossip, that they do not now allow your name to be mentioned.

Gladys searched Mrs. Edwards' face with a peculiarly perplexed look; then in a plainer tone of voice, said: "Mrs. Edwards, it must be that only Negroes possess natural affection. Only think of it, through all the years of my life, and though I have many near relatives, I have been cherished in memory and yearned for by only one of them, and that an old and despised colored woman. The almost infinitesimal drop of her blood in my veins is really the only drop that I can consistently be proud of." Then, springing up, an indecribable glow fairly transfiguring and illuminating her face, she said: "My kind hostess, and comforting friend, I feel that I must tell Paul, but for your sake we will say nothing to the others, and if he does not advise me, yes, command me, to own and cherish that lonely old woman's love, and make happy her declining years, then he is not the man to whom I can or will entrust my love and life."

With burning cheeks, and eyes hiding the stars in their violet depths, her whole countenance glowing with a sense of pride conquered and love exalted, beautiful to see, she turned to Mrs. Edwards and tenderly kissing her, passed softly from the room.

For several moments, Mrs. Edwards stood where Gladys had left her. "Poor deluded girl," she mused. "Paul Westlake is by far one of the truest and noblest young men I have ever known, but let him beware, for there is even now coming to meet him the strongest test of his manhood principles he has ever had to face; beside it, all other perplexing problems must sink into nothingness. Will he be equal to it? We shall soon see."

Gladys, in spite of the sublime courage that had so exalted her but a moment before, felt her resolution weaken with every step. It required almost a super-human will to resist the temptation to silence, so eloquently urged upon her by Mrs. Edwards. But her resolution was not to be thus lightly set aside; it pursued her to her room, translating itself into the persistent thought that if fate is ever to be met and conquered, the time is now; delays are dangerous.

As she was about to leave her room on her mission, impelled by an indefinable sense of farewell, she turned, with her hand upon the door, as if she would include in this backward glance all the dainty furnishings, the taste and elegance everywhere displayed, and of which she had felt so much a part. Finally her wandering gaze fell upon a fine picture of Paul Westlake upon the mantel. Instantly there flashed into her mind the first and only public address she had ever heard Paul make. She had quite forgotten the occasion, except that it had some relation to a so-called "Negro problem." Then out from the past came the rich tones of the beloved voice as with fervid eloquence he arraigned the American people for the wrongs and injustice that had been perpetrated upon a weak and defenseless people through centuries of their enslavement and their few years of freedom.

With much feeling he recounted the pathetic story of this unhappy people when freedom found them, trying to knit together the broken ties of family kinship and their struggles through all the odds and hates of opposition, trying to make a place for themselves in the great family of races. Gladys' awakened conscience quickens the memory of his terrible condemnation of a system and of the men who would willingly demoralize a whole race of women, even at the sacrifice of their own flesh and blood.

With Mrs. Edwards' words still ringing in her ears, the memory of the last few words stings her now as then, except that now she knows why she is so sensitive as to their real import.

This message brought to her from out a happy past by Paul's pictured face, has given to her a light of hope and comfort beyond words. Hastily closing the door of her room, almost eagerly, and with buoyant step, she goes to seek Paul and carry out her mission.

To Paul Westlake's loving heart, Gladys Winne never appeared so full of beauty, curves and graces, her eyes glowing with confidence and love, as when he sprang eagerly forward to greet her on that eventful afternoon. Through all the subsequent years of their lives the tenderness and beauty of that afternoon together never faded from their minds. They seemed, though surrounded by the laughter of friends and festive preparations, quite alone—set apart by the intensity of their love and happiness.

When they were about to separate for the night, Gladys turned to Paul, with ominous seriousness, yet trying to assume a lightness she was far from feeling, saying: "Paul, dear, I am going to put your love to the test tomorrow, may I?" Paul's smiling indifference was surely test enough, if that were all, but she persisted, "I am quite in earnest, dear; I have a confession to make to you. I intended to tell you this afternoon, but I could not cloud this almost our last evening together for a long time perhaps, so I decided to ask you to meet me in the library tomorrow morning at ten o'clock, will you?"

"Will I," Paul replied; "my darling, you know I will do anything you ask; but why tomorrow, and why so serious about the matter; beside, if it be anything that is to affect our future in any way, why not tell it now?" As Gladys was still silent, he added: "Dear, if you will assure me that this confession will not change your love for me in any way, I will willingly wait until tomorrow or next year; any time can you give me this assurance?" Gladys softly answered: "Yes, Paul, my love is yours now and always; that is, if you will always wish it." There was an expression upon her face he did not like, because he could not understand it, but tenderly drawing her to him, he said: "Gladys, dear, can anything matter so long as we love each other? I truly believe it cannot. But tell me this, dear, after this confession do I then hold the key to the situation?" "Yes, Paul,

I believe you do; in fact I know that you will." "Ah, that is one point gained, to-morrow; then it can have no terrors for me," he lightly replied.

Gladys passed an almost sleepless night. Confident, yet fearful, she watched the dawn of the new day. Paul, on the contrary, slept peacefully and rose to greet the morn with confidence and cheer. "If I have Gladys' love," he mused, "there is nothing in heaven or earth for me to fear."

At last the dreaded hour of ten drew near; their "Ides of March" Paul quoted with some amusement over the situation.

The first greeting over, the silence became oppressive. Paul broke it at last, saying briskly: "Now, dear, out with this confession; I am not a success at co-nundrums; another hour of this suspense would have been my undoing," he laughingly said.

Gladys, pale and trembling, felt all of her courage slipping from her; she knew not how to begin. Although she had rehearsed every detail of this scene again and again, she could not recall a single word she had intended to say. Fi-nally she began with the reminder she had intended to use as a last resort: "Paul, do you remember taking me last Spring to hear your first public address; do you remember how eloquently and earnestly you pleaded the cause of the Negro?" Seeing only a growing perplexity upon his face, she cried: "O, my love, can you not see what I am trying to say? O, can you not understand? but no, no, no one could ever guess a thing so awful"; then sinking her voice almost to a whisper and with averted face, she said: "Paul, it was because you were unconsciously pleading for your own Gladys, for I am one of them."

"What nonsense is this," exclaimed Paul, springing from his chair; "it is impossible, worse than improbable, it cannot be true. It is the work of some jealous rival; surely, Gladys, you do not expect me to believe such a wild, un-thinkable story as this!" Then controlling himself, he said: "O, my darling, who could have been so cruel as to have tortured you like this? If any member of this household has done this thing let us leave them in this hour. I confess I do not love the South or a Southerner, with my whole heart, in spite of this 'united country' nonsense; yes, I will say it, and in spite of the apparently gracious hos-pitality of this household."

Gladys, awed by the violence of his indignation, placed a trembling hand upon his arm, saying: "Listen, Paul, do you not remember on the very evening of your arrival here, of my calling your attention to a tall turbaned servant with the piercing eyes? Don't you remember I told you how she annoyed me by fol-lowing me everywhere, and you laughed away my fears, and lovingly quieted my alarm? Now, O Paul, how can I say it, but I must, that woman, that Negress, who was once a slave, is my own grandmother." Without waiting for him to re-ply, she humbly but bravely poured into his ears the whole pitiful story, sparing neither father nor mother, but blaming her mother least of all. Ah, the pity of it!

Without a word, Paul took hold of her trembling hands and drawing her toward the window, with shaking hand, he drew aside the heavy drapery; then turning her face so that the full glory of that sunlit morning fell upon it, he looked long and searchingly into the beautiful beloved face, as if studying the minutest detail of some matchless piece of statuary. At last he found words, saying: "You, my flower, is it possible that there can be concealed in this flawless skin, these dear violet eyes, these finely chiseled features, a trace of lineage or blood, without a single characteristic to vindicate its presence? I will not believe it; it cannot be true." Then baffled by Gladys' silence, he added, "and if it be true, surely the Father of us all intended to leave no hint of shame or dishonor on this, the fairest of his creations."

Gladys felt rather than heard a deepened note of tenderness in his voice and her hopes revived. Then suddenly his calm face whitened and an expression terrible to see swept over it. Instinctively Gladys read his thought. She knew that the last unspoken thought was the future, and because she, too, realized that the problem of heredity must be settled outside the realm of sentiment, her breaking heart made quick resolve.

For some moments they sat in unbroken silence; then Gladys spoke: "Good bye, Paul, I see that you must wrestle with this life problem alone as I have; there is no other way. But that you may be wholly untrammelled in your judgment, I want to assure you that you are free. I love you too well to be willing to degrade your name and prospects by uniting them with a taint of blood, of which I was as innocent as yourself, until two days ago.

"May I ask you to meet me once more, and for the last time, at twelve o'clock tonight? I will then abide by your judgment as to what is best for both of us. Let us try to be ourselves today, so that our own heart-aches may not cloud the happiness of others. I said twelve o'clock because I thought we would be less apt to be missed at that hour of general rejoicings than at any other time. Good bye, dear, 'till then." Absently Paul replied: "All right, Gladys, just as you say; I will be here."

At the approach of the midnight hour Paul and Gladys slipped away to the library, which had become to them a solemn and sacred trysting place.

Gladys looked luminously beautiful on this Christmas eve. She wore a black gauze dress flecked with silver, through which her skin gleamed with dazzling fairness. Her only ornaments were sprigs of holly, their brilliant berries adding the necessary touch of color to her unusual pallor. She greeted Paul with gentle sweetness and added dignity and courage shining in her eyes.

Eagerly she scanned his countenance and sought his eyes, and then she shrank back in dismay at his set face and stern demeanor.

Suddenly the strength of her love for him and the glory and tragedy which his love had brought to her life surged through her, breaking down all reserve. "Look at me, Paul," she cried in a tense whisper, "have I changed since yesterday; am I not the same Gladys you have loved so long?" In a moment their positions had changed and she had become the forceful advocate at the bar of love and justice; the love of her heart overwhelmed her voice with a torrent of words, she implored him by the sweet and sacred memories that had enkindled from the first their mutual love; by the remembered kisses, their after-glow flooding her cheeks as she spoke, and "O, my love, the happy days together," she paused, as if the very sweetness of the memory oppressed her voice to silence, and helpless and imploring she held out her hands to him.

Paul was gazing at her as if entranced, a growing tenderness filling and thrilling his soul. Gradually he became conscious of a tightening of the heart at the thought of losing her out of his life. There could be no such thing as life without Gladys, and when would she need his love, his protection, his tenderest sympathy so much as now?

The light upon Paul's transfigured countenance is reflected on Gladys' own and as he moved toward her with outstretched arms, in the adjoining room the magnificent voice of the beautiful singer rises in the Christmas carol, mingling in singular harmony with the plaintive melody as sung by a group of dusky singers beneath the windows.

Katherine Davis Chapman Tillman

The Preacher
At Hill Station

Sunday morning in a little Virginia town nestling among the mountains. A crowd of Negro men and women, coming out of the little Methodist Chapel, discussing in their shrewd humorous manner the new preacher sent to Hill Station Chapel a month previous.

There was plenty of evidence of genuine emotion upon the faces of many of the recent worshippers. Those who enjoyed religion best by shouting were still rejoicing, and their fervent "Praise de Lawds" and "Hallelujahs" seemed but to deepen the troubled looks that were observed upon the faces of several of the "sinnahs" as the impenitent were called.

"Well, Aunt Jennie, do you still think our little elder can't preach?" said Robert Jones, a quiet, little yellow man whose eyes were even now wet with tears to a large black woman with a comely face who chanced to be walking his way.

"Hush, Jones, don' say a word! Ain't I gone an' shouted myse'f cl'ar out of bref, I nebber did feel so much lak flyin' as I did dis mawnin'. Ef it jes' hadn' ben for Mose an' de chillen, I'd ben willin' fer ole Marse to let down his golden chariot an' let me step on bo'd. Oh, glory!"

First published in *A.M.E. Church Review* 19 (Jan. 1903): 634–43

"De elder certn'y was in de sperit," remarked Jones, meditatively.

"An' ter think how I wo'ked against dat blessed man 'case ole Lias done tole me dat our minister was one ob dem edjercated fools, an' when he come to de chapel we ole folks gwine be put back in de corner."

"It was certn'y a wonderful sermon," said Jones, "I've hearn Ward, Wayman,—some ob de bigges' guns in de chu'ch, an' I aint nebber hearn a feelinger sermon dan I hearn dis mawnin'. Well, I guess I'll tu'n off heah."

"Tu'n off nothin'; come rite along home wid me. I prepahed dinnah fo' de elder ter day, but he couldn't come an somebody's got to he'p eat dat chicken an' apple-dumplin's 'sides Mose an' de chillen?"

The fame of Aunt Jennie's cooking was too well assured for Jones to think of refusing the invitation, so he walked on with her saying gently, "I'm so full ob de sperit that I don' feel a bit hungry. Smith was out dis mawnin'; he mus' felt mighty cheap after sayin' roun' so big to evahbody he never spec' to put his foot inside de chapel agin."

"De bird nevah fly so high but what he hab to come down to de groun fer his feed," said Aunt Jennie oracularly. "Lias Smith got to be sich a good Baptis' inside ob de four weeks dat he hab lef our chu'ch. Why he come to my house a few days ago an' tried to tu'n me, an' I've ben raised on Methodis' doctrine all my days. De Baptis' preacher, Elder Smiles, was wid him; they dropped in 'bout noon an' ob co'se I gib 'em bof dinnah. Seemed lak when Smith's mouth 'gin to close down on de biscuits an' fried bacon I had fer dinnah, dat it 'gan to loosen his tongue. Says he to me, 'Sis Jennie, you'd better come ober to de Baptis' chu'ch an' jine us, you'll get de rite kin of feed. 'Sides dat Elder Smiles dun proved it in de Bible dat day aint no sich church as de Methodis' chu'ch in de Bible, nor dey aint any chu'ch mentioned, but de Baptis! Aint I rite Elder?' 'You's puffe'ly rite,' says Elder Smiles. Well, I was mad as a hornet, but I held in bes' I could an' says, 'How you make dat out, Elder Siles?' 'Well, Sis' Jennie,' he says, 'it's jes' dis way; you knows all de churches 'cep de Baptis' is called Peter Baptist. Now sarch de Bible from kiver to kiver, an' ef you fin' any Peter Baptist, or any other Baptis', 'cep'n one man, John de Baptis' I'll jine yo' chu'ch nex' Sunday.' Well, Jones, it made me mad to think he was settin' thar' at my table, eatin' my grub an' callin' me an' my chu'ch Peter Baptist. Says I, 'Elder Smiles, I want you an' ole two-faced Lias Smith to know dat

> I am Methodis' bred
> An' Methodis' born
> An' when I'm dead,
> Thar's a Methodis' gone.'

"I told 'em what I thought of them bofe, an' dey lef' in a hurry, I tell you.

"You know, 'cause you'se my class leader, dat I ain't been doing my duty fo' de longes' an' my heart riz in my mouf, when I saw Elder Clark comin' fas' as he could.

"He come in, shook han's an axed me what I'se so mad about, an' den I up an' tole him de whole thing, from start to finish. Jones, you orter see de Elder; I thought he'd split hisse'f laffin.

"He hah-hahed an' I got to laffin' too, an' I mos' killed myse'f. Den he sot down an' 'splained de whole mattah 'bout Christ bein' de chief cornah stone ob de chu'ch an' all de members belongin' to one family, till I actually felt sorry fer 'Lias an' his preacher, case I believe Elder Smiles is a good kin' ob a man, but ob cose he ain't got de edjercation our Elder's got.

"I was kinder skittish at fus' dat Elder Clark done come to git aftah me bout not comin' to Chu'ch, but he didn'. He come to see ef I'se willin' to let de chillen come to his school he gwine sta't sence he foun' out the white foks din' 'low us but three months' school.

"Den fo' he lef he tole me 'bout his ole mother down in Washington dat was a slave heah in Virginny jes' lak me an' how dat woman lived in de wash-tub, till he got out ob school, so he could he'p her school de res'. Well, heah we is at last an' I reckon de chillens got evah thing ready by de away de grubs smellin'," and the twain went in to enjoy the feast of good things for which Aunt Jennie's Sunday table was justly famous.

When Clark came to Hill Station, he found the little Methodist Chapel divided into two distinct factions; one formidable and aggressive, led by 'Lias Smith, an unprincipled old Negro, with an intense desire to be known as the "bigges' man in de chu'ch."

This faction was composed of the majority of the older members, who, of course, were the financial strength of the church. The other faction was led by Robert Jones, a man respected alike by black and white for his excellent traits of character. Jones' followers were principally the younger people, who resented 'Lias Smith's coarse bullying manner and demanded a church carried on "lak de white fo'ks carry deirs on."

Aunt Jennie, one of the very strongest pillars of the Chapel, was with Jones at first; but finally fell a victim to the specious wiles of the enemy, becoming a staunch supporter of the Smith faction, which declared that the Bishop need not send them a man from the schools to quench their spirits. They refused to support such a minister; they demanded a man that didn't think he "kno mo' dan fo'ks dat hab ben professin' twenty an' thirty yeahs."

More than that, they demanded a preacher who could preach upon such startling subjects as "Dry Bones in the Valley," "The Sea of Glass" and "Lazarus in Abraham's Bosom"; "For," added 'Lias, "stir dese fo'ks up an' you'll git money, an' ef you don' you won'." He even went so far as to send a badly scrawled petition to the Bishop, describing the kind of a preacher that in *his* opinion, Hill Station required.

Perhaps Jones got some of the young people who taught in the Sunday School to write a petition describing the kind of a preacher that the young people thought was needed. I know not how it was, but the Bishop sent to Hill Station a man fresh from one of the largest and best known of our Negro institutions, a man small and insignificant in stature and withal not very prepossessing in looks; but large of soul, and very much in earnest concerning the needs, bodily and spiritual, of the tiny parish that had been assigned to him.

By persistent kindness, and a refusal to listen to the idle tales of either faction Clark had won the hearts of all of Smith's faction to such an extent that they had, with a few exceptions the most notable of which was 'Lias Smith himself, come back to the church and renewed their allegiance to her courts.

Finding himself defeated and unable, like Lucifer, to draw the third part of the elect with him, the old man took his family from the church and Sunday School, and joined the Rock Daniel Baptist Church which had obtained this queer name from a peculiar custom of this church which required its members to meet at stated intervals and sing and rock Daniel with clasped hands and swaying bodies until they were ready to drop from sheer exhaustion.

In order to combat this and other foolish customs and superstitions, Clark gathered the people together one night in each week and read to them stories of the superstitions of other people, and the way science had made mere bugaboos of them. He read to them stories from ancient mythology, bits of interesting history and short poems, commenting upon them in words that the most ignorant could not fail to comprehend; and when he felt that he had almost exhausted his resources, he called upon several of the white pastors for help and his appeal met with a hearty response.

They, in turn, filled one evening at the Chapel for several weeks, with bright earnest talks upon homely subjects which affected the everyday life of the people; and they were always greeted with an eager appreciative audience.

The week before the delivery of the sermon which had made such an impression upon its hearers, while Clark was returning at four o'clock in the morning from the sick bed of one of his flock, he saw a Negro boy sneaking out of the back gate of one of the white citizens of the place, with a large white rooster.

"Why, why, my boy, what are you up to?" he said, laying his hands upon the boy's shoulder.

"None yer bizness," replied the boy sullenly, with an ugly scowl on his dark face.

"Little brother," said Clark gently, "you are doing wrong; put that rooster back."

"Doin' wrong to take from white fo'ks?" echoed the boy incredulously. "You don' kno' what yer talkin' 'bout; you lemme go."

"Not till you do what is right. Stealing is stealing and it's just as wrong to steal from white folks as it is to steal from black ones. Put it back, and if you are hungry I'll give you money to buy meat," said Clark, willing to sacrifice the meat for his own meagre breakfast in order to enforce a lesson in morals.

"It's a lie; 'tain't wrong to steal from white fo'ks, you ole white fo'ks' nigger," said the boy, and wrenching himself from the minister's grasp, he gave Clark a brutal blow in the face and then ran.

The minister gave chase until he saw the boy disappear in the rear of a house where he had been told his old enemy 'Lias Smith lived. He knocked, and after awhile 'Lias came to the door. "Brother Smith, I came to tell you that your boy is getting into trouble." "How' dat, Elder? Set down."

Clark sat down and related the circumstances. 'Lias looked relieved. "I thought he'd been caught," he said. "See heah, Elder, I mus' say you'se took a heap on yo'se'f to come an' tell me afteh de way I done leff de chu'ch, an' I thank you fer it, but, Elder, you can't make any ob dese ole heds dat went thro' slavery believe dat any thing we takes from white fo'ks is stealing! Whar did dese Virginny white fo'ks from Gawdge Washerton down get what dey got? Dey stole de black fo'ks time an' labor, an' made it off ob dem: dat's whar dey got it."

The minister tried to reason, but apparently with no avail. "Think of the disgrace of your boy being put in prison, if you will not think of his sin," said Clark as he rose to leave, "Sho, dey ain't nevah gwine cotch lil' 'Lias. He's too slick for dat."

But we all know what happened to the pitcher that was carried to the well once too often. A similar fate befell 'Lias, Jr., for he was caught red-handed a few days later, while making an early morning trip to a neighboring hen-house, and in spite of his tears and protestations of innocence, landed in the city jail.

Knowing the kind of moral training that the boy had received, Clark again counselled with the white pastors, and persuaded them to assist him in getting 'Lias out of jail. Through their united interposition, 'Lias was released, upon the payment of a fine, his accusers refusing to appear against him, after having been visited by Clark, and 'Lias returned to his home a sadder and, thanks to Clark, a wiser boy.

Clark took the boy and his parents into a quiet place and made them acknowledge their sin and promise to try to raise the other children differently.

That incident was the turning point, the pivotal epoch of young 'Lias life. He looked at the scar on Clark's face which his brutal blow had left, and he seemed to feel that he never could do enough by way of atonement.

He entered Clark's day school, next his Sunday School and a year later his church—but I anticipate; melted down by the incidents referred to and the sermon, the subject of which on that memorable Sunday morning was "Brotherhood," 'Lias came back to the church soon after, bringing his family with him, and for the first time in the history of the church membership, gave some slight evidence of having accepted the teachings of Christ.

Clark had been at the Chapel four years, and according to the rule of his ecclesiastical body, had stayed his time out, and was preparing to leave for good.

He could look back with a certain amount of satisfaction upon his labors at Hill Station. From being a place of purely noisy demonstration of the spirit, either of the good or the evil, the Chapel had grown to be a recognized center for all good enterprise. A six months term of school, a circulating library, and something more than a parrot form of knowledge of the Ten Commandments had been secured.

The membership of the Chapel was trebled, and in addition to the wiping out of their traditional church debt, under Clark's direction, several of the members had succeeded in clearing the titles to their own little homes.

And Clark had grown to love his work, he was constantly being surprised by the nobility he found in the lives of many of the newly freed. Among them was an orphan girl, with a thirst for books, whom he had helped off to school, and who had just returned, after a three years' absence, transformed from a shy country girl into a beautiful woman, not unlike some of the nice girls that Clark had known at Washington.

He was thinking of one of them now, a teacher in the public schools there, and of Ora May, his *protégé*, who gravely assured him that she wanted to go to Africa as a missionary. How pleasant it would be to have Ora as—when suddenly.

"Elder Clark! Elder Clark!" Ora's voice: He opened the door hastily. Ora stood there with wide-open eyes and parted lips, "Polls,—election—riot—'Lias shot!" she gasped. Clark threw on his coat and almost flew past her.

"To think I forgot it was the hour for the election, for the first time in four years! I might have known." The place where the polls were held was a good half mile. Clark ran till he got in sight of the place, then he stopped and a groan of horror burst from his lips.

A party of young white men, considerably the worse for drink, were trying to drive the Negro voters from the polls. The Negroes had refused to go and 'Lias, Jr., had been wounded by one of the drunken fellows. A large number of both black and white were coming upon the scene, and the situation grew more serious each moment. As if emboldened by the presence of more of their kind the young white fellows began to yell "Down with the niggers!" "Don't let them vote." "We'll run them from the polls."

"Don't leave the polls; if we die, let's die like men. Out of one blood hath God created all the nations of the earth. If you are fired upon while doing your duty as American citizens, you must protect yourselves," and placing himself in the lead, Clark led the way to the polls and the Negro men followed him and cast their votes amid derisive yells and a perfect shower of stones. "Kill 'em!" shouted one of the drunken bullies.

"Friends," said Clark, mounting an old box that stood near, "Let me speak."

"Go on, let's hear the nigger preacher!"

"Let my people go home peaceably. They are only doing their duty as freed men and as voters. Who would not despise any man, black or white, who held this great privilege and would not try to use it. Friends, John Brown is dead, but his truth is marching on."

A cheer went up from the black men's throats, but it ended in a wail of anger and despair, for a bullet aimed at Clark's head struck him in his right arm and he fell.

Then, as if the sight of their wounded leader had infused into them a newborn courage, the black men charged upon their enemies, and drove them from the place with sticks, stones, and any weapon that chanced to be available.

Of course, there was a cry of riot and a call for troops to prevent the Negroes from murdering all of the whites, but the better class of Hill Station's white citizens, those who had become intimately acquainted with Clark's work, and knew that he was no politician trying to use his own struggling people as a mere stepping-stone to his ambition, believed Clark's version of the affair, and condemned the white marauders so strongly that some of them left Hill Station for good, and that was the first and last riot that took place in that vicinity.

Neither 'Lias nor the minister was dangerously wounded, and what with the careful nursing Clark received from Aunt Jennie and Ora, and the nursing and petting 'Lias got from his mother and the Chapel girls, they were inclined to think themselves lucky fellows.

Some eight weeks later Clark walked into his Annual Conference amid cheers, that brought tears to his eyes. He brought two trophies that were worthy of the occasion—Ora, the sweetest bride Hill Station ever saw, and 'Lias, as a new messenger of the gospel.

Guests Unexpected

A Thanksgiving Story

*I*na Scott-Craven settled among the rich cushions of her luxurious divan with a distinct sense of well-being. She was a widow with a generous income, left by a man whom she married solely because he was rich. Mr. Scott-Craven had been a very convenient husband, generous and indulgent; so she bore him no grudge when he died a few years after their marriage, leaving her free and contented with life.

In society Mrs. Scott-Craven was neither popular nor unpopular; the paragraphs for which she furnished comment in the smart weeklies devoted more space to her bridge and motor achievements than to her dinners and receptions. She was extremely selfish, but not ill-natured. Her conversation never expanded beyond the recognized topics of the day in her set, racing, chiffons, bridge and motoring, with stray remarks on new books, plays and spicy gossip on the marriages, deaths, debts and divorces of her dearest friends and acquaintances.

Among the new books lately received by Mrs. Scott-Craven was one devoted to the slums, sent by a new acquaintance. The author was soon to lecture in a fashionable drawing-room, and in order to converse intelligently with her

First published in *Colored American Magazine* 14 (Nov. 1908): 614–16

during the subsequent reception Mrs. Scott-Craven deemed it the correct thing to skim through the pages of her gift.

The book was written in the most lurid vein, the heroes and heroines being represented as hopelessly wicked, the men drunken and brutal; the women miserable in appearance and light in conduct.

A perusal of the chapters did not increase Mrs. Scott-Craven's charity nor was she inspired with a desire to help humanity. The pleadings of the author were overdone and she turned with loathing from the description of a state of things which can only be described as bestial, remarking, "How dreadful!"

A servant entered to interrupt her thoughts, and noticing a frown upon the none too handsome countenance of her mistress, hastened to announce that the decorators had finished their work of preparing the dining and reception rooms for the Thanksgiving dinner dance to take place on the following day.

"Very well, Juliette," said Mrs. Scott-Craven. "Tell the decorators to go, and if there are later changes I will telephone for them to return. And, by the way, Juliette," continued the mistress, "you need not come again for two hours. I do not feel well, and hope to go to sleep before dressing for Mrs. Barlow's dinner this evening."

Juliette, a demure damsel, with a coquettish expression in her small, dark eyes, retired, closing the door softly.

Mrs. Scott-Craven, conscious of the luxury of oncoming sleep, reclined deeper among the cushions and straightened out the folds of the beautiful Persian silk dressing gown, which had been a gift from her late husband. The richness of the gown made her think of the donor in a desultory way, but soon she ceased to think connectedly; a great whiteness seemed to spread around her and sleep coursed warmly through her veins.

In her subconsciousness Mrs. Scott-Craven saw gradually moving toward her divan a tall, white-clad form, like that of a conventional male angel with great white feather wings. He was the conventional angel of pictorial art, and yet he reminded her, whimsically enough, of a handsome young man whom she had noticed with the author of the book on slum life a few days ago.

"You must come with me," said the angel, with an air of authority, and she rose upward, followed him without further protest. It was not until they arrived in a strange section of the city that it occurred to her she was attired in dressing gown and slippers. But she was under the influence of the angel and powerless to help herself or offer the least resistance. The streets were narrow and dirty, and the rookeries parading under the names of tenements ill-smelling and stuffy. Following her guide, without a question, she ascended four or five flights of break-neck steps, finally reaching a squalid apartment of two rooms which they entered without the formality of a knock at the door.

On a couch lay a woman, not older than forty-two or three years, though wasted by disease until she appeared sixty. Three small children, the picture of poverty, were gazing pitifully into her face, one of them crying for a piece of bread. An old stove in a corner of the room contained an ordinary bit of candle, which sent out the only heat the occupants of the room felt, while furnishing light at the same time.

Mrs. Scott-Craven, obeying a motion command of the angel, surveyed the dismal picture and her heart sank within her.

Hearing a slight sigh from another corner of the room, she turned to see from whom it escaped, astonished to recognize—as well as she could by the miserable candle light—the figure of a beautiful young girl snuggling to her breast, in an effort to keep it warm, a young baby. Her hair was fluffed out on either side of her head, covering the top halves of her ears, and caught up at the back in an unpretentious knot. Her features were thin, but beautiful, her eyes a mystery, her mouth a flower and her hands, despite the signs of hard work, well shaped and well kept. The expression she wore was one of indescribable sadness; one could easily guess that the responsibility of the entire household devolved upon her and the task was too much for her strength as well as the little money she received for the two or three days' work she was fortunate enough to secure every week.

Mrs. Scott-Craven finally perceived that the little group noticed neither her, her strange attire nor her stranger companion. She evidently was in the spirit world. What would happen next?

The angel left the dingy little tenement, walking a little in front of her, but moving along with swift even strides. Gaining the street, she was led through first one alley and another, interrupting their walks with visits to homes each worse than the preceding one.

Thoroughly frightened and sick at heart, she summoned courage and said:

"I wish you would tell me the meaning of all this? Am I mad or are these people merely visionaries?"

For answer the angel took her by the hand, spread his great bird-like wings and for one giddy moment they hung in space.

"Br-rr, it is freezing here," cried the terrified Mrs. Scott-Craven; "my dressing gown has shrunk to my ankles and the pattern has all washed out. An air journey is worse than traveling through the frightful streets below."

"It is not an air journey," replied the angel. "It is your mental atmosphere. If your inner life had been large and full and beautiful, your outer covering would have been luxuriant. As you may be said to have had no inner life at all, your mental poverty is shown in your scanty drapery. In all of your lifetime you have never made an effort to make those around you happy. The hungry you have turned from your door; the poor you have oppressed."

Then suddenly as they had ascended, the angel released her hand and she felt herself speeding through space, helpless and alone.

"Save me! Save me!" she cried, almost paralyzed with fear.

"What is it, Madame?" asked the surprised voice of Juliette.

It was some time before Mrs. Scott-Craven realized that she had been asleep and dreaming.

A few minutes later Mrs. Scott-Craven received a call from her "Lady of the Slums," as she called the writer of the settlements. And still unstrung by the memory of her vision, she begged to be excused to keep her dinner engagement.

"I have a surprise for you, however," said she to her guest in parting. "I am recalling the invitations to my Thanksgiving dinner dance to-morrow, and my plans, without any rearrangement whatever, are subject to your disposal for your unfortunate charges. My invitations number fifty, but you can increase the number to suit your needs and in future draw upon me for any assistance needed."

The astonishment of Mrs. Scott-Craven's new friend was too great for words, but it did not compare with the sensation created by the announcement in the newspapers the next morning that one of the wealthiest women in the city, who had always attracted society's attention by her independence of action, had decided to abandon the pleasures of fashionable life to devote her time entirely to work among the poor.

Effie Waller Smith

The Judgment of Roxenie

"*A*s the Almighty 's my witness, 'pears to me like you 're a-runnin' religion in the ground, a-settin' so much store by a passel of things that the Lord ain't no-wise pertickler about!"

It was the time of the annual Sacrament and crowds of people had gathered at the Dunkard meeting-house from every ridge and hollow for miles around. Even amid the unusual flutter of life and color that now invested it, the low log building, standing against the sombreness of innumerable pines that cover Bays Mountain, had a bleak and melancholy aspect. In its best days its appearance had not been cheerful, and time and storm had dealt with it hardly, darkening its walls to a sober brown, and seaming them with numberless fissures; here and there the mortar had fallen away from between the logs, leaving unsightly chinks and crannies; and several broken panes of the small window gave jagged glimpses of an austere and gloomy interior.

Under a huge buckeye tree near the meeting-house, three or four people, whose appearance was singularly in keeping with the scene around them, were engaged in earnest discussion. With one exception, they were old men, whose stern, deep-lined faces bore indelible records of the hardship of their long lives

First published in *Putnam's Monthly* 6 (June 1909): 309–17

and the asceticism of their religion. According to Dunkard custom, they wore long hair; and the cut of their beards, closely shaven except for a single gray tuft on the chin, gave an odd, half-monstrous aspect to their faces.

The young man who had just spoken differed from the rest of the group in more respects than his youth. True, his rich hair fell back from his forehead in long waves; and his dress was, like that of the others, rigidly plain even according to the mountain standards of simplicity. Yet his face, for all its seriousness, had a warmth, a suggested capacity for passion and struggle, which his companions had probably never known. As the Brethren put it, Ephraim Utsman looked like a man in whom the old Adam would die hard.

At his passionate words, a shocked murmur came from the listeners. "Who air we," a little fiery-eyed man broke in with shrill vehemence, "who are we to jedge what the Lord is pertickler about! When the Almighty lays His commands on us, what mortal man has got the right to say that ary word of 'em be left out?"

The protest which rose to Ephraim's lips was interrupted by a derisive laugh from one of the deacons. "Ephraim," he sneered, "is it bekase ye 've been keepin' company with Roxenie that yer tongue 's tied so 's you can't reprove her sins? It 's a evil day when a da'ter of the church gits took up with the onrighteous Mammon, and goes to puttin' on breastpins and ruffles; and the wust part of it is, that him that the Brethren 's chose to guide their feet in the straight and narrer path, is upholdin' her in her folly. You 've got to take yer stand on one side or t' other, Ephraim! Ef in yer secret heart you're a-puttin' Roxenie Pulliam afore the Lord's cause, yer sin 's a-goin' to find you out!"

"The Lord knows I ain't a-puttin' Roxenie afore His cause, Deacon Hunley," declared the young pastor, "but it ain't right and jest fer you-uns to be so set agin her. I don't say that she ha'n't got vain and foolish ways, but I 'low she don't mean no rale harm."

"Don't mean no harm!" Deacon Hunley echoed, scornfully. "Can't everybody see that the gal carries a high head and a proud look jest like her pappy and grandpappy did afore her?" The old man's brow darkened with sombre recollection. "I knowed her fore-payrents well enough, and I knowed 'em to my sorrer!"

The rich odor stealing from the meeting-house kitchen announced that the lamb to be used at the supper was now ready. As the men turned toward the low dooray, one of the deacons, whose age-bleached and sharpened features still bore a strong resemblance to Ephraim's own, laid a detaining hand on his arm.

"Be keerful, Ephe," warned the shaking voice, "be mighty keerful that you don't listen to the call o' flesh and blood, 'stid of the voice of the Almighty.

'No man, havin' put his hand to the plow and lookin' back, is fit fer the kingdom of God.'"

"I know, Grandpap," Ephraim murmured sadly, "but I can't decide agin her till I git more light."

On the young man's face a frown of sore perturbation still lingered, as he took his official place at the head of the rude table which, extending down the whole length of the meeting-house, held the steaming dishes of the sacred meal. Plates had been set for all the members of the church, who, as they filed in, sat down at the board, the men on one side and the women on the other.

The conscious color deepened in Ephraim's tanned cheek when his glance, wandering down the table, fell on a young girl seated near the opposite end. Among the faded or phlegmatic countenances around her, the rich bloom and vivacity of her face stood strongly out, reminding Ephraim of a crimson poppy he had once found gleaming amid the humbler growths of the garden. Like the rest of the women, she wore a plain frock of dark calico, and the white head-dress customary on sacramental occasions; but the muslin cap was fastened under her chin with a knot of warm-tinted ribbon, and below it glittered a huge breastpin, resplendent with gold plating and imitation jewels.

A sudden silence fell on the congregation as Ephraim rose and, laying aside his coat, girded a towel around him. Taking a basin of water, he knelt beside the man next him, who chanced to be Deacon Hunley, and washed and dried his feet. Then, rising, he bent his head and solemnly pressed on the old man's weazen lips the kiss of charity.

The shadows of the October afternoon deepened as the rite was passed from one to another around the table; and the first stars had come out above the dusky ridges when, the solemn meal ended, Ephraim made his way to Roxenie's side.

As he came up, his unsmiling eyes rested on a flashily-dressed young man who had been talking with the girl. "Good evenin', Abner," he said, coldly.

Abner Biddle, who, though born and bred a mountaineer, had for some years been employed on the public works at the county seat, had recently come back to the neighborhood of his birth, versed in so many ways of the world and displaying so many strange fashions, as might well dazzle the simple sons and daughters of Bays Mountain. It suddenly occurred to Ephraim that Roxenie's love of finery might have another source than the vanity natural to her years. "The world and the lusts thereof" all at once seemed to him to find concrete embodiment in Abner Biddle.

As Ephraim and Roxenie walked homeward along the laurel-hedged path, the silence was for a time unbroken except by the wind in the pines, and the waters of Laurel Run, dashing over the rocks down the ravine.

At length the young man sighed deeply. "I 'm plumb disheartened about ye, Roxenie. It beats me why you should wear them gewgaws o' your'n to the Seckrement, of all places."

"I can't see as it 's wuss to wear 'em at Seckrement than anywhars else," the girl retorted. "I ain't a-goin' behind the door to hide what I do, and the whole church kin see ef they want to!"

"The whole church is a-seein' your acts, and a-grievin' fer 'em too! In fact," Ephraim's voice fell to an awed undertone, "ef you don't take heed to your ways, the Brethren's a-talkin' about turnin' ye out!"

There was a startled hush, through which Roxenie could hear her own loud-beating heart. To dally with the forbidden allurements of the world from a position of supposed safety, had been diverting enough; but to be called to account, and turned out of the church as an unworthy member, was an appalling prospect, full of terror and shame.

"Who's been talkin' about turnin' me out?" she demanded. "I 'low it 's old Jeremiah Hunley that's at the bottom of it! I seed you and him a-talkin' together, as thick as peas in a pod. And ye washed his feet, and give him the holy kiss! Lordy, ye must hev a strong stomach!"

"The foll'wers of the Lord ortn't to be above washin' nobody's feet, Roxenie. Whose feet did you wash—yer cousin Polly Ann Ledbetter's? That war one of the things the Brethern helt agin ye, that ye never washed nobody's feet at the Seckrement, onless it war some of yer own nigh kin."

"It's Jeremiah Hunley's spite-work a-bringin' up sich things," the girl cried, passionately. "Atter him and pap had that fuss about the line-fence, he never war satisfied till he'd got pap turned out o' the church; and he'll never be satisfied now till he gits me turned out too."

"You nee'n't to lay it all on Jeremiah Hunley, nuther," Ephraim answered, stoutly. "It'll be yer own fault ef you 're turned out. You didn't hev to jine the Brethern, Roxenie; you could 'a' staid out ef you'd 'a' wanted to; but bein' as you air a member, 'pears to me like you ort to do what you bound yerself up to!"

For a moment Roxenie was shocked into silence by the severity of her lover's words. Then her pride rose. "Yes, I could 'a' staid out of the church, Ephraim, and I've wished a heap o' times that I hed! Thar ain't no use in bein' so quair, and different from everybody else! W'y, over in Kingsport, whar I went a-visitin' to Aunt Mirandy Pickens's, 'most every woman at the meetin'-house was a-wearin' gold pins; and they said when a gal promised to marry a feller, it war the reg'lar thing fer him to give her a ring. They 'lowed it war mighty quair that I was promised and didn't hev none, and I felt plumb ashamed." Roxenie laughed significantly. "Abner Biddle's got a pow'ful purty ring—"

She stopped abruptly as the rushing storm of Ephraim's wrath swept down on her. "Ef nothin' else'll do you, you kin hev Abner Biddle and his ring, fer all o' me. I'll never buy a ring fer no woman while the world stands! I've helt up fer you, Roxenie, and tuk your part agin them that was hard down on ye, but I'll do it no more! I've tried to snatch ye as a brand from the burnin', but from now on I'll leave ye to yer own ways. My skyirts is clear o' your blood!"

Roxenie's laugh rang out through the solemnity of the mountain night, clear and scornful, yet with something hollow and forced in its defiant tones. "Yes, your skyirts is clear, and so is Deacon Hunley's! Go ahead and turn me out ef you want to! Jeremiah Hunley'll never pull *me* around atter him with a leadin' string!"

A few days later, two or three Brethren chosen for that purpose called at the Pulliam cabin to talk with Roxenie, and endeavor to persuade her to submit to the church. They were received by Mrs. Pulliam, who, though she went through with all the essentials of mountain hospitality, setting "cheers" on the porch for the visitors, serving them with gourdfuls of water fresh from the spring, and inquiring minutely after their health and the health of their respective families, had about her a resolute frigidity that augured ill for the success of the visit. She was a rigid church member, and under other circumstances Roxenie's delinquencies and the prospect of her expulsion would have brought down a storm of lamentations and reproaches on the girl's head; but the supposition that Deacon Hunley was behind the movement to discipline Roxenie, awakening in the old woman dark memories of the grudge that had begun in her husband's lifetime, rendered her even more stubborn and defiant than her daughter.

"Jeremiah Hunley'll never run rough-shod over me and mine while my head's hot," she had declared.

Roxenie listened to her visitors in silence, making to their exhortations the unvarying response that she hidn't done nothin' much wrong as she could see, and she wa'n't agoin' to make no acknowledgments to the church. The Brethren knew, as they walked down the rugged path from the house, that their mission had failed.

On the next preaching day, the meeting-house was crowded to overflowing; for the news that Roxenie Pulliam was to be "drawed before the brethen" had gone far and wide over the ridges, and even the most careless churchgoer had felt it incumbent on him to be present.

As the girl walked down the aisle on that eventful morning, there was a sudden stir of interest in the congregation, followed by a hush of utter amazement. Never before had such a vision appeared on Bays Mountain. Roxenie's calico dress and square cut, unfrilled Dunkard bonnet had been laid aside, and she shone dazzlingly forth in brilliant and heavily flounced sateen, while on her head rested the supreme sacrilege of a gaily trimmed hat bought at a fabulous price from a store in the valley. The much-offending breastpin flaunted itself on her bosom, and on one of her little brown hands glittered the blue stones of the ring Abner Biddle had given her. Something like a groan passed over the devouter portion of the congregation; and from that moment the result of the trial was foreseen.

During what followed, she sat haughtily erect. Only once did her resolution falter. When, at the close of the trial, Ephraim Utsman, as paster of the church, rose to pronounce the solemn sentence, her glance met his agonized face, turned in passionate pity upon her. Her head drooped for an instant, and a sudden tremor shook the blossoms on her gorgeous hat. Then she looked up as proudly as ever; and a defiant smile parted her lips as she passed through the crowd of brethren and sisters, to whose fellowship she belonged no more. It was not until she was well on her homeward road and the heavy underbrush had screened her from all eyes, that the angry pride which had sustained Roxenie fell away from her. The face above the scarlet ribbons grew strangely white; and the eyes she lifted to the accusing heavens were suddenly full of terror and remorse.

"O Lordy, what hev I done?" she moaned. "I've give up Ephraim and lost my own soul, too, fer ought I know, all fer a passel of trash that ain't wuth no more 'n those dead leaves in the holler down yander!'

In a wild revulsion of feeling she tore off the brooch and the ring, and flung them far down the Laurel Run ravine.

"Roxenie Pulliam's reapin' the reward of her doin 's! It's a judgment of the Lord, ef ever I knowed of one!"

The speaker was a withered and rawboned old woman, who, on her way up the steep mountain road, had stopped to rest and chat at the corn pile, where the entire Utsman family were busy harvesting their fall crop. Ephraim and his father, with an old mule and a primitive "slide," were hauling the pumpkins and spindling corn down from the new ground on top of the ridge; while Mrs. Utsman and the younger children, a numerous company of all ages and sizes, were "shucking" the gathered ears and storing them in the crib.

At the visitor's words, uttered with an air of melancholy triumph befitting an annunciator of the judgments of the Lord, there was an astounded pause among the workers. Mr. Utsman, in the act of unloading a huge pumpkin, dropped it back on the sled; the children stood wide-eyed and open-mouthed, for once unrebuked by their mother for the suspension of their labors; and a gray shadow crept over Ephraim's face.

"Lordy, mussy," cried Mrs. Utsman, "I allus knowed that gal 'u'd come to no good eend! But tell us what's happened, Mis' Landers."

The news-bringer seated herself on the corn-pile, panting with excitement and the fatigue of her recent climb. "You-uns all know," she began, "about that thar ring, that Abner Biddle give Roxenie, and that she was a-flauntin' round so high, the day the brethren turned her out. Well, that ring war *stole!* Abner Biddle stole it from a man down about Rogersville that he'd been a-workin' fer. Thar ain't never been no sich ring in these parts afore. It was rale gold, and the sets in it war wuth away up yander, 'most fifty dollars!"

A gasp of astonishment went round the corn-pile. That there could be a ring worth fifty dollars had never occurred to the wildest imaginings of Bay Mountain.

"The feller that he stole it from," Mrs. Landers continued, "got to suspicionin' that mebbe Abner had tuk the ring, and so he come up here on a still hunt fer it. Do you mind that dressed-up man person, with eye-glasses, Mis' Utsman, that set at the back eend of the meetin'-house at Roxenie's trial? Well, that was him, and he seed his ring on the gal's hand that day. And this mornin', early, a officer rid up on hossback to Mis' Pulliam's, with a writ fer Roxenie. She's summoned fer trial over at Squair Riggs' on Beech Creek and the Lord only knows whar she'll eend up at!"

"What's 'come of Abner Biddle?" demanded Ephraim, sternly. "Whar's the no-count pup that done the devilment, and then put it on Roxenie to tote his load!"

Mrs. Landers gazed on the young man with the icy severity justly due an interrupter of important news. "I don't know whar Abner Biddle is, and I hain't hed no pertickler call to find out. The officer stopped at his pap's, I heerd, but Abner hedn't been there since Sunday. But as fer as totin' Abner's load is concerned, Roxenie'll hev enough to do ef she totes her own load, accordin' to *my* count."

"The gal can't be sent to the pen, onless she tuk the ring a-known' it war stole."

Mr. Utsman, whose father had once been sheriff's deputy for a brief time, delivered this bit of inherited knowledge with befitting gravity. "But, o' course, she'll hev to restore the proputty."

The visitor bending forward lifted a mysteriously significant forefinger. "You-uns, mark my words," she said, her voice sinking to an impressive whisper, "Roxenie'll never restore the proputty! She hain't got no notion of givin' up that ring. Accordin' to her tale, she's throwed it away and can't find it no more!"

"Throwed it away!" exclaimed Mrs. Utsman, derisively. "Don't tell me that a gal that loves finery like Roxenie Pulliam does, would throw away a ring! She never would 'a' gone so fur as to be turned out of the church fer it, ef she'd 'a' aimed to throw it away."

"That's what I told 'em when I fust heerd it," corroborated Mrs. Landers, "and everybody on Bays Mounting is a-sayin' the same. Lordy, Lordy," the old woman shook her head dismally, "when a immortal soul gits started down hill, thar don't 'pear to be no stoppin'-place!"

Ephraim's face was tense with anguish, as he turned hurriedly away from the gossiping group. All the jealousy that had stirred him on the night of his quarrel with Roxenie was swallowed up in remorse for his delinquency as pastor, and anxiety for the erring girl.

"Whatever she comes to, it's my fault, leastways part of it is," he muttered. I ort n't never to 'a' forsook her when she war so sore tempted. 'The hirelin' fleeth.' I han't been nothin' but a hirelin' over the Lord's flock!"

An hour later, Roxenie was slowly descending the ridge on her way to the 'Squire's for trial. Behind her came the constable together with her uncle, Crit Ledbetter, who had promised to accompany her to Beech Creek. She had chosen to ride in advance in order, so far as possible, to escape the old man's long-winded exhortations. "I 'low I'll be 'most glad to go to the pen, jest to git shet of mam's and Uncle Crit's jaw, fer a spell," she had declared, while a forlorn little smile trembled on her pale lips.

Around her the words were bare in the desolation of late autumn, and a blue haze, dim and infinitely mournful, filled the valleys and shrouded the distant peaks. As her eyes fell listlessly on the altered aspect of the autumnal woods, the girl's mind was occupied with more momentous changes. "Ain't it quair," she murmured, "how everything is turned round since we come along this road from the Seckrement! Jest five weeks ago a-Saturday, and it feels like fifty year!"

A horseman was approaching down one of the bridle-paths that led to the main road. Long before he reached her, Roxenie knew that it was Ephraim Utsman.

He drew back a moment at sight of the girl's stricken face. "You ort n't to git too much pestered about what's happened," he said, gently. "Folks ain't apt to come to harm onless they mean harm theirselves. And I can't never believe you meant much wrong, Roxenie."

A gleam of surprise lighted the blank hopelessness of her countenance. "I don't know how come ye to say that, Ephraim. Thar ain't nary other soul on Bays Mounting that's said as much. They all 'low it's a made-up tale about losin' the ring, and say I'm a-keepin' it hid some'r's."

"What defence air ye aimin' to make afore the 'Squair?"

The girl's pale face grew paler.

"Folks is a-sayin'," she answered in a low, awed voice, "that it's a jedgment of the Lord that's come on me; and ef it is, it won't do not good to fight agin it. But I 'lowed, bein' as I'd throwed the man's ring away, I'd ort to pay him fer it." Bending down, she laid a caressing hand on her mare's glossy neck. "Old Bet's wuth what the ring cost, and more too. Ef the man'll be satisfied to take her in place of what he's lost, we'll be square; and ef he won't I'm at the eend of my row," she added, despairingly.

"Roxenie," the young man's voice was full of passionate sorrow, "you ain't the only one that's a-deservin' of the jedgment of the Most High! I'm a-goin' with ye to the trial, and ef any harm befalls ye, I pray it may light on me, too. I war in fault. I turned agin ye and let ye stray from the Lord's fold, bekase I war mad and jealous, a-thinkin' ye loved Abner."

"Loved Abner!" Something of Roxenie's old spirit flashed into her eyes. "I ha'n't never been that bad off fer a feller yit! Ye must 'a' 'lowed I war purty fur gone, to take up with the likes of Abner Biddle!"

A sudden light came into Ephraim's troubled face. "Tell me why you throwed the ring away, Roxenie!" he demanded, eagerly. "Could it 'a' been bekase ye hated it—bekase ye war sorry fer what ye 'd done?"

Roxenie's composure, which she had kept so resolutely through all that had befallen, was giving way at last. Dropping the reins on her mare's neck, she buried her face in her hands. "Sorry! O Ephraim," she sobbed, "you can't know—nobody can't know—how sorry I was!"

It was nearly ten o'clock on the following morning when Mrs. Pulliam, coming to the door, peered out with eyes that were red from a night of weeping. Many times, during the past twenty-four hours, she had thus stepped forth, scanning the narrow road, or listening intently for every footstep or distant barking of dogs that might foretoken news of Roxenie. Now, as she stood on the porch, listening, she fancied she heard the sound of hoofs coming up from the hollow; and a few moments later, Crit Ledbetter's mule appeared over the slope.

When she saw that Roxenie was not with her uncle, the old woman threw her apron over her head, and broke into loud lamentation. "I knowed it 'u'd turn out that way!" she wailed. "I knowed when the pore gal started off, that she 'd never set foot on Bays Mounting agin!"

Crit Ledbetter gave a bluff, reassuring laugh, "You nee'n't to pester nary bit about Roxenie. She's a-comin' on behind, and old Bet's a-comin' too. The feller that Abner stole from war a pow'ful clever man. When Roxenie d' told him all about the ring, and offered him the old mare to make up fer it, he would n't hev the nag at all. He said he'd like mightly well to git a holt of the rascal that stole his proputty, but he didn't hev no notion of sendin' a innicent gal to the pen, nor of takin' a widder woman's hoss, nuther. And he hed the trial called right spang off, and paid the costs hisself!"

"Air ye tellin' me the truth, Crit?" the old woman cried, incredulously. "Ef nothin's happened to Roxenie, why hain't she come back along o' you?"

A sly smile wrinkled Crit Ledbetter's brown visage. "The gal's all right," he answered, "but they was delayed by hevin' to wait till the license come from town. You see, atter the trial was called off, her and Ephraim 'lowed they 'd git married while they was over thar, bein' thar wa'n't no use in makin' all that long trip to the 'Squair's fer nothin'!"

Annie McCary

Breaking the Color-line

"*C*oach Hardy has selected for the two-mile relay team to go against Gale, Carter, Pratt, Staunton and Thacker, to run in the order named. Payne, you will 'sub'."

"Captain Pratt, I certainly object to that nigger's presence on the team. Whom do I mean? Thacker, of course, he's a nigger, and no southern gentleman would compete against or run with a nigger and I—"

"Now, Staunton, none of your southern idiosyncrasies go here," cut in Pratt. "You know we want to win that relay, and Gale is priming her best half-milers for the race and since Thacker can do the half in less that two minutes, take it from me, so long as I'm captain, he runs."

"Then I quit," and red as a beet, Staunton sat down.

"Quit, then, if you want to!" thundered Pratt.

"Hold on, Pratt, we're all white fellows together and there's no need of our having a row over a colored chap. You know, I'm from Texas anyway, and I want to say that here in Starvard we've never had any colored fellows on the track team in the three years I've been here, and I'm hanged if I see why we've

First published in *Crisis* 9 (Feb. 1915): 193-95

got to start now. These niggers are always trying to get out of their place," said Payne, the junior who had been crowded off the team by Thacker.

"Well by Jove, he seems to have pushed you out of *your* place on the team. He's beaten you more than once in the time trials and—"

"Just a minute," a calm voice put in, and Thacker came into the meeting. "I did not hear the beginning of this discussion, but I did hear some remarks and I judge that I am considered objectionable as a member of the relay because of—surely not the color of my skin [for he was as fair as any of the other fellows there] but because I have Negro blood in my veins." Every man was breathless. "Let me say this one thing, that *nigger* or not, I have won the place on the team but rather than cause any discord which might end in Starvard's losing the meet to Gale, I'll quit!" he swung on his heel and strode from the gym.

As the door slammed the storm broke.

"I didn't know he was colored," said one.

"Well, he is," answered Staunton.

"Well, he's whiter than you both in skin and in heart, Phil Staunton," yelled Pratt.

"You are insulting me, you Yank," and Staunton sprang at Pratt. The other men jumped in and held the two apart. Finally, quiet was restored and Payne was replaced on the team.

The meet was to come off a week from the coming Saturday. This was on Wednesday. Saturday, Gale had a dual meet with East Point, and Pratt and the coach, Hardy, went down to look over Gale's two-mile relay team and get a general line on the rest of the men. Silently they watched Gale win 69 to 20. On the return to Wainbridge, Hardy said: "Pratt, you fellows are all sorts of fools to let that man Thacker get off the team. Why, he's the fastest half-miler I've seen. I bet you he walks away with the half—if his heart isn't taken out by this dirty work," he added in an undertone.

"Hardy, you know I did all I could but he stuck out. He's as proud as the deuce, and as for those Southerners, they stuck out, too. They're always trying to make it hard for these colored boys. Oh, they make me sick!"

"Well, he's going to win that half in a walk, although Price ran a pretty race against those soldiers. Well, here's my jumping off place, Pratt," and the coach swung off the trolley.

"Curse the luck! Hardy doesn't want to own it, but we can't beat that Gale team."

The day of the meet came. Gale was down, brimming over with confidence, for the news that the crack half-miler on the relay was not going to run had spread like wild fire. Gale had no opinion, Starvard was divided.

At 1:30 the pistol cracked for the start of the hundred yard dash. Gale took first, but Starvard got second and third. Engle, of Gale, won the 120 hurdles,

Wilson and Desmond, of Starvard, second and third. In the broad jump Bates and Hines of Starvard took first and third, but again Gale took first in the hammer throw.

The quarter-mile was next. In a close and exciting race Chalmers of Starvard "brought home the bacon" in 50 flat. Starvard began to hope. She grew frantic as she landed first in the high jump, although Gale took second and third.

Then came the half mile. The pride of Gale, Price's equal, Simpson, followed by his teammates, Parsons and Terry, sprang out to toe the mark. James and Keele threw off their crimson sweaters and a third Starvard man stepped up. It was Thacker. He was an ideal half-miler, five feet eleven inches, lean of face, broad shouldered, slender waisted, and with great long tapering legs. Simpson was short and stocky with a choppy stride with which he hoped to break Thacker.

All six got off to a good start. Thacker set the pace for the first lap. Then he seemed to slow up and Simpson and Terry drew up. Terry was now two feet ahead of Thacker, and Simpson stride and stride, with Parsons pushing him hard. Keele was out of it. As they turned in the last stretch, pandemonium broke loose in the Gale stands. Starvard cheered on her men. Thacker had seen Staunton leer at him and his heart gave a great jump and his feet responded to the call. His big lead was gone and it would be no easy matter to get in first in the short distance remaining. Teeth set, head back, he began a great sprint. With forty yards to go Terry and Simpson were leading, Terry a good two feet in front of Simpson and Thacker a yard behind. Three great strides and the red and blue jerseys were neck and neck. The stands were hushed. Nothing was heard but the pat-pat-pat of the spikes on the cinders. All three runners were straining every muscle, calling on their reserve strength, holding on by sheer nerve. Five great jumps and Thacker toppled over a winner in 1:58 flat, Simpson dropped a hand's breadth behind, and Terry was all in as he fell across.

Starvard cheered and cheered Thacker. Rooters jumped from the stands to pat Thacker on the back. Hardy drove them off and arm in arm he and Thacker went to see to a rub down.

"All out for the 220 high hurdles!" Payne and Gardner showed Starvard's crimson, while Kittredge and Fields wore the Gale blue. Payne was showing an easy first with Gardner and Fields neck and neck, with Kittredge a good third. As Payne took the last hurdle, Starvard's cheers turned to groans, for Payne stumbled and fell. In a flash he was up, just to limp across the finish behind Gardner, who was trailing the Gale man. Gloom pervaded the Starvard stands when the news spread that Payne, the anchor man of the two-mile relay was out with a sprained ankle. Second and third in the 120 high hurdles gave Starvard four points to Gale's five. Gale took first and third in the mile and first in the pole vault.

There was but one event left on the program—the two-mile relay. In the stands it was figured that Gale was three points to the good: Starvard 48, Gale 51.

"Who's going to take Payne's place?" was the question in the Starvard stands. Then calls for "Thacker! Thacker!" came from the crimson supporters. For if Starvard took the relay, the meet was hers by a scant two points. If Gale won, the meet was *hers*, together with the Eastern championship.

"Hardy, do you suppose Thacker *could* run *another* half against Price, who is perfectly fresh?"

"Pratt, I'd think you fellows would be so ashamed of the dirt you've done Thacker that you'd go hide yourselves. I won't ask him, I'll tell you, but—" here the coach looked straight into Pratt's eyes, "I bet you he'll run, and mark my words, he'll beat Price, if it kills him. Now, go ask him."

Pratt came back looking relieved. "All right, Hardy!"

Carter toed the mark against Steen, the first Gale runner. Crack! went the pistol, off they sped.

"Staunton, Thacker takes the baton from you," called Pratt. Staunton looked sullen. Down the home stretch came Carter and Steen, Carter giving Pratt a good five-yard lead which he held and increased by five, and then Staunton took up the running. Archer brought joy to Gale as he cut down Staunton's lead yard by yard. Then he tore down to give Price an eight-yard start. Thacker snatched the baton from Staunton and sped away on a seemingly impossible task.

"Can he catch him? Will he hold out?"

Thacker seemed to be oblivious to the fact that the heat was terrific, of everything indeed, but the eight-yard lead he had to cut down. What difference did it make that his throat was parched, his head was splitting, that Price was the fastest man in the East and this was *his* first year in collegiate circles? He had to win. He had to make good, even under handicaps. Starvard thundered encouragement as he tore after the flying Price. After the first hundred yards, he began a terrific pace. His feet seemed to barely touch the ground. All thoughts of his blood gone, Starvard cheered him on: "Keep it up! Thack, old boy, go it! Come on, old man!"

He heard nothing. He thought he had cut down the lead by two yards. He prayed for strength: "Oh, Lord, just let me catch him and I can pass him!" On and on they flew. No cheering now, for the stands had settled down to watch a match between two strong men. The great stadium was silent save for the crunching of the cinders. Thacker was crawling up, foot by foot. Yard after yard

was covered at this murderous pace. Around the last turn they sped, Price running easily, Thacker glassy-eyed, hollow-cheeked but still flying. One hundred
yards to go—Thacker's breath was coming hot and fast, his knees felt as if they
must give way, yet he spurred his failing strength for one last great sprint. He
again increased his speed, to the amazement of the stands. Half-way down he
seemed almost gone. Forty yards—two more yards to make up on Price, who,
although tiring was beginning a spurt. Twenty-five yards—he was just behind
Price but his chin had dropped on his chest, his mouth hung open, and his eyes
were blinded with tears as he felt unable to pass Price, laboring at his side. Eight
yards—he was growing weaker stride by stride, but Price had slipped an inch or
so behind. Thacker no longer heard the heavy breathing of Price and raised his
eyes to see whether he was in front. Nothing in front but that bit of worsted
which marked the finish. He threw up his arms and Hardy caught him as he fell
unconscious, breasting the tape, and breaking the color line.

Adeline F. Ries

Mammy

A Story

Mammy's heart felt heavy indeed when (the time was now two years past) marriage had borne Shiela, her "white baby," away from the Governor's plantation to the coast. But as the months passed, the old colored nurse became accustomed to the change, until the great joy brought by the news that Shiela had a son, made her reconciliation complete. Besides, had there not always been Lucy, Mammy's own "black baby," to comfort her?

Yes, up to that day there had always been Lucy; but on that very day the young Negress had been sold—sold like common household ware!—and (the irony of it chilled poor Mammy's leaden heart)—she had been sold to Shiela as nurse to the baby whose birth, but four days earlier had caused Mammy so much rejoicing. The poor slave could not believe that it was true, and as she buried her head deeper into the pillows, she prayed that she might wake to find it all a dream.

But a reality it proved and a reality which she dared not attempt to change. For despite the Governor's customary kindness, she knew from experience, that any interference on her part would but result in serious floggings. One morning each week she would go to his study and he would tell her the news from the coast and then with a kindly smile dismiss her.

First published in *Crisis* 13 (Jan. 1917) 117–18

So for about a year, Mammy feasted her hungering soul with these meagre scraps of news, until one morning, contrary to his wont, the Governor rose as she entered the room, and he bade her sit in a chair close to his own. Placing one of his white hands over her knotted brown ones, he read aloud the letter he held in his other hand:

"Dear Father:—

"I can hardly write the sad news and can, therefore, fully appreciate how difficult it will be for you to deliver it verbally. Lucy was found lying on the nursery floor yesterday, dead. The physician whom I immediately summoned pronounced her death a case of heart-failure. Break it gently to my dear old mammy, father, and tell her too, that the coach, should she wish to come here before the burial, is at her disposal.

"Your daughter,
"SHIELA."

While he read, the Governor unconsciously nerved himself to a violent outburst of grief, but none came. Instead, as he finished, Mammy rose, curtsied, and made as if to withdraw. At the door she turned back and requested the coach, "if it weren't asking too much," and then left the room. She did not return to her cabin; simply stood at the edge of the road until the coach with its horses and driver drew up and then she entered. From that time and until nightfall she did not once change the upright position she had assumed, nor did her eyelids once droop over her staring eyes. "They took her from me an' she died"—"They took her from me an' she died"—over and over she repeated the same sentence.

When early the next morning Mammy reached Shiela's home, Shiela herself came down the road to meet her, ready with words of comfort and love. But as in years gone by, it was Mammy who took the golden head on her breast, and patted it, and bade the girl to dry her tears. As of old, too, it was Mammy who first spoke of other things; she asked to be shown the baby, and Shiela only too willingly led the way to the nursery where in his crib the child lay cooing to itself. Mammy took up the little body and again and again tossed it up into the air with the old cry, "Up she goes, Shiela," till he laughed aloud.

Suddenly she stopped, and clasping the child close she took a hurried step towards the open window. At a short distance from the house rolled the sea and Mammy gazed upon it as if fascinated. And as she stared, over and over the words formed themselves: "They took her from me an' she died,"—"They took her from me an' she died."

From below came the sound of voices, "They're waiting for you, Mammy,"—it was Shiela's soft voice that spoke—"to take Lucy—you understand, dear."

Mammy's eyes remained fixed upon the waves,—"I can't go—go foh me, chile, won't you?" And Shiela thought that she understood the poor woman's feelings and without even pausing to kiss her child she left the room and joined the waiting slaves.

Mammy heard the scraping as of a heavy box upon the gravel below; heard the tramp of departing footsteps as they grew fainter and fainter until they died away. Then and only then, did she turn her eyes from the wild waters and looking down at the child in her arms, she laughed a low, peculiar laugh. She smoothed back the golden ringlets from his forehead, straightened out the little white dress, and then, choosing a light covering for his head, she descended the stairs and passed quietly out of the house.

A short walk brought Mammy and her burden to the lonely beach; at the water's edge she stood still. Then she shifted the child's position until she supported his weight in her hands and with a shrill cry of "Up she goes, Shiela," she lifted him above her head. Suddenly she flung her arms forward, at the same time releasing her hold of his little body. A large breaker caught him in its foam, swept him a few feet towards the shore and retreating, carried him out into the sea—

A few hours later, two slaves in frantic search for the missing child found Mammy on the beach tossing handfuls of sand into the air and uttering loud, incoherent cries. And as they came close, she pointed towards the sea and with the laugh of a mad-woman shouted: "They took her from me an' she died!"

Jessie Fauset

Mary Elizabeth

A Story

M ary Elizabeth was late that morning. As a direct result, Roger left for work without telling me good-bye, and I spent most of the day fighting the headache which always comes if I cry.

For I cannot get a breakfast. I can manage a dinner,—one just puts the roast in the oven and takes it out again. And I really excel in getting lunch. There is a good delicatessen near us, and with dainty service and flowers, I get along very nicely. But breakfast! In the first place, it's a meal I neither like nor need. And I never, if I live a thousand years, shall learn to like coffee. I suppose that is why I cannot make it.

"Roger," I faltered, when the awful truth burst upon me and I began to realize that Mary Elizabeth wasn't coming, "Roger, couldn't you get breakfast downtown this morning? You know last time you weren't so satisfied with my coffee."

Roger was hostile. I think he had just cut himself, shaving. Anyway, he was horrid.

"No, I can't get my breakfast downtown!" He actually snapped at me. "Really, Sally, I don't believe there's another woman in the world who would

First published in *Crisis* 19 (Dec. 1919): 51–56

send her husband out on a morning like this on an empty stomach. I don't see how you can be so unfeeling."

Well, it wasn't "a morning like this," for it was just the beginning of November. And I had only proposed his doing what I knew he would have to do eventually.

I didn't say anything more, but started on that breakfast. I don't know why I thought I had to have hot cakes! The breakfast really was awful! The cakes were tough and gummy and got cold one second, exactly, after I took them off the stove. And the coffee boiled, or stewed, or scorched, or did whatever the particular thing is that coffee shouldn't do. Roger sawed at one cake, took one mouthful of the dreadful brew, and pushed away his cup.

"It seems to me you might learn to make a decent cup of coffee," he said icily. Then he picked up his hat and flung out of the house.

I think it is stupid of me, too, not to learn how to make coffee. But, really, I'm no worse than Roger is about lots of things. Take "Five Hundred." Roger knows I love cards, and with the Cheltons right around the corner from us and as fond of it as I am, we could spend many a pleasant evening. But Roger will not learn. Only the night before, after I had gone through a whole hand with him, with hearts as trumps, I dealt the cards around again to imaginary opponents and we started playing. Clubs were trumps, and spades led. Roger, having no spades, played triumphantly a Jack of Hearts and proceeded to take the trick.

"But, Roger," I protested, "you threw off."

"Well," he said, deeply injured, "didn't you say hearts were trumps when you were playing before?"

And when I tried to explain, he threw down the cards and wanted to know what difference it made; he'd rather play casino, anyway! I didn't go out and slam the door.

But I couldn't help from crying this particular morning. I not only value Roger's good opinion, but I hate to be considered stupid.

Mary Elizabeth came in about eleven o'clock. She is a small, weazened woman, very dark, somewhat wrinkled, and a model of self-possession. I wish I could make you see her, or that I could reproduce her accent, not that it is especially colored,—Roger's and mine are much more so—but her pronunciation, her way of drawing out her vowels, is so distinctively Mary Elizabethan!

I was ashamed of my red eyes and tried to cover up my embarrassment with sternness.

"Mary Elizabeth," said I, "you are late!" Just as though she didn't know it.

"Yas'm, Mis' Pierson," she said, composedly, taking off her coat. She didn't remove her hat,—she never does until she has been in the house some two or three hours. I can't imagine why. It is a small, black, dusty affair, trimmed with black ribbon, some dingy white roses and a sheaf of wheat. I give Mary Elizabeth a dress and hat now and then, but, although I recognize the dress from time to time, I never see any change in the hat. I don't know what she does with my ex-millinery.

"Yas'm," she said again, and looked comprehensively at the untouched breakfast dishes and the awful viands, which were still where Roger had left them.

"Looks as though you'd had to git breakfast yoreself," she observed brightly. And went out in the kitchen and ate all those cakes and drank that unspeakable coffee! Really she did, and she didn't warm them up either.

I watched her miserably, unable to decide whether Roger was too finicky or Mary Elizabeth a natural-born diplomat.

"Mr. Gales led me an awful chase last night," she explained. "When I got home yistiddy evenin', my cousin whut keeps house fer me (!) tole me Mr. Gales went out in the mornin' en hadn't come back."

"Mr. Gales," let me explain, is Mary Elizabeth's second husband, an octogenarian, and the most original person, I am convinced, in existence.

"Yas'm," she went on, eating a final cold hot-cake, "en I went to look fer 'im, en had the whole perlice station out all night huntin' 'im. Look like they wusn't never goin' to find 'im. But I ses, 'Jes' let me look fer enough en long enough en I'll find 'im,' I ses, en I did. Way out Georgy Avenue, with the hat on ole Mis' give 'im. Sent it to 'im all the way fum Chicaga. He's had it fifteen years,—high silk beaver. I knowed he wusn't goin' too fer with that hat on.

"I went up to 'im, settin' by a fence all muddy, holdin' his hat on with both hands. En I ses, 'Look here, man, you come erlong home with me, en let me put you to bed.' En he come jest as meek! No-o-me, I knowed he wusn't goin' fer with ole Mis' hat on."

"Who was old 'Mis,' Mary Elizabeth?" I asked her.

"Lady I used to work fer in Noo York," she informed me. "Me en Rosy, the cook, lived with her fer years. Old Mis' was turrible fond of me, though her en Rosy used to querrel all the time. Jes' seemed like they couldn't git erlong. 'Member once Rosy run after her one Sunday with a knife, en I kep 'em apart. Reckon Rosy musta bin right put out with ole Mis' that day. By en by her en Rosy move to Chicaga, en when I married Mr. Gales, she sent 'im that hat. That old white woman shore did like me. It's so late, reckon I'd better put off sweepin' tel termorrer, ma'am."

I acquiesced, following her about from room to room. This was partly to get away from my own doleful thoughts—Roger really had hurt my feelings— but just as much to hear her talk. At first I used not to believe all she said, but after I investigated once and found her truthful in one amazing statement, I capitulated.

She had been telling me some remarkable tale of her first husband and I was listening with the stupefied attention, to which she always reduces me. Remember she was speaking of her first husband.

"En I ses to 'im, I ses, 'Mr. Gale,—'"

"Wait a moment, Mary Elizabeth," I interrupted, meanly delighted to have caught her for once. "You mean your first husband, don't you?"

"Yas'm," she replied. "En I ses to 'im, 'Mr. Gale! I ses—'"

"But, Mary Elizabeth," I persisted, "that's your second husband, isn't it,—Mr. Gale?"

She gave me her long-drawn "No-o-me! My first husband was Mr. Gale and my second is Mr. *Gales*. He spells his name with a Z, I reckon. I ain't never see it writ. Ez I wus sayin', I ses to Mr. Gale—"

And it was true! Since then I have never doubted Mary Elizabeth.

She was loquacious that afternoon. She told me about her sister, "where's got a home in the country and where's got eight children." I used to read Lucy Pratt's stories about little Ephraim or Ezekiel, I forget his name, who always said "where's" instead of "who's," but I never believed it really till I heard Mary Elizabeth use it. For some reason or other she never mentions her sister without mentioning the home, too. "My sister where's got a home in the country" is her unvarying phrase.

"Mary Elizabeth," I asked her once, "does your sister live in the country, or does she simply own a house there?"

"Yas'm," she told me.

She is fond of her sister. "If Mr. Gales wus to die," she told me complacently, "I'd go to live with her."

"If he should die," I asked her idly, "would you marry again?"

"Oh, no-o-me!" She was emphatic. "Though I don't know why I shouldn't, I'd come by it hones'. My father wus married four times."

That shocked me out of my headache. "Four times, Mary Elizabeth, and you had all those stepmothers!" My mind refused to take it in.

"Oh, no-o-me! I always lived with mamma. She was his first wife."

I hadn't thought of people in the state in which I had instinctively placed Mary Elizabeth's father and mother as indulging in divorce, but as Roger says slangily, "I wouldn't know."

Mary Elizabeth took off the dingy hat. "You see, papa and mamma—" the ineffable pathos of hearing this woman of sixty-four, with a husband of eighty, use the old childish terms!

"Papa and mamma wus slaves, you know, Mis' Pierson, and so of course they wusn't exackly married. White folks wouldn't let 'em. But they wus awf'ly in love with each other. Heard mamma tell erbout it lots of times, and how papa wus the han'somest man! Reckon she wus long erbout sixteen or seventeen then. So they jumped over a broomstick, en they wus jes as happy! But not long after I come erlong, they sold papa down South, and mamma never see him no mo' fer years and years. Thought he was dead. So she married again."

"And he came back to her, Mary Elizabeth?" I was overwhelmed with the woefulness of it.

"Yas'm. After twenty-six years. Me and my sister where's got a home in the country—she's really my half-sister, see Mis' Pierson,—her en mamma en my step-father en me wus all down in Bumpus, Virginia, workin' fer some white folks, and we used to live in a little cabin, had a front stoop to it. En one day an ole cullud man come by, had a lot o' whiskers. I'd saw him lots of times there in Bumpus, lookin' and peerin' into every cullud woman's face. En jes' then my sister she call out, 'Come here, you Ma'y Elizabeth,' en that old man stopped, en he looked at me en he looked at me, en he ses to me, 'Chile, is yo' name Ma'y Elizabeth?'

"You know, Mis' Pierson, I thought he wus jes' bein' fresh, en I ain't paid no 'tention to 'im. I ain't sed nuthin' ontel he spoke to me three or four times, en then I ses to 'im, 'Go 'way fum here, man, you ain't got no call to be fresh with me. I'm a decent woman. You'd oughta be ashamed of yoreself, an ole man like you.'"

Mary Elizabeth stopped and looked hard at the back of her poor wrinkled hands.

"En he says to me, 'Daughter,' he ses, jes' like that, 'daughter,' he ses, 'hones' I ain't bein' fresh. Is you' name shore enough Ma'y Elizabeth?'

"En I tole him, 'Yas'r.'

"'Chile,' he ses, 'whaar is yo' daddy?'

"'Ain't got no daddy,' I tole him peart-like. 'They done tuk 'im away fum me twenty-six years ago, I wusn't but a mite of a baby. Sol' 'im down the river. My mother often talks about it.' And, oh, Mis' Pierson, you shoulda see the glory come into his face!

"'Yore mother!' he ses, kinda out of breath, 'yore mother! Ma'y Elizabeth, whar is your mother?'

"'Back thar on the stoop,' I tole 'im. 'Why, did you know my daddy?'

"But he didn't pay no 'tention to me, jes' turned and walked up the stoop whar mamma wus settin'! She was feelin' sorta porely that day. En you oughta see me steppin' erlong after 'im.

"He walked right up to her and giv' her one look. 'Oh, Maggie,' he shout out, 'oh, Maggie! Ain't you know me? Maggie, ain't you know me?'

"Mamma look at 'im and riz up outa her cheer. 'Who're you?' she ses kinda trimbly, 'callin' me Maggie thata way? Who're you?'

"He went up real close to her, then, 'Maggie,' he ses jes' like that, kinda sad 'n tender, 'Maggie!' And hel' out his arms.

"She walked right into them. 'Oh,' she ses, 'it's Cassius! It's Cassius! It's my husban' come back to me! It's Cassius!' They wus like two mad people.

"My sister Minnie and me, we jes' stood and gawped at 'em. There they wus, holding on to each other like two pitiful childrun, en he tuk her hands and kissed 'em.

"'Maggie,' he ses, 'you'll come away with me, won't you? You gona take me back, Maggie? We'll go away, you en Ma'y Elizabeth en me. Won't we, Maggie?'

"Reckon my mother clean fergot my stepfather. 'Yes, Cassius,' she ses, 'we'll go away.' And then she sees Minnie, en it all comes back to her. 'Oh, Cassius,' she ses, 'I cain't go with you, I'm married again, en this time fer real. This here gal's mine and three boys, too, and another chile comin' in November!'"

"But she went with him, Mary Elizabeth," I pleaded.

"Surely she went with him after all those years. He really was her husband."

I don't know whether Mary Elizabeth meant to be sarcastic or not. "Oh, no-o-me, mamma couldn't a done that. She wus a good woman. Her ole master, whut done sol' my father down river, brung her up too religious fer that, en anyways, papa was married again, too. Had his fourth wife there in Bumpus with 'im."

The unspeakable tragedy of it!

I left her and went up to my room, and hunted out my dark-blue serge dress which I had meant to wear again that winter. But I had to give Mary Elizabeth something, so I took the dress down to her.

She was delighted with it. I could tell she was, because she used her rare untranslatable expletive.

"Haytian!" she said. "My sister where's got a home in the country, got a dress looks somethin' like this, but it ain't as good. No-o-me. She got hers to wear at a friend's weddin',—gal she was riz up with. Thet gal married well, too, lemme tell you; her husband's a Sunday School sup'rintendent."

I told her she needn't wait for Mr. Pierson, I would put dinner on the table. So off she went in the gathering dusk, trudging bravely back to her Mr. Gales and his high silk hat.

I watched her from the window till she was out of sight. It had been such a long time since I had thought of slavery. I was born in Pennsylvania, and neither my parents nor grandparents had been slaves; otherwise I might have had the same tale to tell as Mary Elizabeth, or worse yet, Roger and I might have lived in those black days and loved and lost each other and futilely, damnably, met again like Cassius and Maggie.

Whereas it was now, and I had Roger and Roger had me.

How I loved him as I sat there in the hazy dusk. I thought of his dear, bronze perfection, his habit of swearing softly in excitement, his blessed stupidity. Just the same I didn't meet him at the door as usual, but pretended to be busy. He came rushing to me with the *Saturday Evening Post*, which is more to me than rubies. I thanked him warmly, but aloofly, if you can get that combination.

We ate dinner almost in silence for my part. But he praised everything,— the cooking, the table, my appearance.

After dinner we went up to the little sitting-room. He hoped I wasn't tired,—couldn't he fix the pillows for me? So!

I opened the magazine and the first thing I saw was a picture of a woman gazing in stony despair at the figure of a man disappearing around the bend of the road. It was too much. Suppose that were Roger and I! I'm afraid I sniffled. He was at my side in a moment.

"Dear loveliest! Don't cry. It was all my fault. You aren't any worse about coffee than I am about cards! And anyway, I needn't have slammed the door! Forgive me, Sally. I always told you I was hard to get along with. I've had a horrible day,—don't stay cross with me, dearest."

I held him to me and sobbed outright on his shoulder. "It isn't you, Roger," I told him, "I'm crying about Mary Elizabeth."

I regret to say he let me go then, so great was his dismay. Roger will never be half the diplomat that Mary Elizabeth is.

"Holy smokes!" he groaned. "She isn't going to leave us for good, is she?"

So then I told him about Maggie and Cassius. "And oh, Roger," I ended futilely, "to think that they had to separate after all those years, when he had come back, old and with whiskers!" I didn't mean to be so banal, but I was crying too hard to be coherent.

Roger had got up and was walking the floor, but he stopped then aghast.

"Whiskers!" he moaned. "My hat! Isn't that just like a woman?" He had to clear his throat once or twice before he could go on, and I think he wiped his eyes.

"Wasn't it the—" I really can't say what Roger said here,—"wasn't it the darndest hard luck that when he did find her again, she should be married? She might have waited."

I stared at him astounded. "But, Roger," I reminded him, "he had married three other times, he didn't wait."

"Oh—!" said Roger, unquotably, "married three fiddlesticks! He only did that to try to forget her."

Then he came over and knelt beside me again. "Darling, I do think it is a sensible thing for a poor woman to learn how to cook, but I don't care as long as you love me and we are together. Dear loveliest, if I had been Cassius,"—he caught my hands so tight that he hurt them,"—and I had married fifty times and had come back and found you married to someone else, I'd have killed you, killed you."

Well, he wasn't logical, but he was certainly convincing.

So thus, and not otherwise, Mary Elizabeth healed the breach.

Angelina Weld Grimké

Goldie

H e had never thought of the night, before, as so sharply black and white; but then, he had never walked before, three long miles, after midnight, over a country road. A short distance only, after leaving the railroad station, the road plunged into the woods and stayed there most of the way. Even in the day, he remembered, although he had not traveled over it for five years, it had not been the easiest to journey over. Now, in the almost palpable darkness, the going was hard, indeed; and he was compelled to proceed, it almost seemed to him, one careful step after another careful step.

Singular fancies may come to one, at such times: and, as he plodded forward, one came, quite unceremoniously, quite unsolicited, to him and fastened its tentacles upon him. Perhaps it was born of the darkness and the utter windlessness with the resulting great stillness; perhaps—but who knows from what fancies spring? At any rate, it seemed to him, the woods, on either side of him, were really not woods at all but an ocean that had flowed down in a great rolling black wave of flood to the very lips of the road itself and paused there as though suddenly arrested and held poised in some strange and sinister spell. Of course, all of this came, he told himself over and over, from having such a cursed imagination; but whether he would or not, the fancy persisted and the growing feeling with it, that he, Victor Forrest, went in actual danger, for at any second the

First published in *Birth Control Review* 4 (Nov.–Dec. 1920)

spell might snap and with that snapping, this boundless, deep upon deep of horrible, waiting sea, would move, rush, hurl itself heavily and swiftly together from the two sides, thus engulfing, grinding, crushing, blotting out all in its path, not excluding what he now knew to be that most insignificant of insignificant pigmies, Victor Forrest.

But there were bright spots, here and there in the going—he found himself calling them white islands of safety. These occurred where the woods receded at some little distance from the road.

"It's as though," he thought aloud, "they drew back here in order to get a good deep breath before plunging forward again. Well, all I hope is, the spell holds O.K. beyond."

He always paused, a moment or so, on one of these islands to drive out expulsively the dank, black oppressiveness of the air he had been breathing and to fill his lungs anew with God's night air, that, here, at least, was sweet and untroubled. Here, too, his eyes were free again and he could see the dimmed white blur of road for a space each way; and, above, the stars, millions upon millions of them, each one hardly brilliant, stabbing its way whitely through the black heavens. And if the island were large enough there was a glimpse, scarcely more, of a very pallid, slightly crumpled moon sliding furtively down the west.—Yes, sharply black and sharply white, that was it, but mostly it was black.

And as he went, his mind busy enough with many thoughts, many memories, subconsciously always the aforementioned fancy persisted, clung to him; and he was never entirely able to throw off the feeling of his very probably and imminent danger in the midst of this arrested wood-ocean.

—Of course, he thought, it was downright foolishness, his expecting Goldie, or rather Cy, to meet him. He hadn't written or telegraphed.—Instinct he guessed, must have warned him that wouldn't be safe; but, confound it all! This was the devil of a road.—Gosh! What a lot of noise a man's feet could make—couldn't they?—All alone like this—Well, Goldie and Cy would feel a lot worse over the whole business than he did.—After all it was only once in a lifetime, wasn't it?—Hoofing it was good for him, anyway.—No doubt about his having grown soft.—He'd be as lame as the dickens tomorrow.—Well, Goldie would enjoy that—liked nothing better than fussing over a fellow.—If (But he very resolutely turned away from that if.)

—In one way, it didn't seem like five years and yet, in another, it seemed longer—since he'd been over this road last. It had been the sunshiniest and the saddest May morning he ever remembered.—He'd been going in the opposite direction, then; and that little sister of his, Goldie, had been sitting very straight beside him, the two lines held rigidly in her two little gold paws and her little gold face stiff with repressed emotion. He felt a twinge, yet, as he remembered her face and the way the great tears would well up and run over down her cheeks at intervals.—Proud little thing!—She had disdained even to notice them and treated them as a matter with which she had no concern.—No, she hadn't wanted him to go.—Good, little Goldie!—Well, she never knew, how close, how very close he had been to putting his hand out and telling her to turn back—he'd changed his mind and wasn't going after all.—

He drew a sharp breath.—He hadn't put out his hand.

—And at the station, her face there below him, as he looked down at her through the open window of the train.—The unwavering way her eyes had held his—and the look in them, he hadn't understood them, or didn't now, for that matter.

"Don't," he had said, "Don't Goldie!"

"I must. Vic, I must.—I don't know—Don't you understand I may never see you again?"

"Rot!" he had said. "Am I not going to send for you?"

—And then she had tried to smile and that had been worse than her eyes.

"You think so, now, Vic,—but will you?"

"Of course."

"Vic!"

"Yes."

"Remember, whatever it is—it's all right. *It's all right.*—I mean it.—See! I couldn't smile—could I?—If I didn't?"

And then, when it had seemed as if he couldn't stand any more—he had leaned over, even to pick up his bag to get off, give it all up—the train had started and it was too late. The last he had seen of her, she had been standing there, very straight, her arms at her sides and her little gold paws two little tight fists.—And her eyes!—And her twisted smile!—God! that was about enough of that.—He was going to her, now, wasn't he?

—Had he been wrong to go?—Had he?—Somehow, now, it seemed that way.—And yet, at the time, he had felt he was right.—He still did for that matter.—His chance, that's what it had meant.—Oughtn't he to have had it?—Certainly a colored man couldn't do the things that counted in the South.—To live here, just to *live* here, he had to swallow his self-respect.—Well, he had tried, honestly, too, for Goldie's sake, to swallow his.—The trouble was he couldn't keep it swallowed—it nauseated him.—The thing for him to have done, he saw that now, was to have risked everything and taken Goldie with him.—He shouldn't have waited, as he had from year to year, to send for her.—It would have meant hard sledding, but they could have managed somehow.—Of course, it wouldn't have been the home she had had with her Uncle Ray and her Aunt Millie, still.—Well, there wasn't any use in crying over spilt milk. One thing was certain, never mind how much you might wish to, you couldn't recall the past.—

—Two years ago—(Gosh!) but time flew!—When her letter had come telling him she had married Cy Harper.—Queer thing, this life!—Darned queer thing!—Why he had been in the very midst of debating whether or not he could afford to send for her—had almost decided he could.—Well, sisters, even the very best of them, it turned out, weren't above marrying and going off and leaving you high and dry—just like this.—Oh! of course, Cy was a good enough fellow, clean, steady going, true, and all the rest of it;—no one could deny that—still, confound it all! how could Goldie prefer a fathead like Cy to him.—Hm!—peeved yet, it seemed!—Well, he'd acknowledge it—he was peeved all right.

Involuntarily he began to slow up.

—Good! since he was acknowledging things—why not get along and acknowledge the rest.—Might just as well have this out with himself here and now.—Peeved first, then, what?

He came to an abrupt stop in the midst of the black silence of the arrested wood-ocean.

—There was one thing, it appeared, a dark road could do for you—it could make it possible for you to see yourself quite plainly—almost too plainly.—Peeved first, then what?—No blinking now, the truth.—He'd evaded himself very cleverly—hadn't he?—up until tonight?—No use any more.—Well, what was he waiting for?—Out with it.—Peeved first; go ahead, now.—Louder!—*Relief!*—Honest, at last.—Relief! Think of it, he had felt relief when he had learned he wasn't to be bothered, after all, with little, loyal, big-hearted Goldie.—*Bothered!*—And he had prided himself upon being rather a decent, upright, respectable fellow.—Why, if he had heard this about anybody else, he wouldn't have been able to find language strong enough to describe him—A rotter, that's what he was, and a cad.

"And Goldie would have sacrificed herself for you any time, and gladly, and you know it."

To his surprise he found himself speaking aloud.

—Why once, when the kid had been only eight years old and he had been taken with a cramp while in swimming, she had jumped in too!—Goldie, who couldn't swim a single stroke!—Her screams had done it and they were saved. He could see his mother's face yet, quizzical, a little puzzled, a little worried.

"But what on earth, Goldie, possessed you to jump in too?" she had asked. "Didn't you *know* you couldn't save him?"

"Yes, I know it."

"Then, why?"

"I don't know. It just seemed that if Vic had to drown, why I had to drown with him.—Just couldn't live *afterwards,* Momsey. If I lived *then* and he drowned."

"Goldie! Goldie!—If Vic fell out of a tree, would you have to fall out too?"

"Proberbly." Goldie had never been able to master "probably," but it fascinated her.

"Well, for Heavens' sake. Vic, do be careful of yourself hereafter. You see how it is," his mother had said.

And Goldie had answered—how serious, how quaint, how true her little face had been.—

"Yes, that's how it is, isn't it?" Another trick of hers, ending so often what she had to say with a question.—And he hadn't wished to be bothered with her!—

He groaned and started again.

—Well, he'd try to even up things a little, now.—He'd show her (there was a lump in his throat) if he could.—

For the first time Victor Forrest began to understand the possibilities of tragedy that may lie in those three little words. "If I can."

—Perhaps Goldie had understood and married Cy so that he needn't bother any more about having to have her with him. He hoped, as he had never hoped, for anything before that this hadn't been her reason. She was quite equal to marrying, he knew, for such a motive—and so game, too, you'd never dream it was a sacrifice she was making. He'd rather believe, even, that it had been just to get the little home all her own.—When Goldie was only a little thing and you asked her want she wanted most in all the world when she grew up, she had always answered:

"Why, a little home—all my own—a cunning one—and young things in it and about it."

And if you asked her to explain, she had said:

"Don't you *know?*—not *really?*"

And, then, if you had suggested children, she had answered:

"Of course, all my own; and kittens and puppies and little fluffy chickens and ducks and little birds in my trees, who will make little nests and little songs there because they will know that the trees near the little home all my own are the very nicest ever and ever."—

—Once, she must have been around fifteen, then—how well he remembered that once—he had said:

"Look here, Goldie, isn't this an awful lot you're asking God to put over for you?"

Only teasing, he had been—but Goldie's face!

"Oh! Vic, am I?—Do you *really* think that?"

And then, before he could reply in little, eager, humble rushes:

"I hadn't thought of it—*that* way—before.—Maybe you're right.—If—if—I gave up something, perhaps—the ducks—or the chickens—or the—birds—or the kittens—or the puppies?"

Then very slowly:

"Or-the-children?—Oh!—but I couldn't!—Not any of them.—Don't you think, perhaps,—just perhaps, Vic,—if—if—I'm—good—always—from now on—that—that—maybe—maybe—sometime, Vic, sometime—I—I—might?—Oh! don't you?"—

He shut his mouth hard.

—Well, she had had the little home all her own. Cy had made a little clearing, she had written, just beyond the great live oak. Did he remember it? And did he remember, too, how much Cy loved the trees?—

—No, he hadn't forgotten that live oak—not the way he had played in it—and carved his initials all over it; and he hadn't forgotten Cy and the trees, either.—Silly way, Cy had had, even after he grew up, of mooning among them.

"Talk to me—they do—sometimes.—Tell me big, quiet things, nice things."

—Gosh! after *his* experience, *this* night among them. *Love* 'em!—Hm!—Damned, waiting, greedy things!—Cy could have them and welcome.—

—It had been last year Goldie had written about the clearing with the little home all her own in the very "prezact" middle of it.—They had had to wait a whole year after they were married before they could move in—not finished or something—he'd forgotten the reason.—How had the rest of that letter gone?—Goldie's letters were easy to remember—had, somehow, a sort of burrlike quality about them. He had it, now, something like this:

She wished she could tell him how cunning the little home all her own was, but there was really no cunning word cunning enough to describe it.—Why even the very trees came right down to the very edges of the clearing on all four sides just to look at it.—If he could only *see* how proudly they stood there and nodded their entire approval one to the other!—

Four rooms, the little home, all her own, had.—Four!—And a little porch in the front and a "littler" one in the back, and a hall that had really the most absurd way of trying to get out both the front and rear doors at the same time. Would he believe it, they had to keep both the doors shut tight in order to hold that ridiculous hall in? Had he ever, in all his life, heard of such a thing? And just off of this little hall, at the right of the front door, was their bedroom, and back of this, at the end of this same very silly hall was their dining-room and opposite, across the hall again—she hoped he saw how this hall simply refused to be ignored—again—opposite was the kitchen.—He was, then, to step back into the hall once more, but *this* time he was to pretend very hard not to see it. There was no telling, it's vanity was so great, if you paid too much attention to it, what it might do. Why, the unbearable little thing might rise up, break down the front and back doors and escape; and then where'd they be, she'd like to know, without any little hall at all?—He was to step, then, quite nonchalantly—if he knew what that was, back into the hall and come forwards but this time he was to look at the room at the left of the front door; and *there*, if he pleased, he would see something really to repay him for his trouble, for here he would behold her sitting room and parlor both in one. And if he couldn't believe how perfectly adorable this little room could be and was, why she was right there to tell him all about it.—Every single bit of the little home all her own was built just as she had wished and furnished just as she had hoped. And, well, to sum it all up, it wasn't safe, if you had any kind of heart trouble at all, to stand in the road in front of the little home all her own, because it had such a way of calling you that before you knew it, you were running to it and running fast. She could vouch for the absolute truth of this statement.

And she had a puppy, yellow all over, all but his little heart—she dared him even to suggest such a thing!—with a funny wrinkled forehead and a most impudent grin. And he insisted upon eating up all the uneatable things they possessed, including Cy's best straw had and her own Sunday-go-to-meeting slippers; And she had a kitten, a grey one; and the busiest things he did were to eat and sleep. Sometimes he condescended to play with his tail and to keep the puppy in his place. He had a way of looking at you out of blue, very young, very innocent eyes that you knew perfectly well were not a bit young nor yet a bit innocent. And she had the darlingest, downiest, little chickens and ducks and a canary bird, that Emma Elizabeth lent her sometimes when she went away to work, and the canary had been made of two golden songs. And outside of the little home all her own—in the closest trees, the birds were, lots of them, and they had nested there.—If, of a morning, he could only hear them singing!—As if they knew—and did it on purpose—just as she had wished.—How happy it had all sounded—and yet—and yet—once or twice—he had had the feeling that something wasn't quite right.

—He hoped it didn't mean she wasn't caring for Cy.—He would rather believe it was because there hadn't been children.—The latter could be remedied—from little hints he had been gathering lately, he rather thought it was already being remedied; but if she didn't *care* for Cy, there wasn't much to be done about that.—Well, he was going to her, at last.—She couldn't fool him—

couldn't Goldie—; and if that fathead, Cy, couldn't take care of her, now. Just let somebody start somebody start something.—

—That break ahead there, in the darkness, ought to be just about where the settlement was.—No one need ever tell *him* again it was only three miles from the station—he guessed he knew better.—More like ten or twenty.—The settlement, all right.—Thought he hadn't been mistaken.—So far, then, so good.

The road, here, became the main street of the little colored settlement. Three or four smaller ones cut it at right angles and, then, ran off into the darkness. The houses, for the most part, sat back, not very far apart; and, as the shamed moon had entirely disappeared, all he could make out of them was their silent, black little masses. His quick eyes and his ears were busy. No sound broke the stillness. He drew a deep breath of relief. As nearly as he could make out everything was as it should be.

He did not pause until he was about midway of the settlement. Here he set his bag down, sat on it and looked at the illuminated hands of his watch. It was half past two. In the woods he had found it almost cold, but, in this spot, the air was warm and close. He pulled out his handkerchief, took off his hat, mopped his face, head and neck, finally the sweatband of his hat.

—Queer!—but he wouldn't have believed that the mere sight of all this, after five years, could make him feel this way. There was something to this home idea, after all.—Didn't feel, hardly, as though he had ever been away.—

Suddenly he wondered if old man Tom Jackson had fixed that gate of his yet. Curiosity got the better of him. He arose, went over and looked. Sure enough the gate swung outward on a broken hinge. Forrest grinned.

"Don't believe over much here, in change, do they?—That gate was that way ever since I can remember.—Bet every window is shut tight too. 'Turrible; the night air always used to be.—Wonder if my people will ever get over these things."

He came back and sat down again. He was facing a house that his eyes had returned to more than any other.

"Looks just the same.—Wonder who lives there, now.—Suppose some one does.—Looks like it.—Mother sure had courage—more that I would have had—to give up a good job in the North, teaching school to come down here and marry a poor doctor in a colored settlement. I give it to her.—Game!—Goldie's just like her—she'd have done it too."

—How long had it been since his father had died?—Nine—ten—why, it was ten years and eight since his mother—. They'd both been born there—he and Goldie.—That was that story his mother had used to tell about him when he had first been brought in to see her?—He had been six at the time.

"Mother," he had asked, "is her gold?"

"What, Son?"

"I say, is her gold?"

"Oh! I see," his mother had said and smiled, he was sure, that very nice understanding smile of hers. "Why, she *is* gold, isn't she?"

"Yes, all of her. What's her name?"

"She hasn't any, yet, Son."

"He aint got no name?—Too bad!—I give her one. Hers name's Goldie, 'cause."

"All right, Son, Goldie it shall be." And Goldie it had always been.—

—No, you couldn't call Goldie pretty exactly.—Something about her, though, mighty attractive.—Different looking!—that was it.—Like herself.— She had never lost that beautiful even gold color of hers.—Even her hair was "goldeny" and her long eye-lashes. Nice eyes, Goldie had, big and brown with flecks of gold in them—set in a little wistful, pointed face.—

He came to his feet suddenly and picked up his bag. He moved swiftly, now, but not so swiftly as not to notice things still as he went.

"Why, hello!" he exclaimed and paused a second or so before going on again. "What's happened to Uncle Ray's house?—Something's not the same.— Seems larger, somehow.—Wonder what it is?—Maybe a porch.—So they do change here a little.—That there ought to be Aunt Phoebe's house.—But she must be dead—though I don't remember Goldie's saying so.—Why, she'd be way over ninety.—Used to be afraid of the dark or something and never slept without a dime light.—Gosh! if there isn't the light—just the same as ever.— And way over ninety.—Whew!—Wonder how it feels to be that old.—Bet I wouldn't like it.—Gee! what's that?"

Victor Forrest stopped short and listened. The sound was muffled but continuous, it seemed to come from the closed faintly lighted pane of Aunt Phoebe's room. It was a sound, it struck him, remarkably like the keening he had heard in an Irish play. It died out slowly and though he waited it did not begin again.

"Probably dreaming or something and woke herself up," and he started on once more.

He soon left the settlement behind and, continuing along the same road found himself, (he hoped for the last time) in the midst of the arrested wood-ocean.

But the sound of that keening, although he had explained it quite satisfactorily to himself had left him disturbed. Thoughts, conjectures, fears that he had refused, until now, quite resolutely to entertain no longer would be denied. They were rooted in Goldie's two last letters, the cause of his hurried trip South.

"Of course, there's no *real* danger.—I'm foolish, even, to entertain such a thought.—Women get like that sometimes—nervous and overwrought.—And if it is with her as I suspect and hope—why the whole matter's explained.—Why it had really sounded *frightened!*—and parts of it were—hm!—almost incoherent.—The whole thing's too ridiculous however, to believe.—Well, when she sees me we'll have a good big laugh over it all.—Just the same, I'm glad I came.—Rather funny—somehow—thinking of Goldie—with a kid—in her arms.—Nice, though.—"

—Lafe Coleman!—Lafe Coleman!—He seemed to remember dimly a stringy, long white man with stringy colorless hair, quite disagreeably under-clean; eyes a pale grey and fishlike.—He associated a sort of toothless grin with that face.—No, that wasn't it, either,—Ah! that was it!—He had it clearly, now.—The grin was all right but it displayed the dark and rotting remains of tooth stumps.—

He made a grimace of strong disgust and loathing.

—And—this—this—*thing* had been annoying Goldie, had been in fact, for years.—She hadn't told anybody, it seems, because she had been able to take care of herself.—But since she had married and been living away, from the set-tlement—it had been easier for him, and much more difficult for her. He wasn't to worry, though, for the man was stupid and so far she'd always been able to outwit,—What she feared was Cy. It was true Cy was amiability itself—but—well—she had seen him angry once.—Ought she to tell him?—She didn't be-lieve Cy would kill the creature—not outright—but it would be pretty close to it.—The feeling between the races was running higher than it used to.—There had been a very terrible lynching in the next county only last year.—She hadn't spoken of it before—for there didn't seem any use going into it.—As he had never mentioned it, she supposed it had never gotten into the papers. Nothing, of course, had been done abut it, nothing ever was. Everybody knew who were in the mob.—Even he would be surprised at some of the names.—The brother of the lynched man, quite naturally, had tried to bring some of the leaders to jus-tice; and he, too, had paid with his life. Then the mob, not satisfied, had threat-ened, terrorized, cowed all the colored people in the locality.—He was to remember that when you were under the heel it wasn't the most difficult of mat-ters to be terrorized and cowed. There was absolutely no law, as he knew, to pro-tect a colored man.—That was one of the reasons she had hesitated to tell Cy, for not only Cy and she might be made to pay for what Cy might do, but the lit-tle settlement as well. Now, keeping all this in mind, ought she to tell Cy?

And the letter had ended:

"I'm a little nervous, Vic, and frightened and not quite sure of my judg-ment. Whatever you advise me to do, I am sure will be right."

—On the very heels of this had come the "special" mailed by Goldie in another town.—She hadn't dared, it seemed, to post it in Hopewood.—It had contained just twelve words, but they had brought him South on the next train.

"Cy knows," it had said, "and O! Vic, if you love me, come, come, come!"

Way down, inside of him, in the very depths, a dull cold rage began to glow, but he banked it down again, carefully, very carefully, as he had been able to do, so far, each time before that the thoughts of Lafe Coleman and little Goldie's helplessness had threatened anew to stir it.

—That there ought to be the great live oak—and beyond should be the clearing, in the very "prezact" middle of which should be the little home all Goldie's own.—

For some inexplicable reason his feet suddenly began to show a strange reluctance to go forward.

"Damned silly ass!" he said to himself. "There wasn't a thing wrong with the settlement. That ought to be a good enough sign for anybody with a grain of sense."

And then, quite suddenly, he remembered the keening.

He did not turn back to pause, still his feet showed no tendency to hasten. Of necessity, however, it was only a matter of time before he reached the live oak. He came to a halt beside it, ears and every sense keenly on the alert. Save for the stabbing, white stars above the clearing, there was nothing else in all the world, it seemed, but himself and the heavy black silence.

Once more he advanced but, this time, by an act of sheer will. He paused, set his jaw and faced the clearing. In the very centre was a dark small mass, it must be the little home. The breath he had drawn in sharply, while turning, he emitted in a deep sigh. His knees felt strangely weak.—What he had expected to see exactly, he hardly knew. He was almost afraid of the reaction going on inside of him. The relief, the blessed relief at merely finding it there, the little house all her own!

It made him feel suddenly very young and joyous and the world, bad as it was, a pretty decent old place after all. Danger!—of course, there was no danger.—How could he have been so absurd?—Just wait until he had teased Goldie a plenty about this. He started to laugh aloud but caught himself in time.

—No use awaking them.—He'd steal up and sit on the porch, there'd probably be a chair there or something, and wait until dawn.—They shouldn't be allowed to sleep one single second after that.—And then he'd bang on their window, and call out quite casually:

"O, Goldie Harper, this is a nice way—isn't it?—to treat a fellow; not even to leave the latch string out for him?"

He could hear Goldie's little squeal now.

And then he'd say to Cy:

"Hello, you big fathead, you!—what do you mean, anyhow, by making a perfectly good brother-in-law hoof it the whole way here, like this?"

He had reached the steps by this time and he began softly to mount them. It was very dark on the little porch and he wished he dared to light a match, but he mustn't risk anything that might spoil the little surprise he was planning. He transferred his bag from his right to his left hand, the better to feel his way. With his fingers outstretched in front of him he took a cautious step forward and stumbled over something.

"Clumsy chump!" he exclaimed below his breath, "that will about finish your little surprise I am thinking." He stood stockstill for several seconds, but there was no sound.

"Some sleepers," he commented.

He leaned over to find out what it was he had stumbled against and discovered that it was a broken chair lying on its side. Slowly he came to a standing posture. He was not as happy for some reason. He stood there, very quiet, for several moments. Then his hand stretched out before, he started forward again. This time, after only a couple of steps, his hand came in contact with the housefront. He was feeling his way along, cautiously still, when all of a sudden his fingers encountered nothing but air. Surprised, he paused. He thought, at first, he had come to the end of the porch. He put out a carefully exploring foot only to find firm boards beneath. A second time he experimented with the same result. And then, as suddenly, he felt the housefront once more beneath his fingers. Gradually it came to him where he must be. He was standing before the door and it was open, wide open!

He could not have moved if he had wished. He made no sound and none broke the blackness all about.

It was sometime afterwards when he put his bag down upon the porch, took a box of matches out of his pocket, lit one and held it up. His hand was trembling, but he managed, before it burned his fingers and he blew it out automatically, to see four things—two open doors to right and left, a lamp in a bracket just beyond the door at the left and a dirty mudtrodden floor.

The minutes went by and then, it seemed to him, somebody else called out:

"Goldie! Cy!" This was followed by silence only.

Again the voice tried, a little louder this time:

"Goldie! Cy!" —There was no response.

———————

This other person who seemed, somehow, to have entered into his body, moved forward, struck another match, lit the lamp and took it down out of the bracket. Nothing seemed to make very much difference to this stranger. He moved his body stiffly; his eyes felt large and dry. He passed through the open door at the left and what he saw there did not surprise him in the least. In some dim way, only he knew that it affected him.

There was not, in this room, one single whole piece of furniture. Chairs, tables, a sofa, a whatnot, all had been smashed, broken, torn apart; the stuffing of the upholstery, completely ripped out; and the entirety thrown, scattered, here, there and everywhere. The piano lay on one side, its other staved in.—Something, it reminded him of—something to do with a grin—the black notes like the rotting stumps of teeth. Oh! yes, Lafe Coleman!—that was it. The thought aroused no particular emotion in him. Only, again he knew it affected him in some far off way.

Every picture on the walls had been wrenched down and the moulding with it, the pictures, themselves, defaced and torn, and the glass splintered and crushed under foot. Knick-knacks, vases, a china clock, all lay smashed and broken. Even the rug upon the floor had not escaped, but had been ripped up, torn into shreds and fouled by many dirty feet. The frail white curtains and window shades had gone down too in this human whirlwind; not a pane of glass was whole. The white woodwork and the white walls were soiled and smeared. Over and over the splay-fingered imprint of one dirty hand repeated itself on the walls. A wanton boot had kicked through the plastering in places.

This someone else went out of the door, down the hall, into the little kitchen and dining-room. In each room he found precisely the same conditions prevailing.

There was one left, he remembered, so he turned back into the hall, went along it to the open door and entered in.—What was the matter, here, with the air?—He raised the lamp higher above his head. He saw the same confusion as elsewhere. A brass bed was overturned and all things else shattered and topsy-turvy. There was something dark at the foot of the bed. He moved nearer, and understood why the air was not pleasant. The dark object was a little dead dog, a yellow one, with a wrinkled forehead. His teeth were bared in a snarl. A kick in the belly had done for him. He leaned over; the little leg was quite stiff. Less dimly, this time, he knew that this affected him.

He straightened up. When he had entered the room there had been something he had noticed for him to do. But, what was it? This stranger's memory was not all that it should be.—Oh! yes, he knew, now. The bed. He was to right the bed. With some difficulty he cleared a space for the lamp and set it down carefully. He raised the bed. Nothing but the mattress and the rumpled and twisted bed clothing. He didn't know exactly just what this person was expecting to find.

He was sitting on the steps, the extinguished lamp at his side. It was dawn. Everything was veiled over with grey. As the day came on a breeze followed softly after, and with the breeze there came to him there on the steps a creaking, two creakings!—Some where there to the right, they were, among the trees. They grey world became a shining green one. Why were the birds singing like that, he wondered.—It didn't take the day long to get here—did it?—once it started. A second time his eyes went to the woods at the right. He was able to see, now. Nothing there, as far as he could make out. His eyes dropped from the trees to the ground and he beheld what looked to him like a trampled path. It began, there at the trees: it approached the house: it passed over a circular bed of little pansies. It ended at the steps. Again his eyes traversed the path, but this time from the steps to the trees.

Quite automatically he arose and followed the path. Quite automatically he drew the branches aside and saw what he saw. Underneath those two terribly mutilated swinging bodies, lay a tiny unborn child, its head crushed in by a deliberate heel.

Something went very wrong in his head. He dropped the branches, turned and sat down. A spider, in the sunshine, was reweaving the web some one had just destroyed while passing through the grass. He sat slouched far forward watching the spider for hours. He wished the birds wouldn't sing so.—Somebody had said something once about them. He wished, too, he could remember who it was.

About midday, the children of the colored settlement, playing in the road looked up and saw a man approaching. There was something about him that frightened them, the little ones in particular, for they ran screaming to their mothers. The larger ones drew back as unobtrusively as possible into their own yards. The man came on with a high head and an unhurried gait. His should have been a young face, but it was not. Out of its set sternness looked his eyes, and they were very terrible eyes indeed. Mothers with children hanging to them from behind and peering around, came to their doors. The man was passing through the settlement, now. A woman, startled, recognized him and called the news out shrilly to her man eating his dinner within. He came out, went down to the road rather reluctantly. The news spread. Other men from other houses followed the first man's example. They stood abut him, quite a crowd of them. The stranger of necessity, came to a pause. There were no greetings on either side. He eyed them over, this crowd, coolly, appraisingly, contemptuously. They eyed him, in turn, but surreptitiously. They were plainly very uncomfortable.

Wiping their hands on aprons, women joined the crowd. A larger child or two dared the outskirts. No one would meet his eye.

Suddenly a man was speaking. His voice came sharply, jerkily. He was telling a story. Another took it up and another.

One added a detail here; one a detail there. Heated arguments arose over insignificant particulars; angry words were passed. Then came too noisy explanations, excuses, speeches in extenuation of their own actions, pleas, attempted exoneration of themselves. The strange man said never a word. He listened to each and to all. His contemptuous eyes made each writhe in turn. They had finished. There was nothing more, that they could see to be said. They waited, eyes on the ground, for him to speak.

But what he said was:

"Where is Uncle Ray?"

Uncle Ray, it seemed was away—had been for two weeks. His Aunt Millie with him. No one had written to him for his address was not known.

The strange man made no comment.

"Where is Lafe Coleman?" he asked.

No one there knew where he was to be found—not one. They regretted the fact, they were sorry, but they couldn't say. They spoke with lowered eyes, shifting their bodies uneasily from foot to foot.

Watching their faces he saw their eyes suddenly lift, as if with one accord and focus upon something behind him and to his right. He turned his head. In the brilliant sunshine, a very old, very bent form leaning heavily on a cane was coming down the path from the house in whose window he had seen the dimmed light. It was Aunt Phoebe.

He left the crowd abruptly and went to meet her. When she was quite sure he was coming she paused where she was, bent over double, her two hands, one over the other, on the knob of her cane, and waited for him. No words, either, between these two. He looked down at her and she bent back her head, tremulous from age, and looked up at him.

The wrinkles were many and deep-bitten in Aunt Phoebe's dark skin. A border of white wool fringed the bright bandana tied tightly around her head. There were grey hairs in her chin; two blue rings encircled the irises of her dim eyes. But all her ugliness could not hide the big heart of her, kind yet, and brave, after ninety years on earth.

And as he stood gazing down at her, quite suddenly he remembered what Goldie had once said about those circled eyes.

"Kings and Queens may have *their* crowns and welcome. What's there to *them?*—But the kind Aunt Phoebe wears—that different. She earned hers, Vic, earned them through many years and long of sorrow, and heartbreak and bitter,

bitter tears. She bears with her the unforgetting heart.—And though they could take husband and children and sell them South, though she lost them in the body—Never a word of them, since—she keeps them always in her heart.—I knew, Vic, I know—and God who is good and God who is just touched her eyes, both of them and gave her blue crowns, beautiful ones, a crown for each. Don't you *see she is of God's Elect?*"

For a long time Victor Forrest stood looking down into those crowned eyes. No one disturbed these two in the sun drenched little yard. They, in the road, drew closer together and watched silently.

And then he spoke:

"You are to tell me, Aunt Phoebe—aren't you?—where I am to find Lafe Coleman?"

Aunt Phoebe did not hesitate a second. "Yes," she said and told him.

The crowd in the road moved uneasily, but no one spoke.

And, then, Victor Forrest did a thing he had never done before, he leaned over swiftly and kissed the wrinkled parchment cheek of Aunt Phoebe.

"Goldie loved you," he said and straightened up, turned on his heel without another word and went down the path to the road. Those there made no attempt to speak. They drew closer together and made way for him. He looked neither to the right nor to the left. He passed them without a glance. He went with a steady, purposeful gait and a high head. All watched him for they knew they were never to see him alive again. The woods swallowed Victor Forrest. A low keening was to be heard. Aunt Phoebe had turned and was going more feebly, more slowly than ever towards her house.

Those that know whereof they speak say that when Lafe Coleman was found he was not a pleasant object to see. There was no bullet in him—nothing like that. It was the marks upon his neck and the horror of his blackened face.

And Victor Forrest died, as the other two had died, upon another tree.

There is a country road upon either side of which grow trees even to its very edges. Each tree has been chosen and transplanted here for a reason and the reason is that at some time each has borne upon its boughs a creaking victim. Hundreds of these trees, there are, thousands of them. They form a forest—"Creaking Forrest" it is called. And over this road many pass, very, very many. And they go jauntily, joyously here—even at night. They do not go as Victor Forrest went,—they do not sense the things that Victor Forrest sensed. If their souls were not deaf, there would be many things for them to hear in

"Creaking Forest." At night the trees become an ocean dark and sinister, for it is made up of all the evil in all the hearts of all the mobs that have done to death their creaking victims. It is an ocean arrested at the very edges of the road by a strange spell. But this spell may snap at any second and with that snapping this sea of evil will move, rush, hurl itself heavily and swiftly together from the two sides of the road, engulfing, grinding, crushing, blotting out all in its way.

Zora Neale Hurston

Isis

"You Isie Watts! Git 'own offen dat gate post an' rake up dis yahd!" The small brown girl perched upon the gate post looked yearningly up the gleaming shell road that lead to Orlando. After awhile, she shrugged her thin shoulders. This only seemed to heap still more kindling on Grandma Potts' already burning ire.

"Lawd a-mussy!" she screamed, enraged—"Heah Joel, gimme dat wash stick. Ah'll show dat limb of Satan she cain't shake herself at *me*. If she ain't down by the time Ah gets dere, Ah'll break huh down in de lines."

"Aw Gran'ma, Ah see Mist' George and Jim Robinson comin' and Ah wanted to wave at 'em," the child said impatiently.

"You jes' wave dat rake at dis heah yahd, madame, else Ah'll take you down a button hole lower. Youse too 'oomanish jumpin' up in everybody's face dat pass."

This struck the child sorely for nothing pleased her so much as to sit atop of the gate post and hail the passing vehicles on their way South to Orlando, or North to Sanford. That white shell road was her great attraction. She raced up and down the stretch of it that lay before her gate like a round-eyed puppy hailing gleefully all travelers. Everybody in the country, white and colored, knew little Isis Watts, Isis the Joyful. The Robinson brothers, white cattlemen, were

First published in *Opportunity Magazine* (Dec. 1924) under the original title "Drenched in Light."

particularly fond of her and always extended a stirrup for her to climb up behind one of them for a short ride, or let her try to crack the long bull whips and *yee whoo* at the cows.

Grandma Potts went inside and Isis literally waved the rake at the 'chaws' of ribbon cane that lay so bountifully about the yard in company with the knots and peelings, with a thick sprinkling of peanut hulls.

The herd of cattle in their envelope of gray dust came alongside and Isis dashed out to the nearest stirrup and was lifted up.

"Hello theah Snidlits, I was wonderin' wheah you was," said Jim Robinson as she snuggled down behind him in the saddle. They were almost out of the danger zone when Grandma emerged. "You Isie," she bawled.

The child slid down on the opposite side of the house and executed a flank movement through the corn patch that brought her into the yard from behind the privy.

"You li'l hasion you! Wheah you been?"

"Out in de back yahd," Isis lied and did a cart wheel and a few fancy steps on her way to the front again.

"If you doan git in dat yahd, Ah make a mommuk of you!"

Isis observed that Grandma was cutting a fancy assortment of switches from peach, guana and cherry trees.

She finished the yard by raking everything under the edge of the porch and began a romp with the dogs, those lean, floppy-eared hounds that all country folks keep. But Grandma vetoed this also.

"Isie, you set on day porch! Uh great big 'leben yeah ole gal racin' an' rompin' lak dat—set 'own!"

Isis flung herself upon the steps.

"Git up offa dem steps, you aggravatin' limb, 'fore Ah git dem hick'ries tuh you, an' set yo' seff on a cheah."

Isis arose, and then sat down as violently as possible in the chair. She slid down, and down, until she all but sat on her own shoulder blades.

"Now look atcher," Grandma screamed, "Put yo' knees together, an' git up offen yo' backbone! Lawd, you know dis hellion is gwine make me stomp huh insides out."

Isis sat bolt upright as if she wore a ramrod down her back and began to whistle. Now there are certain things that Grandma Potts felt no one of this female persuasion should do—one was to sit with the knees separated, 'settin' brazen' she called it; another was whistling, another playing with boys. Finally, a lady must never cross her legs.

Grandma jumped up from her seat to get the switches.

"So youse whistlin' in mah face, huh!" She glared till her eyes were beady and Isis bolted for safety. But the noon hour brought John Watts the widowed father, and this excused the child from sitting for criticism.

Being the only girl in the family, of course she must wash the dishes, which she did in intervals between frolics with the dogs. She even gave Jake, the puppy, a swim in the dishpan by holding him suspended above the water that reeked of 'pot likker'—just high enough so that his feet would be immersed. The deluded puppy swam and swam without ever crossing the pan, much to his annoyance. Hearing Grandma she hurriedly dropped him on the floor, which he tracked-up with feet wet with dishwater.

Grandma took her patching and settled down in the front room to sew. She did this every afternoon, and invariably slept in the big red rocker with her head lolled back over the back, the sewing falling from her hand.

Isis had crawled under the center table with its red plush cover with little round balls for fringe. She was lying on her back imagining herself various personages. She wore trailing robes, golden slippers with blue bottoms. She rode white horses with flaring pink nostrils to the horizon, for she still believed that to be land's end. She was picturing herself gazing over the edge of the world into the abyss when the spool of cotton fell from Grandma's lap and rolled away under the whatnot. Isis drew back from her contemplation of the nothingness at the horizon and glanced up at the sleeping woman. Her head had fallen far back. She breathed with a regular 'mark' intake and 'poosah' exhaust. They were long gray hairs curled every here and there against the dark brown skin. Isis was moved with pity for her mother's mother.

"Poah Gran-ma needs a shave," she murmured, and set about it. Just then Joel, next older than Isis, entered with a can of bait.

"Come on Isie, les' we all go fishin'. The Perch is bitin' fine in Blue Sink."

"Sh-sh—" cautioned his sister, "Ah got to shave Gran'ma."

"Who say so?" Joel asked, surprised.

"Nobody doan hafta tell me. Look at her chin. No ladies don't weah whiskers if they kin help it. But Gran-ma gittin ole an' she doan know how to shave lak *me*."

The conference adjourned to the back porch lest Grandma wake.

"Aw, Isie, you doan know nothin' 'bout shavin' a-tall—but a *man* lak *me*—"

"Ah do so know."

"You don't not. Ah'm goin' shave her mahseff."

"Naw, you won't neither, Smarty. Ah saw her first an' thought it all up first," Isis declared, and ran to the calico-covered box on the wall above the wash basin and seized her father's razor. Joel was quick and seized the mug and brush.

"Now!" Isis cried defiantly, "Ah got the razor."

"Goody, goody, goody, pussy cat, Ah got th' brush an' you can't shave 'thout lather—see! Ah know mo' than you," Joel retorted.

"Aw, who don't know dat?" Isis pretended to scorn. But seeing her progress blocked from lack of lather she compromised.

"Ah know! Les' we all shave her. You lather an' Ah shave."

This was agreeable to Joel. He made mountains of lather and anointed his own chin, and the chin of Isis and the dogs, splashed the wall and at last was persuaded to lather Grandma's chin. Not that he was loath but he wanted his new plaything to last as long as possible.

Isis stood on one side of the chair with the razor clutched cleaver fashion. The niceties of razor-handling had passed over her head. The thing with her was to *hold* the razor—sufficient in itself.

Joel splashed on the lather in great gobs and Grandma awoke.

For one bewildered moment she stared at the grinning boy with the brush and mug but sensing another presence, she turned to behold the business face of Isis and the razor-clutching hand. Her jaw dropped and Grandma, forgetting years and rheumatism, bolted from the chair and fled the house, screaming.

"She's gone to tell papa, Isie. You didn't have no business wid his razor and he's gonna lick yo' hide," Joel cried, running to replace mug and brush.

"You too, chuckle-head, you too," retorted Isis. "You was playin' wid his brush and put it all over the dogs—Ah seen you put in on Ned an' Beulah." Isis shaved and replaced it in the box. Joel took his bait and pole and hurried to Blue Sink. Isis crawled under the house to brood over the whipping she knew would come. She had meant well.

But sounding brass and tinkling cymbal drew her forth. The local lodge of the Grand United Order of Odd Fellows, led by a braying, thudding band, was marching in full regalia down the road. She had forgotten the barbecue and log-rolling to be held today for the benefit of the new hall.

Music to Isis meant motion. In a minute razor and whipping forgotten, she was doing a fair imitation of a Spanish dancer she had seen in a medicine show some time before. Isis' feet were gifted—she could dance most anything she saw.

Up, up, went her spirits, her small feet doing all sorts of intricate things and her body in rhythm, hand curving above her head. But the music was growing faint. Grandma was nowhere in sight. Isis stole out of the gate, running and dancing after the band.

Not far down the road, Isis stopped. She realized she couldn't dance at the carnival. Her dress was torn and dirty. She picked a long-stemmed daisy, and placed it behind her ear, but her dress remained torn and dirty just the same. Then Isis had an idea. Her thoughts returned to the battered, round-topped trunk back in the bedroom. She raced back to the house; then, happier, she raced down the white dusty road to the picnic grove, gorgeously clad. People laughed good-naturedly at her, the band played and Isis danced because she couldn't help it. A crowd of children gathered admiringly about her as she wheeled lightly about, hand on hip, flower between her teeth with the red and white fringe of the tablecloth—Grandma's new red tablecloth that she wore in lieu of a Spanish shawl—trailing in the dust. It was too ample for her meager form, but she wore it like a gypsy. Her brown feet twinkled in and out of the fringe. Some grown people joined the children about her. The Grand Exalted Ruler rose to speak; the band was hushed, but Isis danced on, the crowd clapping their hands for her. No one listened to the Exalted one, for little by little the multitude had surrounded the small brown dancer.

An automobile drove up to the Crown and halted. Two white men and a lady got out and pushed into the crowd, suppressing mirth discretely behind gloved hands. Isis looked up and waved them a magnificent hail and went on dancing until—

Grandma had returned to the house, and missed Isis. She straightaway sought her at the festivities, expecting to find her in her soiled dress, shoeless, standing at the far edge of the crowd. What she saw now drove her frantic. Here was her granddaughter dancing before a gaping crowd in her brand new red tablecloth, and reeking of lemon extract. Isis had added the final touch to her costume. Of course she must also have perfume.

When Isis saw her Grandma, she bolted. She heard her Grandma cry— "Mah Gawd, mah brand new tablecloth Ah just bought f'um O'landah!"—as Isis fled through the crowd and on into the woods.

Isis followed the little creek until she came to the ford in a rutty wagon road that led to Apopka and laid down on the cool grass at the roadside. The April sun was quite warm.

Misery, misery and woe settled down upon her. The child wept. She knew another whipping was in store.

"Oh, Ah wish Ah could die, then Gran'ma an' papa would be sorry they beat me so much. Ah b'leeve Ah'll run away and never go home no mo'. Ah'm goin' drown mahseff in th' creek!"

Isis got up and waded into the water. She routed out a tiny 'gator and a huge bullfrog. She splashed and sang. Soon she was enjoying herself immensely.

The purr of a motor struck her ear and she saw a large, powerful car jolting along the rutty road toward her. It stopped at the water's edge.

"Well, I declare, it's our little gypsy," exclaimed the man at the wheel. "What are you doing here, now?"

"Ah'm killin' mahseff," Isis declared dramatically, "Cause Gran'ma beats me too much."

There was a hearty burst of laughter from the machine.

"You'll last some time the way you are going about it. Is this the way to Maitland? We want to go to the Park Hotel."

Isis saw no longer any reason to die. She came up out of the water, holding up the dripping fringe of the tablecloth.

"Naw, indeedy. You go to Maitlan' by the shell road—it goes by mah house—an' turn off at Lake Sebelia to the clay road that takes you right to the do'."

"Well," went on the driver, smiling furtively, "Could you quit dying long enough to go with us?"

"Yessuh," she said thoughtfully, "Ah wanta go wid you."

The door of the car swung open. She was invited to a seat beside the driver. She had often dreamed of riding in one of these heavenly chariots but never thought she would, actually.

"Jump in then, Madame Tragedy, and show us. We lost ourselves after we left your barbecue."

During the drive Isis explained to the kind lady who smelt faintly of violets and to the indifferent men that she was really a princess. She told them about her trips to the horizon, about the trailing gowns, the gold shoes with blue bottoms—she insisted on the blue bottoms—the white charger, the time when she was Hercules and had slain numerous dragons and sundry giants. At last the car approached her gate over which stood the umbrella chinaberry tree. The car was abreast of the gate and had all but passed when Grandma spied her glorious tablecloth lying back against the upholstery of the Packard.

"You Isie-e!" she bawled, "You li'l wretch you! Come heah *dis instant.*"

"That's me," the child confessed, mortified, to the lady on the rear seat.

"Oh Sewell, stop the car. This is where the child lives. I hate to give her up though."

"Do you wanta keep me?" Isis brightened.

"Oh, I wish I could. Wait, I'll try to save you a whipping this time."

She dismounted with the gaudy lemon-flavored culprit and advanced to the gate where Grandma stood glowering, switches in hand.

"You're gointuh ketchit f'um yo' haid to yo' heels m'lady. Jes' come in heah."

"Why, good afternoon," she accosted the furious grandparent. "You're not going to whip this poor little thing, are you?" the lady asked in conciliatory tones.

"Yes, Ma'am. She's de wustest li'l limb dat ever drawed bref. Jes' look at mah new tablecloth, dat ain't never been washed. She done traipsed all over de woods, uh dancin' an' uh prancin' in it. She done took a razor to me t'day an' Lawd knows whut mo'."

Isis clung to the stranger's hand fearfully.

"Ah wuzn't gointer hurt Gran'ma, miss—Ah wuz just gointer shave her whiskers fuh huh 'cause she's old an' can't."

The white hand closed tightly over the little brown one that was quite soiled. She could understand a voluntary act of love even though it miscarried.

"Now, Mrs. er-er-I didn't get the name—how much did your tablecloth cost?"

"One whole big silvah dollar down at O'landah—ain't had it a week yit."

"Now here's five dollars to get another one. I want her to go to the hotel and dance for me. I could stand a little light today—"

"Oh, yessum, yessum," Grandma cut in, "Everything's alright, sho' she kin' go, yessum."

Feeling that Grandma had been somewhat squelched did not detract from Isis' spirit at all. She pranced over to the waiting motor-car and this time seated herself on the rear seat between the sweet-smiling lady and the rather aloof man in gray.

"Ah'm gointer stay wid you all," she said with a great deal of warmth, and snuggled up to her benefactress. "Want me tuh sign a song fuh you?"

"There, Helen, you've been adopted," said the man with a short, harsh laugh.

"Oh, I hope so, Harry." She put her arm about the red-draped figure at her side and drew it close until she felt the warm puffs of the child's breath against her side. She looked hungrily ahead of her and spoke into space rather than to anyone in the car. "I would like just a little of her sunshine to soak into my soul. I would like that alot."

Nella Larsen

Sanctuary

One

On the Southern coast, between Merton and Shawboro, there is a strip of desolation some half a mile wide and nearly ten miles long between the sea and old fields of ruined plantations. Skirting the edge of this narrow jungle is a partly grown-over road which still shows traces of furrows made by the wheels of wagons that have long since rotted away or been cut into firewood. This road is little used, now that the state has built its new highway a bit to the west and wagons are less numerous than automobiles.

In the forsaken road a man was walking swiftly. But in spite of his hurry, at every step he set down his feet with infinite care, for the night was windless and the heavy silence intensified each sound; even the breaking of a twig could be plainly heard. And the man had need of caution as well as haste.

Before a lonely cottage that shrank timidly back from the road the man hesitated a moment, then struck out across the patch of green in front of it. Stepping behind a clump of bushes close to the house, he looked in through the lighted window at Annie Poole, standing at her kitchen table mixing the supper biscuits.

First published in *The Forum* (Vol. LXXXIII, No. 1: Jan. 1930)

He was a big, black man with pale brown eyes in which there was an odd mixture of fear and amazement. The light showed streaks of gray soil on his heavy, sweating face and great hands, and on his torn clothes. In his woolly hair clung bits of dried leaves and dead grass.

He made a gesture as if to tap on the window, but turned away to the door instead. Without knocking he opened it and went in.

Two

The woman's brown gaze was immediately on him, though she did not move. She said, "You ain't in no hurry, is you, Jim Hammer?" It wasn't, however, entirely a question.

"Ah's in trubble, Mis' Poole," the man explained, his voice shaking, his fingers twitching.

"W'at you done done now?"

"Shot a man, Mis' Poole."

"Trufe?" The woman seemed calm. But the word was spat out.

"Yas'm. Shot 'im." In the man's tone was something of wonder, as if he himself could not quite believe that he had really done this thing which he affirmed.

"Daid?"

"Dunno, Mis' Poole. Dunno."

"White man o' niggah?"

"Cain't say, Mis' Poole. White man, Ah reckons."

Annie Poole looked at him with cold contempt. She was a tiny, withered woman—fifty perhaps—with a wrinkled face the color of old copper, framed by a crinkly mass of white hair. But about her small figure was some quality of hardness that belied her appearance of frailty. At last she spoke, boring her sharp little eyes into those of the anxious creature before her.

"An' w'at am you lookin' foh me to do 'bout et?"

"Jes' lemme stop till dey's gone by. Hide me till dey passes. Reckon dey ain't fur off now." His begging voice changed to a frightened whimper. "Foh de Lawd's sake, Mis' Poole, lemme stop."

And why, the woman inquired caustically, should she run the dangerous risk of hiding him?

"Obadiah, he'd lemme stop ef he was to home," the man whined.

Annie Poole sighed. "Yas," she admitted slowly, reluctantly, "Ah spec' he would. Obadiah, he's too good to youall no 'count trash." Her slight shoulders lifted in a hopeless shrug. "Yas, Ah reckon he'd do et. Emspecial' seein' how he

allus set such a heap o' store by you. Cain't see w'at foh, mahse'f. Ah shuah don'
see nuffin' in you but a heap o'dirt."

But a look of irony, of cunning, of complicity passed over her face. She
went on, "Still, 'siderin' all an' all, how Obadiah's right fon' o' you, an' how
white folks is white folks, Ah'm a-gwine hide you dis one time."

Crossing the kitchen, she opened a door leading into a small bedroom,
saying, "Git yo'se'f in dat dere feather baid an' Ah'm a-gwine put de clo's on de
top. Don' reckon dey'll fin' you ef dey does look foh you in mah house. An Ah
don' spec' dey'll go foh to do dat. Not lessen you been keerless an' let 'em smell
you out gittin' hyah." She turned on him a withering look. "But you allus been
triflin'. Cain't do nuffin' propah. An' Ah'm a-tellin' you ef dey warn't white
folks an' you a po' niggah, Ah shuah wouldn't be lettin' you mess up mah
feather baid dis ebenin', 'cose Ah jes' plain don' want you hyah. Ah done kep'
mahse'f outen trubble all mah life. So's Obadiah."

"Ah's powahful 'bliged to you, Mis' Poole. You shuah am one good
'oman. De Lawd'll mos' suttinly—."

Annie Poole cut him off. "Dis ain't no time foh all dat kin' o' fiddle-de-
roll. Ah does mah duty as Ah sees et 'thout no thanks from you. Ef de Lawd had
gib you a white face 'stead o' dat dere black one, Ah shuah would turn you out.
Now hush yo' mouf an' git yo'se'f in. An' don' git movin' and scrunchin' undah
dose covahs and git yo'se'f kotched in mah house."

Without further comment the man did as he was told. After he had laid his
soiled body and grimy garments between her snowy sheets, Annie Poole carefully rearranged the covering and placed piles of freshly laundered linen on top.
Then she gave a pat here and there, eyed the result, and, finding it satisfactory,
went back to her cooking.

Three

Jim Hammer settled down to the racking business of waiting until the approaching danger should have passed him by. Soon savory odors seeped in to
him and he realized that he was hungry. He wished that Annie Poole would
bring him something to eat. Just one biscuit. But she wouldn't, he knew. Not
she. She was a hard one, Obadiah's mother.

By and by he fell into a sleep from which he was dragged back by the rum-
bling sound of wheels in the road outside. For a second fear clutched so tightly
at him that he almost leaped from the suffocating shelter of the bed in order to
make some active attempt to escape the horror that his capture meant. There
was a spasm at his heart, a pain so sharp, so slashing, that he had to suppress an

impulse to cry out. He felt himself falling. Down, down, down…Everything grew dim and very distant in his memory….Vanished…Came rushing back.

Outside there was silence. He strained his ears. Nothing. No footsteps. No voices. They had gone on then. Gone without even stopping to ask Annie Poole if she had seen him pass that way. A sigh of relief slipped from him. His thick lips curled in an ugly, cunning smile. It had been smart of him to think of coming to Obadiah's mother's to hide. She was an old demon, but he was safe in her house.

He lay a short while longer, listening intently, and, hearing nothing, started to get up. But immediately he stopped, his yellow eyes glowing like pale flames. He had heard the unmistakable sound of men coming toward the house. Swiftly he slid back into the heavy, hot stuffiness of the bed and lay listening fearfully.

The terrifying sounds drew nearer. Slowly. Heavily. Just for a moment he thought they were not coming in—they took so long. But there was a light knock and the noise of a door being opened. His whole body went taut. His feet felt frozen, his hands clammy, his tongue like a weighted, dying thing. His pounding heart made it hard for his straining ears to hear what they were saying out there.

"Ebenin', Mistah Lowndes." Annie Pooles' voice sounded as it always did, sharp and dry.

There was no answer. Or had he missed it? With slow care he shifted his position, bringing his head nearer the edge of the bed. Still he heard nothing. What were they waiting for? Why didn't they ask about him?

Annie Poole, it seemed, was of the same mind. "Ah don' reckon youall done traipsed way out hyah jes' foh yo' healf," she hinted.

"There's bad news for you, Annie, I'm 'fraid." The sheriff's voice was low and queer.

Jim Hammer visualized him standing out there—a tall, stooped man, his white tobacco-stained mustache drooping limply at the ends, his nose hooked and sharp, his eyes blue and cold. Bill Lowndes was a hard one too. And white.

"W'atall bad news, Mistah Lowndes?" The woman put the question quietly, directly.

"Obadiah—" the sheriff began—hesitated—began again. "Obadiah—ah—er—he's outside, Annie. I'm 'fraid—"

"Shucks! You done missed. Obadiah, he ain't done nuffin', Mistah Lowndes. Obadiah!" she called stridently, "Obadiah! git hyah an' splain yo'se'f."

But Obadiah didn't answer, didn't come in. Other men came in. Came in with steps that dragged and halted. No one spoke. Not even Annie Poole. Something was laid carefully upon the floor.

"Obadiah, chile," his mother said softly, "Obadiah, chile." Then, with sudden alarm, "He ain't daid, is he? Mistah Lowndes! Obadiah, he ain't daid?"

Jim Hammer didn't catch the answer to that pleading question. A new fear was stealing over him.

"There was a to-do, Annie," Bill Lowndes explained gently, "at the garage back o' the factory. Fellow tryin' to steal tires. Obadiah heerd a noise an' run out with two or three others. Scared the rascal all right. Fired off his gun an' run. We allow et to be Jim Hammer. Picked up his cap back there. Never was no 'count. Thievin' an' sly. But we'll git 'im, Annie. We'll git 'im."

The man huddled in the feather bed prayed silently. "Oh, Lawd! Ah didn't go to do et. Not Obadiah, Lawd. You knows dat. You knows et." And into his frenzied brain came the thought that it would be better for him to get up and go out to them before Annie Poole gave him away. For he was lost now. With all his great strength he tried to get himself out of the bed. But he couldn't.

"Oh, Lawd!" he moaned. "Oh, Lawd!" His thoughts were bitter and they ran through his mind like panic. He knew that it had come to pass as it said somewhere in the Bible about the wicked. The Lord had stretched out his hand and smitten him. He was paralyzed. He couldn't move hand or foot. He moaned again. It was all there was left for him to do. For in the terror of this new calamity that had come upon him he had forgotten the waiting danger which was so near out there in the kitchen.

His hunters, however, didn't hear him. Bill Lowndes was saying, "We been a-lookin' for Jim out along the old road. Figured he'd make tracks for Shawboro. You ain't noticed anybody pass this evenin', Annie?"

The reply came promptly, unwaveringly. "No, Ah ain't sees nobody pass. Not yet."

Four

Jim Hammer caught his breath.

"Well," the sheriff concluded, "we'll be gittin' along. Obadiah was a mighty fine boy. Ef they was all like him—I'm sorry, Annie. Anything I c'n do, let me know."

"Thank you, Mistah Lowndes."

With the sound of the door closing on the departing men, power to move came back to the man in the bedroom. He pushed his dirt-caked feet out from the covers and rose up, but crouched down again. He wasn't cold now, but hot all over and burning. Almost he wished that Bill Lowndes and his men had taken him with them.

Annie Poole had come into the room.

It seemed a long time before Obadiah's mother spoke. When she did there were no tears, no reproaches; but there was a raging fury in her voice as she lashed out, "Git outer mah feather baid, Jim Hammer, an' outen mah house, an' don' nevah stop thankin' yo' Jesus he done gib you dat black face."

Ann Petry

Doby's Gone

When Doby first came into Sue Johnson's life her family were caretakers on a farm way up in New York State. And because Sue had no one else to play with, the Johnsons reluctantly accepted Doby as a member of the family.

The spring that Sue was six they moved to Wessex, Connecticut—a small New England town whose neat colonial houses cling to a group of hills overlooking the Connecticut River. All that summer Mrs. Johnson had hoped that Doby would vanish long before Sue entered school in the fall. He would only complicate things in school.

For Doby wasn't real. He existed only in Sue's mind. He had been created out of her need for a friend her own age—her own size. And he had gradually become an escape from the very real world that surrounded her. She first started talking about him when she was two and he had been with her ever since. He always sat beside her when she ate and played with her during the day. At night he slept in a chair near her bed so that they awoke at the same time in the morning. A place had to be set for him at mealtime. A seat had to be saved for him on trains and buses.

After they moved to Wessex, he was still her constant companion just as he had been when she was three and four and five.

First Published in *Phylon* V (1944):361–66

On the morning that Sue was to start going to school she said, "Doby has a new pencil, too. And he's got a red plaid shirt just like my dress."

"Why can't Doby stay home?" Mrs. Johnson asked.

"Because he goes everywhere I go," Sue said in amazement.

"Of course he's going to school. He's going to sit right by me."

Sue watched her mother get up from the breakfast table and then followed her upstairs to the big front bedroom. She saw with surprise that her mother was putting on her going-out clothes.

"You have to come with me, Mommy?" she asked anxiously.

She had wanted to go with Doby. Just the two of them. She had planned every step of the way since the time her mother told her she would start school in the fall.

"No, I don't have to, but I'm coming just the same. I want to talk to your teacher." Mrs. Johnson fastened her coat and deftly patted a loose strand of hair in place.

Sue looked at her and wondered if the other children's mothers would come to school, too. She certainly hoped so because she wouldn't want to be the only one there who had a mother with her.

Then she started skipping around the room holding Doby by the hand. Her short black braids jumped as she skipped. The gingham dress she wore was starched so stiffly that the hemline formed a wide circular frame for her sturdy dark brown legs as she bounced up and down.

"Ooh," she said suddenly. "Doby pulled off one of my hair ribbons." She reached over and picked it up from the floor and came to stand in front of her mother while the red ribbon was retied into a crisp bow.

Then she was walking down the street hand in hand with her mother. She held Doby's hand on the other side. She decided it was good her mother had come. It was better that way. The street would have looked awfully long and awfully big if she and Doby had been by themselves, even though she did know exactly where the school was. Right down the street on this side. Past the post office and town hall that sat so far back with green lawn in front of them. Past the town pump and the old white house on the corner, past the big empty lot. And there was the school.

It had a walk that went straight down between the green grass and was all brown-yellow gravel stuff—coarser than sand. One day she had walked past there with her mother and stopped to finger the stuff the walk was made of, and her mother had said, "It's gravel."

She remembered how they'd talked about it. "What's gravel?" she asked.

"The stuff in your hand. It's like sand, only coarser. People use it for driveways and walks," her mother had said.

Gravel. She liked the sound of the word. It sounded like pebbles. Gravel. Pebble. She said the words over to herself. You gravel and pebble. Pebble said to gravel. She started making up a story. Gravel said to pebble, "You're a pebble." Pebble said back, "You're a gravel."

"Sue, throw it away. It's dirty and your hands are clean," her mother said.

She threw it down on the sidewalk. But she kept looking back at it as she walked along. It made a scattered yellow-brown color against the rich brown-black of the dirt path.

She held on to Doby's hand a little more tightly. Now she was actually going to walk up that long gravel walk to the school. She and Doby would play there every day when school was out.

The school yard was full of children. Sue hung back a little looking at them. They were playing ball under the big maple trees near the back of the yard. Some small children were squatting near the school building, letting gravel trickle through their fingers.

"I want to play, too." She tried to free her hand from her mother's firm grip.

"We're going inside to see your teacher first." And her mother went on walking up the school steps holding on to Sue's hand.

Sue stared at the children on the steps. "Why are they looking so hard?" she asked.

"Probably because you're looking at them so hard. Now come on," and her mother pulled her through the door. The hall inside was dark and very long. A neat white sign over a door to the right said FIRST GRADE in bold black letters.

Sue peered inside the room while her mother knocked on the door. A pretty lady with curly yellow hair got up from a desk and invited them in. While the teacher and her mother talked grown-up talk, Sue looked around. She supposed she'd sit at one of those little desks. There were a lot of them and she wondered if there would be a child at each desk. If so then Doby would have to squeeze in beside her.

"Sue, you can go outside and play. When the bell rings you must come in," the teacher said.

"Yes, teacher," Sue started out the door in a hurry.

"My name is Miss Whittier," the teacher said. "You must call me that."

"Yes, Miss Whittier. Good-bye, Mommy," she said, and went quickly down the hall and out the door.

"Hold my hand, Doby," she said softly under her breath.

Now she and Doby would play in the gravel. Squeeze it between their fingers, pat it into shapes like those other children were doing. Her short starched skirt stood out around her legs as she skipped down the steps. She watched the children as long as she could without saying anything.

"Can we play, too?" she asked finally.

A boy with a freckled face and short stiff red hair looked up at her and frowned. He didn't answer but kept ostentatiously patting at a little mound of gravel.

Sue walked over a little closer, holding Doby tightly by the hand. The boy ignored her. A little girl in a blue and white checked dress stuck her tongue out.

"Your legs are black," she said suddenly. And then when the others looked up she added, "Why, look, she's black all over. Looky, she's black all over."

Sue retreated a step away from the building. The children got up and followed her. She took another backward step and they took two steps forward. The little girl who had stuck her tongue out began a chant, "Look, look. Her legs are black. Her legs are black."

The children were all saying it. They formed a ring around her and they were dancing up and down and screaming, "Her legs are black. Her legs are black."

She stood in the middle of the circle completely bewildered. She wanted to go home where it was safe and quiet and where her mother would hold her tight in her arms. She pulled Doby nearer to her. What did they mean her legs were black? Of course, they were. Not black but dark brown. Just like these children were white some other children were dark like her. Her mother said so. But her mother hadn't said anyone would make her feel bad about being a different color. She didn't know what to do; so she just stood there watching them come closer and closer to her—their faces red with excitement, their voices hoarse with yelling.

Then the school bell rang. And the children suddenly plunged toward the building. She was left alone with Doby. When she walked into the school room she was crying.

"Don't you mind, Doby," she whispered. "Don't you mind. I won't let them hurt you."

Miss Whittier gave her a seat near the front of the room. Right near her desk. And she smiled at her. Sue smiled back and carefully wiped away the wet on her eyelashes with the back of her hand. She turned and looked around the room. There were no empty seats. Doby would have to stand up.

"You stand right close to me and if you get tired just sit on the edge of my seat," she said.

She didn't go out for recess. She stayed in and helped Miss Whittier draw on the blackboard with colored chalk—yellow and green and red and purple and brown. Miss Whittier drew the flowers and Sue colored them. She put a small piece of crayon out for Doby to use. And Miss Whittier noticed it. But she didn't say anything, she just smiled.

"I love her," Sue thought. "I love my teacher." And then again, "I love Miss Whittier, my teacher."

At noon the children followed her halfway home from school. They called after her and she ran so fast and so hard that the pounding in her ears cut off the sound of their voices.

"Go faster, Doby," she said. "You have to go faster." And she held his hand and ran until her legs ached.

"How was school, Sue?" asked her mother.

"It was all right," she said slowly. "I don't think Doby likes it very much. He likes Miss Whittier though."

"Do you like her?"

"Oh, yes," Sue let her breath come out with a sigh.

"Why are you panting like that?" her mother asked.

"I ran all the way home," she said.

Going back after lunch wasn't so bad. She went right in to Miss Whittier. She didn't stay out in the yard and wait for the bell.

When school was out, she decided she'd better hurry right home and maybe the children wouldn't see her. She walked down the gravel path taking quick little looks over her shoulder. No one paid any attention and she was so happy that she gave Doby's hand a squeeze.

And then she saw that they were waiting for her right by the vacant lot. She hurried along trying not to hear what they were saying.

"My mother says you're a little nigger girl," the boy with the red hair said.

And then they began to shout: "Her legs are black. Her legs are black."

It changed suddenly. "Run. Go ahead and run." She looked over her shoulder. A boy was coming toward her with a long switch in his hand. He raised it in a threatening gesture and she started running.

For two days she ran home from school like that. Ran until her short legs felt as though they couldn't move another step.

"Sue," her mother asked anxiously, watching her try to catch her breath on the front steps, "what makes you run home from school like this?"

"Doby doesn't like the other children very much," she said panting.

"Why?"

"I don't think they understand about him," she said thoughtfully. "But he loves Miss Whittier."

The next day the children waited for her right where the school's gravel walk ended. Sue didn't see them until she was close to them. She was coming slowly down the path hand in hand with Doby trying to see how many of the big pebbles they could step on without stepping on any of the finer, sandier gravel.

She was in the middle of the group of children before she realized it. They started off slowly at first. "How do you comb that kind of hair?" "Does that black color wash off?" And then the chant began and it came faster and faster: "Her legs are black. Her legs are black."

A little girl reached out and pulled one of Sue's braids. Sue tried to back away and the other children closed in around her. She rubbed the side of her head—it hurt where her hair had been pulled. Someone pushed her. Hard. In the middle of her back. She was suddenly outraged. She planted her feet firmly on the path. She started hitting out with her fists. Kicking. Pulling hair. Tearing at clothing. She reached down and picked up handfuls of gravel and aimed it at eyes and ears and noses.

While she was slapping and kicking at the small figures that encircled her she became aware that Doby had gone. For the first time in her life he had left her. He had gone when she started to fight.

She went on fighting—scratching and biting and kicking—with such passion and energy that the space around her slowly cleared. The children backed away. And she stood still. She was breathing fast as though she had been running.

The children ran off down the street—past the big empty lot, past the old white house with the green shutters. Sue watched them go. She didn't feel victorious. She didn't feel anything except an aching sense of loss. She stood there panting, wondering about Doby.

And then, "Doby," she called softly. Then louder, "Doby! Doby! Where are you?"

She listened—cocking her head on one side. He didn't answer. And she felt certain he would never be back because he had never left her before. He had gone for good. And she didn't know why. She decided it probably had something to do with growing up. And she looked down at her legs hoping to find they had grown as long as her father's. She saw instead that her dress was torn in three different places, her socks were down around her ankles, there were long angry scratches on her legs and on her arms. She felt for her hair—the red hair ribbons were gone and her braids were coming undone.

She started looking for the hair ribbons. And as she looked she saw that Daisy Bell, the little girl who had stuck her tongue out that first day of school, was leaning against the oak tree at the end of the path.

"Come on, let's walk home together," Daisy Bell said matter-of-factly.

"All right," Sue said.

As they started past the empty lot, she was conscious that someone was tagging along behind them. It was Jimmie Piebald, the boy with the stiff red hair. When she looked back he came up and walked on the other side of her.

They walked along in silence until they came to the town pump. They stopped and looked deep down into the well. And spent a long time hallooing down into it and listening delightedly to the hollow funny sound of their voices.

It was much later than usual when Sue got home. Daisy Bell and Jimmie walked up to the door with her. Her mother was standing on the front steps waiting for her.

"Sue," her mother said in a shocked voice. "What's the matter? What happened to you?"

Daisy Bell put her arm around Sue. Jimmie started kicking at some stones in the path.

Sue stared at her mother, trying to remember. There was something wrong but she couldn't think what it was. And then it came to her. "Oh," she wailed, "Doby's gone. I can't find him anywhere."

Alice Childress

In The Laundry Room

M arge...Sometimes it seems like the devil and all his imps are tryin' to wear your soul case out....Sit down, Marge, and act like you got nothin' to do....No, don't make no coffee, just sit....

Today was laundry day and I took Mrs. M...'s clothes down to the basement to put them in the automatic machine. In a little while another houseworker comes down—a white woman. She dumps her clothes on the bench and since my bundle is already in the washer I go over to sit down on the bench and happen to brush against her dirty clothes....Well sir! She gives me a kinda sickly grin and snatched her clothes away quick....

Now, you know, Marge, that it was nothin' but the devil in her makin' her snatch that bundle away 'cause she thought I might give her folks gallopin' pellagra or somethin'. Well, honey, you know what the devil in me wanted to do!...You are right!...My hand was just itchin' to pop her in the mouth, but I remembered how my niece Jean has been tellin' me that *poppin'* people is not the way to solve problems....So I calmed myself and said, "Sister, why did you snatch those things and look so flustered?" She turned red and says, "I was just

First published in *Like One of the Family: Conversations from a Domestic's Life*. Boston: Beacon, 1986

makin' room for you." Still keepin' calm, I says, "You are a liar."...And then she hung her head.

"Sister," I said, "you are a houseworker and I am a houseworker—now will you favor me by answering some questions?" She nodded her head....The first thing I asked her was how much she made for a week's work and, believe it or not, Marge, she earns less than I do and *that ain't easy*....Then I asked her, "Does the woman you work for ask you in a *friendly* way to do extra things that ain't in the bargain and then later on get *demandin'* about it?"...She nods, yes... "Tell me, young woman," I went on, "does she cram eight hours of work into five and call it *part time?*"...She nods yes again....

Then, Marge, I added, "I am not your enemy, so don't get mad with me just because you ain't free!"...Then she speaks up fast, "I am free!"...."All right," I said. "How about me goin' over to your house tonight for supper?"..."Oh," she says, "I room with people and I don't think they..." I cut her off...."If you're free," I said, "you can pick your own friends without fear."

Wait a minute, Marge, let me tell it now...."How come," I asked her, "the folks I work for are willin' to have me put my hands all over their chopped meat patties and yet ask me to hang my coat in the kitchen closet instead of in the hall with theirs?"...By this time, Marge, she looked pure bewildered...."Oh," she said, "it's all so mixed up I don't understand!"

"Well, it'll all get clearer as we go along," I said...."Now when you got to plunge your hands in all them dirty clothes in order to put them in the machine...how come you can't see that it's a whole lot safer and makes more sense to put your hand in mine and be friends?" Well, Marge, she took my hand and said, "I want to be friends!"

I was so glad I hadn't popped her, Marge. The good Lord only knows how hard it is to do things the right way and make peace....All right now, let's have the coffee, Marge.

Paule Marshall

Brooklyn

A summer wind, soaring just before it died, blew the dusk and the first scattered lights of downtown Brooklyn against the shut windows of the classroom, but Professor Max Berman—B.A., 1919, M.A., 1921, New York; Docteur de l'Université, 1930, Paris—alone in the room, did not bother to open the windows to the cooling wind. The heat and airlessness of the room, the perspiration inching its way like an ant around his starched collar were discomforts he enjoyed; they obscured his larger discomfort: the anxiety which chafed his heart and tugged his left eyelid so that he seemed to be winking, roguishly, behind his glasses.

To steady his eye and ease his heart, to fill the time until his students arrived and his first class in years began, he reached for his cigarettes. As always he delayed lighting the cigarette so that his need for it would be greater and, thus, the relief and pleasure it would bring, fuller. For some time he fondled it, his fingers shaping soft, voluptuous gestures, his warped old man's hands looking strangely abandoned on the bare desk and limp as if the bones had been crushed, and so white—except for the tobacco burn on the index and third fingers—it seemed his blood no longer traveled that far.

He lit the cigarette finally and as the smoke swelled his lungs, his eyelid stilled and his lined face lifted, the plume of white hair wafting above his narrow

First published in *Soul Clap Hands and Sing* by Paule Marshall. Chatham: The Chatham Bookseller, 1961

brow; his body—short, blunt, the shoulders slightly bent as if in deference to his sixty-three years—settled back in the chair. Delicately Max Berman crossed his legs and, looking down, examined his shoes for dust. (The shoes were of a very soft, fawn-colored leather and somewhat foppishly pointed at the toe. They had been custom made in France and were his one last indulgence. He wore them in memory of his first wife, a French Jewess from Alsace-Lorraine whom he had met in Paris while lingering over his doctorate and married to avoid returning home. She had been gay, mindless and very excitable—but at night, she had also been capable of a profound stillness as she lay in bed waiting for him to turn to her, and this had always awed and delighted him. She had been a gift—and her death in a car accident had been a judgment on him for never having loved her, for never, indeed, having even allowed her to matter.) Fastidiously Max Berman unbuttoned his jacket and straightened his vest, which had a stain two decades old on the pocket. Through the smoke his veined eyes contemplated other, more pleasurable scenes. With his neatly shod foot swinging and his cigarette at a rakish tilt, he might have been an old *boulevardier* taking the sun and an absinthe before the afternoon's assignation.

A young face, the forehead shiny with earnestness, hung at the half-opened door. "Is this French Lit, fifty-four? Camus and Sartre?"

Max Berman winced at the rawness of the voice and the flat "a" in Sartre and said formally, "This is Modern French Literature, number fifty-four, yes, but there is some question as to whether we will take up Messieurs Camus and Sartre this session. They might prove hot work for a summer-evening course. We will probably do Gide and Mauriac, who are considerably more temperate. But come in nonetheless...."

He was the gallant, half rising to bow her to a seat. He knew that she would select the one in the front row directly opposite his desk. At the bell her pen would quiver above her blank notebook, ready to commit his first word—indeed, the clearing of his throat—to paper, and her thin buttocks would begin sidling toward the edge of her chair.

His eyelid twitched with solicitude. He wished that he could have drawn the lids over her fitful eyes and pressed a cool hand to her forehead. She reminded him of what he had been several lifetimes ago: a boy with a pale, plump face and harried eyes, running from the occasional taunts at his yamilke along the shrill streets of Brownsville in Brooklyn, impeded by the heavy satchel of books which he always carried as proof of his scholarship. He had been proud of his brilliance at school and the Yeshiva, but at the same time he had been secretly troubled by it and resentful, for he could never believe that he had come by it naturally or that it belonged to him alone. Rather, it was like a heavy medal his father had hung around his neck—the chain bruising his flesh—and constantly exhorted him to wear proudly and use well.

The girl gave him an eager and ingratiating smile and he looked away. During his thirty years of teaching, a face similar to hers had crowded his vision whenever he had looked up from a desk. Perhaps it was fitting, he thought, and lighted another cigarette from the first, that she should be present as he tried again at life, unaware that behind his rimless glasses and within his ancient suit, he had been gutted.

He thought of those who had taken the last of his substance—and smiled tolerantly. "The boys of summer," he called them, his inquisitors, who had flailed him with a single question: "Are you now or have you ever been a member of the Communist party?" Max Berman had never taken their question seriously—perhaps because he had never taken his membership in the party seriously—and he had refused to answer. What had disturbed him, though, even when the investigation was over, was the feeling that he had really been under investigation for some other offense which did matter and of which he was guilty; that behind their accusations and charges had lurked another which had not been political but personal. For had he been disloyal to the government? His denial was a short, hawking laugh. Simply, he had never ceased being religious. When his father's God had become useless and even a little embarrassing, he had sought others: his work for a time, then the party. But he had been middle-aged when he joined and his faith, which had been so full as a boy, had grown thin. He had come, by then, to distrust all pieties, so that when the purges in Russia during the thirties confirmed his distrust, he had withdrawn into a modest cynicism.

But he had been made to answer for that error. Ten years later his inquisitors had flushed him out from the small community college in upstate New York where he had taught his classes from the same neat pack of notes each semester and had led him bound by subpoena to New York and bandied his name at the hearings until he had been dismissed from his job.

He remembered looking back at the pyres of burning autumn leaves on the campus his last day and feeling that another lifetime had ended—for he had always thought of his life as divided into many small lives, each with its own beginning and end. Like a hired mute, he had been present at each dying and kept the wake and wept professionally as the bier was lowered into the ground. Because of this feeling, he told himself that his final death would be anticlimactic.

After his dismissal he had continued living in the small house he had built near the college, alone except for an occasional visit from a colleague, idle but for some tutoring in French, content with the income he received from the property his parents had left him in Brooklyn—until the visits and tutoring had tapered off and a silence had begun to choke the house, like weeds springing up around a deserted place. He had begun to wonder then if he were still alive. He would wake at night from the recurrent dream of the hearings, where he was being accused of an unstated crime, to listen for his heart, his hand fumbling among the bedclothes to press the place. During the day he would pass repeatedly in front of the mirror with the pretext that he might have forgotten to shave that morning or that something had blown into his eye. Above all, he had begun to think of his inquisitors with affection and to long for the sound of their voices. They, at least, had assured him of being alive.

As if seeking them out, he had returned to Brooklyn and to the house in Brownsville where he had lived as a boy and had boldly applied for a teaching post without mentioning the investigation. He had finally been offered the class which would begin in five minutes. It wasn't much: a six-week course in the summer evening session of a college without a rating, where classes were held in a converted factory building, a college whose campus took in the bargain department stores, the five-and-dime emporiums and neon-spangled movie houses of downtown Brooklyn.

Through the smoke from his cigarette, Max Berman's eyes—a waning blue that never seemed to focus on any one thing—drifted over the students who had gathered meanwhile. Imbuing them with his own disinterest, he believed that even before the class began, most of them were longing for its end and already anticipating the soft drinks at the soda fountain downstairs and the synthetic dramas at the nearby movie.

They made him sad. He would have liked to lead them like a Pied Piper back to the safety of their childhoods—all of them: the loud girl with the formidable calves of an athlete who reminded him, uncomfortably, of his second wife (a party member who was always shouting political heresy from some picket line and who had promptly divorced him upon discovering his irreverence); the two sallow-faced young men leaning out the window as if searching for the wind that had died; the slender young woman with crimped black hair who sat very still and apart from the others, her face turned toward the night sky as if to a friend.

Her loneliness interested him. He sensed its depth and his eye paused. He saw then that she was a Negro, a very pale mulatto with skin the color of clear, polished amber and a thin, mild face. She was somewhat older than the others in the room—a schoolteacher from the South, probably, who came north each summer to take courses toward a graduate degree. He felt a fleeting discomfort and irritation: discomfort at the thought that although he had been sinned against as a Jew he still shared in the sin against her and suffered from the same vague guilt, irritation that she recalled his own humiliations: the large ones, such as the fact that despite his brilliance he had been unable to get into a medical school as a young man because of the quota on Jews (not that he had wanted to be a doctor; that had been his father's wish) and had changed his studies from medicine to French; the small ones which had worn him thin: an eye widening imperceptibly as he gave his name, the savage glance which sought the Jewishness in his nose, his chin, in the set of his shoulders, the jokes snuffed into silence at his appearance....

Tired suddenly, his eyelid pulsing, he turned and stared out the window at the gaudy constellation of neon lights. He longed for a drink, a quiet place and then sleep. And to bear him gently into sleep, to stay the terror which bound his heart then reminding him of those oleographs of Christ with the thorns binding his exposed heart—fat drops of blood from one so bloodless—to usher him into sleep, some pleasantly erotic image: a nude in a boudoir scattered with her frilled garments and warmed by her frivolous laugh, with the sun like a voyeur at the half-closed shutters. But this time instead of the usual Rubens nude with thighs like twin portals and a belly like a huge alabaster bowl into which he poured himself, he chose Gauguin's Aita Parari, her languorous form in the straight-back chair, her dark, sloping breasts, her eyes like the sun under shadow.

With the image still on his inner eye, he turned to the Negro girl and appraised her through a blind of cigarette smoke. She was still gazing out at the night sky and something about her fixed stare, her hands stiffly arranged in her lap, the nerve fluttering within the curve of her throat, betrayed a vein of tension within the rock of her calm. It was as if she had fled long ago to a remote region within herself, taking with her all that was most valuable and most vulnerable about herself.

She stirred finally, her slight breasts lifting beneath her flowered summer dress as she breathed deeply—and Max Berman thought again of Gauguin's girl with the dark, sloping breasts. What would this girl with the amber-colored skin be like on a couch in a sunlit room, nude in a straight-back chair? And as the question echoed along each nerve and stilled his breathing, it seemed suddenly that life, which had scorned him for so long, held out her hand again— but still a little beyond his reach. Only the girl, he sensed, could bring him close enough to touch it. She alone was the bridge. So that even while he repeated to himself that he was being presumptuous (for she would surely refuse him) and ridiculous (for even if she did not, what could he do—his performance would be a mere scramble and twitch), he vowed at the same time to have her. The challenge eased the tightness around his heart suddenly; it soothed the damaged muscle of his eye and as the bell rang he rose and said briskly, "Ladies and gentlemen, may I have your attention, please. My name is Max Berman. The course is Modern French Literature, number fifty-four. May I suggest that you check your program cards to see whether you are in the right place at the right time."

Her essay on Gide's *The Immoralist* lay on his desk and the note from the administration informing him, first, that his past political activities had been brought to their attention and then dismissing him at the end of the session weighed the inside pocket of his jacket. The two, her paper and the note, were linked in his mind. Her paper reminded him that the vow he had taken was still an empty one, for the term was half over and he had never once spoken to her (as if she understood his intention she was always late and disappeared as soon as the closing bell rang, leaving him trapped in a clamorous circle of students around his desk), while the note which wrecked his small attempt to start anew suddenly made that vow more urgent. It gave him the edge of desperation he needed to act finally. So that as soon as the bell rang, he returned all the papers but hers, announced that all questions would have to wait until their next meeting and, waving off the students from his desk, called above their protests, "Miss Williams, if you have a moment, I'd like to speak with you briefly about your paper."

She approached his desk like a child who has been cautioned not to talk to strangers, her fingers touching the backs of the chair as if for support, her gaze following the departing students as though she longed to accompany them.

Her slight apprehensiveness pleased him. It suggested a submissiveness which gave him, as he rose uncertainly, a feeling of certainty and command. Her hesitancy was somehow in keeping with the color of her skin. She seemed to bring not only herself but the host of black women whose bodies had been despoiled to make her. He would not only possess her but them also, he thought (not really thought, for he scarcely allowed these thoughts to form before he snuffed them out). Through their collective suffering, which she contained, his own personal suffering would be eased; he would be pardoned for whatever sin it was he had committed against life.

"I hope you weren't unduly alarmed when I didn't return your paper along with the others," he said, and had to look up as she reached the desk. She was taller close up and her eyes, which he had thought were black, were a strong, flecked brown with very small pupils which seemed to shrink now from the sight of him. "But I found it so interesting I wanted to give it to you privately."

"I didn't know what to think," she said, and her voice—he heard it for the first time for she never recited or answered in class—was low, cautious, Southern.

"It was, to say the least, refreshing. It not only showed some original and mature thinking on your part, but it also proved that you've been listening in class—and after twenty-five years and more of teaching it's encouraging to find that some students do listen. If you have a little time I'd like to tell you, more specifically, what I liked about it...."

Talking easily, reassuring her with his professional tone and a deft gesture with his cigarette, he led her from the room as the next class filed in, his hand cupped at her elbow but not touching it, his manner urbane, courtly, kind. They paused on the landing at the end of the long corridor with the stairs piled in steel tiers above and plunging below them. An intimate silence swept up the stairwell in a warm gust and Max Berman said, "I'm curious. Why did you choose *The Immoralist?*"

She started suspiciously, afraid, it seemed, that her answer might expose and endanger the self she guarded so closely within.

"Well," she said finally, her glance reaching down the stairs to the door marked EXIT at the bottom, "when you said we could use anything by Gide I decided on *The Immoralist,* since it was the first book I read in the original French when I was in undergraduate school. I didn't understand it then because my French was so weak, I guess, but I always thought about it afterward for some odd reason. I was shocked by what I did understand, of course, but something else about it appealed to me, so when you made the assignment I thought I'd try reading it again. I understood it a little better this time. At least I think so...."

"Your paper proves you did."

She smiled absently, intent on some other thought. Then she said cautiously, but with unexpected force, "You see, to me, the book seems to say that the only way you begin to know what you are and how much you are capable of is by daring to try something, by doing something which tests you...."

"Something bold," he said.

"Yes."

"Even sinful."

She paused, questioning this, and then said reluctantly, "Yes, perhaps even sinful."

"The salutary effects of sin, you might say." He gave the little bow.

But she had not heard this; her mind had already leaped ahead. "The only trouble, at least with the character in Gide's book, is that what he finds out about himself is so terrible. He is so unhappy...."

"But at least he knows, poor sinner." And his playful tone went unnoticed.

"Yes," she said with the same startling forcefulness. "And another thing, in finding out what he is, he destroys his wife. It was as if she had to die in order for him to live and know himself. Perhaps in order for a person to live and know himself somebody else must die. Maybe there's always a balancing out.... In a way"—and he had to lean close now to hear her—"I believe this."

Max Berman edged back as he glimpsed something move within her abstracted gaze. It was like a strong and restless seed that had taken root in the darkness there and was straining now toward the light. He had not expected so subtle and complex a force beneath her mild exterior and he found it disturbing and dangerous, but fascinating.

"Well, it's a most interesting interpretation," he said. "I don't know if M. Gide would have agreed, but then he's not around to give his opinion. Tell me, where did you do your undergraduate work?"

"At Howard University."

"And you majored in French?"

"Yes."

"Why, if I may ask?" he said gently.

"Well, my mother was from New Orleans and could still speak a little Creole and I got interested in learning how to speak French through her, I guess. I teach it now at a junior high school in Richmond. Only the beginner courses because I don't have my master's. You know, *je vais, tu vas, il va* and *Frère Jacques.* It's not very inspiring."

"You should do something about that then, my dear Miss Williams. Perhaps it's time for you, like our friend in Gide, to try something new and bold."

"I know," she said, and her pale hand sketched a vague, despairing gesture. "I thought maybe if I got my master's...that's why I decided to come north this summer and start taking some courses...."

Max Berman quickly lighted a cigarette to still the flurry inside him, for the moment he had been awaiting had come. He flicked her paper, which he still held. "Well, you've got the makings of a master's thesis right here. If you like I will suggest some ways for you to expand it sometime. A few pointers from an old pro might help."

He had to turn from her astonished and grateful smile—it was like a child's. He said carefully, "The only problem will be to find a place where we can talk quietly. Regrettably, I don't rate an office...."

"Perhaps we could use one of the empty classrooms," she said.

"That would be much too dismal a setting for a pleasant discussion."

He watched the disappointment wilt her smile and when he spoke he made certain that the same disappointment weighed his voice. "Another difficulty is that the term's half over, which gives us little or no time. But let's not give up. Perhaps we can arrange to meet and talk over a weekend. The only hitch there is that I spend weekends at my place in the country. Of course you're perfectly welcome to come up there. It's only about seventy miles from New York, in the heart of what's very appropriately called the Borsch Circuit, even though, thank God, my place is a good distance away from the borsch. That is, it's very quiet and there's never anybody around except with my permission.

She did not move, yet she seemed to start; she made no sound, yet he thought he heard a bewildered cry. And then she did a strange thing, standing there with the breath sucked into the hollow of her throat and her smile, that had opened to him with such trust, dying—her eyes, her hands faltering up begged him to declare himself.

"There's a lake near the house," he said, "so that when you get tired of talking—or better, listening to me talk—you can take a swim, if you like. I would very much enjoy that sight." And as the nerve tugged at his eyelid, he seemed to wink behind his rimless glasses.

Her sudden, blind step back was like a man groping his way through a strange room in the dark, and instinctively Max Berman reached out to break her fall. Her arms, bare to the shoulder because of the heat (he knew the feel of her skin without even touching it—it would be like a rich, fine-textured cloth which would soothe and hide him in its amber warmth), struck out once to drive him off and then fell limp at her side, and her eyes became vivid and convulsive in her numbed face. She strained toward the stairs and the exit door at the bottom, but she could not move. Nor could she speak. She did not even cry. Her eyes remained dry and dull with disbelief. Only her shoulders trembled as though she was silently weeping inside.

It was as though she had never learned the forms and expressions of anger. The outrage of a lifetime, of her history, was trapped inside her. And she stared at Max Berman with this mute, paralyzing rage. Not really at him but to his side, as if she caught sight of others behind him. And remembering how he had imagined a column of dark women trailing her to his desk, he sensed that she glimpsed a legion of old men with sere flesh and lonely eyes flanking him: "old lechers with a love on every wind..."

"I'm sorry, Miss Williams," he said, and would have welcomed her insults, for he would have been able, at least, to distill from them some passion and a kind of intimacy. It would have been, in a way, like touching her. "It was only that you are a very attractive young woman and although I'm no longer young"—and he gave the tragic little laugh which sought to dismiss that fact— "I can still appreciate and even desire an attractive woman. But I was wrong...." His self-disgust, overwhelming him finally, choked off his voice. "And so very crude. Forgive me. I can offer no excuse for my behavior other than my approaching senility."

He could not even manage the little marionette bow this time. Quickly he shoved the paper on Gide into her lifeless hand, but it fell, the pages separating, and as he hurried past her downstairs and out the door, he heard the pages scattering like dead leaves on the steps.

She remained away until the night of the final examination, which was also the last meeting of the class. By that time Max Berman, believing that she would not return, had almost succeeded in forgetting her. He was no longer even certain of how she looked, for her face had been absorbed into the single, blurred, featureless face of all the women who had ever refused him. So that she startled him as much as a stranger would have when he entered the room that night and found her alone amid a maze of empty chairs, her face turned toward the window as on the first night and her hands serene in her lap. She turned at his footstep and it was as if she had also forgotten all that had passed between them. She waited until he said, "I'm glad you decided to take the examination. I'm sure you won't have any difficulty with it"; then she gave him a nod that was somehow reminiscent of his little bow and turned again to the window.

He was relieved yet puzzled by her composure. It was as if during her three-week absence she had waged and won a decisive contest with herself and was ready now to act. He was wary suddenly and all during the examination he tried to discover what lay behind her strange calm, studying her bent head amid the shifting heads of the other students, her slim hand guiding the pen across the page, her legs—the long bone visible, it seemed, beneath the flesh. Desire flared and quickly died.

"Excuse me, Professor Berman, will you take up Camus and Sartre next semester, maybe?" The girl who sat in front of his desk was standing over him with her earnest smile and finished examination folder.

"That might prove somewhat difficult, since I won't be here."

"No more?"

"No."

"I mean, not even next summer?"

"I doubt it."

"Gee, I'm sorry. I mean, I enjoyed the course and everything."

He bowed his thanks and held his head down until she left. Her compliment, so piteous somehow, brought on the despair he had forced to the dim rear of his mind. He could no longer flee the thought of the exile awaiting him when the class tonight ended. He could either remain in the house in Brooklyn, where the memory of his father's face above the radiance of the Sabbath candles haunted him from the shadows, reminding him of the certainty he had lost and never found again, where the mirrors in his father's room were still shrouded with sheets, as on the day he lay dying and moaning into his beard that his only son was a bad Jew; or he could return to the house in the country, to the silence shrill with loneliness.

The cigarette he was smoking burned his fingers, rousing him, and he saw over the pile of examination folders on his desk that the room was empty except for the Negro girl. She had finished—her pen lay aslant the closed folder on her desk—but she had remained in her seat and she was smiling across the room at him—a set, artificial smile that was both cold and threatening. It utterly denuded him and he was wildly angry suddenly that she had seen him give way to despair; he wanted to remind her (he could not stay the thought; it attacked him like an assailant from a dark turn in his mind) that she was only black after all.... His head dropped and he almost wept with shame.

The girl stiffened as if she had seen the thought and then the tiny muscles around her mouth quickly arranged the bland smile. She came up to his desk, placed her folder on top of the others and said pleasantly, her eyes like dark, shattered glass that spared Max Berman his reflection, "I've changed my mind. I think I'd like to spend a day at your place in the country if your invitation still holds."

He thought of refusing her, for her voice held neither promise nor passion, but he could not. Her presence, even if it was only for a day, would make his return easier. And there was still the possibility of passion despite her cold manner and the deliberate smile. He thought of how long it had been since he had had someone, of how badly he needed the sleep which followed love and of awakening certain, for the first time in years, of his existence.

"Of course the invitation still holds. I'm driving up tonight."

"I won't be able to come until Sunday," she said firmly. "Is there a train then?"

"Yes, in the morning," he said, and gave her the schedule.

"You'll meet me at the station?"

"Of course. You can't miss my car. It's a very shabby but venerable Chevy."

She smiled stiffly and left, her heels awakening the silence of the empty corridor, the sound reaching back to tap like a warning finger on Max Berman's temple.

The pale sunlight slanting through the windshield lay like a cat on his knees, and the motor of his old Chevy, turning softly under him could have been the humming of its heart. A little distance from the car a log-cabin station house—the logs blackened by the seasons—stood alone against the hills, and the hills, in turn, lifted softly, still green although the summer was ending, into the vague autumn sky.

The morning mist and pale sun, the green that was still somehow new, made it seem that the season was stirring into life even as it died, and this contradiction pained Max Berman at the same time that it pleased him. For it was his own contradiction after all: his desires which remained those of a young man even as he was dying.

He had been parked for some time in the deserted station, yet his hands were still tensed on the steering wheel and his foot hovered near the accelerator. As soon as he had arrived in the station he had wanted to leave. But like the girl that night on the landing, he was too stiff with tension to move. He could only wait, his eyelid twitching with foreboding, regret, curiosity and hope.

Finally and with no warning the train charged through the fiery green, setting off a tremor underground. Max Berman imagined the girl seated at a window in the train, her hands arranged quietly in her lap and her gaze scanning the hills that were so familiar to him, and yet he could not believe that she was really there. Perhaps her plan had been to disappoint him. She might be in New York or on her way back to Richmond now, laughing at the trick she had played on him. He was convinced of this suddenly, so that even when he saw her walking toward him through the blown steam from under the train, he told himself that she was a mirage created by the steam. Only when she sat beside him in the car, bringing with her, it seemed, an essence she had distilled from the morning air and rubbed into her skin, was he certain of her reality.

"I brought my bathing suit but it's much too cold to swim," she said and gave him the deliberate smile.

He did not see it; he only heard her voice, its warm Southern lilt in the chill, its intimacy in the closed car—and an excitement swept him, cold first and then hot, as if the sun had burst in his blood.

"It's the morning air," he said. "By noon it should be like summer again."

"Is that a promise?"

"Yes."

By noon the cold morning mist had lifted above the hills and below, in the lake valley, the sunlight was a sheer gold net spread out on the grass as if to dry, draped on the trees and flung, glinting, over the lake. Max Berman felt it brush his shoulders gently as he sat by the lake waiting for the girl, who had gone up to the house to change into her swimsuit.

He had spent the morning showing her the fields and small wood near his house. During the long walk he had been careful to keep a little apart from her. He would extend a hand as they climbed a rise or when she stepped uncertainly over a rock, but he would not really touch her. He was afraid that at his touch, no matter how slight and casual, her scream would spiral into the morning calm, or worse, his touch would unleash the threatening thing he sensed behind her even smile.

He had talked of her paper and she had listened politely and occasionally even asked a question or made a comment. But all the while detached, distant, drawn within herself as she had been that first night in the classroom. And then halfway down a slope she had paused and, pointing to the canvas tops of her white sneakers, which had become wet and dark from the dew secreted in the grass, she had laughed. The sound, coming so abruptly in the midst of her tense quiet, joined her, it seemed, to the wood and wide fields, to the hills; she shared their simplicity and held within her the same strong current of life. Max Berman had felt privileged suddenly, and humble. He had stopped questioning her smile. He had told himself then that it would not matter even if she stopped and picking up a rock bludgeoned him from behind.

"There's a lake near my home, but it's not like this," the girl said, coming up behind him. "Yours is so dark and serious-looking."

He nodded and followed her gaze out to the lake, where the ripples were long, smooth welts raised by the wind, and across to the other bank, where a group of birches stepped delicately down to the lake and bending over touched the water with their branches as if testing it before they plunged.

The girl came and stood beside him now—and she was like a pale-gold naiad, the spirit of the lake, her eyes reflecting its somber autumnal tone and her body as supple as the birches. She walked slowly into the water, unaware, it seemed, of the sudden passion in his gaze, or perhaps uncaring; and as she walked she held out her arms in what seemed a gesture of invocation (and Max Berman remembered his father with the fringed shawl draped on his out-stretched arms as he invoked their God each Sabbath with the same gesture); her head was bent as if she listened for a voice beneath the water's murmurous surface. When the ground gave way she still seemed to be walking and listening, her arms outstretched. The water reached her waist, her small breasts, her shoulders. She lifted her head once, breathed deeply and disappeared.

She stayed down for a long time and when her white cap finally broke the water some distance out, Max Berman felt strangely stranded and deprived. He understood suddenly the profound cleavage between them and the absurdity of his hope. The water between them became the years which separated them. Her white cap was the sign of her purity, while the silt darkening the lake was the flotsam of his failures. Above all, their color—her arms a pale, flashing gold in the sunlit water and his bled white and flaccid with the veins like angry blue penciling—marked the final barrier.

He was sad as they climbed toward the house late that afternoon and trou-bled. A crow cawed derisively in the bracken, heralding the dusk which would not only end their strange day but would also, he felt, unveil her smile, so that he would learn the reason for her coming. And because he was sad, he said wryly, "I think I should tell you that you've been spending the day with some-thing of an outcast."

"Oh," she said and waited.

He told her of the dismissal, punctuating his words with the little hoarse, deprecating laugh and waving aside the pain with his cigarette. She listened, polite but neutral, and because she remained unmoved, he wanted to confess all the more. So that during dinner and afterward when they sat outside on the porch, he told her of the investigation.

"It was very funny once you saw it from the proper perspective, which I did, of course," he said. "I mean here they were accusing me of crimes I couldn't remember committing and asking me for the names of people with whom I had never associated. It was pure farce. But I made a mistake. I should have done something dramatic or something just as farcical. Bared my breast in the public market place or written a tome on my apostasy, naming names. It would have been a far different story then. Instead of my present ignominy I would have been offered a chairmanship at Yale.... No? Well, Brandeis then. I would have been draped in honorary degrees...."

"Well, why didn't you confess?" she said impatiently.

"I've often asked myself the same interesting question, but I haven't come up with a satisfactory answer yet. I suspect, though, that I said nothing because none of it really mattered that much."

"What did matter?" she asked sharply.

He sat back, waiting for the witty answer, but none came, because just then the frame upon which his organs were strung seemed to snap and he felt his heart, his lungs, his vital parts fall in a heap within him. Her question had dealt the severing blow, for it was the same question he understood suddenly that the vague forms in his dream asked repeatedly. It had been the plaintive undercurrent to his father's dying moan, the real accusation behind the charges of his inquisitors at the hearing.

For what had mattered? He gazed through his sudden shock at the night squatting on the porch steps, at the hills asleep like gentle beasts in the darkness, at the black screen of the sky where the events of his life passed in a mute, accusing review—and he saw nothing there to which he had given himself or in which he had truly believed since the belief and dedication of his boyhood.

"Did you hear my question?" she asked, and he was glad that he sat within the shadows clinging to the porch screen and could not be seen.

"Yes, I did," he said faintly, and his eyelid twitched. "But I'm afraid it's another one of those I can't answer satisfactorily." And then he struggled for the old flippancy. "You make an excellent examiner, you know. Far better than my inquisitors."

"What will you do now?" Her voice and cold smile did not spare him.

He shrugged and the motion, a slow, eloquent lifting of the shoulders, brought with it suddenly the weight and memory of his boyhood. It was the familiar gesture of the women hawkers in Belmont Market, of the men standing outside the temple on Saturday mornings, each of them reflecting his image of

God in their forbidding black coats and with the black, tumbling beards in which he had always imagined he could hide as in a forest. All this had mattered, he called loudly to himself, and said aloud to the girl, "Let me see if I can answer this one at least. What *will* I do?" He paused and swung his leg so that his foot in the fastidious French shoe caught the light from the house. "Grow flowers and write my memoirs. How's that? That would be the proper way for a gentleman and scholar to retire. Or hire one of those hefty housekeepers who will bully me and when I die in my sleep draw the sheet over my face and call my lawyer. That's somewhat European, but how's that?"

When she said nothing for a long time, he added soberly, "But that's not a fair question for me any more. I leave all such considerations to the young. To you, for that matter. What will you do, my dear Miss Williams?"

It was as if she had been expecting the question and had been readying her answer all the time that he had been talking. She leaned forward eagerly and with her face and part of her body fully in the light, she said, "I will do something. I don't know what yet, but something."

Max Berman started back a little. The answer was so unlike her vague, resigned "I know" on the landing that night when he had admonished her to try something new.

He edged back into the darkness and she leaned further into the light, her eyes overwhelming her face and her mouth set in a thin, determined line. "I will do something," she said, bearing down on each word, "because for the first time in my life I feel almost brave."

He glimpsed this new bravery behind her hard gaze and sensed something vital and purposeful, precious, which she had found and guarded like a prize within her center. He wanted it. He would have liked to snatch it and run like a thief. He no longer desired her but it, and starting forward with a sudden envious cry, he caught her arm and drew her close, seeking it.

But he could not get to it. Although she did not pull away her arm, although she made no protest as his face wavered close to hers, he did not really touch her. She held herself and her prize out of his desperate reach and her smile was a knife she pressed to his throat. He saw himself for what he was in her clear, cold gaze: an old man with skin the color and texture of dough that had been kneaded by the years into tragic folds, with faded eyes adrift behind a pair of rimless glasses and the roughened flesh at his throat like a bird's wattles. And as the disgust which he read in her eyes swept him, his hand dropped from her arm. He started to murmur, "Forgive me..." when suddenly she caught hold of his wrist, pulling him close again, and he felt the strength which had borne her swiftly through the water earlier hold him now as she said quietly and without passion, "And do you know why, Dr. Berman, I feel almost brave today?

Because ever since I can remember my parents were always telling me, 'Stay away from white folks. Just leave them alone. You mind your business and they'll mind theirs. Don't go near them.' And they made sure I didn't. My father, who was the principal of a colored grade school in Richmond, used to drive me to and from school every day. When I needed something from downtown my mother would take me and if the white saleslady asked me anything she would answer....

"And my parents were also always telling me, 'Stay away from niggers,' and that meant anybody darker than we were." She held out her arm in the light and Max Berman saw the skin almost as white as his but for the subtle amber shading. Staring at the arm she said tragically, "I was so confused I never really went near anybody. Even when I went away to college I kept to myself. I didn't marry the man I wanted to because he was dark and I knew my parents would disapprove...." She paused, her wistful gaze searching the darkness for the face of the man she had refused, it seemed, and not finding it she went on sadly, "So after graduation I returned home and started teaching and I was just as confused and frightened and ashamed as always. When my parents died I went on the same way. And I would have gone on like that the rest of my life if it hadn't been for you, Dr. Berman"—and the sarcasm leaped behind her cold smile. "In a way you did me a favor. You let me know how you—and most of the people like you—see me."

"My dear Miss Williams, I assure you I was not attracted to you because you were colored...." And he broke off, remembering just how acutely aware of her color he had been.

"I'm not interested in your reasons!" she said brutally. "What matters is what it meant to me. I thought about this these last three weeks and about my parents—how wrong they had been, how frightened, and the terrible thing they had done to me...And I wasn't confused any longer." Her head lifted, tremulous with her new assurance. "I can do something now! I can begin," she said with her head poised. "Look how I came all the way up here to tell you this to your face. Because how could you harm me? You're so old you're like a cup I could break in my hand." And her hand tightened on his wrist, wrenching the last of his frail life from him, it seemed. Through the quick pain he remembered her saying on the landing that night: "Maybe in order for a person to live someone else must die" and her quiet "I believe this" then. Now her sudden laugh, an infinitely cruel sound in the warm night, confirmed her belief.

Suddenly she was the one who seemed old, indeed ageless. Her touch became mortal and Max Berman saw the darkness that would end his life gathered in her eyes. But even as he sprang back, jerking his arm away, a part of him rushed forward to embrace that darkness, and his cry, wounding the night, held both ecstasy and terror.

"That's all I came for," she said, rising. "You can drive me to the station now."

They drove to the station in silence. Then, just as the girl started from the car, she turned with an ironic, pitiless smile and said, "You know, it's been a nice day, all things considered. It really turned summer again as you said it would. And even though your lake isn't anything like the one near my home, it's almost as nice."

Max Berman bowed to her for the last time, accepting with that gesture his responsibility for her rage, which went deeper than his, and for her anger, which would spur her finally to live. And not only for her, but for all those at last whom he had wronged through his indifference: his father lying in the room of shrouded mirrors, the wives he had never loved, his work which he had never believed in enough and, lastly (even though he knew it was too late and he would not be spared), himself.

Too weary to move, he watched the girl cross to the train which would bear her south, her head lifted as though she carried life as lightly there as if it were a hat made of tulle. When the train departed his numbed eyes followed it until its rear light was like a single firefly in the immense night or the last flickering of his life. Then he drove back through the darkness.

Ann Allen Shockley

The Funeral

T he death of Melissa's grandmother had been expected. She had been ailing a long time, beset with the genealogical diseases of the old: arthritis, high blood pressure, and diabetes advanced by her eighty years, until these were finally laid to rest by a heart attack.

The funeral was already paid for. *Had* been paid for years ago through the fifty-cents-a-week policy taken out with the Black Brothers Burial Society. Undertaker C.B. Brown had nothing to worry about along those lines. Neither did the Reverend Thomas Cooke have reason to fret over the funeral services because all that information had been foretold to him time before time and locked in the Zion Methodist Church's metal strongbox.

The occasion had been prepared for well, and all involved rose nobly to meet it. Even the tired decrepit four-room house, whose once white frame was archaically grimy with red dust from the patch of yard surrounding it—where no grass appeared ever to be able to grow—managed to look less worn, less dull, to accommodate the throngs of people stopping by to share the grief. Helpful neighbors and friends came in hushed, sad-eyed groups, bringing plates of fried chicken, potato salad, greens, and homemade pastries to Melissa, too bereaved to bother with the mundane.

There was more food than Melissa could ever eat, since with her grandmother dead, she was left alone. If there were any other relatives, Melissa knew

First published in *Phylon* 28 (Vol. 1: Spring 1967)

nothing about them, scattered here and yond up north and east and God-knows-where.

There had only been the two of them living in the house. Just the two of them facing each other in the evenings in the small living room with the shades tightly drawn: Granny rocking slowly back and forth in the ancient rocker with its high straight arrow back, and Melissa, absorbing herself in preparing for the next day which would end like the day before.

Granny sewed when the arthritic pain wasn't drawing her hands, brown fingers weaving in and out, no longer swift, only halfway sure. But when the pain was there curling up the gnarled hands that had known work since thoughts could remember—cleaning up the big house for the white folks and making their children spotless—Granny would open the frayed family Bible scrawled with census records, and slowly, very slowly form the biblical words aloud with her lips. Frequently she paused to peer over at Melissa, shakily pointing to a passage she wanted read at her funeral.

Granny talked a lot to Melissa about the funeral. Especially about the clothes she wanted to be buried in—an old black satin with a lace embroidered shawl, and the black square-heel shoes kept shiny under her bed. When talking about the funeral, Granny's skinny flat chest would heave with tiny ripples like a small wind trying to press the sea into waves.

Melissa would listen sometimes, and sometimes she wouldn't. The woman was old and Melissa could smell death around her. Once in a while even see it—dismal shadow hovering near. There were unjust moments when she wished the shadow would stay so she could make the lamps brighter and turn the tiny boxlike radio up to cheerful sounds. Now she couldn't. Bright lights hurt Granny's cataracts, and the blaring music wasn't the sound of the Lord's.

Now and then some evenings when Granny talked about the funeral, Melissa would stare blankly at her with the hand-knitted robe thrown across her lap winter and summer, focusing her eyes dreamily at the vacant corner behind the rocker where she hoped to put a secondhand television—after it was over.

"That song, Melissa. Don't forget I want Sister Smith to sing *Just a Closer Walk with Thee* right before the preaching. You hear me?" Granny's voice would rise, squeaking in the manner of a worn out reed.

"Sure, Granny, sure."

After various intervals, Melissa would get up and go through the plastic curtain door to the kitchen on the pretense of getting a glass of water. There she would turn on the faucet vigorously while reaching quickly behind the flour can for the pint of Gordon's gin. She would hurriedly gulp down the drink, choking in her haste, then return to the room, smiling a little now, able to endure the talk and the death in the chair whose cushion had long worn down with the weight and the words.

In the chair was where she died: the thin, wasted body crumpled in the rocker, head down, white hair straggling outrageously from its knot, just as if she had nodded to sleep.

Now there was no longer the quietness in the house. The door was left unlocked to admit the endless string of church members and lodge sisters, and even some of the white folks for whom Granny had scrubbed and worked and fussed over.

Granny had insisted on being laid out at the house—no funeral parlor where it was unfriendly and reeking with embalming fluid—but laid out in her satin dress with her hands crossed to show the round tarnished wedding band right in her own living room.

Since that was where she wanted to be, the living room was always the one papered each year to keep down the smoke stain ruins of the potbellied coal stove fired in the winters. The coffin was large for the room and the couch had to be moved into the bedroom to make space. Extra folding chairs were brought in by the undertaker and cardboard fans advertising C.B. Brown's Funeral Home ALWAYS THE FAMILY FIRST were distributed noticeably even though there was no need.

Melissa stayed in the bedroom, letting the visitors feel free to drift in and sign the register while Undertaker Brown stood solemnly at the door, neatly attired in his navy suit, whispering professional instructions. Across from him was stalwart Sister Mary Smith, head of the church's stewardess board, in her stiff white uniform, handling the viewers with equal aplomb.

Watching the people drift in and out, leaving behind the soft rustle of dresses and ragged shuffling of feet moving past the body, Melissa could tell the town remembered and loved Miss Eliza. That was what they all called her—Miss Eliza—young, old, white folks alike. She had been a fixture in the town like the Confederate soldier in front of the court house. A born and bred fixture claimed by time.

Melissa could hear the laments as they filed by:

"Don't she look nat-u-ral?"

"Poor Miss Eliza. God's restin' her now. Put her out of her mis-ery." And the younger ones, impatiently: "Wonder if'n I'll live to get *that* old?"

An answering giggle. "Not at the rate you goin' now!"

"Please..." the smooth articulate voice of the undertaker, "move on by the casket and sign the register. Others are waiting...."

A tray of hot food was brought to Melissa, urged upon her, heedless of her feeble sign of refusal. But finally the aroma of hot bread and chicken pressed close to her nose made her relent.

"We goin' to stay all night for the wake, honey," one of the lodge sisters murmured consolingly. "Now you lay down 'n rest. Don't cry now. The Lord giveth and the Lord taketh away."

"Give her a hot toddy..." another voice suggested. "That *always* helps at times like these."

The undertaker thrust his head into the room. "Is Miss Melissa all right?"

"Doin' fine."

Melissa sipped the toddy, feeling a warm glow kindle within her, spreading some life into her tired body.

"Wait! Undertaker Brown..." she called, beckoning him back. "Don't forget the expensive hearse tomorrow. The *Cad-il-lac*. Granny always said that that'd be the one time she rode in style. Even if it was to her grave."

"Of course...of course."

"And all the white folks' messages read *first*."

"Naturally."

Melissa drank longer on the toddy, not minding the burning hot sting this time, talking excitedly now like Granny used to do. "That pretty white spray of carnations from the white folks I work for I want right in *front*."

The undertaker nodded affirmatively, his shining bald head bobbing quickly. "Thy will be done."

A small tuneless wail suddenly rose in the outer room, coiling in a feverish pitch. "Oh Lord...Lordy...po' Melissa. Where's the chile?"

A stooped old woman bundled in a threadbare coat groped into the room towards Melissa. "Chile...chile...I knowed your grandmother ever since we wuz chillen. I'm goin' next. I can feel it in my bones. Death don't never stop at one. It takes more 'n more...."

"Sh-h-h, Miss Reva, don't cry," Melissa consoled, hugging the woman close to her. "You go on home and get a good night's sleep. You to ride with me tomorrow. You an old friend of the family. I ain't got nothing but old friends to ride with me."

Sobbing louder, the woman was aided out. "Oh, Lord, God help us all."

Melissa stretched out on the bed. Someone threw a quilt over her, persuading her to sleep. She heard the women's preparations of turning off the lamp by the bed and quietly closing the door, leaving her alone to rest. A thin shred of light shone vigilantly under the door where Granny was, and watching it, she found it hard to sleep.

The morning of the funeral was cold and gray, hanging heavily with impending rain.

"A good sign," one lodge sister said, looking out the window. "When it rains, they goin' to heaven."

Melissa sighed, fumbling with her black veil, feeling weak and worn from the four-day ordeal of death. The house reeked nauseously, emanating the sweet odors of the myriad sprays. Her arms and legs felt lifeless, debilitated by people and emotions. But inwardly she had the sensation of being alive with excitement and anticipation over the drama orbiting around her.

"Everything is in readiness," Undertaker Brown murmured gently, glancing anxiously at her. "The cars are waiting."

Melissa lowered her head in what she judged to be a proper angle, not too low or too high, but leveled to see her steps and that around her too. Sister Mary Ellen and a nurse supported her on each side as she moved falteringly on her Sunday best heels into the gray foggy mist.

The black Cadillac hearse gleamed brilliantly, and seeing it, Melissa knew how proud Granny would be. She got in the sleek family limousine whose interior was spotless. Undertaker Brown sure kept his cars up nice, she thought. Granny always said that, and Granny ought to know because she never missed a funeral. "Goin' to ever'body's. I got no folks livin' I know of 'cept you. If I go to other peoples', they'll come to mine," Granny used to say.

True to Granny's words, they were there, Melissa noticed as the car came slowly to a stop in front of the church. People were standing on the outside and in the church's doorway. Melissa furtively lifted her veil to survey the scene as the other cars came slowly to a stop behind them in the section reserved.

The sounds of sobs and moans surrounded her, reminding her of those beside her. She took a deep harsh breath, letting herself be half lifted out of the luxuriously plush seat that was better than a sofa.

"Steady...steady," the undertaker whispered, stationing her at the head to lead the long line of lodge sisters, friends, and members of the burying order into the church. "The procession is now ready to begin...."

The church organist was softly playing the piece Granny wanted, *Nearer My God to Thee*. Melissa sniffled, fumbling for her handkerchief. Arms tightened around her shoulders and gently guided her through the parting crowd to the front pew by the casket.

The Reverend Cooke cleared his throat and stretched his black robed arms wide in twin hawk's wings, engulfing the congregation. "Jesus said, 'I am the resurrection, and the life: he that believeth in Me, though he were dead, yet shall he live; and whosoever liveth and believeth in Me shall never die.' Let us pray. Our Father...."

Melissa's fingers tightly gripped her wet handkerchief, twisting it to dabble at her eyes. Moments later, the loud resounding voice of Sister Smith filled the church with Granny's favorite hymn, *Just a Closer Walk with Thee*, punctuated by foot tapping rhythm and shouts:

"Sing it, Sister, sing it."

"She's gone...*gone.*"

"Oh, God, have mercy."

Melissa swayed and the nurse pushed a bottle of smelling salts under her nose.

The Reverend rose again, paused, and in deep sonorous tones started his eulogy. "A good and Godly woman was Sister Eliza. Loved by all who knew her. A fine church worker has left us, who God has called to work in His heavenly church above."

"A-men."

The words of the preacher drifted around her in swelling billows that would not stop long enough for her to grasp them. So she sat still, eyes downcast, thoughts locked in nothingness.

In what seemed like a long time, the choir later began to sing softly as the minister called for the president of the Burial Society to read the obituary. The acknowledgement of cards and flowers followed, given by the head of the church's stewardess board.

"They goin' to view the body now," the nurse said softly, looking anxiously at Melissa.

Melissa heard the organist playing *Steal Away* as she half watched the long column of men, women, and children filing past to gaze one last time at Granny. A female voice shrieked hysterically, and Melissa pushed her head slightly forward to see who it was.

And last, the family. Strong capable hands clutched Melissa, and she found herself being shelteringly steeled against a large warm bosom, steadying her to look down upon Granny's sleeping face. The face was peaceful, serene, no longer complaining of the ache in her joints—especially on rainy days like this. This was one rainy day when Granny wouldn't have an ache.

Melissa reached out to touch Granny for the last time, just once more. That's what Granny had asked her to do: reach out and touch her. Melissa's hand moved slowly, hesitantly, and suddenly paused in midair, a breath away from the sunken brown cheek. She *couldn't*. A drowning siege of dizziness covered her, a temporary black cloud passing over to hover for a tiny vacuous second before going beyond.

Then poised as a tense wary bird for sudden flight, one finger extended out from the rounded mold of her hand to gently touch the cheek. And when she did, she knew that she would never forget its unyielding tough chill. Far off, she imagined hearing Granny saying, "Well done, chile, well done."

Laboriously she sat back on the bench, now aware of its hardness, and that her feet ached in the shoes she seldom wore, and the girdle was making ridges around her stomach.

The funeral had been long. Outside, rain pushed harder against the multicolored stained windows, as if to intrude with sound if nothing else. She realized by the beginning restless stirrings many of the women were listening to it and becoming angry because their hair would get wet standing in the graveyard.

There was an indistinct prayer mumbled by the minister, and through the light pressure of the protective hands beside her, she understood that it was all over. The choir rose to sing *Swing Low, Sweet Chariot,* just as Granny wanted.

They had gone. The house was the same once again, quiet, still, but not the same either. She had told them there was no need to stay with her tonight. They were being nice and polite, but the commotion was over. They had to get back to their normal routines of work and everyday living until the next funeral which would come in a manner of a charging white horse to interrupt the dull monotony of their plodding lives. Then again, they would be rejuvenated in baking their pies, caring for the living, and crying for the dead.

It was still raining, an all-night incessant dirge. She was glad everything had been carried out as Granny wished: a big expensive funeral to put her at rest in the family plot. Granny was now covered by a blanket of dirt. Ashes to ashes, dust to dust, just like the preacher said at the grave.

Melissa rose slowly and went to the kitchen, taking down a fresh bottle of gin. Pouring a drink, she started to down it quickly to keep Granny from calling and asking why she was so long in the kitchen.

Then remembering, she shrugged, picked up the bottle and glass, and went back to the living room. Wearily she sat down in the rocker which seemed still warmed by Granny's long sitting and waiting.

She began to rock slowly back and forth in Granny's rhythm with her head resting against the chair. The blinds were drawn and the room was half shadowed in illusions. She closed her eyes, listening to the measured screaks of the old rocker, a soft sound from the past, and began to wonder what would happen when she was gone someday. For everybody's got to go—someday.

Louise M. Meriwether

A Happening in Barbados

*T*he best way to pick up a Barbadian man, I hoped, was to walk alone down the beach with my tall, brown frame squeezed into a skin-tight bathing suit. Since my hotel was near the beach and Dorothy and Alison, my two traveling companions, had gone shopping, I managed this quite well. I had not taken more than a few steps on the glittering, white sand before two black men were on either side of me vying for attention.

I chose the tall, slim-hipped one over the squat, muscle-bound man who was also grinning at me. But apparently they were friends because Edwin had no sooner settled me under his umbrella than the squat one showed up with a beach chair and two other boys in tow.

Edwin made the introductions. His temporary rival was Gregory, and the other two were Alphonse and Dimitri.

Gregory was ugly. He had thick, rubbery lips, a scarcity of teeth, and a broad nose splattered like a pyramid across his face. He was all massive shoulders and bulging biceps. No doubt he had a certain animal magnetism, but personally I preferred a lean man like Edwin, who was well built but slender, his

---

First published in *The Antioch Review* (Vol. 27, No. 3: 1968)

whole body fitting together like a symphony. Alphonse and Dimitri were clean-cut and pleasant looking.

They were all too young—twenty to twenty-five at the most—and Gregory seemed the oldest. I inwardly mourned their youth and settled down to make the most of my catch.

The crystal blue sky rivaled the royal blue of the Caribbean for beauty, and our black bodies on the white sand added to the munificence of colors. We ran into the sea like squealing children when the sudden raindrops came, then shivered on the sand under a makeshift tent of umbrellas and damp towels waiting for the sun to reappear while nourishing ourselves with straight Barbados rum.

As with most of the West Indians I had already met on my whirlwind tour of Trinidad and Jamaica who welcomed American Negroes with open arms, my new friends loved their island home, but work was scarce and they yearned to go to America. They were hungry for news of how Negroes were faring in the States.

Edwin's arm rested casually on my knee in a proprietary manner, and I smiled at him. His thin, serious face was smooth, too young for a razor, and when he smiled back, he looked even younger. He told me he was a waiter at the Hilton, saving his money to make it to the States. I had already learned not to be snobbish with the island's help. Yesterday's waiter may be tomorrow's prime minister.

Dimitri, very black with an infectious grin, was also a waiter, and lanky Alphonse was a tile setter.

Gregory's occupation was apparently women, for that's all he talked about. He was able to launch this subject when a bony, white woman—more peeling red than white, really—looking like a gaunt cadaver in a loose-fitting bathing suit, came out of the sea and walked up to us. She smiled archly at Gregory.

"Are you going to take me to the Pigeon Club tonight, Sugar?"

"No, mon," he said pleasantly, with a toothless grin. "I'm taking a younger pigeon."

The woman turned a deeper red, if that were possible, and, mumbling something incoherent, walked away.

"That one is always after me to take her some place," Gregory said. "She's rich, and she pays the bills but, mon, I don't want an old hag nobody else wants. I like to take my women away from white men and watch them squirm."

"Come down, mon," Dimitri said, grinning. "She look like she's starving for what you got to spare."

We all laughed. The boys exchanged stories about their experiences with predatory white women who came to the islands looking for some black action.

But, one and all, they declared they liked dark-skinned meat the best, and I felt like a black queen of the Nile when Gregory winked at me and said: "The blacker the berry, mon, the sweeter the juice."

They had all been pursued and had chased some white tail, too, no doubt, but while the others took it all in good humor, it soon became apparent that Gregory's exploits were exercises in vengeance.

Gregory was saying: "I told that bastard, 'You in my country now, mon, and I'll kick your ass all the way back to Texas. The girl agreed to dance with me, and she don't need your permission.' That white man's face turned purple, but he sat back down, and I danced with his girl. Mon, they hate to see me rubbing bellies with their women 'cause they know once she rub bellies with me she wanna rub something else, too."

He laughed, and we all joined in. Serves the white men right, I thought. Let's see how they liked licking *that* end of the stick for a change.

"Mon, you gonna get killed yet," Edwin said, moving closer to me on the towel we shared. "You're crazy. You don't care whose woman you mess with. But it's not gonna be a white man who kills you but some bad Bajian."

Gregory led in the laughter, then held us spellbound for the next hour with intimate details of his affair with Glenda, a young white girl spending the summer with her father on their yacht. Whatever he had, Glenda wanted it desperately, or so Gregory told it.

Yeah, I thought to myself, like LSD, a black lover is the thing this year. I had seen the white girls in the Village and at off-Broadway theatres clutching their black men tightly while I, manless, looked on with bitterness. I often vowed I would find me an ofay in self-defense, but I could never bring myself to condone the wholesale rape of my slave ancestors by letting a white man touch me.

We finished the rum, and the three boys stood up to leave, making arrangements to get together later with us and my two girl friends and go clubbing.

Edwin and I were left alone. He stretched out his smoothly muscled leg and touched my toes with his. I smiled at him and let our thighs come together. Why did he have to be so damned young? Then our lips met, his warm and demanding, and I thought, what the hell, maybe I will.

I was thirty-nine—goodbye, sweet bird of youth—an ungay divorcee, up tight and drinking too much, trying to disown the years which had brought only loneliness and pain. I had clawed my way up from the slums of Harlem via night school and was now a law clerk on Wall Street. But the fight upward had taken its toll. My husband, who couldn't claw as well as I, got lost somewhere in that concrete jungle. The last I saw of him he was peering under every skirt around, searching for his lost manhood.

I had always felt contempt for women who found their kicks by robbing the cradle. Now here I was on a Barbados beach with an amorous child young enough to be my son. Two sayings flitted unbidden across my mind: "Judge not that ye be not judged," and "The thing which I feared is come upon me." I thought, ain't it the goddamned truth?

Edwin kissed me again, pressing the length of his body against mine.

"I've got to go," I gasped. "My friends have probably returned and are looking for me. About ten, tonight?"

He nodded. I smiled at him and ran all the way to my hotel.

At exactly ten o'clock the telephone in our room announced we had company downstairs.

"Hot damn," Alison said, putting on her eyebrows in front of the mirror. "We're not going to be stood up."

"Island men," I said loftily, "are dependable, not like the bums you're used to in America."

Alison, freckled and willowy, had been married three times and was looking for her fourth. Her motto was, if at first you don't succeed, find another mother. She was a real estate broker in Los Angeles, and we had been childhood friends in Harlem.

"What I can't stand," Dorothy said from the bathroom, "are those creeps who come to *your* apartment, drink up *your* liquor, then dirty up *your* sheets. You don't even get a lousy dinner out of the deal."

She came out of the bathroom in her slip. Petite and delicate with a pixie grin, at thirty-five Dorothy looked more like one of the high school girls she taught than their teacher. She had never been married. Years ago, while she was holding onto her virginity with a miser's grip, her fiancé had messed up and knocked up one of her friends. Since then, all of Dorothy's affairs had been with married men, displaying perhaps a subconscious vendetta against all wives.

By ten-twenty we were downstairs and I was introducing the girls to our four escorts who eyed us with unconcealed admiration. We were looking good in our Saks Fifth Avenue finery. They were looking good, too, in soft shirts and loose slacks, all except Gregory, whose bulging muscles confined in clothing made him seem more gargantuan.

We took a cab and a few minutes later were squeezing behind a table in a small, smoky room called the Pigeon Club. A Trinidad steel band was blasting out the walls, and the tiny dance area was jammed with wiggling bottoms and shuffling feet. The white tourists, trying to do the hip-shaking calypso, were having a ball and looking awkward.

I got up to dance with Edwin. He had a natural grace and was easy to follow. Our bodies found the rhythm and became one with it while our eyes locked in silent, ancient combat, his pleading, mine teasing.

We returned to our seats and to tall glasses of rum and cola tonic. The party had begun.

I danced every dance with Edwin, his clasp becoming gradually tighter until my face was smothered in his shoulder, my arms locked around his neck. He was adorable. Very good for my ego. The other boys took turns dancing with my friends, but soon preferences were set—Alison with Alphonse and Dorothy with Dimitri. With good humor Gregory ordered another round and didn't seem to mind being odd man out, but he wasn't alone for long.

During the floor show featuring the inevitable limbo dancers, a pretty white girl, about twenty-two, with straight, red hair hanging down to her shoulder, appeared at Gregory's elbow. From his wink at me and self-satisfied grin, I knew this was Glenda from the yacht.

"Hello," she said to Gregory. "Can I join you, or do you have a date?"

Well, I thought, that's the direct approach.

"What are you doing here?" Gregory asked.

"Looking for you."

Gregory slid over on the bench next to the wall, and Glenda sat down as he introduced her to the rest of us. Somehow her presence spoiled my mood. We had been happy being black, and I resented this intrusion from the white world. But Glenda was happy. She had found the man she set out to find and a swinging party to boot. She beamed a dazzling smile around the table.

Alphonse led Alison onto the dance floor, and Edwin and I followed. The steel band was playing a wild calypso, and I could feel my hair rising with the heat as I joined in the wildness.

When we returned to the table, Glenda applauded us, then turned to Gregory. "Why don't you teach me to dance like that?"

He answered with his toothless grin and a leer, implying he had better things to teach her.

White women were always snatching our men, I thought, and now they want to dance like us.

I turned my attention to Edwin and met his full stare.

"I want you," he said, his tone as solemn as if he were in church.

I teased him with a smile, refusing to commit myself. He had a lusty, healthy appetite, which was natural, I supposed, for a twenty-one-year-old lad. Lord, but why did he have to be *that* young? I stood up to go to the ladies' room.

"Wait for me," Glenda cried, trailing behind me.

The single toilet stall was occupied, and Glenda leaned against the wall waiting for it while I flipped open my compact and powdered my grimy face.

"You married?" she asked.

"Divorced."

"When I get married, I want to stay hooked forever."

"That's the way I planned it, too," I said drily. "What I mean," she rushed on, "is that I've gotta find a cat who wants to groove only with me."

Oh Lord, I thought, don't try to sound like us, too. Use your own sterile language.

"I really dug this guy I was engaged to," Glenda continued, "but he couldn't function without a harem. I could have stood that maybe, but when he didn't mind if I made it with some other guy, too, I knew I didn't want that kind of life."

I looked at her in the mirror as I applied my lipstick. She had been hurt, and badly. Shook right down to her naked soul. So she was dropping down a social notch, according to her scale of values, and trying to repair her damaged ego with a black brother.

"You gonna make it with Edwin?" she asked, as if we were college chums comparing dates.

"I'm not a one-night stand." My tone was frigid. That's another thing I can't stand about white people. Too familiar, just because we're colored.

"I dig Gregory," she said, pushing her hair out of her eyes. "He's kind of rough, but who wouldn't be, the kind of life he's led."

"And what kind of life is that?" I asked.

"Didn't you know? His mother was a whore in an exclusive brothel for white men only. That was before, when the British owned the island."

"I take it you like rough men?" I asked.

"There's usually something gentle and lost underneath," she replied.

A white woman came out of the toilet, and Glenda went in. Jesus, I thought. Gregory, gentle? The woman walked to the basin, flung some water in the general direction of her hands, and left.

"Poor Daddy is having a fit," Glenda volunteered from the john, "but there's not much he can do about it. He's afraid I'll leave him again, and he gets lonely without me, so he just tags along and tries to keep me out of trouble."

"And pays the bills?"

She answered with a laugh. "Why not? He's loaded."

Why not, I thought with bitterness. You white women have always managed to have your cake and eat it, too. The toilet flushed with a roar like Niagara Falls. I opened the door and went back to our table. Let Glenda find her way back alone.

Edwin pulled my chair out and brushed his lips across the nape of my neck as I sat down. He still had not danced with anyone else, and his apparent desire was flattering. For a moment I considered it. That's what I really needed, wasn't it? To walk down the moonlit beach wrapped in his arms, making it to some pad to be made? It would be a delightful story to tell at bridge sessions. But I shook my head at him, and this time my smile was more sad than teasing.

Glenda came back and crawled over Gregory's legs to the seat beside him. The bastard. He made no pretense of being a gentleman. Suddenly, I didn't know which of them I disliked the most. Gregory winked at me. I don't know where he got the impression I was his conspirator, but I got up to dance with him.

"That Glenda," he grinned, "she's the one I was on the boat with last night. I banged her plenty, in the room right next to her father. We could hear him coughing to let us know he was awake, but he didn't come in."

He laughed like a naughty schoolboy, and I joined in. He was a nerveless bastard all right, and it served Glenda right that we were laughing at her. Who asked her to crash our party, anyway? That's when I got the idea to take Gregory away from her.

"You gonna bang her again tonight?" I asked, a new teasing quality in my voice. "Or are you gonna find something better to do?" To help him get the message I rubbed bellies with him.

He couldn't believe this sudden turn of events. I could almost see him thinking. With one stroke he could slap Glenda down a peg and repay Edwin for beating out his time with me on the beach that morning.

"You wanna come with me?" he asked, making sure of his quarry.

"What you got to offer?" I peered at him through half-closed lids.

"Big Bamboo," he sang, the title of a popular calypso. We both laughed.

I felt a heady excitement of impending danger as Gregory pulled me back to the table.

The men paid the bill, and suddenly we were all standing outside the club in the bright moonlight. Gregory deliberately uncurled Glenda's arm from his and took a step toward me. Looking at Edwin and nodding in my direction, he said: "She's coming with me. Any objections?"

Edwin inhaled a mouthful of smoke. His face was inscrutable. "You want to go with him?" he asked me quietly.

I avoided his eyes and nodded. "Yes."

He flipped the cigarette with contempt at my feet and lit another one. "Help yourself to the garbage," he said, and leaned back against the building, one leg braced behind him. The others suddenly stilled their chatter, sensing trouble.

I was holding Gregory's arm now, and I felt his muscles tense. "No," I said, as he moved toward Edwin. "You've got what you want. Forget it."

Glenda was ungracious in defeat. "What about me?" she screamed. She stared from one black face to another, her

glance lingering on Edwin. But he wasn't about to come to her aid and take Gregory's leavings.

"You can go home in a cab," Gregory said, pushing her ahead of him and pulling me behind him to a taxi waiting at the curb.

Glenda broke from his grasp. "You bastard. Who in the hell do you think you are, King Solomon? You can't dump me like this." She raised her hands as if to strike Gregory on the chest, but he caught them before they landed.

"Careful, white girl," he said. His voice was low but ominous. She froze.

"But why," she whimpered, all hurt child now. "You liked me last night. I know you did. Why are you treating me like this?"

"I didn't bring you here," his voice was pleasant again, "so don't be trailing me all over town. When I want you, I'll come to that damn boat and get you. Now get in that cab before I throw you in. I'll see you tomorrow night. Maybe."

"You go to hell." She eluded him and turned on me, asking with incredible innocence: "What did I ever do to you ?" Then she was running past us toward the beach, her sobs drifting back to haunt me like a forlorn melody.

What had she ever done to me? And what had I just done? In order to degrade her for the crime of being white I had sunk to the gutter. Suddenly Glenda was just another woman, vulnerable and lonely, like me.

We were sick, sick, sick. All fucked up. I had thought only Gregory was hung up in his love-hate, black-white syndrome, decades of suppressed hatred having sickened his soul. But I was tainted, too. I had forgotten my own misery long enough to inflict it on another woman who was only trying to ease her loneliness by making it with a soul brother. Was I jealous because she was able to function as a woman where I couldn't, because she realized that a man is a man, color be damned, while I was crucified on my anti-white-man cross? What if she were going black trying to repent for some ancient Nordic sin? How else could she atone except with the gift of herself? And if some black brother wanted to help a chick off her lily-white pedestal, he was entitled to that freedom, and it was none of my damned business anyway.

"Let's go, baby," Gregory said, tucking my arm under his.

The black bastard. I didn't even like the ugly ape. I backed away from him. "Leave me alone," I screamed. "Goddammit, just leave me alone!"

For a moment we were all frozen into an absurd fresco—Alison, Dorothy, and the two boys looking at me in shocked disbelief, Edwin hiding behind a nonchalant smoke screen, Gregory off balance and confused, reaching out toward me.

I moved first, toward Edwin, but I had slammed that door behind me. He laughed, a mirthless sound in the stillness. He knew.I had forsaken him, but at least not for Gregory.

Then I was running down the beach looking for Glenda, hot tears of shame burning my face. How could I have been such a bitch? But the white beach, shimmering in the moonlight, was empty. And once again, I was alone.

Mom Luby and the Social Worker

P uddin' and I been livin' with Mom Luby three years, ever since our mother
died. We like it fine. But when Mom Luby took us down to the Welfare,
we thought our happy days were over and our troubles about to begin.

"Chirren," she said that day, "I got to get some of this State Aid so I can
give you everything you need. Shoes for you, Elijah, and dresses for Puddin'
now she's startin' school. And lunch money and carfare and stuff like that. But
the only way I can get it is to say I'm your mother. So don't mess up my lie."

Mom Luby is old as Santa Claus, maybe older, with hair like white cotton
and false teeth that hurt so much she takes them out and gums her food. But
she's strong as a young woman and twice as proud. Much too proud to say she's
our grandmother, which is something the Welfare people might believe.

So we went down there scared that morning, Puddin' holding tight onto
both our hands. But we was lucky. The lady behind the desk didn't even look at
us, and we got out of that gloomy old State Building safe and free. Man! Was I
glad to get back to Division Street where people don't ask questions about your
business.

First published in *Guests in the Promised Land* by Kristin Hunter. New York: Charles
Scribner's Sons, 1968

When we got home, a whole bunch of people was waiting for Mom to let them in the speakeasy she runs in the back room. Jake was there, and Sissiemae, and Bobo and Walter and Lucas and Mose and Zerline. They are regular customers who come every evening to drink the corn liquor Mom gets from down South and eat the food she fixes, gumbo and chicken wings and ribs and potato salad and greens.

Bobo picked Puddin' up to see how much she weighed (a lot), until she hollered to be let down. Jake gave me a quarter to take his shoes down to Gumby's Fantastic Shoe Shine Parlor and get them shined and keep the change. We let the people in the front door and through the red curtain that divides the front room from the back. Soon they were settled around the big old round table with a half-gallon jar of corn. Then Sissiemae and Lucas wanted chicken wings, and I had to collect the money while Mom heated them up on the stove. There was so much to do, I didn't pay no attention to the tapping on the front door.

But then it came again, louder, like a woodpecker working on a tree.

"Elijah," Mom says, "run see who it is trying to chip a hole in that door. If it be the police, tell them I'll see them Saturday."

But it wasn't the cops, who come around every Saturday night to get their money and drink some of Mom's corn and put their big black shoes up on the table. It was a little brownskin lady with straightened hair and glasses and black high-top shoes. She carried a big leather envelope and was dressed all in dark blue.

"Good afternoon," she says. "I am Miss Rushmore of the Department of Child Welfare, Bureau of Family Assistance. Is Mrs. Luby at home?"

"I am she," says Mom. "Never been nobody else. Come in, honey, and set yourself down. Take off them shoes, they do look like real corn-crushers to me."

"No thank you," says Miss Rushmore. She sits on the edge of one of Mom's chairs and starts pulling papers out of the envelope. "This must be Elijah."

"Yes ma'am," I say.

"And where is Arlethia?"

"Taking her nap," says Mom, with a swat of the broom at the middle of the curtain, which Puddin' was peeking through. She's five and fat, and she loves to hang around grownups. Especially when they eating.

Mom hit the curtain with the broom again, and Puddin' ran off. The lady didn't even notice. She was too busy peeking under the lids of the pots on the stove.

"Salt pork and lima beans," she says. "Hardly a proper diet for growing children."

"Well," says Mom, "when i get me some of this State Aid, maybe I can afford to get them canned vegetables and box cereal. Meanwhile you welcome to what we have."

The lady acted like she didn't hear that. She just wrinkled up her nose like she smelled something bad.

"First," she says, "we must have a little talk about your budget. Do you understand the importance of financial planning?"

"Man arranges and God changes," says Mom. "When I got it, I spends it, when I don't, I do without."

"That," says the lady, "is precisely the attitude I am here to correct." She pulls out a big yellow sheet of paper. "Now this is our Family Budget Work Sheet. What is your rent?"

"I ain't paid it in so long I forgot," Mom says. Which set me in a fit because everybody but this dumb lady knows Mom owns the house. Behind her back Mom gave me a whack that stopped my giggles.

The lady sighed. "We'll get to the budget later," she says. "First, there are some questions you left blank today. How old were you when Elijah was born?"

"Thirty-two," says Mom.

"And he is now thirteen, which would make you forty-five," says the lady.

"Thirty-eight," says Mom without batting an eye.

"I'll put down forty-five," says the lady, giving Mom a funny look. "No doubt your hard life has aged you beyond your years. Now, who is the father, and where is he?"

"Lemme see," says Mom, twisting a piece of her hair. "I ain't seen Mr. Luby since 1942. He was a railroad man, you see, and one time he just took a train out of here and never rode back."

"1942," Miss Rushmore wrote on the paper. And then said, "But that's impossible!"

"The dear Lord do teach us," says Mom, "that nothing in life is impossible if we just believe enough."

"Hey, Mom, we're out of corn!" cries Lucas from the back room.

Miss Rushmore looked very upset. "Why," she says, "you've got a man in there."

"Sure do sound like it, don't it?" Mom says. "Sure do. You got one too, honey?"

"That's my business," says the lady.

"I was just trying to be sociable," says Mom pleasantly. "You sure do seem interested in mine."

I ran back there and fetched another mason jar of corn from the shed kitchen. I told Lucas and Bobo and them to be quiet. Which wasn't going to be easy, cause them folks get good and loud when they get in a card game. I also dragged Puddin' away from the potato salad bowl, where she had stuck both her hands, and brought her in the front room with me. She was bawling. The lady gave her a weak smile.

"Now," Mom says. "About these shoes and school clothes."

"I am not sure," Miss Rushmore says, "that you can get them. There is something wrong in this house that I have not yet put my finger on. But this is what you do. First you fill out Form 905, which you get at the Bureau of Family Assistance, room 1203. Then you call the Division of Child Welfare and make an appointment with Mr. Jenkins. He will give you Form 202 to fill out. Then you go to the fifth floor, third corridor on the left, turn right, go in the second door. You stand at the first desk and fill out Form 23-B, Requisition for Clothing Allowance. You take *that* to Building Three, room 508, third floor, second door, fourth desk and then—"

"Lord," Mom says, "By the time we get clothes for these chirren, they will have done outgrowed them."

"I don't make the rules," the lady says.

"Well, honey," says Mom, "I ain't got time to do all that, not right now. Tonight I got to go deliver a baby. Then I got to visit a sick old lady and work on her with some herbs. Then I got to go down to the courthouse and get a young man out of jail. He's not a bad boy, he's just been keepin' bad company. *Then* I got to preach a funeral."

The lady looked at Mom like she was seeing a spirit risen from the dead. "But you can't do those things!" she says.

But I happen to know Mom Luby *can*. She's a midwife and a herb doctor and an ordained minister of the Gospel, besides running a place to eat and drink after hours. And she wouldn't need Welfare for us if people would only pay her sometimes.

Mom says, "Honey, just come along and watch me."

She picked up her old shopping bag full of herbs and stuff. Miss Rushmore picked up her case and followed like somebody in a trance. Mom has that effect on people sometimes.

They were gone about two hours, and me and Puddin' had a good time eating and joking and looking into everybody's card hands.

I was surprised to see Mom bring Miss Rushmore straight into the back room when they got back. She sat her down at the table and poured her a drink of corn. To tell the truth, that lady looked like she needed it. Her glasses was crooked, and her shoes were untied, and her hair had come loose form its pins. She looked kind of pretty, but lost.

"Mrs. Luby," she said after a swallow of corn, "you don't need my help."

"Ain't it the truth," says Mom.

"I came here to help you solve your problems. But now I don't know where to begin."

"What problems?" Mom asks.

"You are raising these children in an unhealthy atmosphere. I am not even sure they are yours. And you are practicing law, medicine, and the ministry without a license. I simply can't understand it."

"Can't understand what, honey?"

The lady sighed. "How you got more done in two hours than I ever get done in two years."

"You folks oughta put me on the payroll," says Mom with a chuckle.

"We can't," says Miss Rushmore. "You're not qualified."

Lucas started laughing, and Bobo joined in, and then we all laughed, Mose and Zerline and Jake and Sissiemae and Puddin' and me. We laughed so hard we rocked the room and shook the house and laughed that social worker right out the door.

"She got a point though," Mom says after we finished laughing. "You need an education to fill out forty pieces of paper for one pair of shoes. Never you mind, chirren. We'll make out fine, like we always done. Cut the cards, Bobo. Walter, deal."

The Library

A lot of folks ask me about that and I really haven't thought about it a whole lot. You know how you just go along and try not to get on folks' nerves and never think about it much anymore 'cause it'll just make you unhappy. When I was real little nobody much was talking bout Black is Beautiful and Black Power and Think Black and stuff. Nobody even talked about White Power or how the system could maybe be wrong and how much it hurts to be lynched and burned and to lose your father in a war that you don't even understand way away from home and then the government in Washington gives you a couple of thousand dollars for him but he won't be back to play with you or even to fuss at your mommy. No, when I was a little girl, we just were unhappy by ourselves and we tried not to let anybody know how unhappy we were 'cause America was the land of the brave and we wanted to be the bravest of them all. So we never talked about our History at all except sometimes during Brotherhood Week or Negro History Week and sometimes, if you lived in a hometown like mine, we celebrated Emancipation Day and THEY let us go to WhiteWash, the big amusement park.

I would hear Mommy and Aunt Bertha saying that Negroes don't know nothing about themselves, so I wasn't completely dumb about us 'cause I knew that I didn't know anything and that's really a good thing to know, I think. And once during a really phosphoresce period—I think that's what they called it,

First published in *Brothers and Sisters,* edited by A. Adoff. New York: Macmillan, 1970

you know, during The Teapot Dome Scandal and all—there was this man named Andrew Carnegie who gave lots of money for libraries 'cause he had been dumb once himself and he wanted everybody to have an equal chance like he didn't have. In my hometown the Carnegie library is for COLORED ONLY so Mommy took me there one day after I was pestering her to tell me something about Negroes. The first thing the librarian did was to give us a book called *Up from Slavery* which was by a very great man named Booker T. Washington. He pulled himself up by practically nothing at all to be the biggest and most important Negro in maybe the whole world. And he told us not to fool with politics and stuff but to lay our burden down, I mean to put our loaves afloat—that is, to cast the first stone where we were and the Southern people would be good to us and understand that we were just like their children. My mommy liked Dr. Washington very much and was a truly great follower of his, 'cause she worked two jobs every day and a half a day on Sunday. Dr. Washington said if we worked really hard and didn't get on anybody's nerves we would soon live in peace and comfort. When I read him and the big speech he gave in Atlanta, Georgia, I just laughed and laughed 'cause I knew how hard my mommy worked and we not only didn't have nothing but we didn't have no peace! And honest, we never meant to get on anybody's nerves; but as Mommy would say, Folks are just naturally mean and some folks are just naturally meaner than others. So no matter how hard we tried we just never had no peace.

I went back to the library by myself and told the librarian that I didn't like that book 'cause he didn't tell the whole truth. I mean, if it would've been the whole truth we would've been living in peace and comfort 'cause not Mommy or Daddy or even Gram and Granpapa ever bothered anybody except for that time Deacon Wright stole the church money and you couldn't say we were wrong for getting upset 'bout folks mistreating God! Or folks mistreating folks for that matter. I heard Mommy talking 'bout Daddy going over to fight Hitler for rights that we didn't have and Double V and all 'cause war is awful and if we can't get something good out of a war we shouldn't fight anyway. That's what Mommy said. So I went and got a book by a real smart man named Dr. DuBois. He said we must fight for our manhood rights and learn about politics and Africa 'cause these were the most important things in the world. He said Dr. Washington had political power already and was just being selfish if he didn't let other Negroes get political power. Dr. Dubois started The National Association for Colored People to Advance By and then THEY got mad at him and he left home and lived in Africa. I liked him a lot but we still were in a lot of trouble 'cause we were trying to prove by science methods that we were human and it doesn't seem the sort of thing that we can prove. I mean, how can you prove that you are human and all when you are there talking to folks and they are talking to you? Plus they sure passed a lot of laws that said we couldn't do stuff that only humans could do. Like Dr. Frederick Douglass said, why would they pass a law saying that we couldn't marry them if we weren't human? 'Cause a bull couldn't marry them, could he? I mean, not to really live with them and raise a family and go to church and all.

So I wanted to know lots more about us and I asked the librarian what she thought would be real good. She looked at me real hard, then shook her head...then looked real hard again and scratched her head and started mumbling 'bout what an old fool she is. Then told me to come back about closing time. I went down to the drugstore and bought a *Screen Stories* and went back to the lawn area and read it until it was time to see her. When I went back in she asked if anyone had seen me come in. I said no. Then she closed up the library and looked around again. She asked me if I would promise not to tell anyone what she was going to show me. And I promised and crossed my heart three times while facing east. So we went down to the basement where Mommy's Lodge used to hold meetings. She had a flashlight so that we could see. Right there where the TV sat was a door. She took the key off the wall and we went into the door. She told me the door was a part of the underground railroad which was not in use at this time. We walked about five minutes in the tunnel and I must admit it was a bit scary. I had read about Harriet Tubman, how she was my friend and all but it was still cold and scary down there. Then we came to another door and the librarian stopped and looked at me and asked me again if I would promise not to tell what she was about to show me. I swore on the Bible that Dr. Sweet Daddy Grace once used and she started chanting:

> *Ole Nat Turner still alive*
> *Got him one, wants to get five*
>
> *Denmark Vesey sitting nifty*
> *Got one hundred wants one fifty*
>
> *Gabriel, Gabriel, you our man*
> *If you don't get them Garvey can*

And all the while she was talking her hair was turning fuzzy on her head and wasn't long like it had been, and all the makeup was disappearing from her face and the dress she had on turned to a gunny-sack dress and then to a long gown that looked real strange to me. Her shoes went away and she looked like an African or something. Now, I really did want another book to read but I was scared about all the funny things that were going on and I was getting ready to run home. Just then the door opened and she pushed me inside. The room was huge like a museum and all around on the walls were books, higher than I would ever reach. She told me this was the Black Museum that held *The Great Black Book*. Most of the books the people didn't even know about 'cause they wouldn't be published 'til much later when we were ready for them. Some others had already been outside but THEY had tried to destroy them and books have feelings like everybody else. So they had come home 'til we were ready for them. The librarian had shown this room to only one other person and that's the one we call Crazy Butch, 'cause he just mumbles to himself all the time and people don't understand him. It gave me a real queasy feeling to be there. There were books about Africa and Asia and South America and China. There were books by Ronald Fair and John Killens and Lerone Bennett and LeRoi Jones. Ed Bullins and Larry Neal and Etheridge Knight and Diane Oliver and lots and lots of people. There were big picture books with lots of maps and there were books with lots of writing without anything to see but the words. There were children's books and grown-up books and books about cooking the kind of foods we like to eat. And just every book in the world that we would ever write. And then there was *The Great Black Book*. I asked if I could touch it. It was taller than me and it sat all by itself in a corner on the floor. I wiped my hands on my dress and touched it once. It opened to the year when I was born and there was everything that had happened to us in that year. It didn't say anything about me but I still liked it. Then it flipped ten years and showed everything that was happening then. I started to turn to see what would happen in the future but the librarian stopped me to warn me. If you look in the future of *The Great Black Book* wherever you are in the real world will be where you stay. Like if you are ten years old then you will always act like a ten-year-old on the outside even though you could know what will happen in the next century. I thought about Crazy Butch for a little minute and I knew what was wrong with him. It's because he knows everything and nobody else understands that. I guess that's how come people say too much learning will drive you crazy. But I wanted to know 'cause I think it's very important that you know as much as you can. Plus, when the year gets to where you stopped reading in the future all of a sudden you will be making sense on the outside and people will quit laughing at you. So I read all the way up to 1970 and boy! You should see what will happen. I read about Floyd McKissick and a little boy named Stokely Carmichael. I read about The Black, Shining Prince and Rap Brown. I read all about how they would help us a whole lot. And then there are these people called Vietnamese who will fight with the US and a little puppet called Tshombe who will have to run a lot 'cause he won't act nice at home. Plus there are some really funny stories about the 35th President and how the 36th got to take his place. Boy! You should see those. But I can't talk anymore 'cause it's time for us to pack up and move on. I don't mind being in a circus, I guess, but I really wish they'd let me out of this cage every now and then.

After Saturday Night Comes Sunday

*I*t had all started at the bank. She wuzn't sure, but she thot it had. At that crowded bank where she had gone to clear up the mistaken notion that she wuz $300.00 overdrawn in her checking account.

Sandy had moved into that undersized/low expectation of niggahs/being able to save anything bank/meanly. She wuz tired of people charging her fo they own mistakes. She had seen it wid her own eyes, five checks: four fo $50 the other one fo $100 made out to an Anthony Smith. It wuz Winston's signature. Her stomach jumped as she added and re-added the figures. Finally she dropped the pen and looked up at the business/suited/man sitten across from her wid crossed legs and eyes. And as she called him faggot in her mind, watermelon tears gathered round her big eyes and she just sat.

Someone had come for her at the bank. A friend of Winston's helped her to his car. It wuz the wite/dude who followed Winston constantly wid his eyes. Begging eyes she had once called em, half in jest, half seriously. They wuz begging now, along wid his mouth, begging Sandy to talk. But she cudn't. The words had gone away, gotten lost, drowned by the warm/april/rain dropping

First published in *Black World* 20 (Vol. 5: March 1971)

in on her as she watched the car move down the long/unbending/street. It was her first Spring in Indianapolis. She wondered if it wud be beautiful.

He wuz holding her. Crying in her ear. Loud cries, almost louder than the noise already turning in her head. Yeh. He sed between the cries that he had messed up the money. He had…he had…oh babee. *C'mon Sandy and talk. Talk to me. Help me, babee. Help me to tell you what I got to tell you for both our sakes.* He stretched her out on the green/oversized/couch that sat out from the wall like some displaced trailer waiting to be parked.

I'm hooked, he sed. I'm hooked again on stuff. It's not like befo though when I wuz 17 and just beginning. This time it's different. I mean it has to do now wid me and all my friends who are still on junk. You see I got out of the joint and looked around and saw those brothers who are my friends all still on the stuff and I cried inside. I cried long tears for some beautiful dudes who didn't know how the man had 'em by they balls. Baby I felt so sorry for them and they wuz so turned around that one day over to Tony's crib I got high wid 'em. That's all babee. I know I shouldn't have done that. You and the kids and all. But they wuz dudes I wuz in the joint wid. My brothers who wuz still unaware. I can git clean, babee. I mean, I don't have a long jones. I ain't been on it too long. I can kick now. Tomorrow. You just say it. Give me the word/sign that you understand, forgive me for being one big asshole and I'll start kicking tomorrow. For you babee. I know I been laying some heavy stuff on you. Spending money we ain't even got—I'll git a job too next week— staying out all the time. Hitting you fo telling me the truth 'bout myself. My actions. Babee, it's you I love in spite of my crazy actions. It's you I love. Don't nobody else mean to me what you do. It's just that I been acting crazy but I know I can't keep on keepin' on this way and keep you and the children. Give me a whole lot of slack during this time and I can kick it, babee. I love you. You so good to me. The meanest thing that done ever happened to me. You the best thing that ever happened to me in all of my 38 years and I'll take better care of you. Say something Sandy. Say you understand it all. Say you forgive me. At least that, babee.

He raised her head from the couch and kissed her. It was a short cooling kiss. Not warm. Not long. A binding kiss. She opened her eyes and looked at him, and the bare room that somehow now complemented their lives, and she started to cry again. And as he grabbed her and rocked her, she spoke fo the first time since she had told that wite/collar/man in the bank that the bank was wrong.

The-the-the-the bab-bab-bab-ies. Ar-ar-ar-are th-th-th-they o-o-okay? Oh my god. I'm stuttering. Stuttering, she thot. Just like when I wuz little. Stop talking. Stop talking girl. Write what you have to say. Just like you used to when you wuz little and you got tired of people staring at you while you pushed words out of an unaccommodating mouth. Yeh. That was it, she thot. Stop talking and write what you have to say. Nod yo/head to all of this madness. But rest yo/head and use yo/hands till you git it all straight again.

She pointed to her bag and he handed it to her. She took out a pen and notebook and wrote that she wuz tired, that her head hurt and wuz spinning, and that she wanted to sleep fo awhile. She turned and held his face full of little sores where he had picked fo ingrown hairs the nite befo. She kissed them and let her tongue move over his lips, wetting them. He smiled at her and sed he wud git her a coupla sleeping pills. He wud also pick up some dollies fo himself cuz Saturday was kicking time fo him. As he went out the door he turned and sed, *Lady, you some lady. I'm a lucky M.F. to have found you.* She watched him from the window and the sun hit the gold of his dashiki and made it bleed yellow raindrops.

She must have dozed. She knew it wuz late. It was dark outside. The room was dark also and she wondered if he had come in and gone upstairs where the children were napping. What a long nap the boys were taking. They wud be up all nite tonite if they didn't wake up soon. Maybe she shud wake them up, but she decided against it. Her body wuz still tired and she heard footsteps on the porch.

His voice was light and cracked a little as he explained his delay. He wuz high. She knew it. He sounded like he sounded on the phone when he called her late in the nite from some loud place and complimented her fo understanding his late hours. She hadn't understood them, she just hated to be a complaining bitch. He had no sleeping pills, but he had gotten her something as good. A morphine tablet. She watched his face as he explained that she cud swallow it or pop it into the skin. He sed it worked better if you stuck it in yo/arm. As he took the tablet out of the cellophane paper of his cigarettes, she closed her eyes and fo a moment, she thot she heard someone crying outside the house. She opened her eyes.

His body hung loose as he knelt by the couch. He took from his pocket a manila envelope. It had little spots of blood on it and as he undid the rubber hands, she saw two needles, a black top wid two pieces of dirty, wite cotton balls in it. She knew this wuz what he used to git high wid.

I-I-I-I-I don-don-don-don't wa-wa-want none o-o-o-of that stuff, ma-a-a-a-a-n. Ain't th-th-th-that do-do-do-dope, too? I-I-I-I-I just just just just wa-wa-wa-nnnt-ted to sleep. I'm o-o-o-kay now. She picked up her notebook and pen and started to write again.

I slept while you wuz gone, man. I drifted on off as I looked for you to walk up the steps. I don't want that stuff. Give me a cold beer though, if there's any in the house. I'll drink that. But no stuff man, she wrote. I'm yo/woman. You shudn't be giving me any of that stuff. Throw the pill away. We don't need it. You don't need it any mo. You gon kick and we gon move on. Keep on being baddDDD togetha. I'll help you, man, cuz I know you want to kick. Flush it down the toilet! You'll start kicking tomorrow and I'll get a babysitter and take us fo a long drive in the country and we'll move on the grass and make it move wid us, cuz we'll be full of living/alive/thots and we'll stop and make love in the middle of nowhere, and the grass will stop its wintry/brown/chants and become green as our Black bodies sing. Heave. Love each other. Throw that stuff away, man, cuz we got more important/beautiful/things to do.

As he read the note his eyes looked at hers in a half/clear/way and he got up and walked slowly to the john. She heard the toilet flushing and she heard the refrigerator door open and close. He brought two cold beers and, as she opened hers, she sat up to watch him rock back and forth in the rocking chair. And his eyes became small and sad as he sed, half-jokingly, *Hope I don't regret throwing that stuff in the toilet,* and he leaned back and smiled sadly as he drank his beer. She turned the beer can up to her lips and let the cold evening foam wet her mouth and drown the gathering stutters of her mind.

The sound of cries from the second floor made her move. As she climbed the stairs she waved to him. But his eyes were still closed. He wuz somewhere else, not in this house she thot. He wuz somewhere else, floating among past dreams she had never seen or heard him talk about. As she climbed the stairs, the boys' screams grew louder. *Wow. Them boys got some strong lungs,* she thot. And smiled.

It wuz 11:30 and she had just put the boys in their cribs. She heard them sucking on their bottles, working hard at nourishing themselves. She knew the youngest twin wud finish his bottle first and cry out fo more milk befo he slept. She laughed out loud. He sho cud grease.

He wuz in the bathroom. She knocked on the door, but he sed for her not to come in. She stood outside the door, not moving, and knocked again. *Go and turn on the TV,* he said, *I'll be out in a few minutes.*

It wuz 30 minutes later when he came out. His walk wuz much faster than befo and his voice wuz high, higher than the fear moving over her body. She ran to him, threw her body against him and held on. She kissed him hard and moved her body 'gainst him til he stopped and paid attention to her movements. They fell to the floor. She felt his weight on her as she moved and kissed him. She wuz feeling good and she cudn't understand why he stopped. In the midst of pulling off her dress he stopped and took out a cigarette and lit it while she undressed to her bra and panties. She felt naked all of a sudden and sat down and drew her legs up against her chest and closed her eyes. She reached for a cigarette and lit it.

He stretched out next to her. She felt very ashamed, as if she had made him do something wrong. She wuz glad that she cudn't talk cuz that way she didn't have to explain. He ran his hand up and down her legs and touched her soft wet places.

It's just, babee, that this stuff kills any desire for THAT! I mean, I want you and all that but I can't quite git it up to perform. He lit another cigarette and sat up. *Babee, you sho know how to pick 'em. I mean, wuz you born under an unlucky star or sumthin'? First, you had a nigguh who preferred a rich/wite/woman to you and Blackness. Now you have a junkie who can't even satisfy you when you need satisfying.* And his laugh wuz harsh as he sed again, *You sho know how to pick 'em, lady.* She didn't know what else to do so she smiled a nervous smile that made her feel, remember times when she wuz little and she had stuttered thru a sentence and the listener had acknowledged her accomplishment wid a smile and all she cud do was smile back.

He turned and held her and sed, *Stay up wid me tonite, babee. I got all these memories creeping in on me. Bad ones. They's the things that make kicking hard, you know. You begin remembering all the mean things you've done to yo/family/friends who dig you. I'm remembering now all the heavee things I done laid on you in such a short time. You hardly had a chance to catch yo/breath when I'd think of sum new game to lay on you. Help me, Sandy. Listen to my talk. Hold my hand when I git too sad. Laugh at my fears that keep poppin' out on me like some childhood disease. Be my vaccine, babee. I need you. Don't ever leave me, babee, cuz I'll never have a love like you again. I'll never have another woman again if you leave me.* He picked up her hands and rubbed them in his palms as he talked, and she listened until he finally slept and morning crept in through the shades and covered them.

He threw away his works when he woke up. He came over to where she wuz feeding the boys and kissed her and walked out to the backyard and threw the manila envelope into the middle can. He came back inside, smiled and took a dollie wid a glass of water, and fell on the couch.

Sandy put the boys in their strollers in the backyard where she cud watch them as she cleaned the kitchen. She saw Snow, their big/wite/dog, come round the corner of the house to sit in front of them. They babbled words to him but he sat still guarding them from the backyard/evils of the world.

She moved fast in the house, had a second cup of coffee, called their babysitter and finished straightening up the house. She put on a short dress which showed her legs, and she felt good about her black/hairy legs. She laughed as she remembered that the young brothers on her block used to call her a big/legged/momma as she walked in her young ways.

They never made the country. Their car refused to start and Winston wuz too sick to push it to the filling station for a jump. So they walked to the park. He pushed her in the swing and she pumped herself higher and higher and higher till he told her to stop. She let the swing come slowly to a stop and she jumped out and hit him on the behind and ran. She heard him gaining on her and she tried to dodge him but they fell laughing and holding each other. She looked at him and her eyes sed, *I wish you cud make love to me man.* As she laughed and pushed him away she thot, *but just you wait til you all right Winston, I'll give you a workout you'll never forget,* and they got up and walked till he felt badly and went home.

He stayed upstairs while she cooked. When she went upstairs to check on him, he was curled up, wrapped tight as a child in his mother's womb. She wiped his head and body full of sweat and kissed him and thought how beautiful he wuz and how proud she wuz of him. She massaged his back and went away. He called fo her as she wuz feeding the children and asked for the wine. He needed somethin' else to relieve this saturday/nite/pain that was creeping up on him. He looked bad, she thot, and raced down the stairs and brought him the sherry. He thanked her as she went out the door and she curtsied, smiled and sed, *Any ol time, man.* She noticed she hadn't stuttered and felt good.

By the time she got back upstairs he was moaning and turning back and forth on the bed. He had drunk half the wine in the bottle, now he wuz getting up to bring it all up. When she came back up to the room he sed he was cold, so she got another blanket for him. He wuz still cold, so she took off her clothes and got under the covers wid him and rubbed her body against him. She wuz scared. She started to sing a Billie Holiday song. Yeh. God bless the child that's got his own. She cried in between the lyrics as she felt his big frame trembling and heaving. *Oh god,* she thot, *am I doing the right thing?* He soon quieted down and got up to go to the toilet. She closed her eyes as she waited fo him. She closed her eyes and felt the warmth of the covers creeping over her. She remembered calling his name as she drifted off to sleep. She remembered how quiet everything finally wuz.

One of the babies woke her up. She went into the room, picked up his bottle and got him more milk. It wuz while she wuz handing him the milk that she heard the silence. She ran to their bedroom and turned on the light. The bed wuz empty. She ran down the stairs and turned on the lights. He was gone. She saw her purse on the couch. Her wallet wuz empty. Nothing was left. She opened the door and went out on the porch, and she remembered the lights were on and that she wuz naked. But she stood fo a moment looking out at the flat/Indianapolis/street and she stood and let the late/nite/air touch her body and she turned and went inside.

Alice Walker

Nineteen Fifty-Five

1955

*T*he car is a brandnew red Thunderbird convertible, and it's passed the house more than once. It slows down real slow now, and stops at the curb. An older gentleman dressed like a Baptist deacon gets out on the side near the house, and a young fellow who looks about sixteen gets out on the driver's side. They are white, and I wonder what in the world they doing in this neighborhood.

Well, I say to J.T., put your shirt on, anyway, and let me clean these glasses offa the table.

We had been watching the ballgame on TV. I wasn't actually watching, I was sort of daydreaming, with my foots up in J.T.'s lap.

I seen 'em coming on up the walk, brisk, like they coming to sell something, and then they rung the bell, and J.T. declined to put on a shirt but instead disappeared into the bedroom where the other television is. I turned down the one in the living room; I figured I'd be rid of these two double quick and J.T. could come back out again.

Are you Gracie Mae Still? asked the old guy, when I opened the door and put my hand on the lock inside the screen.

First published in *Ms.* 9 (March 1981)

And I don't need to buy a thing, said I.

What makes you think we're sellin'? he asks, in that hearty Southern way that makes my eyeballs ache.

Well, one way or another and they're inside the house and the first thing the young fellow does is raise the TV a couple of decibels. He's about five feet nine, sort of womanish looking, with real dark white skin and a red pouting mouth. His hair is black and curly and he looks like a Loosianna creole.

About one of your songs, says the deacon. He is maybe sixty, with white hair and beard, white silk shirt, black linen suit, black tie and black shoes. His cold gray eyes look like they're sweating.

One of my songs?

Traynor here just loves your songs. Don't you, Traynor? He nudges Traynor with his elbow. Traynor blinks, says something I can't catch in a pitch I don't register.

The boy learned to sing and dance livin' round you people out in the country. Practically cut his teeth on you.

Traynor looks up at me and bites his thumbnail.

I laugh.

Well, one way or another they leave with my agreement that they can record one of my songs. The deacon writes me a check for five hundred dollars, the boy grunts his awareness of the transaction, and I am laughing all over myself by the time I rejoin J.T.

Just as I am snuggling down beside him though I hear the front door bell going off again.

Forgit his hat? asks J.T.

I hope not, I say.

The deacon stands there leaning on the door frame and once again I'm thinking of those sweaty-looking eyeballs of his. I wonder if sweat makes your eyeballs pink because his are sure pink. Pink and gray and it strikes me that nobody I'd care to know is behind them.

I forgot one little thing, he says pleasantly. I forgot to tell you Traynor and I would like to buy up all of those records you made of the song. I tell you we sure do love it.

Well, love it or not, I'm not so stupid as to let them do that without making 'em pay. So I says, Well, that's gonna cost you. Because, really, that song never did sell all that good, so I was glad they was going to buy it up. But on the other hand, them two listening to my song by themselves, and nobody else getting to hear me sing it, give me a pause.

Well, one way or another the deacon showed me where I would come out ahead on any deal he had proposed so far. Didn't I give you five hundred dollars? he asked. What white man—and don't even need to mention colored—would give you more? We buy up all your records of that particular song: first, you git royalties. Let me ask you, how much you sell that song for in the first place? Fifty dollars? A hundred, I say. And no royalties from it yet, right? Right. Well, when we buy up all of them records you gonna git royalties. And that's gonna make all them race record shops sit up and take notice of Gracie Mae Still. And they gonna push all them other records of yourn they got. And you no doubt will become one of the big name colored recording artists. And then we can offer you another five hundred dollars for letting us do all this for you. And by God you'll be sittin' pretty! You can go out and buy you the kind of outfit a star should have. Plenty sequins and yards of red satin.

I had done unlocked the screen when I saw I could get some more money out of him. Now I held it wide open while he squeezed through the opening between me and the door. He whipped out another piece of paper and I signed it.

He sort of trotted out to the car and slid in beside Traynor, whose head was back against the seat. They swung around in a u-turn in front of the house and then they was gone.

J.T. was putting his shirt on when I got back to the bedroom. Yankees beat the Orioles 10–6, he said. I believe I'll drive out to Paschal's pond and go fishing. Wanta go?

While I was putting on my pants J.T. was holding the two checks.

I'm real proud of a woman that can make cash money without leavin' home, he said. And I said *Umph.* Because we met on the road with me singing in first one little low-life jook after another, making ten dollars a night for myself if I was lucky, and sometimes bringin' home nothing but my life. And J.T. just loved them times. The way I was fast and flashy and always on the go from one town to another. He loved the way my singin' made the dirt farmers cry like babies and the womens shout Honey, hush! But that's mens. They loves any style to which you can get 'em accustomed.

1956

My little grandbaby called me one night on the phone: Little Mama, Little Mama, there's a white man on the television singing one of your songs! Turn on channel 5.

Lord, if it wasn't Traynor. Still looking half asleep from the neck up, but kind of awake in a nasty way from the waist down. He wasn't doing too bad with my song either, but it wasn't just the song the peope in the audience was screeching and screaming over, it was that nasty little jerk he was doing from the waist down.

Well, Lord have mercy, I said, listening to him. If I'da closed my eyes, it could have been me. He had followed every turning of my voice, side streets, avenues, red lights, train crossings and all. It gave me a chill.

Everywhere I went I heard Traynor singing my song, and all the little white girls just eating it up. I never had so many ponytails switched across my line of vision in my life. They was so *proud.* He was a *genius.*

Well, all that year I was trying to lose weight anyway and that and high blood pressure and sugar kept me pretty well occupied. Traynor had made a smash from a song of mine, I still had seven hundred dollars of the original one thousand dollars in the bank, and I felt if I could just bring my weight down, life would be sweet.

1957

I lost ten pounds in 1956. That's what I give myself for Christmas. And J.T. and me and the children and their friends and grandkids of all description had just finished dinner—over which I had put on nine and a half of my lost ten—when who should appear at the front door but Traynor. Little Mama, Little Mama! It's that white man who sings _____ _____ _____. The children didn't call it my song anymore. Nobody did. It was funny how that happened. Traynor and the deacon had bought up all my records, true, but on his record he had put "written by Gracie Mae Still." But that was just another name on the label, like "produced by Apex Records."

On the TV he was inclined to dress like the deacon told him. But now he looked presentable.

Merry Christmas, said he.

And same to you, Son.

I don't know why I called him Son. Well, one way or another they're all our sons. The only requirement is that they be younger than us. But then again, Traynor seemed to be aging by the minute.

You looks tired, I said. Come on in and have a glass of Christmas cheer.

J.T. ain't never in his life been able to act decent to a white man he wasn't working for, but he poured Traynor a glass of bourbon and water, then he took all the children and grandkids and friends and whatnot out to the den. After while I heard Traynor's voice singing the song, coming from the stereo console. It was just the kind of Christmas present my kids would consider cute.

I looked at Traynor, complicit. But he looked like it was the last thing in the world he wanted to hear. His head was pitched forward over his lap, his hands holding his glass and his elbows on his knees.

I done sung that song seem like a million times this year, he said. I sung it on the Grand Ole Opry, I sung it on the Ed Sullivan show. I sung it on Mike Douglas, I sung it at the Cotton Bowl, the Orange Bowl. I sung it at Festivals. I sung it at Fairs. I sung it overseas in Rome, Italy, and once in a submarine *underseas*. I've sung it and sung it, and I'm making forty thousand dollars a day offa it, and you know what, I don't have the faintest notion what that song means.

Whatchumean, what do it mean? It mean what is says. All I could think was: These suckers is making forty thousand a *day* offa my song and now they gonna come back and try to swindle me out of the original thousand.

It's just a song, I said. Cagey. When you fool around with a lot of no count mens you sing a bunch of 'em. I shrugged.

Oh, he said. Well. He started brightening up. I just come by to tell you I think you are a great singer.

He didn't blush, saying that. Just said it straight out.

And I brought you a little Christmas present too. Now you take this little box and you hold it until I drive off. Then you take it outside under that first streetlight back up the street aways in front of that green house. Then you open the box and see...Well, just *see*.

What had come over this boy, I wondered, holding the box. I looked out the window in time to see another white man come up and get in the car with him and then two more cars full of white mens start out behind him. They was all in long black cars that looked like a funeral procession.

Little Mama, Little Mama, what it is? One of my grandkids come running up and started pulling at the box. It was wrapped in gay Christmas paper—the thick, rich kind that it's hard to picture folks making just to throw away.

J.T. and the rest of the crowd followed me out the house, up the street to the streetlight and in front of the green house. Nothing was there but somebody's gold-grilled white Cadillac. Brandnew and most distracting. We got to looking at it so till I almost forgot the little box in my hand. While the others were busy making 'miration I carefully took off the paper and ribbon and folded them up and put them in my pants pocket. What should I see but a pair of genuine solid gold caddy keys.

Dangling the keys in front of everybody's nose, I unlocked the caddy, motioned for J.T. to git in on the other side, and us didn't come back home for two days.

1960

Well, the boy was sure nuff famous by now. He was still a mite shy of twenty but already they was calling him the Emperor of Rock and Roll.

Then what should happen but the draft.

Well, says J.T. There goes all this Emperor of Rock and Roll business.

But even in the army the womens was on him like white on rice. We watched it on the News.

Dear Gracie Mae [he wrote from Germany],

How you? Fine I hope as this leaves me doing real well. Before I come in the army I was gaining a lot of weight and gitting jittery from making all them dumb movies. But now I exercise and eat right and get plenty of rest. I'm more awake than I been in ten years.

I wonder if you are writing any more songs?

> *Sincerely,*
> *Traynor*

I wrote him back:

Dear Son,

We is all fine in the Lord's good grace and hope this finds you the same. J.T. and me be out all times of the day and night in that car you give me—which you know you didn't have to do. Oh, and I do appreciate the mink and the new self-cleaning oven. But if you send anymore stuff to eat from Germany I'm going to have to open up a store in the neighborhood just to get rid of it. Really, we have more than enough of everything. The Lord is good to us and we don't know Want.

Glad to here you is well and gitting your right rest. There ain't nothing like exercising to help that along. J.T. and me work some part of every day that we don't go fishing in the garden.

Well, so long Soldier.

> *Sincerely,*
> *Gracie Mae*

He wrote:

Dear Gracie Mae,

I hope you and J.T. like that automatic power tiller I had one of the stores back home send you. I went through a mountain of catalogs looking for it—I wanted something that even a woman can use.

I've been thinking about writing some songs of my own but every time I finish one it don't seem to be about nothing I've actually lived myself. My agent keeps sending me other people's songs but they just sound mooney. I can hardly git through 'em without gagging.

Everybody still loves that song of yours. They ask me all the time what do I think it means, really. I mean, they want to know just what I want to know. Where out of your life did it come from?

Sincerely,
Traynor

1968

I didn't see the boy for seven years. No. Eight. Because just about everybody was dead when I saw him again. Malcolm X, King, the president and his brother, and even J.T. J.T. died of a head cold. It just settled in his head like a block of ice, he said, and nothing we did moved it until one day he just leaned out the bed and died.

His good friend Horace helped me put him away, and then about a year later Horace and me started going together. We was sitting out on the front porch swing one summer night, dust-dark, and I saw this great procession of lights winding to a stop.

Holy Toledo! said Horace. (He's got a real sexy voice like Ray Charles.) Look *at* it. He meant the long line of flashy cars and the white men in white summer suits jumping out on the drivers' sides and standing at attention. With wings they could pass for angels, with hoods they could be the Klan.

Traynor comes waddling up the walk.

And suddenly I know what it is he could pass for. An Arab like the ones you see in storybooks. Plump and soft and with never a care about weight. Because with so much money, who cares? Traynor is almost dressed like someone from a storybook too. He has on, I swear, about ten necklaces. Two sets of bracelets on his arms, at least one ring on every finger, and some kind of shining buckles on his shoes, so that when he walks you get quite a few twinkling lights.

Gracie Mae, he says, coming up to give me a hug. J.T.

I explain that J.T. passed. That this is Horace.

Horace, he says, puzzled but polite, sort of rocking back on his heels, Horace.

That's it for Horace. He goes in the house and don't come back.

Looks like you and me is gained a few, I say.

He laughs. The first time I ever heard him laugh. It don't sound much like a laugh and I can't swear that it's better than no laugh a'tall.

He's gitting fat for sure, but he's still slim compared to me. I'll never see three hundred pounds again and I've just about said (excuse me) fuck it. I got to thinking about it one day an' I thought: aside from the fact that they say it's unhealthy, my fat ain't never been no trouble. Mens always have loved me. My kids ain't never complained. Plus they's fat. And fat like I is I looks distinguished. You see me coming and know somebody's *there*.

Gracie Mae, he says, I've come with a personal invitation to you to my house tomorrow for dinner. He laughed. What did it sound like? I couldn't place it. See them men out there? he asked me. I'm sick and tired of eating with them. They don't never have nothing to talk about. That's why I eat so much. But if you come to dinner tomorrow we can talk about the old days. You can tell me about that farm I bought you.

I sold it, I said.

You did?

Yeah, I said, I did. Just cause I said I liked to exercise by working in a garden didn't mean I wanted five hundred acres! Anyhow, I'm a city girl now. Raised in the country it's true. Dirt poor—the whole bit—but that's all behind me now.

Oh well, he said, I didn't mean to offend you.

We sat a few minutes listening to the crickets.

Then he said: You wrote that song while you was still on the farm, didn't you, or was it right after you left?

You had somebody spying on me? I asked.

You and Bessie Smith got into a fight over it once, he said.

You *is* been spying on me!

But I don't know what the fight was about, he said. Just like I don't know what happened to your second husband. Your first one died in the Texas electric chair. Did you know that? Your third one beat you up, stole your touring costumes and your car and retired with a chorine to Tuskegee. He laughed. He's still there.

I had been mad, but suddenly I calmed down. Traynor was talking very dreamily. It was dark but seems like I could tell his eyes weren't right. It was like some*thing* was sitting there talking to me but not necessarily with a person behind it.

You gave up on marrying and seem happier for it. He laughed again. I married but it never went like it was supposed to. I never could squeeze any of my own life either into it or out of it. It was like singing somebody else's record.

I copied the way it was sposed to be *exactly* but I never had a clue what marriage meant.

I bought her a diamond ring big as your fist. I bought her clothes. I built her a mansion. But right away she didn't want the boys to stay there. Said they smoked up the bottom floor. Hell, there were *five* floors.

No need to grieve, I said. No need to. Plenty more where she come from.

He perked up. That's part of what that song means, ain't it? No need to grieve. Whatever it is, there's plenty more down the line.

I never really believed that way back when I wrote that song, I said. It was all bluffing then. The trick is to live long enough to put your young bluffs to use. Now if I was to sing that song today I'd tear it up. 'Cause I done lived long enough to know it's *true*. Them words could hold me up.

I ain't lived that long, he said.

Look like you on your way, I said. I don't know why, but the boy seemed to need some encouraging. And I don't know, seem like one way or another you talk to rich white folks and you end up reassuring *them*. But what the hell, by now I feel something for the boy. I wouldn't be in his bed all alone in the middle of the night for nothing. Couldn't be nothing worse than being famous the world over for something you don't even understand. That's what I tried to tell Bessie. She wanted that same song. Overheard me practicing it one day, said, with her hands on her hips: Gracie Mae, I'ma sing your song tonight. I *likes* it.

Your lips be too swole to sing, I said. She was mean and she was strong, but I trounced her.

Ain't you famous enough with your own stuff? I said. Leave mine alone. Later on, she thanked me. By then she was Miss Bessie Smith to the World, and I was still Miss Gracie Mae Nobody from Notasulga.

The next day all these limousines arrived to pick me up. Five cars and twelve bodyguards. Horace picked that morning to start painting the kitchen.

Don't paint the kitchen, fool, I said. The only reason that dumb boy of ours is going to show me his mansion is because he intends to present us with a new house.

What you gonna do with it? he asked me, standing there in his shirtsleeves stirring the paint.

Sell it. Give it to the children. Live in it on weekends. It don't matter what I do. He sure don't care.

Horace just stood there shaking his head. Mama you sure looks *good*, he says. Wake me up when you git back.

Fool, I say, and pat my wig in front of the mirror.

The boy's house is something else. First you come to this mountain, and then you commence to drive and drive up this road that's lined with magnolias. Do magnolias grow on mountains? I was wondering. And you come to lakes and you come to ponds and you come to deer and you come up on some sheep. And I figure these two is sposed to represent England and Wales. Or something out of Europe. And you just keep on coming to stuff. And it's all pretty. Only the man driving my car don't look at nothing but the road. Fool. And then *finally*, after all this time, you begin to go up the driveway. And there's more magnolias—only they're not in such good shape. It's sort of cool up this high and I don't think they're gonna make it. And then I see this building that looks like if it had a name it would be The Tara Hotel. Columns and steps and outdoor chandeliers and rocking chairs. Rocking chairs? Well, and there's the boy on the steps dressed in a dark green satin jacket like you see folks wearing on TV late at night, and he looks sort of like a fat dracula with all that house rising behind him, and standing beside him there's this little white vision of loveliness that he introduces as his wife.

He's nervous when he introduces us and he says to her: This is Gracie Mae Still, I want you to know me. I mean...and she gives him a look that would fry meat.

Won't you come in, Gracie Mae, she says, and that's the last I see of her.

He fishes around for something to say or do and decides to escort me to the kitchen. We go through the entry and the parlor and the breakfast room and the dining room and the servants' passage and finally get there. The first thing I notice is that, altogether, there are five stoves. He looks about to introduce me to one.

Wait a minute, I say. Kitchens don't do nothing for me. Let's go sit on the front porch.

Well, we hike back and we sit in the rocking chairs rocking until dinner.

Gracie Mae, he says down the table, taking a piece of fried chicken from the woman standing over him, I got a little surprise for you.

It's a house, ain't it? I ask, spearing a chitlin.

You're getting *spoiled*, he says. And the way he says *spoiled* sounds funny. He slurs it. It sounds like his tongue is too thick for his mouth. Just that quick he's finished the chicken and is now eating chitlins *and* a pork chop. *Me* spoiled, I'm thinking.

I already got a house. Horace is right this minute painting the kitchen. I bought that house. My kids feel comfortable in that house.

But this one I bought you is just like mine. Only a little smaller.

I still don't need no house. And anyway who would clean it?

He looks surprised.

Really, I think, some peoples advance *so* slowly.

I hadn't thought of that. But what the hell, I'll get you somebody to live in.

I don't want other folks living 'round me. Makes me nervous.

You *don't?* It *do?*

What I want to wake up and see folks I don't even know for?

He just sits there downtable staring at me. Some of that feeling is in the song, ain't it? Not the words, the *feeling.* What I want to wake up and see folks I don't even know for? But I see twenty folks a day I don't even know, including my wife.

This food wouldn't be bad to wake up to though, I said. The boy had found the genius of corn bread.

He looked at me real hard. He laughed. Short. They want what you got but they don't want you. They want what I got only it ain't mine. That's what makes 'em so hungry for me when I sing. They getting the flavor of something but they ain't getting the thing itself. They like a pack of hound dogs trying to gobble up a scent.

You talking 'bout your fans?

Right. Right. He says.

Don't worry 'bout your fans, I say. They don't know their asses from a hole in the ground. I doubt there's a honest one in the bunch.

That's the point. Dammit, that's the point! He hits the table with his fist. It's so solid it don't even quiver. You need a honest audience! You can't have folks that's just gonna lie right back to you.

Yeah, I say, it was small compared to yours, but I had one. It would have been worth my life to try to sing 'em somebody else's stuff that I didn't know nothing about.

He must have pressed a buzzer under the table. One of his flunkies zombies up.

Git Johnny Carson, he says.

On the phone? asks the zombie.

On the phone, says Traynor, what you think I mean, git him offa the front porch? Move your ass.

So two weeks later we's on the Johnny Carson show.

Traynor is all corseted down nice and looks a little bit fat but mostly good. And all the women that grew up on him and my song squeal and squeal. Traynor says: The lady who wrote my first hit record is here with us tonight, and she's agreed to sing it for all of us, just like she sung it forty-five years ago. Ladies and Gentlemen, the great Gracie Mae Still!

Well, I had tried to lose a couple of pounds my own self, but failing that I had me a very big dress made. So I sort of rolls over next to Traynor, who is dwarfed by me, so that when he puts his arm around back of me to try to hug me it looks funny to the audience and they laugh.

I can see this pisses him off. But I smile out there at 'em. Imagine squealing for twenty years and not knowing why you're squealing? No more sense of endings and beginnings than hogs.

It don't matter, Son, I say. Don't fret none over me.

I commence to sing. And I sound——wonderful. Being able to sing good ain't all about having a good singing voice a'tall. A good singing voice helps. But when you come up in the Hard Shell Baptist church like I did you understand early that the fellow that sings is the singer. Them that waits for programs and arrangements and letters from home is just good voices occupying body space.

So there I am singing my own song, my own way. And I give it all I got and enjoy every minute of it. When I finish Traynor is standing up clapping and clapping and beaming at first me and then the audience like I'm his mama for true. The audience claps politely for about two seconds.

Traynor looks disgusted.

He comes over and tries to hug me again. The audience laughs.

Johnny Carson looks at us like we both weird.

Traynor is mad as hell. He's supposed to sing something called a love ballad. But instead he takes the mike, turns to me and says: Now see if my imitation still holds up. He goes into the same song, *our* song, I think, looking out at his flaky audience. And he sings it just the way he always did. My voice, my tone, my inflection, everything. But he forgets a couple of lines. Even before he's finished the matronly squeals begin.

He sits down next to me looking whipped.

It don't matter, Son, I say, patting his hand. You don't even know those people. Try to make the people you know happy.

Is that in the song? he asks.

Maybe. I say.

1977

For a few years I hear from him, then nothing. But trying to lose weight takes all the attention I got to spare. I finally faced up to the fact that my fat is the hurt

I don't admit, not even to myself, and that I been trying to bury it from the day I was born. But also when you git real old, to tell the truth, it ain't as pleasant. It gits lumpy and slack. Yuck. So one day I said to Horace, I'ma git this shit offa me.

And he fell in with the program like he always try to do and Lord such a procession of salads and cottage cheese and fruit juice!

One night I dreamed Traynor had split up with his fifteenth wife. He said: *You meet 'em for no reason. You date 'em for no reason. You marry 'em for no reason. I do it all but I swear it's just like somebody else doing it. I feel like I can't remember Life.*

The boy's in trouble, I said to Horace.

You've always said that, he said.

I have?

Yeah. You always said he looked asleep. You can't sleep through life if you wants to live it.

You not such a fool after all, I said, pushing myself up with my cane and hobbling over to where he was. Let me sit down on your lap, I said, while this salad I ate takes effect.

In the morning we heard Traynor was dead. Some said fat, some said heart, some said alcohol, some said drugs. One of the children called from Detroit. Them dumb fans of his is on a crying rampage, she said. You just ought to turn on the t.v.

But I didn't want to see 'em. They was crying and crying and didn't even know what they was crying for. One day this is going to be a pitiful country, I thought.

Toni Cade Bambara

The Lesson

Back in the days when everyone was old and stupid or young and foolish and me and Sugar were the only ones just right, this lady moved on our block with nappy hair and proper speech and no makeup. And quite naturally we laughed at her, laughed the way we did at the junk man who went about his business like he was some big-time president and his sorry-ass horse his secretary. And we kinda hated her too, hated the way we did the winos who cluttered up our parks and pissed on our handball walls and stank up our hallways and stairs so you couldn't halfway play hide-and-seek without a goddamn gas mask. Miss Moore was her name. The only woman on the block with no first name. And she was black as hell, cept for her feet, which were fish-white and spooky. And she was always planning these boring-ass things for us to do, us being my cousin, mostly, who lived on the block cause we all moved North the same time and to the same apartment then spread out gradual to breathe. And our parents would yank our heads into some kinda shape and crisp up our clothes so we'd be presentable for travel with Miss Moore, who always looked like she was going to church, though she never did. Which is just one of things the grown-ups talked about when they talked behind her back like a dog. But when she came calling with some sachet she'd sewed up or some gingerbread she'd made or some book, why then they'd all be too embarrassed to turn her down and we'd get handed

First published in *Gorilla, My Love and Other Stories* by Toni Cade Bambara. New York: Random House, 1972 over all spruced up. She'd been to college and said it was only right that she should take responsibility for the young ones' education, and she not even related by marriage or blood. So they'd go for it. Specially Aunt Gretchen. She was the main gofer in the family. You got some ole dumb shit foolishness you want somebody to go for, you send for Aunt Gretchen. She been screwed into the go-along for so long, it's a blood-deep natural thing with her. Which is how she got saddled with me and Sugar and Junior in the first place while our mothers were in a la-de-da apartment up the block having a good ole time.

So this one day Miss Moore rounds us all up at the mailbox and it's pure-dee hot and she's knockin herself out about arithmetic. And school suppose to let up in summer I heard, but she don't never let up. And the starch in my pinafore scratching the shit outta me and I'm really hating this nappy-head bitch and her goddamn college degree. I'd much rather go to the pool or to the show where it's cool. So me and Sugar leaning on the mailbox being surly, which is a Miss Moore word. And Flyboy checking out what everybody brought for lunch. And Fat Butt already wasting his peanut-butter-and-jelly sandwich like the pig he is. And Junebug punchin on Q.T.'s arm for potato chips. And Rosie Giraffe shifting from one hip to the other waiting for somebody to step on her foot or ask her if she from Georgia so she can kick ass, preferably Mercedes'. And Miss Moore asking us do we know what money is, like we a bunch of retards. I mean real money, she say, like it's only poker chips or monopoly papers we lay on the grocer. So right away I'm tired of this and say so. And would much rather snatch Sugar and go to the Sunset and terrorize the West Indian kids and take their hair ribbons and their money too. And Miss Moore files that remark away for next week's lesson brotherhood, I can tell. And finally I say we oughta get to the subway cause it's cooler and besides we might meet some cute boys. Sugar done swiped her mama's lipstick, so we ready.

So we heading down the street and she's boring us silly about what things cost and what our parents make and how much goes for rent and how money ain't divided up right in this country. And then she gets to the part about we all poor and live in the slums, which I don't feature. And I'm ready to speak on that, but she steps out in the street and hails two cabs just like that. Then she hustles half the crew in with her and hands me a five-dollar bill and tells me to calculate 10 percent tip for the driver. And we're off. Me and Sugar and Junebug and Flyboy hangin out the window and hollering to everybody, putting lipstick on each other cause Flyboy a faggot anyway, and making farts with our sweaty armpits. But I'm mostly trying to figure how to spend this money. But they all fascinated with the meter ticking and Junebug starts laying bets as to how much it'll read when Flyboy can't hold his breath no more. Then Sugar lays bets as to how much it'll be when we get there. So I'm stuck. Don't nobody want to go for my plan, which is to jump out at the next light and run off to the first bar-b-que we can find. Then the driver tells us to get the hell out cause we there already. And the meter reads eighty-five cents. And I'm stalling to figure out the tip and Sugar say give him a dime. And I decide he don't need it bad as I do, so later for him. But then he tries to take off with Junebug foot still in the door so we talk about his mama something ferocious. Then we check out that we on Fifth Avenue and everybody dressed up in stockings. One lady in a fur coat, hot as it is. White folks crazy.

"This is the place," Miss Moore say, presenting it to us in the voice she uses at the museum. "Let's look in the windows before we go in."

"Can we steal?" Sugar asks very serious like she's getting the ground rules squared away before she plays. "I beg your pardon," say Miss Moore, and we fall out. So she leads us around the windows of the toy store and me and Sugar screamin, "This is mine, that's mine, I gotta have that, that was made for me, I was born for that," till Big Butt drowns us out.

"Hey, I'm goin to buy that there."

"That there? You don't even know what it is, stupid."

"I do so," he say punchin on Rosie Giraffe. "It's a microscope."

"Whatcha gonna do with a microscope, fool?"

"Look at things."

"Like what, Ronald?" ask Miss Moore. And Big Butt ain't got the first notion. So here go Miss Moore gabbing about the thousands of bacteria in a drop of water and the somethinorother in a speck of blood and the million and one living things in the air around us is invisible to the naked eye. And what she say that for? Junebug go to town on that "naked" and we rolling. Then Miss Moore ask what it cost. So we all jam into the window smudgin it up and the price tag say $300. So then she ask how long'd take for Big Butt and Junebug to save up their allowances. "Too long," I say. "Yeh," adds Sugar, "Outgrown it by that time." And Miss Moore say no, you never outgrow learning instruments. "Why, even medical students and interns and," blah, blah, blah. And we ready to choke Big Butt for bringing it up in the first damn place.

"This here costs four hundred eighty dollars," say Rosie Giraffe. So we pile up all over her to see what she pointin out. My eyes tell me it's a chunk of glass cracked with something heavy, and different-color inks dripped into the splits, then the whole thing put into a oven or something. But for $480 it don't make sense.

"That's a paperweight made of semi-precious stones fused together under tremendous pressure," she explains slowly, with her hands doing the mining and all the factory work.

"So what's a paperweight?" asks Rosie Giraffe.

"To weigh paper with, dumbbell," say Flyboy, the wise man from the East.

"Not exactly," say Miss Moore, which is what she say when you warm or way off too. "It's to weigh paper down so it won't scatter and make your desk untidy." So right away me and Sugar curtsy to each other and than to Mercedes who is more the tidy type.

"We don't keep paper on top of the desk in my class," say Junebug, figuring Miss Moore crazy or lyin one.

"At home, then," she say. "Don't you have a calendar and a pencil case and a blotter and a letter-opener on your desk at home where you do your homework?" And she know damn well what our homes look like cause she nosys around in them every chance she gets.

"I don't even have a desk," say Junebug. "Do we?"

"No. And I don't get no homework neither," say Big Butt.

"And I don't even have a home," say Flyboy like he do at school to keep the white folks off his back and sorry for him. Send this poor kid to camp posters, is his specialty.

"I do," says Mercedes. "I have a box of stationery on my desk and a picture of my cat. My godmother bought the stationery and the desk. There's a big rose on each sheet and the envelopes smell like roses."

"Who wants to know about your smelly-ass stationery," say Rosie Giraffe fore I can get my two cents in.

"It's important to have a work area all your own so that..."

"Will you look at this sailboat, please," say Flyboy, cuttin her off and pointin to the thing like it was his. So once again we tumble all over each other to gaze at this magnificent thing in the toy store which is just big enough to maybe sail two kittens across the pond if you strap them to the posts tight. We all start reciting the price tag like we in assembly. "Handcrafted sailboat of fiberglass at one thousand one hundred ninety-five dollars."

"Unbelievable," I hear myself say and am really stunned. I read it again for myself just in case the group recitation put me in a trance. Same thing. For some reason this pisses me off. We look at Miss Moore and she lookin at us, waiting for I dunno what.

Who'd pay all that when you can buy a sailboat set for a quarter at Pop's, a tube of glue for a dime, and a ball of string for eight cents? "It must have a motor and a whole lot else besides," I say. "My sailboat cost me about fifty cents."

"But will it take water?" say Mercedes with her smart ass.

"Took mine to Alley Pond Park once," say Flyboy. "String broke. Lost it. Pity."

"Sailed mine in Central Park and it keeled over and sank. Had to ask my father for another dollar."

"And you got the strap," laugh Big Butt. "The jerk didn't even have a string on it. My old man wailed on his behind."

Little Q.T. was staring hard at the sailboat and you could see he wanted it bad. But he too little and somebody'd just take it from him. So what the hell. "This boat for kids, Miss Moore?"

"Parents silly to buy something like that just to get all broke up," say Rosie Giraffe.

"That much money it should last forever," I figure.

"My father'd buy it for me if I wanted it."

"Your father, my ass," say Rosie Giraffe getting a chance to finally push Mercedes.

"Must be rich people shop here," say Q.T.

"You are a very bright boy," say Flyboy. "What was your first clue?" And he rap him on the head with the back of his knuckles, since Q.T. the only one he could get away with. Though Q.T. liable to come up behind you years later and get his licks in when you half expect it.

"What I want to know is," I says to Miss Moore though I never talk to her, I wouldn't give the bitch that satisfaction, "is how much a real boat costs? I figure a thousand'd get you a yacht any day."

"Why don't you check that out," she says, "and report back to the group?" Which really pains my ass. If you gonna mess up a perfectly good swim day least you could do is have some answers. "Let's go in," she say like she got something up her sleeve. Only she don't lead the way. So me and Sugar turn the corner to where the entrance is, but when we get there I kinda hang back. Not that I'm scared, what's there to be afraid of, just a toy store. But I feel funny, shame. But what I got to be shamed about? Got as much right to go in as anybody. But somehow I can't seem to get hold of the door, so I step away for Sugar to lead. But she hangs back too. And I look at her and she looks at me and this is ridiculous. I mean, damn, I have never ever been shy about doing nothing or going nowhere. But then Mercedes steps up and then Rosie Giraffe and Big Butt crowd in behind and shove, and next thing we all stuffed into the doorway with only Mercedes squeezing past us, smoothing out her jumper and walking right down the aisle. Then the rest of us tumble in like a glued-together jigsaw done all wrong. And people lookin at us. And it's like the time me and Sugar crashed into the Catholic church on a dare. But once we got in there and everything so hushed and holy and the candles and the bowin and the handkerchiefs on all the drooping heads, I just couldn't go through with the plan. Which was for me to run up to the altar and do a tap dance while Sugar played the nose flute and messed around in the holy water. And Sugar kept givin me the elbow. Then later teased me so bad I tied her up in the shower and turned it on and locked her in.

And she'd be there till this day if Aunt Gretchen hadn't finally figured I was lyin about the boarder takin a shower.

Same thing in the store. We all walkin on tiptoe and hardly touchin the games and puzzles and things. And I watched Miss Moore who is steady watchin us like she waitin for a sign. Like Mama Drewery watches the sky and sniffs the air and takes note of just how much slant is in the bird formation. Then me and Sugar bump smack into each other, so busy gazing at the toys, 'specially the sailboat. But we don't laugh and go into our fat-lady bump-stomach routine. We just stare at that price tag. Then Sugar run a finger over the whole boat. And I'm jealous and want to hit her. Maybe not her, but I sure want to punch somebody in the mouth.

"Watcha bring us here for, Miss Moore?"

"You sound angry, Sylvia. Are you mad about something?" Givin me one of them grins like she tellin a grown-up joke that never turns out to be funny. And she's lookin very closely at me like maybe she plannin to do my portrait from memory. I'm mad, but I won't give her that satisfaction. So I slouch around the store bein very bored and say, "Let's go."

Me and Sugar at the back of the train watchin the tracks whizzin by large then small then gettin gobbled up in the dark. I'm thinkin about this tricky toy I saw in the store. A clown that somersaults on a bar then does chin-ups just cause you yank lightly at his leg. Cost $35. I could see me askin my mother for a $35 birthday clown. "You wanna who that costs what?" she'd say, cocking her head to the side to get a better view of the hole in my head. Thirty-five dollars could buy new bunk beds for Junior and Gretchen's boy. Thirty-five dollars and the whole household could go visit Granddaddy Nelson in the country. Thirty-five dollars would pay for the rent and the piano bill too. Who are these people that spend that much for performing clowns and $1,000 for toy sailboats? What kinda work they do and how they live and how come we ain't in on it? Where we are is who we are, Miss Moore always pointin out. But it don't necessarily have to be that way, she always adds then waits for somebody to say that poor people have to wake up and demand their share of the pie and don't none of us know what kind of pie she talkin about in the first damn place. But she ain't so smart cause I still got her four dollars from the taxi and she sure ain't gettin it. Messin up my day with this shit. Sugar nudges me in my pocket and winks.

Miss Moore lines us up in front of the mailbox where we started from, seem like years ago, and I got a headache for thinkin so hard. And we lean all over each other so we can hold up under the draggy-ass lecture she always finishes us off with at the end before we thank her for borin us to tears. But she just looks at us like she readin tea leaves. Finally she say, "Well, what did you think of F.A.O. Schwartz?"

Rosie Giraffe mumbles, "White folks crazy."

"I'd like to go there again when I get my birthday money," says Mercedes, and we shove her out the pack so she has to lean on the mailbox by herself.

"I'd like a shower. Tiring day," say Flyboy.

Then Sugar surprises me by sayin, "You know, Miss Moore, I don't think all of us here put together eat in a year what that sailboat costs." And Miss Moore lights up like somebody goosed her. "And?" she say, urging Sugar on. Only I'm standin on her foot so she don't continue.

"Imagine for a minute what kind of society it is in which some people can spend on a toy what it would cost to feed a family of six or seven. What do you think?"

"I think," say Sugar pushing me off her feet like she never done before, cause I whip her ass in a minute, "that this is not much of a democracy if you ask me. Equal chance to pursue happiness means an equal crack crack at the dough, don't it?" Miss Moore is besides herself and I am disgusted with Sugar's treachery. So I stand on her foot one more time to see if she'll shove me. She shuts up, and Miss Moore looks at me, sorrowfully I'm thinkin. And somethin weird is goin on, I can feel it in my chest.

"Anybody else learn anything today?" lookin dead at me. I walk away and Sugar has to run to catch up and don't even seem to notice when I shrug her arm off my shoulder.

"Well, we got four dollars anyway," she says.

"Uh hunh."

"We could go to Hascombs and get half a chocolate layer and then go to the Sunset and still have plenty money for potato chips and ice-cream sodas."

"Uh-hunh."

"Race you to Hascombs," she say.

We start down the block and she gets ahead which is O.K. by me cause I'm goin to the West End and then over to the Drive to think this day through. She can run if she want to and even run faster. But ain't nobody gonna beat me at nuthin.

Kiswana Browne

From the window of her sixth-floor studio apartment, Kiswana could see over the wall at the end of the street to the busy avenue that lay just north of Brewster Place. The late-afternoon shoppers looked like brightly clad marionettes as they moved between the congested traffic, clutching their packages against their bodies to guard them from sudden bursts of the cold autumn wind. A portly mailman had abandoned his cart and was bumping into indignant window-shoppers as he puffed behind the cap that the wind had snatched from his head. Kiswana leaned over to see if he was going to be successful, but the edge of the building cut him off from her view.

A pigeon swept across her window, and she marveled at its liquid movements in the air waves. She placed her dreams on the back of the bird and fantasized that it would glide forever in transparent silver circles until it ascended to the center of the universe and was swallowed up. But the wind died down, and she watched with a sigh as the bird beat its wings in awkward, frantic movements to land on the corroded top of a fire escape on the opposite building. This brought her back to earth.

Humph, it's probably sitting over there crapping on those folks' fire escape, she thought. Now, that's a safety hazard. ...And her mind was busy again, creating flames and smoke and frustrated tenants whose escape was being hin-

First published in *The Women of Brewster Place* by Gloria Naylor. New York: Viking, Penguin, 1980

dered because they were slipping and sliding in pigeon shit. She watched their cussing, haphazard descent on the fire escapes until they had all reached the bottom. They were milling around, oblivious to their burning apartments, angrily planning to march on the mayor's office about the pigeons. She materialized placards and banners for them, and they had just reached the corner, boldly sidestepping fire hoses and broken glass, when they all vanished.

A tall copper-skinned woman had met this phantom parade at the corner, and they had dissolved in front of her long, confident strides. She plowed through the remains of their faded mists, unconscious of the lingering wisps of their presence on her leather bag and black fur-trimmed coat. It took a few seconds for this transfer from one realm to another to reach Kiswana, but then suddenly she recognized the woman.

"Oh, God, it's Mama!" She looked down guiltily at the forgotten newspaper in her lap and hurriedly circled random job advertisements.

By this time Mrs. Browne had reached the front of Kiswana's building and was checking the house number against a piece of paper in her hand. Before she went into the building she stood at the bottom of the stoop and carefully inspected the condition of the street and the adjoining property. Kiswana watched this meticulous inventory with growing annoyance but she involuntarily followed her mother's slowly rotating head, forcing herself to see her new neighborhood through the older woman's eyes. The brightness of the unclouded sky seemed to join forces with her mother as it highlighted every broken stoop railing and missing brick. The afternoon sun glittered and cascaded across even the tiniest fragments of broken bottle, and at that very moment the wind chose to rise up again, sending unswept grime flying into the air, as a stray tin can left by careless garbage collectors went rolling noisily down the center of the street.

Kiswana noticed with relief that at least Ben wasn't sitting in his usual place on the old garbage can pushed against the far wall. He was just a harmless old wino, but Kiswana knew her mother only needed one wino or one teenager with a reefer within a twenty-block radius to decide that her daugher was living in a building seething with dope factories and hang-outs for derelicts. If she had seen Ben, nothing would have made her believe that practically every apartment contained a family, a Bible, and a dream that one day enough could be scraped from those meager Friday night paychecks to make Brewster Place a distant memory.

As she watched her mother's head disappear into the building, Kiswana gave silent thanks that the elevator was broken. That would give her at least five minutes' grace to straighten up the apartment. She rushed to the sofa bed and hastily closed it without smoothing the rumpled sheets and blanket or removing her nightgown. She felt that somehow the tangled bedcovers would give away the fact that she had not slept alone last night. She silently apologized to Abshu's memory as she heartlessly crushed his spirit between the steel springs of the couch. Lord, that man was sweet. Her toes curled involuntarily at the passing thought of his full lips moving slowly over her instep. Abshu was a foot man, and he always started his lovemaking from the bottom up. For that reason Kiswana changed the color of the polish on her toenails every week. During the course of their relationship she had gone from shades of red to brown and was now into the purples. I'm gonna have to start mixing them soon, she thought aloud as she turned from the couch and raced into the bathroom to remove any traces of Abshu from there. She took up his shaving cream and razor and threw them into the bottom drawer of her dresser beside her diaphragm. Mama wouldn't dare pry into my drawers right in front of me, she thought as she slammed the drawer shut. Well, at least not the *bottom* drawer. She may come up with some sham excuse for opening the top drawer, but never the bottom one.

When she heard the first two short raps on the door, her eyes took a final flight over the small apartment, desperately seeking out any slight misdemeanor that might have to be defended. Well, there was nothing she could do about the crack in the wall over that table. She had been after the landlord to fix it for two months now. And there had been no time to sweep the rug, and everyone knew that off-gray always looked dirtier than it really was. And it was just too damn bad about the kitchen. How was she expected to be out job-hunting every day and still have time to keep a kitchen that looked like her mother's, who didn't even work and still had someone come in twice a month for general cleaning. And besides…

Her imaginary argument was abruptly interrupted by a second series of knocks, accompanied by a penetrating, "Melanie, Melanie, are you there?"

Kiswana strode toward the door. She's starting before she even gets in here. She knows that's not my name anymore.

She swung the door open to face her slightly flushed mother. "Oh, hi, Mama. You know, I thought I heard a knock, but I figured it was for the people next door, since no one hardly ever calls me Melanie." Score one for me, she thought.

"Well, it's awfully strange you can forget a name you answered to for twenty-three years," Mrs. Browne said, as she moved past Kiswana into the apartment. "My, that was a long climb. How long has your elevator been out? Honey, how do you manage with your laundry and groceries up all those steps? But I guess you're young, and it wouldn't bother you as much as it does me." This long string of questions told Kiswana that her mother had no intentions of beginning her visit with another argument about her new African name.

"You know I would have called before I came, but you don't have a phone yet. I didn't want you to feel that I was snooping. As a matter of fact, I didn't expect to find you home at all. I thought you'd be out looking for a job." Mrs. Browne had mentally covered the entire apartment while she was talking and taking off her coat.

"Well, I got up late this morning. I thought I'd buy the afternoon paper and start early tomorrow."

"That sounds like a good idea." Her mother moved toward the window and picked up the discarded paper and glanced over the hurriedly circled ads. "Since when do you have experience as a fork-lift operator?"

Kiswana caught her breath and silently cursed herself for her stupidity. "Oh, my hand slipped-I meant to circle file clerk." She quickly took the paper before her mother could see that she had also marked cutlery salesman and chauffeur.

"You're sure you weren't sitting her moping and daydreaming again?" Amber specks of laughter flashed in the corner of Mrs. Browne's eyes.

Kiswana threw her shoulders back and unsuccessfully tried to disguise her embarrassment with indignation.

"Oh, God, Mama! I haven't done that in years—it's for kids. When are you going to realize that I'm a woman now?" She sought desparately for some womanly thing to do and settled for throwing herself on the couch and crossing her legs in what she hoped looked like a nonchalant arc.

"Please, have a seat," she said, attempting the same tones and gestures she'd seen Bette Davis use on the late movies.

Mrs. Browne, lowering her eyes to hide her amusement, accepted the invitation and sat at the window, also crossing her legs. Kiswana saw immediately how it should have been done. Her celluloid poise clashed loudly against her mother's quiet dignity, and she quickly uncrossed her legs. Mrs. Browne turned her head toward the window and pretended not to notice.

"At least you have a halfway decent view from here. I was wondering what lay beyond that dreadful wall—it's the boulevard. Honey, did you know that you can see the trees in Linden Hills from here?"

Kiswana knew that very well, because there were many lonely days that she would sit in her gray apartment and stare at those trees and think of home, but she would rather have choked than admit that to her mother.

"Oh, really, I never noticed. So how is Daddy and things at home?"

"Just fine. We're thinking of redoing one of the extra bedrooms since you children have moved out, but Wilson insists that he can manage all that work alone. I told him that he doesn't really have the proper time or energy for all that. As it is, when he gets home from the office, he's so tired he can hardly move. But you know you can't tell your father anything. Whenever he starts complaining about how stubborn you are, I tell him the child came by it honestly. Oh, and your brother was by yesterday," she added, as if it had just occurred to her.

So that's it, thought Kiswana. That's why she's here.

Kiswana's brother, Wilson, had been to visit her two days ago, and she had borrowed twenty dollars from him to get her winter coat out of layaway. That son-of-a-bitch probably ran straight to Mama—and after he swore he wouldn't say anything. I should have known, he was always a snotty-nosed sneak, she thought.

"Was he?" she said aloud. "He came by to see me, too, earlier this week. And I borrowed some money from him because my unemployment checks hand't cleared in the bank, but now they have and everything's just fine." There, I'll beat you to that one.

"Oh, I didn't know that," Mrs. Browne lied. "He never mentioned you. He had just heard that Beverly was expecting again, and he rushed over to tell us."

Damn. Kiswana could have strangled herself.

"So she's knocked up again, huh?" she said irritably.

Her mother started. "Why do you always have to be so crude?"

"Personally, I don't see how she can sleep with Willie. He's such a dishrag."

Kiswana still resented the stance her brother had taken in college. When everyone at school was discovering their blackness and protesting on campus, Wilson never took part; he had even refused to wear an Afro. This had outraged Kiswana because, unlike her, he was dark-skinned and had the type of hair that was thick and kinky enough for a good "Fro." Kiswana had still insisted on cutting her own hair, but it was so thin and fine-textured, it refused to thicken even after she washed it. So she had to brush it up and spray it with lacquer to keep it from lying flat. She never forgave Wilson for telling her that she didn't look African, she looked like an electrocuted chicken.

"Now that's some way to talk. I don't know why you have an attitude against your brother. He never gave me a restless night's sleep, and now he's settled with a family and a good job."

"He's an assistant to an assistant junior partner in a law firm. What's the big deal about that?"

"The job has a future, Melanie. And at least he finished school and went on for his law degree."

"In other words, not like me, huh?"

"Don't put words into my mouth, young lady. I'm perfectly capable of saying what I mean."

Amen, thought Kiswana.

"And I don't know why you've been trying to start up with me from the moment I walked in. I didn't come here to fight with you. This is your first place away from home, and I just wanted to see how you were living and if you're doing all right. And I must say, you've fixed this apartment up very nicely."

"Really, Mama?" She found herself softening in the light of her mother's approval.

"Well, considering what you had to work with." This time she scanned the apartment openly.

"Look, I know it's not Linden Hills, but a lot can be done with it. As soon as they come and paint, I'm going to hang my Ashanti print over the couch. And I thought a big Boston Fern would go well in that corner, what do you think?"

"That would be fine, baby. You always had a good eye for balance."

Kiswana was beginning to relax. There was little she did that attracted her mother's approval. It was like a rare bird, and she had to tread carefully around it lest it fly away.

"Are you going to leave that statue out like that?"

"Why, what's wrong with it? Would it look better somewhere else?"

There was a small wooden reproduction of a Yoruba goddess with large protruding breasts on the coffee table.

"Well," Mrs. Browne was beginning to blush, "it's just that it's a bit suggestive, don't you think? Since you live alone now, and I know you'll be having male friends stop by, you wouldn't want to be giving them any ideas. I mean, uh, you know, there's no point in putting yourself in any unpleasant situations because they may get the wrong impressions and uh, you know, I mean, well..." Mrs. Browne stammered on miserably.

Kiswana loved it when her mother tried to talk about sex. It was the only time she was at a loss for words.

"Don't worry, Mama." Kiswana smiled. "That wouldn't bother the type of men I date. Now maybe if it had big feet..." And she got hysterical, thinking of Abshu.

Her mother looked at her sharply. "What sort of gibberish is that about feet? I'm being serious, Melanie."

"I'm sorry, Mama." She sobered up. "I'll put it away in the closet," she said, knowing that she wouldn't.

"Good," Mrs. Browne said, knowing that she wouldn't either. "I guess you think I'm too picky, but we worry about you over here. And you refuse to put in a phone so we can call and see about you."

"I haven't refused, Mama. They want seventy-five dollars for a deposit, and I can't swing that right now."

"Melanie, I can give you the money."

"I don't want you to be giving me money—I've told you that before. Please, let me make it by myself."

"Well, let me lend it to you, then."

"No!"

"Oh, so you can borrow money from your brother, but not from me."

Kiswana turned her head from the hurt in her mother's eyes. "Mama, when I borrow from Willie, he makes me pay him back. You never let me pay you back," she said into her hands.

"I don't care. I still think it's downright selfish of you to be sitting over here with no phone, and sometimes we don't hear from you in two weeks— anything could happen—especially living among these people."

Kiswana snapped her head up. "What do you mean, *these people*. They're my people and yours, too, Mama—we're all black. But maybe you've forgotten that over in Linden Hills."

"That's not what I'm talking about, and you know it. These streets—this building—it's so shabby and rundown. Honey, you don't have to live like this."

"Well, this is how poor people live."

"Melanie, you're not poor."

"No, Mama, *you're* not poor. And what you have and I have are two totally different things. I don't have a husband in real estate with a five-figure income and a home in Linden Hills—*you* do. What I have is a weekly unemployment check and an overdrawn checking account at United Federal. So this studio on Brewster is all I can afford."

"Well, you could afford a lot better," Mrs. Browne snapped, "if you hadn't dropped out of college and had to resort to these dead-end clerical jobs."

"Uh-huh, I knew you'd get around to that before long." Kiswana could feel the rings of anger begin to tighten around her lower backbone, and they sent her forward onto the couch. "You'll never understand, will you? Those bourgie schools were counterrevolutionary. My place was in the streets with my people, fighting for equality and a better community."

"Counterrevolutionary!" Mrs. Browne was raising her voice. "Where's your revolution now, Melanie? Where are all those black revolutionaries who were shouting and demonstrating and kicking up a lot of dust with you on that campus? Huh? They're sitting in wood-paneled offices with their degrees in mahogany frames, and they won't even drive their cars past this street because the city doesn't fix potholes in this part of town."

"Mama," she said, shaking her head slowly in disbelief, "how can you—a black woman—sit there and tell me that what we fought for during the Movement wasn't important just because some people sold out?"

"Melanie, I'm not saying it wasn't important. It was damned important to stand up and say that you were proud of what you were and to get the vote and other social opportunities for every person in this country who had it due. But you kids thought you were going to turn the world upside down, and it just wasn't so. When all the smoke had cleared, you found yourself with a fistful of new federal laws and a country still full of obstacles for black people to fight their way over—just because they're black. There was no revolution, Melanie, and there will be no revolution."

"So what am I supposed to do, huh? Just throw up my hands and not care about what happens to my people? I'm not supposed to keep fighting to make things better?"

"Of course, you can. But you're going to have to fight within the system, because it and these so-called 'bourgie' schools are going to be here for a long time. And that means that you get smart like a lot of your old friends and get an important job where you can have some influence. You don't have to sell out, as you say, and work for some corporation, but you could become an assembly-woman or a civil liberties lawyer or open a freedom school in this very neighbor-hood. That way you could really help the community. But what help are you going to be to these people on Brewster while you're living hand-to-mouth on file-clerk jobs waiting for a revolution? You're wasting your talents, child."

"Well, I don't think they're being wasted. At least I'm here in day-to-day contact with the problems of my people. What good would I be after four or five years of a lot of white brainwashing in some phony, prestige institution, huh? I'd be like you and Daddy and those other educated blacks sitting over there in Linden Hills with a terminal case of middle-class amnesia."

"You don't have to live in a slum to be concerned about social conditions, Melanie. Your father and I have been charter members of the NAACP for the last twenty-five years."

"Oh, God!" Kiswana threw her head back in exaggerated disgust. "That's being concerned? That middle-of-the-road, Uncle Tom dumping ground for black Republicans!"

"You can sneer all you want, young lady, but that organization has been working for black people since the turn of the century, and it's still working for them. Where are all those radical groups of yours that were going to put a Cadil-lac in every garage and Dick Gregory in the White House? I'll tell you where."

I knew you would, Kiswana thought angrily.

"They burned themselves out because they wanted too much too fast. Their goals weren't grounded in reality. And that's always been your problem."

"What do you mean, my problem? I know exactly what I'm about."

"No, you don't. You constantly live in a fantasy world—always going to extremes—turning butterflies into eagles, and life isn't about that. It's accepting what is and working from that. Lord, I remember how worried you had me, putting all that lacquered hair spray on your head. I thought you were going to get lung cancer—trying to be what you're not."

Kiswana jumped up from the couch. "Oh, God, I can't take this anymore. Trying to be something I'm not—trying to be something I'm not, Mama! Trying to be proud of my heritage and the fact that I was of African descent. If that's being what I'm not, then I say fine. But I'd rather be dead than be like you—a white man's nigger who's ashamed of being black!"

Kiswana saw streaks of gold and ebony light follow her mother's flying body out of the chair. She was swung around by the shoulders and made to face the deadly stillness in the angry woman's eyes. She was too stunned to cry out from the pain of the long fingernails that dug into her shoulders, and she was brought so close to her mother's face that she saw her reflection, distorted and wavering, in the tears that stood in the older woman's eyes. And she listened in that stillness to a story she had heard from a child.

"My grandmother," Mrs. Browne began slowly in a whisper, "was a full-blooded Iroquois, and my grandfather a free black from a long line of journeymen who had lived in Connecticut since the establishment of the colonies. And my father was a Bajan who came to this country as a cabin boy on a merchant mariner."

"I know all that," Kiswana said, trying to keep her lips from trembling.

"Then, know this." And the nails dug deeper into her flesh. "I am alive because of the blood of proud people who never scraped or begged or apologized for what they were. They lived asking only one thing of this world—to be allowed to be. And I learned through the blood of these people that black isn't beautiful and it isn't ugly—black is! It's not kinky hair and it's not straight hair—it just is.

"It broke my heart when you changed your name. I gave you my grandmother's name, a woman who bore nine children and educated them all, who held off six white men with a shotgun when they tried to drag one of her sons to jail for 'not knowing his place.' Yet you needed to reach into an African dictionary to find a name to make you proud.

"When I brought my babies home from the hospital, my ebony son and my golden daughter, I swore before whatever gods would listen—those of my mother's people or those of my father's people—that I would use everything I had and could ever get to see that my children were prepared to meet this world on its own terms, so that no one could sell them short and make them ashamed of what they were or how they looked—whatever they were or however they looked. And Melanie, that's not being white or red or black—that's being a mother."

Kiswana followed her reflection in the two single tears that moved down her mother's cheeks until it blended with them into the woman's copper skin. There was nothing and then so much that she wanted to say, but her throat kept closing up every time she tried to speak. She kept her head down and her eyes closed, and thought, Oh, God, just let me die. How can I face her now?

Mrs. Browne lifted Kiswana's chin gently. "And the one lesson I wanted you to learn is not to be afraid to face anyone, not even a crafty old lady like me who can outtalk you." And she smiled and winked.

"Oh, Mama, I..." and she hugged the woman tightly.

"Yeah, baby." Mrs. Browne patted her back. "I know."

She kissed Kiswana on the forehead and cleared her throat. "Well, now, I better be moving on. It's getting late, there's dinner to be made, and I have to get off my feet—these new shoes are killing me."

Kiswana looked down at the beige leather pumps. "Those are really classy. They're English, aren't they?"

"Yes, but, Lord, do they cut me right across the instep." She removed the shoe and sat on the couch to massage her foot.

Bright red nail polish glared at Kiswana through the stockings. "Since when do you polish your toenails?" she gasped. "You never did that before."

"Well..." Mrs. Browne shrugged her shoulders, "your father sort of talked me into it, and, uh, you know, he likes it and all, so I thought, uh, you know, why not, so..." And she gave Kiswana an embarrassed smile.

I'll be damned, the young woman thought, feeling her whole face tingle. Daddy's into feet! And she looked at the blushing woman on her couch and suddenly realized that her mother had trod through the same universe that she herself was now traveling. Kiswana was breaking no new trails and would eventually end up just two feet away on that couch. She stared at the woman she had been and was to become.

"But I'll never be a Republican," she caught herself saying aloud.

"What are you mumbling about, Melanie?" Mrs. Browne slipped on her shoe and got up from the couch.

She went to get her mother's coat. "Nothing, Mama. It's really nice of you to come by. You should do it more often."

"Well, since it's not Sunday, I guess you're allowed at least one lie."

They both laughed.

After Kiswana had closed the door and turned around, she spotted an envelope sticking between the cushions of her couch. She went over and opened it up; there was seventy-five dollars in it.

"Oh, Mama, darn it!" She rushed to the window and started to call to the woman, who had just emerged from the building, but she suddenly changed her mind and sat down in the chair with a long sigh and caught in the upward draft of the autumn wind and disappeared over the top of the building.

Becky Birtha

Johnnieruth

S ummertime. Nightime. Talk about steam heat. This whole city get like the
bathroom when somebody in there taking a shower with the door shut.
Nights like that, can't nobody sleep. Everybody be outside, sitting on they
steps or else dragging half they furniture out on the sidewalk—kitchen chairs, card
tables—even bringing TVs outside.

Womenfolks, mostly. All the grown women around my way look just the
same. They all big—stout. They got bosoms and big hips and fat legs, and they
always wearing runover house shoes and them shapeless, flowered numbers
with the buttons down the front. 'Cept on Sunday. Sunday morning they all
turn into glamour girls, in them big hats and long gloves, with they skinny high
heels and they skinny selves in them tight girdles—wouldn't nobody ever know
what they look like the rest of the time.

When I was a little kid, I didn't wanna grow up, 'cause I never wanted to
look like them ladies. I heard Miz Jenkins down the street one time say she
don't mind being fat 'cause that way her husband don't get so jealous. She say
it's more than one way to keep a man. Me, I don't have me no intentions of
keeping no man. I never understood why they was in so much demand anyway,
when it seem like all a woman can depend on 'em for is making sure she keep on
having babies.

First published in *Lover's Choice* by Becky Birtha. Seattle: Seal Press, 1987

We got enough children in my neighborhood. In the summertime even the little kids allowed to stay up till eleven or twelve o'clock at night—playing in the street and hollering and carrying on—don't never seem to get tired. Don't nobody care, long as they don't fight.

Me—I don't hang around no front steps no more. Hot nights like that, I get out my ten-speed and I be gone.

That's what I like to do more than anything else in the whole world. Feel that wind in my face keeping me cool as a air conditioner, shooting along like a snowball. My bike light as a kite. I can really get up some speed.

All the guys around my way got ten-speed bikes. Some of the girls got 'em, too, but they don't ride 'em at night. They pedal around during the day, but at nighttime they just hang around out front, watching babies and running they mouth. I didn't get my Peugeot to be no conversation piece.

My mama don't like me to ride at night. I tried to point out to her that she ain't never said nothing to my brothers, and Vincent a year younger than me. (And Langston two years older, in case "old" is the problem.) She say, "That's different, Johnnieruth. You're a girl." Now I wanna know how is anybody gonna know that. I'm skinny as a knifeblade turned sideways, and all I ever wear is blue jeans and a Wrangler jacket. But if I bring that up, she liable to get started in on how come I can't be more of a young lady, and fourteen is old enough to start taking more pride in my appearance, and she gonna be ashamed to admit I'm her daughter.

I just tell her that my bike be moving so fast can't nobody hardly see me, and couldn't catch me if they did. Mama complain to her friends how I'm wild and she can't do nothing with me. She know I'm gonna do what I want no matter what she say. But she know I ain't getting in no trouble, neither.

Like some of the boys I know stole they bikes, but I didn't do nothing like that. I'd been saving my money ever since I can remember, every time I could get a nickel or a dime outta anybody.

When I was a little kid, it was hard to get money. Seem like the only time they ever give you any was on Sunday morning, and then you had to put it in the offering. I used to hate to do that. In fact, I used to hate everything about Sunday morning. I had to wear all them ruffly dresses—that shiny slippery stuff in the wintertime that got to make a noise every time you move your ass a inch on them hard old benches. And that scratchy starchy stuff in the summertime with all them scratchy crinolines. Had to carry a pocketbook and wear them shiny shoes. And the church we went to was all the way over on Summit Avenue, so the whole damn neighborhood could get a good look. At least all the other kids'd be dressed the same way. The boys think they slick 'cause they get to wear pants, but they still got to wear a white shirt and a tie; and them dumb hats they wear can't hide them baldheaded haircuts, 'cause they got to take the hats off in church.

There was one Sunday when I musta been around eight. I remember it was before my sister Corletta was born, 'cause right around then was when I put my foot down about that whole sanctimonious routine. Anyway, I was dragging my feet along Twenty-fifth Street in back of Mama and Vincent and them, when I spied this lady. I only seen her that one time, but I still remember just how she look. She don't look like nobody I ever seen before. I *know* she don't live around here. She real skinny. But she ain't no real young woman, neither. She could be old as my mama. She ain't nobody's mama—I'm sure. And she ain't wearing Sunday clothes. She got on blue jeans and a man's blue working shirt, with the tail hanging out. She got patches on her blue jeans, and she still got her chin stuck out like she some kinda African royalty. She ain't carrying no shiny pocketbook. It don't look like she care if she got any money or not, or who knows it, if she don't. She ain't wearing no house shoes, or stockings or high heels neither.

Mama always speak to everybody, but when she pass by this lady she make like she ain't even seen her. But I get me a real good look, and the lady stare right back at me. She got a funny look on her face, almost like she think she know me from someplace. After she pass on by, I had to turn around to get another look, even though Mama say that ain't polite. And you know what? She was turning around, too, looking back at me. And she give me a great big smile.

I didn't know too much in them days, but that's when I first got to thinking about how it's got to be different ways to be, from the way people be around my way. It's got to be places where it don't matter to nobody if you all dressed up on Sunday morning or you ain't. That's how come I started saving money. So, when I got enough, I could go away to someplace like that.

Afterwhile I begun to see there wasn't no point in waiting around for handouts, and I started thinking of ways to earn my own money. I used to be running errands all the time—mailing letters for old Grandma Whittaker and picking up cigarettes and newspapers up the corner for everybody. After I got bigger, I started washing cars in the summer, and shoveling people sidewalk in the wintertime. Now I got me a newspaper route. Ain't never been no girl around here with no paper route, but I guess everybody got it figured out by now that I ain't gonna be like nobody else.

The reason I got me my Peugeot was so I could start to explore. I figured I better start looking around right now, so when I'm grown, I'll know exactly where I wanna go. So I ride around every chance I get.

Last summer I used to ride with the boys a lot. Sometimes eight or ten of us just go cruising around the streets together. All of a sudden my mama decide she don't want me to do that no more. She say I'm too old to be spending so much time with boys. (That's what they tell you half the time, and the other half the time they worried 'cause you ain't interested in spending more time with boys. Don't make much sense.) She want me to have some girl friends, but I never seem to fit in with none of the things the girls doing. I used to think I fit in more with the boys.

But I seen how Mama might be right, for once. I didn't like the way the boys was starting to talk about girls sometimes. Talking about what some girl be like from the neck on down, and talking all up underneath somebody clothes and all. Even though I wasn't really friends with none of the girls, I still didn't like it. So now I mostly just ride around by myself. And Mama don't like that neither—you just can't please her.

This boy that live around the corner on North Street, Kenny Henderson, started asking me one time if I don't ever be lonely, 'cause he always see me by myself. He say don't I ever think I'd like to have me somebody special to go places with and stuff. Like I'd pick him if I did! Made me wanna laugh in his face. I do be lonely, a lotta times, but I don't tell nobody. And I ain't met nobody yet that I'd really rather be with than be by myself. But I will someday. When I find that special place where everybody different, I'm gonna find somebody there I can be friends with. And it ain't gonna be no dumb boy.

I found me one place already that I like to go to a whole lot. It ain't even really that far away—by bike—but it's on the other side of the Avenue. So I don't tell Mama and them I go there, 'cause they like to think I'm right around the neighborhood someplace. But this neighborhood too dull for me. All the houses look just the same—no porches, no yards, no trees—not even no parks around here. Every block look so much like very other block it hurt your eyes to look at afterwhile. So I ride across Summit Avenue and go down that big steep hill there, and then make a sharp right at the bottom and cross the bridge over the train tracks. Then I head on out the boulevard—that's the nicest part, with all them big trees making a tunnel over the top, and lightning bugs shining in the bushes. At the end of the boulevard you get to this place call the Plaza.

It's something like a little park—the sidewalks is all bricks and they got flowers planted all over the place. The same kind my mama grow in that painted-up tire she got out front masquerading like a garden decoration—only seem like they smell sweeter here. It's a big high fountain right in the middle, and all the streetlights is the real old-fashion kind. That Plaza is about the prettiest place I ever been.

Sometimes something going on there. Like a orchestra playing music or some man or lady singing. One time they had a show with some girls doing some kinda foreign dances. They look like they were around my age. They all had on these fancy costumes, with different color ribbons all down they back. I wouldn't wear nothing like that, but it looked real pretty when they was dancing.

I got me a special bench in one corner where I like to sit, 'cause I can see just about everything, but wouldn't nobody know I was there. I like to sit still and think, and I like to watch people. A lotta people be coming there at night— to look at the shows and stuff, or just to hang out and cool off. All different kinda people.

This one night when I was sitting over in that corner where I always be at, there was this lady standing right near my bench. She mostly had her back turned to me and she didn't know I was there, but I could see her real good. She had on this shiny purple shirt and about a million silver bracelets. I kinda liked the way she look. Sorta exotic, like she maybe come from California or one of the islands. I mean she had class—standing there posing with her arms folded. She walk away a little bit. Then turn around and walk back again. Like she waiting for somebody.

Then I spotted this dude coming over. I spied him all the way 'cross the Plaza. Looking real fine. Got on a three-piece suit. One of them little caps sitting on a angle. Look like leather. He coming straight over to this lady I'm watching and then she seen him, too, and she start to smile, but she don't move till he get right up next to her. And then I'm gonna look away, 'cause I can't stand to watch nobody hugging and kissing on each other, but all of a sudden I see it ain't no dude at all. It's another lady.

Now I can't stop looking. They smiling at each other like they ain't seen one another in ten years. Then the one in the purple shirt look around real quick—but she don't look just behind her—and sorta pull the other one right back into the corner where I'm sitting at, and then they put they arms around each other and kiss—for a whole long time. Now I really know I oughtta turn away, but I can't. And I know they gonna see me when they finally open they eyes. And they do.

They both kinda gasp and back up, like I'm the monster that just rose up outta the deep. And then I guess they can see I'm only a girl, and they look at one another—and start to laugh! Then they just turn around and start to walk away like it wasn't nothing at all. But right before they gone, they both look around again, and see I still ain't got my eye muscles and my jaw muscles working right again yet. And the one lady wink at me. And the other one say, "Catch you later."

I can't stop staring at they backs, all the way across the Plaza. And then, all of a sudden, I feel like I got to be doing something, got to be moving.

I wheel on outta the Plaza and I'm just concentrating on getting up my speed. 'Cause I can't figure out what to think. Them two women kissing and then, when they get caught, just laughing about it. And here I'm laughing, too, for no reason at all. I'm sailing down the boulevard laughing like a lunatic, and then I'm singing at the top of my lungs. And climbing that big old hill up to Summit Avenue is just as easy as being on a escalator.

Fifth Sunday

*T*he church stood on a hill all to itself, at the intersection of Prospect and Maple. Opposite the broad, shallow steps and the three sets of double doors was a small ash-and-gravel parking lot, room for only a handful of cars; the minister and his assistants had reserved spaces, while the rest of the congregation used the side streets. Valerie's father always parked parallel to Prospect, nosing the sleek car down the steep brick road lined by abandoned houses and devil-strips overgrown to knee-level, weeds topped by sinister furred knobs.

Catercorner from the church was a park. It was everything a park should be: green, shaded, quiet. Stout black poles marked its perimeter at regular intervals, and strung between each pole were two chains, one at waist-level and another six inches from the ground. The park itself was segmented by two concrete paths that cut it on the diagonals, like a huge envelope. The paths seemed to serve no other purpose than help people walk through the park as quickly as possible: there were no animals, no vendors, no bandstand; Valerie could not remember ever seeing anyone sitting on the few chilly benches.

Valerie and the other young people of the church used the park as a short-cut to the all-night coffeehouse on East Exchange Street. "Max's Diner" was connected to a motel; each Sunday morning an exciting, bedraggled assortment

First published in *Fifth Sunday: Stories by Rita Dove*. Callaloo Fiction Series (Vol. 1), Lexington: University of Kentucky Press, 1985 of people could be found at the L-shaped counter. The waitress was called Vera; her upswept blonde hair resembled a fanciful antique urn. She was friendly; sometimes she even let them sit at the counter.

Usually they didn't have time to take a seat. Main Service began at eleven sharp; and though Sunday School was supposed to be over at 10:30, often their teacher, Mr. Brown, got so carried away that they had to resort to coughs and exaggerated glances at the clock before he caught on and let them loose—but not before a five minute lecture on obedience and diligence that made it nearly eleven by the time they got to Max's....

Of course, it hadn't always been like that. When she was little, Valerie wouldn't have dared slip off to anyplace as worldly as a diner. But now that she had been promoted to the Upper Sunday School, it was a matter of course to have a Mounds bar for furtive munching during church. The park hadn't always been a thoroughfare, either. Many, many years ago Valerie's mother had first been kissed there. She had been in the junior choir, and there was a boy among the tenors named John, with light brown eyes and long dark lashes. Choir rehearsals were on Tuesday evenings; before rehearsals the two of them, Valerie's mother and John, had taken to walking in the park. It was summer; the birds sat as if drugged in the trees. He touched her hand and then her cheek, and then he kissed her.

What was it like? "Nice—a kiss," was all her mother had to say about it. Valerie was fourteen and had never been kissed. It was impossible to imagine it ever happening. How did one go about it? Sure, there were plenty of boys around who wanted to—loud boys with scabs on their knuckles. No, she would have to like a boy before she let him kiss her. But as soon as she started to like someone, she got shy and tongue-tied whenever he tried to talk to her. What other choice did he have but to lose interest? No one can like a stone.

Church was the most glorious part of her existence. Her schoolmates she saw every day, in the halls or around the neighborhood—but when Sunday came, she would put on her best clothes and ride to the other side of the city. Deep familial traditions gave the church a varied congregation—people from all parts of town and all social and economic levels filled the dark waxed pews, so that once a week Valerie had friends who were different and met boys who played basketball in rival high schools. No wonder she scorned her classmates and looked forward to Sunday as if to a party.

She was not in the choir but in the junior ushers. Ever since she could remember, Valerie knew she would join one or the other. Whenever the choir stood up, their blue silk robes swaying slightly as they rocked to the beat, an amorphous yearning would surge in her, crystallizing to a single thought: *I can sing!* she would whisper, and bite her lip. Everyone knew, though, that most of the girls in the junior choir were "fast;" nowadays it was no honor to be associated with it.

Andrew was another reason for joining the usher board. He was the president. He was also the minister's son, and as such the undisputed leader of the male youth. He was very ugly—a pasty yellow color, and he wore his sandy hair in a short squarish afro, since it was too kinky to wear fuller. An overlarge lower lip pulled his mouth open slightly, exposing a row of widely-spaced teeth. His ears stood out and the lobes were covered with tiny indentations, as if someone had pricked them with a fork, like a pie shell. And he was blind in one eye. The story went that when he was ten he had been in a snowball fight; somebody threw a snowball with a stone in it. Valerie had to catch her breath whenever she thought of it. Imagine—you're playing outside with no other thought but fun when suddenly, from nowhere, a hard coldness slams into you—an arrow of ice—and when it's all over, you've lost half your sight. It must be horrible. It must be something you could never forget. Valerie found herself staring at Andrew. Of a mottled gray-blue color, both eyes were so beautifully vague that when the light struck them they seemed to disappear. If she watched closely she could pick up the slightly slower reaction of one iris, the minute flagging of the right eyelid when he looked sideways.

It endears him to me, Valerie said silently to herself as they drove home from church. After the car had crunched through the gravel driveway and she was safely in her room and had slipped off her patent-leather T-straps, she looked earnestly into the mirror and said, aloud this time: *It endears him to me.* She studied the tiny pearl earrings her parents had given her for graduation from grade school; she took them off, unscrewing the silver fastenings and locking them in the padded jewelry box. Andrew was seventeen. She had no chance.

She clutched to her passion like a pillow or a torch. On long Saturday afternoons she dreamed about the kiss to come—there was the park, there were the smoke-and-sky eyes to replace the light brown ones. Only when she daydreamed did Valerie experience the power of hope, a sense of luxurious apprehension.

One Saturday night the young people of the white Lutheran church one block over invited the black youth to see a movie on Martin Luther King. Valerie's mother dropped her off. It was still a little early, so she walked over to Prospect and stood for a while on the corner, looking down the hill.

This was not the choked, winding alley where her father parked—here the road fell straight and sharply into the city below. And she was on top of it, looking down. She really didn't know why she had walked to the church—maybe on the chance that the minister was inside working, and that Andrew might come walking out—maybe. But as she stood there looking down at the flushed sky and the indistinct trees clumped below it and below them, the tiny gray houses in the tiny gray streets, she felt a glow inside her chest—like a net with a brilliant fish struggling to escape—and she felt strong. Even the cool white steps of the church were not her equal.

She went back to the Lutheran church, where everyone had gathered in the basement. There were introductions, then the announcement for the start of the movie. Valerie was about to sit next to the aisle when Andrew came up and asked if she minded him sitting next to her. "Of course not," she said, and broke into a sweat behind her knees. She scooted over, trying to regain her composure. But Andrew would not wait for that. He plied her with questions—what kind of music did she like? Was she going to the high school track meet next week? He was sitting to her right, so the good eye could see every movement she made—still, whenever he said something, he turned so that they were face-to-face, the unresponsive eye giving him a vulnerable look. Then the lights went out. He crossed his legs and leaned back, throwing his left arm across the back of her chair; terrified, Valerie sat very still and tried to concentrate on the movie. From time to time Andrew would take away his arm, lean forward, and whisper in her ear; his comments were so hilarious that she could hardly keep from laughing out loud, and before the film was over she even managed a few witticisms of her own.

The next day was Fifth Sunday. Whenever there was a fifth Sunday in a month, the young people presided over the main service. They ushered, provided music, read the text from the Scriptures, passed the collection plate—even led the congregation in prayer for the sick and shut-in. The only thing they did not do was give the sermon. Valerie was so excited from the previous evening that she barely ate anything at breakfast. She had slept very little; and at seven she finally got up to press the knife-pleated white skirt. She hated their uniforms. The skirt was made from some synthetic material that stuck to her legs; the baggy white blouse was not cool at all. Besides, her period had started, which meant that she would have to wear the plastic-lined panties that made her feel like a baby in diapers.

Today, however, even that could not discourage her. Andrew would forego ushering to help at the altar, so today she could look at him as much as she pleased.

It was a hot, humid morning, and by 10:30 everyone looked limp and disgruntled. As on every Sunday when they ushered, the junior ushers did not go to Max's but convened in the small lounge off the main lobby. The decision who was going to "key" had to be made, and it was always a controversial one. There were four aisles to be covered. The side aisles had the least traffic and the windows. The right middle aisle was called the "key." Most of the people came down this aisle. The old, respected members had their regular seats in the front pews; the choir marched down this aisle and up into the chancel; all the fashionable middle class who'd come to show off their new clothes wanted seats in the middle section where they could be seen. The key usher had to remember where the regulars sat, get out of the way of the choir, gesture grandly to the bourgeoise's chosen pew, and take messages to the pulpit. Nobody wanted to be key.

Valerie was assigned aisle three. Of course she was glad she didn't have to key. But almost as many people came down her aisle as down the other middle aisle. It was strange how people always streamed toward the middle of anyplace. At the supermarket they fought for a parking space in the thick of all the other cars; after church in the lobby or on the steps they gravitated toward the largest groups, squeezing through the outer fringe to get a better angle on the discussion in the inner circle. But at least—even if she didn't have a window—she had an unobstructed view of the altar. Except when the congregation stood up to sing, she could see Andrew clearly. He wore a light blue suit with a yellow shirt just a shade brighter than his skin. He looked self-confident, compassionate. He caught her glance and smiled.

The doors opened and people poured in. Valerie was shy of them. They were always in a hurry to be seated and never really looked at her. Today, though, she felt she was getting through it fairly well—although once when there was a crush of people, she had trouble with an old man whose cane kept getting jammed between the pews and some woman in a pink silk hat squeezed past Valerie impatiently, the thick scent of her perfume trailing her like fame itself. Valerie's stomach was growling; she hoped no one could hear it.

Sunlight bowled through the vaulted windows; sweat stood out in delicate beaded patterns on the powdered brows of the women; the cardboard fans in the hands of the junior choir members flitted at an amazing rate, like small scared birds. Valerie felt the dampness under her arms, between her shoulder blades, inside the plastic pants. Her stockings felt like they had been dragged in wet sand—in fact she itched all over, and she kept shifting her weight from one foot to the other and adjusting her white gloves. *I'll stick it out until this song is over and then I'll leave the floor,* she thought; but when the congregation had regained their seats Valerie felt that would look too conspicuous; so she decided to wait until the responsive reading was over. She tried concentrating on a sunbeam that bisected the small table where the gleaners were arrayed. *After the responsive reading,* she thought, *the little girls in their white robes will march up to the altar, and each one will take a gleaner and pass it from row to row, and each person will take out a dime or a nickel and drop it in the slot...*Valerie thought of the sound all those coins clinking against glass would make. The sunbeam had separated into tiny glowing dots, and there were particles of dust suspended between the spots—the sun glancing off of all that silver made her dizzy....

How cool it had become suddenly, and a breeze too! It was a relief to be able to take her mind off her problems. At any rate, she was glad the weather had broken. Now she was lying in a hammock on the back porch with a tall cool glass of punch beside her. As she rocked back and forth, the wind—no, no more than a breath, a zephyr!—lifted her hair to dry her forehead, then dropped each strand gently back into place. Faraway the doorbell rang. She heard her mother's voice, then footsteps growing louder and the screen door slamming; she swooned in delicious anticipation, and then Andrew was beside her with a cool hand for her forehead and a gaze of tender solicitude radiating from the watery depths of his eyes....

Why did she feel so terrible all of a sudden, and why had the sun come back? For a moment there was nothing but a piercing whiteness, and Valerie felt as if she were floating—but badly, in jerks and bobs. Someone was whispering below her...what were they saying? *She must have fainted.*

No! Valerie tried to lift her head but only succeeded in looking down the length of her own body, which was stiff as a board. Several men were carrying her down the aisle. The service had stopped; she lifted her head again, and this time saw the choir's and the minister's startled faces suspended at the far end of the aisle. Then they were gone.

She was laid out on a couch in the lounge and a fat woman in white with a businesslike manner stuck something under her nose. An electric shock jolted her to the base of her spine. After the coolness and the dream of Andrew, this nausea! She felt wounded in her soul. More than anything she was ashamed.

Faces mooned above her and hands undid her collar, rubbed her wrists. None of their administrations did anything but agitate her still further, and she was about to tell them so (if she could only get her mouth to cooperate), when a woman Valerie did not recognize appeared at the foot of the couch and leaned over her. The woman made no attempt to help; she looked Valerie up and down with a hard cool stare and said, "Who knows? Maybe she's pregnant."

Valerie sputtered, struggling onto her elbows, but the nurse held her down. "It's not true!" she gasped and tried to get up again. The circle of faces closed in on her, whispering soothing things she could not understand. The woman had disappeared. No one would tell Valerie her name, though she thrashed and pleaded.

Valerie's parents had arrived. Her father stood awkwardly to one side as her mother knelt beside the couch and looked at her with large, troubled eyes. Valerie barely noticed them; she was thinking of the woman spitting that word over her like a pronouncement: *pregnant.* Well, the bitch wouldn't get away with it. There weren't that many people in this church she didn't know—she'd find out who she was. She'd make them tell. Bitch. She'd find her. She'd find her.

J. California Cooper

The Life You Live
(May Not Be Your Own)

L ove, marriage, and friendship are some of the most important things in your life…if you ain't sick or dyin'! And, Lord knows, you gotta be careful, careful 'cause you sometimes don't know you been wrong 'bout one of them till after the mistake shows up! Sometimes it takes years to find out, and all them years are out of your own life! It's like you got to be careful what life you live, 'cause it may not be your own! Some love, marriage, or friend done led you to the wrong road, 'cause you trusted 'em!

Of course, I'm talkin' 'bout myself, but I'm talkin' 'bout my friend and neighbor, Isobel, too. Maybe you, too! Anyway, if the shoe don't fit, don't put it on!

I might as well start at the beginning. See, Isobel and I went to school together, only I lived in town and she came in from the country. Whenever she came. Her daddy was always keepin' her home from school to do work on that ol' broke-down farm of his. He was a real rude, stocky, solid, bearlike, gray-haired man with red-rimmed eyes. Can't lie about him, he worked all the time hisself. But that's what he wanted to do with his life. His kids, they didn't mind

First Published in *Some Soul to Keep* by J. California Cooper. New York: St. Martin's Press, 1987

workin', but not ALL the time! He never gave them any money to spend on pleasure things like everybody need if they gonna keep workin' all the time.

He was even stingy at the dinner table. Grow it or don't get it! Even his horses and cows was thin. Everything on his farm didn't like him. All his kids he hadn't put out for not workin' left soon as they could, whether they was out of school yet or not! That finally left only Isobel. She did farm work and all the housework, small as she was. Her mother was sickly. I 'magine I'd get sick, too, if I knew that man was comin' home to me every day!

He ran all the boys off who came out to see Isobel. He either put them to work on some odd job or told 'em not to come back. I know, 'cause when we was 'bout sixteen and still in high school I rode out there with one boy who was scared to go by hisself. I wasn't scared of nothin'…then!

I saw that ol' man watchin' and waitin' for us to reach the house. Isobel was standing in the doorway, a pot in her hands and a apron on, getting ready to go slop some pigs. She looked…her face was all cracked, it seemed. Not 'cause she liked that boy so much, but because she wanted to be young, 'stead of old like her father. We left.

Now me, I grew up any which way in my parents' house, full of kids and everybody building their own world right there inside that house. We had the kind of family that when Mama and Daddy was gone off on some business or other and we s'posed to clean the house? we would slop soapy water all over the kitchen floor, put our skates on and have a skating rink party. Oh! That was fun, fun! Then as soon as Mama and Daddy drive up, them skates be off! We could mop, dust, wash dishes, make beds, whatever, before they got in the house! There! Poor, for sure, but happy!

Well, you know you grow up and forget everybody and everything 'cept your own special business. That's what I did. I was grown and married twelve years when Isobel came back into my life. She had been married 'bout seven years then herself.

Tolly was her husband's name, and he had done got to be a good friend of my husband. Tolly was a travelin' salesman, for true. He had traveled right on Isobel's daddy's farm and stole that girl right out from under her daddy's time clock she was still punching at. She was twenty-four years old then, still not ever married. We was both thirty-one or so when they moved next door to me and Gravy.

I was very glad to have a old school chum for a neighbor. I had just at that time left one of them ladies' clubs that ain't nothing but fussing, gossip, and keepin' up with the Joneses type of thing. Not doin' nothin' important! Just getting together to go to each other's houses to see how everybody else was livin'! Stuff like that. My usual best friend had moved away from this town, and

I didn't have a new one I trusted. My mama had told me that I would look up one day and could count my friends on one hand and sometimes one finger! She was right…again.

One day, just before Tolly and Isobel moved in their new house, he was over to see Gravy, and I told him "You all have dinner over here with us on your movin' day. Tell Isobel don't bother with no cookin'!"

He looked at me like I was in space. "Better not do that, Molly. I been puttin' off telling you that for some reason Isobel won't tell me, she does not like you…at all!"

I was honestly shocked. "Not like me? Why?"

He frowned and shook his head. "Won't tell me why. Just got awful upset when I told her you was going to be our neighbor."

I never heard of such a thing! "Upset?"

He nodded his head. "I mean she was! Almost didn't want to move here! There just ain't nowhere else I like right now, and the price is right."

I thought a minute. "Well, when you all move in, I'll find out what's wrong! I can't remember nothing I ever did to her. I was lookin' forward to havin' you two close—"

He cut me off. "Don't count on it! Isobel is kinda sickly, and it makes her awful mean to get along with! Sometimes I want to give up, but we married and I'm gonna make it work, single-handed if I have to!"

I sat down, wondering. In all the time we knew him I never had guessed they had a problem marriage.

He turned to my husband. "Man, you lucky havin' a wife like Molly. Molly got sense. My woman think everybody always lyin' to her!" He turned to me. "If you ever run into her accident'ly don't mention nothin' 'bout my name! She b'lives every woman is after me! Anyway, she say you already done told all kinda lies on her when you all was in school."

I gasped, 'cause it wasn't true!

He kept talkin'. "She told me some terrible things about you! But I know how she lies, so I didn't pay them no mind."

Gravy was looking at him with a funny-lookin' frown on his face. I looked like I was being pushed out of a airplane.

Tolly ended up telling us, as he shook his head sadly, "She goes to bed…and every mornin' when she gets up, the pillowcase be just full of blood. Her mouth bleeds from rotten teeth. Her breath stinks! Bad! She don't never bathe. I have to make her! We don't have kids like you-all 'cause she hates 'em! Hates sex!" He looked at Gravy. "I have to *fight* her to get a little lovin'!"

Oh, he told us so many bad things about his own wife!

When they moved in, I pulled the shades down on that side of the house. And—don't this sound dumb?—we never hardly spoke for twelve years! Twelve years!

If I happen to come out to empty garbage or do something and see her over the hedge, we just did not and sometimes we pretended we didn't see each other. At the market either, or…or anywhere!

Sometimes at some holiday gatherings when we all happen to be there I'd see Isobel. She'd be in a corner somewhere. Sad eyes, mouth always closed, and when she did talk, she put her hand over it. Which made what Tolly said seem true.

Sometimes when I had problems, I'd look over there and wish we were friends. Tolly was gone 'bout four days out of every week. Even when he was home they never went anywhere or had any company. So I knew she had to get lonely sometime. But when Tolly would come over, he always reminded me by some world or other that Isobel did not like me…at all.

The twelve years passed without us ever getting together. Ain't that dumb?

You remember I mentioned my problems? They didn't seem to be big ones. All the ladies said I was lucky to have a husband like Gravy. The fact is I got so many things to tell you that happened all at the same time, I don't know how to start.

Now, Gravy was a good husband, good provider. We raised our kids right. One went to college, one got married. Now we were home alone together.

All down through our married years, he always liked me lookin' kinda messy. Said it made me look homey and woman-warm. He urged me to eat to get meat on my bones till you couldn't tell I had any bones! He liked gray hair, so when mine started turning, he wouldn't let me dye it. He didn't like makeup, so I didn't hardly wear none. Just liked my cooking, so we never went out to dinner, I always cooked! He liked me in comfortable clothes, so I had a lot of baggy dresses. Didn't want me to worry my "pretty head," so he took care of all the money.

I looked, by accident, in the mirror one day…and I cried! I was a fat, sloppy-dressed, house-shoe wearin', gray-haired, old-lookin' woman! I was forty-three and looked fifty-five! Now, ain't nothin' wrong with bein' fifty-five years old if that's where you are. But I wasn't there yet! I had been lookin' in mirrors through the years, and I could see myself then. I felt bad, but I could take it if it made my husband happy. That last day though, I couldn't take it!

That was the day I saw Gravy in the park. A Sunday. He had gone out to do somethin'. Hadn't said what. I was sitting in the park, on a cold bench, by myself. THEY was walkin', laughin' and holding hands. He even peck-kissed her every once in a while, throwing his arm around her shoulders and pulling her to his old slim body. Not a gray hair on his head 'cause he said his job might think he was gettin' old. He dyed his hair. He just liked mine gray.

Let me tell you, PLEASE! She was slim. Wasn't no potatoes, biscuits, and pork chops sittin' on her hips! She had plenty makeup on. I'd say a whole servin'! Black hair without a spot of gray in it! High-heeled shoes and a dress that kept bouncing up so you could see that pretty underwear she had on. She was half his age! Why, she wasn't his type at all! And I could tell by lookin' at her she didn't know how to cook…he took her out!

Big as I was, I jumped behind the bushes and watched 'em slowly pass by, all my weight on my poor little bended knees. Cramped. By the time he got in front of me, I could have yelled a Tarzan holler and leaped on him and beat him into a ass pate.

But…I let them pass. I didn't want HER to see how bad I looked! I know I looked crazy, too, as well as ugly.

When they was well past me, I walked like a ape out of them bushes 'cause I couldn't stand up straight too fast! Some kids saw me come out them bushes and musta thought I had gone to the bathroom in there, 'cause they said something about a "swamp" and ran off laughin'…at me! I cried all the way home.

I'm telling you, I was hurt. Now, you hurt when somebody meets you and loves you up and in a few days you don't hear from them no more. But…this man been lovin' me up twenty-four years! Settin' my life, my looks, and my thoughts! I let him! Well, that hurt filled my whole body and drug my heart down past my toes, and I had to drag it home, forcin' one foot at a time. Going home? Wasn't no home no more. Chile, I hurt! You hear me?!

Now, I'm going to tell you somethin'. If you ain't ready to leave or lose your husband…don't get in his face and tell him nothin'! You wait till you got yourself together in your mind! You wait till you have made your heart understand…you can and will do without him! Otherwise, you may tell him you know what he's doin', thinking YOU smart and he's caught! And HE may say, "Well, since you know, now you know! I ain't giving her up!" Then what you gonna do?

Tell you what I did. But wait, let me tell you first things first. Gravy came home, sat in his favorite chair lookin' at TV, smokin' his pipe. I stared at him, waiting for him to see that I knew. He didn't see me so I got up, put my hands on my fat hips, nose flaring wide open, and I told him I KNEW!

Gravy put his pipe down, just as calm as I ever seen him in my life, turned off the TV, sat back down, put his hands on his knees, and told me…he wanted a divorce.

A DIVORCE?!

I felt like someone had dipped me in cement. I couldn't move. I couldn't speak. I couldn't do nothin' but stare at Gravy. My mind was rushin' back over our years together. Over the last months...looking for signs.

We had been so...comfortable.

He said to me, "You have let yourself go. You make me feel old. You ARE old."

I thought of answers, but my mouth wouldn't act right. He went on and on.

"I ain't got but one life, it ain't over! I got some good years left!" He patted his chest. "I need someone can move on with me. You don't and can't compete with nobody. You don't know how to do nothin' but cook and eat! You ain't healthy! All that fat! Look at your clothes! Look at your head! A lazy woman can't 'spect to keep a man! You been all right...but...I GOT to GO! You tell the kids."

My heart was twistin' around in my breast. I was struck!

He went on and on. "We'll sell this house and each get a new fresh start."

At last my lips moved. "Sell this house? My house? My home?"

His lips moved. "Ain't no home no more. Just a house." He got up talking, putting his foot down. "We gonna sell it and split the money and go each our own way."

I said to myself, This m——f——!

Then I said to him, "You m——f——!"

He walked away. "Ain't no sense in all that. It's too late for sweet names now!"

Now, at first I had been feelin' smart, but that flew out the window. Chile, I lost all my pride, my good sense. Tell you what I did.

I fell out on the couch, cryin', beggin' him to think of our years together, our children, our home, our future, his promises, our dreams. I cried and I begged. Got on my knees, chile! Tears running down, nose running, mouth running, heart stopping. I fought in every way, using everything I could think of to say to hold that man! That man who did not want me! If I had waited till my sense was about me, I'd maybe begin to think of the fact of why was he so much I had to want him? After all, he wasn't no better, no younger than me! I had already had him twenty-four years...maybe that was enough! For him AND for me! But I didn't stop to think that. I just cried and begged.

I had heard some old woman say, "If your man 'bout to fight you or leave you, go somewhere, take your drawers off, go back where he is and fall out on the floor and kick your legs open when you fall back! That'll stop him!" Welllll, it don't always work! It don't always stop him as long as you want it to! Gravy stopped for 'bout thirty minutes, then that was over. I was back where I started.

He left, GOING SOMEWHERE. While I sat in my house that would soon be not mine.

Then I fought for that house like I had fought for him. Why, it stood for my whole life! It's all I had, 'sides my grown children, and they was gone on to live their own lives, have their own children, their own husband and wife.

I was alone.

Just yesterday I had a family. A home. I thought it was the worse moment in my life! But, you see, you never know everything till everything happens!

Then all this stuff started happenin' at the same time! Before my house was sold, when Isobel and Tolly had lived next door twelve years, Tolly died. Had a heart attack. A young man, too! Prove that by the fact that he had that attack in bed with a seventeen-year-old girl! Isobel was forty-three, like me. Now she was alone, I was half dead.

I decided to just go on over there, whether she liked me or not! I baked a cake and went to the wake. She was lookin' like a nervous wreck before Tolly died. Now she still looked a wreck but not so nervous. She looked like she was holdin' up quite well. So well I wished Gravy had died 'stead of getting a divorce. Anyway! She looked at me, her lip dropped, her eyes popped. I slammed the cake down as easy as I could, not to hurt that cake, you know, and said, "Yes, it's me! I'm doin' the neighborly thing whether you like me or not, and whether you eat it or not!" Then I turned to go and she grabbed my arm.

"Whether I like YOU?" she asked.

I turned to her. "Yeah! I don't care if you don't like me. I think all this mess is foolishness! I ain't never done nothin' to you!"

She looked kinda shocked. "Why...you're the one who does not like me! You didn't want to be friends with me! Tolly told me all those bad things you said about me!"

It was my turn to look shocked...again! You might say I was at the time of life where ever' which way I turned, I got shocked.

I gasped. "I never said anything bad about you! I wanted to be your friend."

Her eyes opened wide. "I wanted to be your friend. I needed a friend! I didn't never have nobody by Tolly."

We looked in each other's eyes till we understood that Tolly had planned all this no friendship stuff.

Well, we became friends again. She told me her new name was Belle, said, "Who wants to be named Is-so-bel!" Said, "Now that I am free, I can change my name if I want to! Change my whole life if I want to!" Now!

I learned a lot I did not know, just on account of my not stopping to think for myself. Listenin' to others, taking their words. Trusting them to THINK for me!

Tolly had told Belle the same thing he had told me. PLUS, he ruined that girl's mind! Just shit in it! Told her things like when she talked and opened her mouth, spit stretched from some teeth to some other teeth and just hung there. So she tried never to talk to people.

Told her all kinds of mean, violent things. Every time he went to the store alone, he would tell her stories, like someone was beatin' his wife 'bout tellin' lies. Or someone had killed his wife for lying! Sneaking out on the side! Every day he had things like these to tell her. He would slide out of bed and tell her she was the one left streaks of shit on it, 'cause she didn't wipe herself right! She got where she almost bathed when she went to the bathroom.

He had her believing nobody liked her! Everybody told lies on her! She was weak-minded. A fool about life. Was even ugly. Had a odor. Was very dumb and helpless. That she lost things.

He had taken her wedding rings once, for two years. Hid them. She found them in the bottom of a jar of cold cream. He told her she put them there. She knew she hadn't.

He told her she needed therapy and made her take—GAVE her—hot, hot baths, let the water run out and then he ran cold, cold water on her, holdin' her down in the tub. He threw her food out, said she was tryin' to poison him. Him! Complained he was sick after he would eat somethin' of hers. Whenever they was gettin' along all right and she wanted to go somewhere, he would dress, get to the door, then get very ill. If it was the show, he'd wait till he was in the line almost at the ticket window, then he'd get sick. If they went to the market together, he'd accuse her of talkin' and huggin' a man who had never even been there. He didn't allow her to spend any money except for the house note, food, and insurance. She bought plenty food, paid the house notes, and bought lots of insurance, 'cause that's all she could do!

Wouldn't let her join any clubs. Well, that mighta been good. I was in one at the time I needed to get out of. Tell you about that later!

He kept her up hundreds, thousands of nights, wouldn't let her sleep! Makin' her tell him about her past, and she really didn't have any. From her daddy to him. He had to know that. He did know that! He was sick, crazy. The kind of crazy that can walk around lookin' like everybody else and get away with it! I bet he told Gravy about all them ugly bleeding teeth, bad breath, oh, all them things to keep Gravy away from her when he was out of town!

I never did see her cry.

The slick bastard!

Well, you know. You know all about things like that.

We became friends again. I helped her settle her affairs and all. She said, "I'm gonna sell this prison."

I said, "Sell your only home?" Aghast.

She said, "Money buys another home."

I thought about that!

She said, "Some of the worst times of my life was spent here! First I was glad to leave my daddy's house. Now I'm glad to leave Tolly's! The next house I get is gonna be mine. MINE! I'll live in that one in peace."

I thought about that.

I went to the bank with her to get all the matters set straight. The lady at the desk heard the word *deceased* and looked up in sympathy. But Belle was smiling, a bright, happy smile. She was the happiest woman in the bank!

She sat there in front of that lady, a little ragged, hair undone but neat. Nervous breakdown just leavin', but still showing around the edges. Nails bit off. Lips bit up. Graying hair saying she was older, but bright future-lookin' eyes saying she was ready! MY friend!

That woman really had bought a lot of insurance! Over a hundred thousand dollars' worth! And insurance to pay the house off, the car she couldn't drive yet, off, and any furniture they owed for, off. That's one thing he did for her, he let her buy insurance. And she sure did!

Belle was gaining weight, lookin' way better as time went by. And she was going to the hairdresser, buying clothes, going to shows, nightclubs and restaurants. I went with her most times. I was still in my clubs, a reading club and a social club. I left the reading club 'cause they wanted us to make reports on what we read. I didn't want to make no report! I just wanted to read in peace…exchange books, eat, things like that. I dropped out that club and just started buying my own books.

Both Belle and me was lookin' better, healthier, and was more peaceful every day. She was taking painting lessons now and music appreciation. Tolly hadn't liked her to go to school; she might meet somebody. He always told her as he laughed at her, "What kinda thing you goin' over there to waste time doin'? Showing them people how clumsy and dumb you are! Girl, throw that mess out of your mind!" He put little holes in her plans, and her confidence just leaked out. The desire to go had stayed, though. She was the busiest widow I ever did see! Some people might turn over in their graves, but I knew if Tolly could see her he was spinning in his!

I looked at her livin' her life, and I began to really like what I saw. 'Stead of staying home in case Gravy called, I started goin' to a class to lose weight 'cause Belle said it was healthier and I would look better, too! I started goin' to the hairdresser. Not to dye my hair—that's too much work to keep up—but a natural ain't nothin' but a nappy if you don't take care of it! It's shaped and highlighted now. Belle was learning and showed me how to use a little makeup right. Don't try to hide nothin', just bring out what you got!

She gardened a lot, and I began to help her. We ate fresh vegetables and bought fresh fruit. Dropped them ham hocks and short ribs, chile, less we had a special taste for 'em sometime. I didn't miss 'em! Found out all that rice and gravy and meat was really for Gravy. Wondered how he was eatin' lately, but threw that out my mind 'cause I had to get to my financial-planning class or my jewelry-making class or my self-awareness class. The only one I dropped out of was self-awareness. I knew myself. I was learnin' my strength every day. I already was over my weakness.

I missed a man beside me at night, but I was so busy when I looked up six months had passed and I hadn't cried once.

I didn't fight for the house no more. I wanted it to be sold. I didn't fight for Gravy no more. I was glad he was gone. Mostly. He had done me a big favor by giving me MY life back. You hear me? He handed my life to me and I had fought him! Fought him to take it back! Keep it! Use me some more! Chile, chile, chile.

Gravy noticed when he dropped by to check on the house. He noticed a lot 'bout the new me. He slapped me on my behind. I didn't say nothin'; after all, he had been my husband. I sashayed it in front of him as I walked him to the door. I put him out 'cause I had to get to school or somethin'. Or maybe just lay down in peace and think of my new future. Or take a bath and oil and cream my skin for the next man in my life who I might love…anything! Whatever I want to do! Now!

I prayed for the house to sell. I wanted MY money! 'Cause I had plans.

Belle's house was sold. She moved in my spare rooms while she looked for somethin' she wanted to buy.

I asked her, "You gonna buy a smaller house this time? You don't need much room."

She looked at me thoughtfully. "You know, I been thinking. A house just sits you in one spot and you have to hold your life into that space and around the town it's in. I don't need much room in a house, but I need a lotta space around me."

I thought about that.

Soon after that, she told me she had bought five acres on the edge of a lake. She was goin' to buy a mobile home, nice, roomy, and comfortable. Live there with the lake on one side, the trees on the other, and the town where she could reach it if she wanted to.

I thought about that, liked it, but I couldn't afford that. I told her, "I like that. That's really gonna be nice."

She answered, "Well, come on with me then!"

I know I looked sad. "Girl, my money ain't that heavy. Not for land AND a mobile home. You got over a hundred thousand dollars; I MAY get twenty thousand."

She say, "I can't live all over my five acres. Get you a mobile home and live on my land!" I know I smiled big as she went on talkin'. "Better still, I'll buy your mobile home 'cause you gonna need your money to live on. You buy the landfill I want for the garden 'cause I want to grow my own food."

I thought only a minute; I wanted this to be MY life. So I told her, "The land is yours. If I buy landfill, if I ever leave, I ain't gonna take it with me so it will still be yours, too. Tell you what, I'll buy my mobile home and pay your rent for use of the land. Then if I ever move, you can buy my home, cheap."

She laughed. "Girl, the land is paid for. I don't need no rent for land that's gonna sit there anyway! You my friend! The only one I got now."

I was happy, said, "You my only friend, too!" I was happy 'cause friends are so hard to find. People count their money 'fore they count friends.

Then she was serious. "I want to be alone. Don't want no man, woman, chick or child tellin' me what to do no more!"

I shook my head. "Me neither! Lord, no!"

She went on. "But everybody need some company sometime. You keep me from gettin' lonely enough to run out there in them silly streets and bring somethin' home I don't want!"

I spoke. "You got me started on my new life...school and everything!"

She was still serious. "I trust you."

I got more serious. "I trust you."

She kept talkin'. "I'm goin' to try to pay for everything in cash. Pay it off! Don't want to owe nobody nothin'!"

I added, "And grow our own food."

She nodded. "Come into town for whatever we need or want."

I was eager. "Don't need no fancy clothes."

She smiled. "We can live on a little of nothin'...and be fine! Don't have to go to work or kiss nobody's behind for nothing!"

I laughed out loud. "NOTHIN'!"

You know what we did? We went downtown and bought cowboy jeans, hats, boots, and shirts! We was dressin' for our country life. We was sharp!

It was finally time for her to go, everything ready for her. She drove off with a car full of paints and canvases. I forgot to tell you, she had learned how to drive and had a little red sports car! She wore dark goggles and a long scarf around her neck, just a-flyin' in the wind.

One day, for a minute, just for a minute, she looked sad to me. I looked sad to me. Two older ladies lookin' for a future. Goin' around acting like we was happy. I felt like crying. Belle saw me and asked why, and I told her. Then I did cry.

She put her hands on my shoulders. "Molly? You 'bout forty-five years old."

I corrected her—"Forty-four"—as I sobbed.

She didn't laugh at me. "Well, s'pose you live to be eighty?"

Somethin' in my breast lifted.

She went on. "What you gonna do with them other thirty-five years? What you gonna call 'em if not your future?"

The tears stopped.

But she didn't. "Now, Molly, you my friend. But don't you move out there, away from all your clubs and people, if you gonna be sad. I don't want no sad, depressed killjoy for a neighbor, messin' up my beautiful days! Don't move!"

I could see she meant it. I thought of my clubs where I couldn't stand nobody hardly. I thought of my empty days of food with Gravy. I even thought of my kids who had their own families now. I shook my head so hard. Clearin' it! Shit!

She looked at me steady. "If you even THINK you might want to stay here, PLEASE stay! Till you get all of what you need. 'Cause if you get out there and you got a complaint, I don't want to hear it! 'Less it's 'cause you sick or somethin'!"

She left.

At last my house sold. I went and told the mobile-home man I was ready, gave him a check with no signature on it but mine!

Then I gave my last club meeting, 'cause I knew I was never gonna have to be bothered with them again!

One woman specially, Viola Prunebrough, always was talking 'bout me and laughin' at me. This meeting was specially for her, but the others deserved it, too.

In my reading class we had read Omar Khayyám, and I learned about wrapping food in grape leaves. At the last meeting before this one, I had served them, thinkin' it was some high-class stuff. I didn't know what to put in them, so I stuffed them with chitterlings. It was good to me! Viola had talked about me and laughed all over town. Made me look like a fool in front of everybody. Now you know why I wanted to pay her back. It's ugly, but it's true.

I let everybody in the club know the date for comin'. Then I went to try to find me some marijuana. It was hard to get! Didn't nobody know me that sells the stuff! But I finally got some. A quarter pound! When I prepared the food for that meetin', I mixed that stuff in everything I cooked. I put on a big pot of red beans. No meat, no salt, no onions, no nothin'! Just cooked. I had a plan, see?

When them ladies, all dressed up so nice to show off, got to eatin' all my good food, they went to talkin' loud, laughin', and jumpin' all over the place, saying stupid things. Eatin' and drinkin' everything in sight! I had to snatch some things right off the trays and hurry up and replace 'em 'cause them ladies was gonna eat my dishes and furniture if I didn't! Dainty painted lips just guzzled the wine.

Then I just happen to put on some records by Bobby Blubland. Chile! Them ladies was snapping their fingers, movin' around, shaking their behinds and everythin' else. Dancin' like they hadn't moved in years! Some was singing so loud they drowned Bobby Blubland out. They'd have got me put out if it wasn't my own house. We hadn't had no meeting yet, either!

Then all the food was gone 'cept the beans. The women musta been still starved, 'cause B.B. King was singing when I looked up and ALL them ladies was bearing down, coming on me in the kitchen, lookin' for anything they could get their hands on to eat. That marijuana must be something!

They got hold of them beans and ate them all. Gobbled them, smacking their lips and ohhhhh and ahhhhhing till every bean was gone. I laughed till I cried. Why, these were ladies! Beans were in their clothes, in their shoes, even in one lady's hair. I shoulda felt 'shamed, but I didn't. I didn't eat anything myself! Some of them was getting sleepy. Well, they sure were full! Lou Rawls couldn't keep them up anymore. I told them they better go, and then I fixed something for Viola's stomach: a cup of hot tea with a little Black Draught in it. I rushed her out then. I know when she got home she didn't get no rest! I played music for her exit; she wanted to stay and talk and hug and cry between belches. She danced out the door with her fat self, cramps only beginnin' to hit them beans in her belly. Then they were all gone. When they came to theirselves, to ask me what I had cooked, I was gone, too!

I picked up all the supplies I would need for my jewelry makin'. I had found out I was very good at it. People always wanted to buy whatever I made. I was goin' to make a little livin' on the side!

I moved into my new two-bedroom mobile home with the little fireplace. I always wanted one. As I drove over there for the first time, the smile on my face liked to stretched from here to yonder! I laughed out loud, several times…and wasn't nobody in the car but me!

We each had a little sun porch built facing the lake. Just listen! 'Most every morning we wave to each other as we sit on that porch and watch the sun finish coming up, while we have coffee or tea or whatever! If it's warm, after the sun is up good, I always go for a swim. Belle usually comes out and sets up her painting stuff. Then maybe I fish and catch my lunch. I take her some, or if her sign is out that says "DON'T," then I don't!

Next, maybe I either put on some music I have learned to appreciate or go in my extra bedroom that is my workroom, 'less my kids are here visiting, and make jewelry to sell when I want to. Or I work in the garden, which is full and beautiful. Or I read. The main thing is I do whatever I want to, whenever I want to.

Sometimes I don't see Belle for days. I see her in the distance. We wave, but we don't talk. We ain't had a argument yet, except on where to plant the onions, tomatoes, or potatoes. Something like that.

I'm telling you, life can be beautiful! Peace don't cost as much as people think it does! It depends on what you want. Not money. People with plenty money don't get peace just 'cause they have money. I get lonely, but I never get sad or depressed.

We both got lonely for a man sometime. But we didn't know any that wouldn't come out here and mess things up...in some way.

Then the generator broke down and we had to call in a repairman. He came. A little, thin, bowlegged, slow-walkin', half-ugly man. He was the sweet kind. Anything you need, he wants to fix it for you. Well, there is always something that needs a little fixin'.

He would work, but he wouldn't talk 'bout nothin' but sex while he worked. He talked 'bout how many women loved him. Loved him makin' love to them. What a lover he was. That kinda stuff. He would stop and look for a wrench or screwdriver or hammer, look off in space and tell you 'bout that last beautiful woman who wanted to leave her husband for him, but he don't take nobody's wife! Or the sister who said, as she took off her clothes, "My sister told me how you make her feel. Now you ain't leavin' here till you make me feel that-away, too!"

I don't know was he lyin' all the time, but he did put stuff on your mind.

One day he came back by when everything had been done (and nobody had taken their clothes off once). He went to Belle's. She showed him her shotgun and told him, "If I don't send for you, don't come! I bought this to use and I know how! Don't bring no clouds 'round here, 'cause I will make it rain!" He left, wavin' his hand, telling her he didn't mean nothin' wrong. She thanked him and shut her door.

Now, it had been raining all night and the leaves was dripping over my roof. I could hear the steam sizzle as some of 'em hit my fireplace stack. I had awakened, and instead of putting on Percy Faith or somebody, I had put on B.B. King. When Mr. Repairman passed my house I told him, through the window, I had somethin' needed fixin'! He came on in.

The big LIAR! He couldn't do nothin' he bragged about!

He wanted to lay around in my bed and smoke a cigarette, drink a little wine, and talk. I told him, "You got to go!"

He left, saying, "All you women are crazy! That's why you ain't got no man!" I just laughed.

He still comes to fix the generator when we need him. But that's all!

At that time, Belle's loneliness came out in another way. See, when you have all this space and beauty, it seems to bring you closer to God. Belle decided she ought to know Him better.

This is what she said: "I know the human race ain't no accident. Be 'bout three billion accidents now! And ain't no new kinda accident happenin' all by it-self! Nowhere!"

I started to give my opinion, but she wasn't through.

"And another thing," she went on. "There has got to be some truth some-where! Some of this stuff got to be lies! If we die and rush up to Heaven right away, what is the resurrection for? What is Judgment Day gonna be if everybody is already gone on to Heaven? And if everybody returns to God, then who is on that big, wide road Jesus said would be so packed full of people?"

She made good sense, and it felt warm talking 'bout it. She got some books, and pretty soon she had a Bible study man coming out here. They'd sit on that porch of hers and study, argue, and talk for two or three hours every week. Then she would teach me what she learned. Show it to me in the Bible even! I enjoyed it and was reading the books myself.

On one of Belle's trips to town in her little red sports car she ran into Gravy. He said he needed to see me. She called me and let him talk, 'cause it was my business to give out my own number. I told him he could come out and talk.

He came. He drove up early one morning in a very big, nice blue car. I know he came that early 'cause he wanted to see was anybody there with me. There was only me...and peace. I thought I'd be nervous, but I wasn't.

He stepped in the door, head way out in front of him, looking in and around. His shiny pointy-toe shoe slipped on one of my small steps and he went down on one knee. I know it hurt and he wanted to holler, but he held hisself together and limped on in.

Said, "Hot damn, Molly, you got to do somethin' 'bout that step! Shit!"

I told him, "I ain't never slipped on it. Come on in, sit down. Want some coffee?"

He set. "Yeah, bring me some of that good coffee of yours. You make the best coffee in the world!"

While I got everything together I was lookin' at him lookin' at my place, my home. I really looked at him tryin' to see my twenty-four years. I ain't gonna talk about him. He didn't make me do nothin'. I let everything that happened happen. Other than Mala, his girl. Maybe that, too. Remember, I begged to stay with him even when I knew he had her!

He had changed, naturally, a couple of years had gone by. I looked at his hair. He was letting it go, and it was pretty damn near all gray now. He saw me lookin' and patted his head, sayin', "Mala like this ol' gray hair, say it makes me look mature." He laughed a low, empty, scratchy laugh.

My eyes happen to look down at his stomach when I handed him the napkin. He saw that, too, and said, "Mala say she like a round, cozy stomach. Say it's a sign of satisfaction!"

I thought to myself, Or constipation.

He stirred his coffee. "She like all them hamburgers and hot dogs, boxes of candy, jelly rolls from the bakery. Say all that meat and gravy is too heavy to be healthy." His voice was tryin' to sound happy and young, but it still came out disgusted. He looked at me. I was a slim-plump. Meat all where it ought to be, and healthy!

I sat and crossed my legs, the ones he hadn't seen in twenty-four years. He looked, and took a swallow of hot coffee. It was too hot, but he couldn't spit it out. He finally got it down.

I asked, "How is Mala?"

He put the cup down. Said with a surprised look, "You know, I came down a little sick and she got mad at me for it! Like I could help it! One little ol' operation!"

I said, "For Heaven's sake!"

He said, "Yeah!" He started to take another swallow of the coffee, but put the cup back down.

I asked, "Well, things are better now since you up and all?"

He pursed his lips and rubbed that sore knee. Said, "I don't rightly know. She left me 'bout two months ago." He looked outraged. "Do you know, the judge ain't gonna make her sell that house I bought? 'Cause she got two kids! Them kids ain't mine! Mine is grown and got they own homes! Them some other man's children livin' in my house that she won't let me live in!"

I sat up. "Well, what happened, for God's sake?"

He looked like he could cry. "She told me she like this gray hair...this...this belly and my...my...'scuse me, Molly—my lovin'! Then she got tired of my gray hair, my cozy belly, and my gas, and the way I cough in the bathroom in the mornings! Have you ever heard of such a thing?! You got to cough in the mornings to clear your throat! She crazy! That's what! Crazy!"

I sat back. "Well, I'll be damned!"

He was ready to really talk. "Ain't it a damn shame! And I have seen that man—that boy! She got him coming to MY house after dark! Nothin' but a kid! I could tell him somethin' 'bout what he is gettin' into! She ain't shit! She is a lyin' cracked-butt bitch!"

I sat up. "Don't talk like that in my house, Gravy. I got a special kind of vibration and atmosphere in my house. PEACE. I won't allow it to be disturbed."

He looked at me like I had just said, "Let's get in my flyin' saucer and go to Jupiter today!"

Well, I'm not goin' to bore you with what-all he said. He added up to him and me goin' back together, "like we always shoulda been in the first place." After all, I was the mother of his children. He missed me. When he got to the part where he had always thought of me, even in her arms, I gave him a look that he understood to mean "You are really killin' it!"

I didn't tell him, but I thought clearly, He don't have nothin' to show for twenty-six years of livin' now, 'cept gray hair, potbelly, and a blue car. I had a home…with atmosphere. I had a place where my children and grandchildren come spend the summer. I looked good. Because I was healthy. I ate right. Wasn't gonna go back to cookin' all that shit again!

I didn't need to say all those things. I didn't WANT him. No more, ever again, in this life, or no other life. I didn't love him.

I loved me.

Trying to hug me, he left, saying he'd be back bringing me something pretty. I told him, "Call first, I may be busy." As he drove away, he was the most sad, confused-lookin' man I had seen in a long, long time.

I never let him come back. He had done been free to pick and he had picked.

Belle got married to the Bible study man. She said to me, "Ain't it funny? People go to bars, be around purple-headed, shaved-headed, or even normal-lookin' people, lookin' for a mate. Why do they cry when things go wrong? What did they expect to find in a place like that? Moses?" That's the way she talks. Then she say, "How you doin', girl? Need anything?" That's what she says to me. My friend!

As a matter of fact, I'm doin' all right! I got a couple of fellows I go out with sometime. My jewelry makin' is so good I sell it fast as I can make it.

To think I fought this! Well, I don't know.

I don't have anyone I want to marry. Well, hell, I'm only goin' on fifty. I got a future if I live right. I got dreams. Now I swim in the lake. Maybe someday I'll try a ocean!

I get lonely sometime. But not loooooonely.

I might even get married again someday. That'd be nice, too. Only this time I know what kind of man I'd be lookin' for! 'Cause I have done found ME!

I love myself now...and everything around me...so much.

I know if I got a man there would be just that much more to love. But believe me, I'm doing all right!

You hear me?

Terry McMillan

Ma'Dear

(for Estelle Ragsdale)

L ast year the cost of living crunched me and I got tired of begging from
Peter to pay Paul, so I took in three roomers. Two of 'em is live-in nurses
and only come around here on weekends. Even then they don't talk to me
much, except when they hand me their money orders. One is from Trinidad and
the other is from Jamaica. Every winter they quit their jobs, fill up two and three
barrels with I don't know what, ship 'em home, and follow behind on an airplane.
They come back in the spring and start all over. Then there's the little college girl,
Juanita, who claims she's going for architecture. Seem like to me that was always
men's work, but I don't say nothing. She grown.

I'm seventy-two. Been a widow for the past thirty-two years. Weren't like
I asked for all this solitude, just that couldn't nobody else take Jessie's place is
all. He knew it. And I knew it. He fell and hit his head real bad on the tracks going to fetch us some fresh picked corn and okra for me to make us some succo-
tash, and never come to. I couldn't picture myself with no other man, even
though I looked after a few years of being alone in this big old house, walking
from room to room with nobody to talk to, cook or clean for, and not much
company either.

First published in *Callaloo* (Vol. 10, No. 1: 1987): 71–78

I missed him for the longest time and thought I could find a man just like him, sincerely like him, but I couldn't. Went out for a spell with Esther Davis's ex-husband, Whimpy, but he was crazy. Drank too much bootleg and then started memorizing on World War I and how hard he fought and didn't get no respect and not a ounce of recognition for his heroic deeds. The only war Whimpy been in is with me for not keeping him around. He bragged something fearless about how he coulda been the heavyweight champion of the world. Didn't weigh but 160 pounds and shorter than me.

Chester Rutledge almost worked 'ceptin' he was boring, never had nothing on his mind worth talking about; claimed he didn't think about nothing besides me. Said his mind was always clear and visible. He just moved around like a zombie and worked hard at the cement foundry. Insisted on giving me his paychecks, which I kindly took for a while, but when I didn't want to be bothered no more, I stopped taking his money. He got on my nerves too bad, so I had to tell him I'd rather have a man with no money and a busy mind, least I'd know he's active somewheres. His feelings was hurt bad and he cussed me out, but we still friends to this very day. He in the home, you know, and I visits him regular. Takes him magazines and cuts out his horoscope and the comic strips from the newspaper and lets him read 'em in correct order.

Big Bill Ronsonville tried to convince me that I shoulda married him instead of Jessie, but he couldn't make me a believer of it. All he wanted to do was put his big rusty hands all on me without asking and smile at me with that big gold tooth sparkling and glittering in my face and tell me how lavish I was, lavish being a new word he just learnt. He kept wanting to take me for night rides way out in the country, out there by Smith Creek where ain't nothing but deep black ditches, giant mosquitoes, loud crickets, lightning bugs, and loose pigs, and turn off his motor. His breath stank like whiskey though he claimed and swore on the Bible he didn't drank no liquor. Aside from that his hands were way too heavy and hard, hurt me, sometimes left red marks on me like I been sucked on. I told him finally that I was too light for him, that I needed a smaller, more gentle man, and he said he knew exactly what I meant.

If you want to know the truth, after him I didn't think much about men the way I used to. Lost track of the ones who upped and died or the ones who couldn't do nothing if they was alive nohow. So, since nobody else seemed to be able to wear Jessie's shoes, I just stuck to myself all these years.

My life ain't so bad now 'cause I'm used to being alone and takes good care of myself. Occasionally I still has a good time. I goes to the park and sits for hours in good weather, watch folks move and listen in on confidential conversations. I add up numbers on license plates to keep my mind alert unless they pass too fast. This gives me a clear idea of how many folks is visiting from out of town. I can about guess the color of every state now, too. Once or twice a month I go to the matinee on Wednesdays, providing ain't no long line of senior citizens 'cause they can be so slow; miss half the picture show waiting for them to count their change and get their popcorn.

Sometimes, when I'm sitting in the park, I feed the pigeons old cornbread crumbs, and I wonders what it'll be like not looking at the snow falling from the sky, not seeing the leaves form on the trees, not hearing no car engines, no sirens, no babies crying, not brushing my hair at night, drinking my Lipton tea, and not being able to go to bed early.

But right now, to tell you the truth, it don't bother me all *that* much. What is bothering me is my case worker. She supposed to pay me a visit tomorrow because my nosy neighbor, Clarabelle, saw two big trucks outside, one come right after the other, and she wondered what I was getting so new and so big that I needed trucks. My mama used to tell me that sometimes you can't see for looking. Clarabelle's had it out to do me in ever since last spring when I had the siding put on the house. I used the last of Jessie's insurance money 'cause the roof had been leaking so bad and the wood rotted and the paint chipped so much that it looked like a wicked old witch lived here. The house looked brand-new, and she couldn't stand to see an old woman's house looking better than hers. She know I been had roomers, and now all of a sudden my case worker claim she just want to visit to see how I'm doing, when really what she want to know is what I'm up to. Clarabelle work in her office.

The truth is my boiler broke and they was here to put in a new one. We liked to froze to death in here for two days. Yeah, I had a little chump change in the bank, but when they told me it was gonna cost $2,000 to get some heat, I cried. I had $862 in the bank; $300 of it I had just spent on this couch I got on sale; it was in the other truck. After twenty years the springs finally broke, and I figured it was time to buy a new one 'cause I ain't one for living in poverty, even at my age. I figured $200 was for my church's cross-country bus trip this summer.

Jessie's sister, Willamae, took out a loan for me to get the boiler, and I don't know how long it's gonna take me to pay her back. She only charge me fifteen or twenty dollars a month, depending. I probably be dead by the time it get down to zero.

My bank wouldn't give me the loan for the boiler, but then they keep sending me letters almost every week trying to get me to refinance my house. They must think I'm senile or something. On they best stationery, they write me. They say I'm up in age and wouldn't I like to take that trip I've been putting off because of no extra money. What trip? They tell me if I refinance my house for more than what I owe, which is about $3,000, that I could have enough money left over to go anywhere. Why would I want to refinance my house at fourteen and a half percent when I'm paying four and a half now? I ain't that stupid. They say dream about clear blue water, palm trees, and orange suns. Last night I dreamt I was doing a backstroke between big blue waves and tipped my straw hat down over my forehead and fell asleep under an umbrella. They made me think about it. And they asked me what would I do if I was to die today? They're what got me to thinking about all this dying mess in the first place. It never would've layed in my mind so heavy if they hadn't kept reminding me of it. Who would pay off your house? Wouldn't I feel bad leaving this kind of a burden on my family? What family they talking about? I don't even know where my people is no more.

I ain't gonna lie. It ain't easy being old. But I ain't complaining neither, 'cause I learned how to stretch my social security check. My roomers pay the house note and I pay the taxes. Oil is sky-high. Medicaid pays my doctor bills. I got a letter what told me to apply for food stamps. That case worker come here and checked to see if I had a real kitchen. When she saw I had a stove and sink and refrigerator, she didn't like the idea that my house was almost paid for, and just knew I was lying about having roomers. "Are you certain that you reside here alone?" she asked me. "I'm certain," I said. She searched every inch of my cabinets to make sure I didn't have two of the same kinds of food, which would've been a dead giveaway. I hid it all in the basement inside the washing machine and dryer. Luckily, both of the nurses was in the islands at the time, and Juanita was vising some boy what live in D.C.

After she come here and caused me so much eruptions, I had to make trip after trip down to that office. They had me filling out all kinds of forms and still held up my stamps. I got tired of answering the same questions over and over and finally told 'em to keep their old food stamps. I ain't got to beg nobody to eat. I know how to keep myself comfortable and clean and well fed. I manage to buy my staples and toiletries and once in a while a few extras, like potato chips, ice cream, and maybe a pork chop.

My mama taught me when I was young that, no matter how poor you are, always eat nourishing food and your body will last. Learn to conserve, she said. So I keeps all my empty margarine containers and stores white rice, peas and carrots (my favorites), or my turnips from the garden in there. I can manage a garden when my arthritis ain't acting up. And water is the key. I drinks plenty of it like the doctor told me, and I cheats, eats Oreo cookies and saltines. They fills me right up, too. And when I feels like it, rolls, homemade biscuits, eats them with Alga syrup if I can find it at the store, and that sticks with me most of the day.

Long time ago, used to be I'd worry like crazy about gaining weight and my face breaking out from too many sweets, and about cellulite forming all over my hips and thighs. Of course, I was trying to catch Jessie then, though I didn't know it at the time. I was really just being cute, flirting, trying to see if I could get attention. Just so happens I lucked up and got all of his. Caught him like he was a spider and I was the web.

Lord, I'd be trying to look all sassy and prim. Have my hair all did, it be curled tight in rows that I wouldn't comb out for hours till they cooled off after Connie Curtis did it for a dollar and a Budweiser. Would take that dollar out my special savings, which I kept hid under the record player in the front room. My hair used to be fine, too: long and thick and black, past my shoulders, and mens used to say, "Girl, you sure got a head of hair on them shoulders there, don't it make your neck sweat?" But I didn't never bother answering, just blushed and smiled and kept on walking, trying hard not to switch 'cause mama told me my behind was too big for my age and to watch out or I'd be luring grown mens toward me. Humph! I loved it, though, made me feel pretty, special, like I had attraction.

Ain't quite the same no more, though. I looks in the mirror at myself and I sees wrinkles, lots of them, and my skin look like it all be trying to run down toward my toes but then it changed its mind and just stayed there, sagging and lagging, laying limp against my thick bones. Shoot, mens used to say how sexy I was with these high cheeks, tell me I looked swollen, like I was pregnant, but it was just me, being all healthy and everything. My teeth was even bright white and straight in a row then. They ain't so bad now, 'cause ain't none of 'em mine. But I only been to the dentist twice in my whole life and that was 'cause on Easter Sunday I was in so much pain he didn't have time to take no X-ray and yanked it right out 'cause my mama told him to do anything he had to to shut me up. Second time was the last time, and that was 'cause the whole top row and the fat ones way in the back on the bottom ached me so bad the dentist yanked 'em all out so I wouldn't have to be bothered no more.

Don't get me wrong, I don't miss being young. I did everything I wanted to do and then some. I loved hard. But you take Jessie's niece, Thelma. She pitiful. Only twenty-six, don't think she made it past the tenth grade, got three children by different men, no husband and on welfare. Let her tell it, ain't nothing out here but dogs. I know some of these men out here ain't worth a pot to piss in, but all of 'em ain't dogs. There's gotta be some young Jessies floating somewhere in this world. My mama always told me you gotta have something to give if you want to get something in return. Thelma got long fingernails.

Me, myself, I didn't have no kids. Not 'cause I didn't want none or couldn't have none, just that Jessie wasn't full and couldn't give me the juices

I needed to make no babies. I accepted it 'cause I really wanted him all to myself, even if he couldn't give me no new bloodlines. He was satisfying enough for me, quite satisfying if you don't mind me repeating myself.

I don't understand Thelma, like a lot of these young peoples. I be watching 'em on the streets and on TV. I be hearing things they be doing to themselves when I'm under the dryer at the beauty shop. (I go to the beauty shop once a month 'cause it make me feel like thangs ain't over yet. She give me a henna so the silver have a gold tint to it.) I can't afford it, but there ain't too many luxuries I can. I let her put makeup on me, too, if it's a Saturday and I feel like doing some window shopping. I still know how to flirt and sometimes I get stares, too. It feel good to be looked at and admired at my age. I try hard to keep myself up. Every weekday morning at five-thirty I do exercises with the TV set, when it don't hurt to stretch.

But like I was saying, Thelma and these young people don't look healthy, and they spirits is always so low. I watch 'em on the streets, on the train, when I'm going to the doctor. I looks in their eyes and they be red or brown where they supposed to be milky white and got bags deeper and heavier than mine, and I been through some thangs. I hear they be using these drugs of variety, and I can't understand why they need to use all these thangs to get from day to day. From what I do hear, it's supposed to give 'em much pleasure and make their minds disappear or make 'em not feel the thangs they supposed to be feeling anyway.

Heck, when I was young, we drank sarsaparilla and couldn't even buy no wine or any kind of liquor in no store. These youngsters ain't but eighteen and twenty and buys anything with a bite to it. I've seen 'em sit in front of the store and drank a whole bottle in one sitting. Girls, too.

We didn't have no dreams of carrying on like that, and specially on no corner. We was young ladies and young men with respect for ourselfs. And we didn't smoke none of them funny cigarettes all twisted up with no filters that smell like burning dirt. I ask myself, I say Ma'Dear, what's wrong with these kids? They can read and write and do arithmetic, finish high school, go to college and get letters behind their names, but every day I hear the neighbors complain that one of they youngsters done dropped out.

Lord, what I wouldn'ta done to finish high school and been able to write a full sentence or even went to college. I reckon I'da been a room decorator. I know they calls it be that fancy name now, interior designer, but it boil down to the same thang. I guess it's 'cause I loves so to make my surroundings pleasant, even right pretty, so I feels like a invited guest in my own house. And I always did have a flair for color. Folks used to say, "Hazel, for somebody as poor as a church mouse, you got better taste in thangs than them Rockefellers!" Used to sew up a storm, too. Covered my mama's raggedy duffold and chairs. Made her a bedspread with matching pillowcases. Didn't mix more than two different patterns either. Make you dizzy.

Wouldn't that be just fine, being an interior designer? Learning the proper names of thangs and recognizing labels in catalogs, giving peoples my business cards and wearing a two-piece with white gloves. "Yes, I decorated the Hartleys' and Cunninghams' home. It was such a pleasant experience. And they're such lovely people, simply lovely," I'da said. Coulda told those rich folks just what they needed in their bedrooms, front rooms, and specially in the kitchen. So many of 'em still don't know what to do in there.

But like I was saying before I got all off the track, some of these young people don't appreciate what they got. And they don't know thangs like we used to. We knew about eating fresh vegetables from the garden, growing and picking 'em ourselves. What going to church was, being honest and faithful. Trusting each other. Leaving our front door open. We knew what it was like to starve and get cheated yearly when our crops didn't add up the way we figured. We suffered together, not separately. These youngsters don't know about suffering for any stretch of time. I hear 'em on the train complaining 'cause they can't afford no Club Med, no new record playing albums, cowboy boots, or those Brooke Shields-Calvin Klein blue jeans I see on TV. They be complaining about nonsense. Do they ever read books since they been taught is what I want to know? Do they be learning things and trying to figure out what to do with it?

And these young girls with all this thick makeup caked on their faces, wearing these high heels they can't hardly walk in. Trying to be cute. I used to wear high heels, mind you, with silk stockings, but at least I could walk in 'em. Jessie had a car then. Would pick me up, and I'd walk real careful down the front steps like I just won the Miss America pageant, one step at a time, and slide into his shiny black Ford. All the neighbors peeked through the curtains 'cause I was sure enough riding in a real automobile with my legitimate boyfriend.

If Jessie was here now I'd have somebody to talk to. Somebody to touch my skin. He'd probably take his fingers and run 'em through my hair like he used to; kiss me on my nose and tickle me where it made me laugh. I just loved it when he kissed me. My mind be so light, and I felt tickled and precious. Have to sit down sometime just to get hold of myself.

If he was here, I probably woulda beat him in three games of checkers by now and he'd be trying to get even. But since today is Thursday, I'd be standing in that window over there waiting for him to get home from work, and when I got tired or the sun be in my eyes, I'd hear the taps on his wing tips coming up the front porch. Sometime, even now, I watch for him, but I know he ain't coming back. Not that he wouldn't if he could, mind you, 'cause he always told me I made him feel lightning lighting up his heart.

Don't get me wrong, I got friends, though a heap of 'em is dead or got tubes coming out of their noses or going all through their bodies every which-a-way. Some in the old folks' home. I thank the Lord I ain't stuck in one of them places. I ain't never gonna get that old. They might as well just bury me standing up if I do. I don't want to be no nuisance to nobody, and I can't stand being around a lot of sick people for too long.

I visits Gunther and Chester when I can, and Vivian who I grew up with, but no soon as I walk through them long hallways, I get depressed. They lay there all limp and helpless, staring at the ceiling like they're really looking at something, or sitting stiff in their rocking chairs, pitiful, watching TV and don't be knowing what they watching half the time. They laugh when ain't nothing funny. They wait for it to get dark so they know it's time to go to sleep. They relatives don't hardly come visit 'em, just folks like me. Whimpy don't understand a word I say, and it makes me grateful I ain't lost no more than I have.

Sometime we sits on the sun porch rocking like fools; don't say one word to each other for hours. But last time Gunther told me about his grandson what got accepted to Stanford University, and another one at a university in Michigan. I asked him where was Stanford and he said he didn't know. "What difference do it make?" he asked. "It's one of those uppity schools for rich smart white people," he said. "The important thang is that my black grandson won a scholarship there, which mean he don't have to pay a dime to go." I told him I know what a scholarship is. I ain't stupid. Gunther said he was gonna be there for at least four years or so, and by that time he would be a professional. "Professional what?" I asked. "Who cares, Ma'Dear, he gonna be a professional at whatever it is he learnt." Vivian started mumbling when she heard us talking, 'cause she still like to be the center of attention. When she was nineteen she was Miss Springfield Gardens. Now she can't stand the thought that she old and wrinkled. She started yakking about all the places she'd been to, even described the landscape like she was looking at a photograph. She ain't been but twenty-two miles north of here in her entire life, and that's right there in that home.

Like I said, and this is the last time I'm gonna mention it. I don't mind being old, it's just that sometime I don't need all this solitude. You can't do everything by yourself and expect to have as much fun if somebody was there doing it with you. That's why when I'm feeling jittery or melancholy for long stretches, I read the Bible, and it soothes me. I water my morning glories and amaryllis. I baby-sit for Thelma every now and then, 'cause she don't trust me with the kids for too long. She mainly call on holidays and my birthday. And she the only one who don't forget my birthday: August 19th. She tell me I'm a Leo, that I got fire in my blood. She may be right, 'cause once in a while I gets a churning desire to be smothered in Jessie's arms again.

Anyway, it's getting late, but I ain't tired. I feel pretty good. That old case worker think she gonna get the truth out of me. She don't scare me. It ain't none of her business that I got money coming in here besides my social security check. How they 'spect a human being to live off $369 a month in this day and age is what I wanna know. Every time I walk out my front door it cost me at least two dollars. I bet she making thousands and got credit cards galore. Probably got a summer house on the Island and goes to Florida every January. If she found out how much I was getting from my roomers, the government would make me pay back a dollar for every two I made. I best to get my tail on upstairs and clear everything off their bureaus. I can hide all the nurse's stuff in the attic; they won't be back till next month. Juanita been living out of trunks since she got here, so if the woman ask what's in 'em, I'll tell her, old sheets and pillow-cases and memories.

On second thought, I think I'm gonna take me a bubble bath first, and dust my chest with talcum powder, then I'll make myself a hot cup of Lipton's and paint my fingernails clear 'cause my hands feel pretty steady. I can get up at five and do all that other mess; case worker is always late anyway. After she leave, if it ain't snowing too bad, I'll go to the museum and look at the new paintings in the left wing. By the time she get here, I'ma make out like I'm a lonely old widow stuck in a big old house just sitting here waiting to die.

Charlotte Watson Sherman

Emerald City: Third & Pike

This is Oya's corner. The pin-striped young executives and sleek-pumped clerk-typists, the lacquered-hair punk boys and bleached blondes with safety pins dangling from multi-holed earlobes, the frantic-eyed woman on the corner shouting obscenities, and the old-timers rambling past new high-rise fantasy hotels—all belong to Oya even though she's the only one who knows it.

Oya sits on this corner 365 days of the year, in front of the new McDonald's, with everything she needs bundled inside two plastic bags by her side. Most people pretend they don't even see Oya sitting there like a Buddha under that old green Salvation Army blanket.

Sometimes Oya's eyes look red and wild, but she won't say anything to anybody. Other times her eyes are flat, black and still as midnight outside the mission, and she talks up a furious wind.

She tells them about her family—her uncle who was a cowboy, her grandfather who fought in the Civil War, her mother who sang dirges and blues songs on the Chitlin Circuit, and her daddy who wouldn't "take no stuff from nobody," which is why they say some people got together and broke his back.

First published in *Killing Color* by Charlotte Watson Sherman. Corvallis: Calyx Books, 1992

"Oh yeah, Oya be tellin them folks an earful if they'd ever stop to listen, but she don't pay em no mind. Just keeps right on talkin, keeps right on tellin it."

One day when Oya's eyes were flat and black and she was in a preaching mood, I walked down Third & Pike, passed her as if I didn't know her. Actually I didn't. But Oya turned her eyes on me and I could feel her looking at me and I knew I couldn't just walk past this woman without saying something. So I said, "Hello."

Oya looked at me with those flat black eyes and motioned for me to take a seat by her.

Now, usually I'm afraid of folks who sit on the sidewalks downtown and look as if they've never held a job or have not place to go, but something about her eyes made me sit.

I felt foolish. I felt my face growing warm and wondered what people walking by must think of me sitting on the street next to this woman who looked as if she had nowhere to go. But after sitting there for a few minutes, it seemed as if they didn't think more or less of me than when I was walking down the street. No one paid any attention to us. That bothered me. What if I really needed help or something? What if I couldn't talk, could only sit on that street?

"Don't pay them fools no mind, daughter. They wouldn't know Moses if he walked down Pike Street and split the Nordstrom Building right down the middle. You from round here?"

I nodded my head.

"I thought so. You look like one of them folks what's been up here all they lives, kinda soft-lookin like you ain't never knowed no hard work."

I imediately took offense because I could feel the inevitable speech coming on: "There ain't no real black people in Seattle."

"Calm down, daughter, I don't mean to hurt your feelings. It's just a fact, that's all. You folks up here too cushy, too soft. Can't help it. It's the rainwater does it to you, all that water can't help but make a body soggy and spineless."

I made a move to get up.

"Now wait a minute, just wait a minute. Let me show you somethin."

She reached in her pocket and pulled out a crumpled newspaper clipping. It held a picture of a grim-faced young woman and a caption that read: "DOMESTIC TO SERVE TIME IN PRISON FOR NEAR-MURDER."

"That's me in that picture. Now ain't that somethin?"

Sure is, I thought and wondered how in the world I would get away from this woman before she hurt me.

"Them fools put me in the jail for protectin my dreams. Humph, they the only dreams I got, so naturally I'm gonna protect em. Nobody else gonna do it for me, is they?"

"But how could somebody put you in jail for protectin your dreams? That paper said you almost killed somebody."

I didn't want to seem combative but I didn't know exactly what this lady was talking about and I was feeling pretty uneasy after she'd almost insulted me then showed me evidence she'd been in jail for near-murder, no less.

"Now, I know you folks up here don't know much bout the importance of a body's dreams, but where I come from dreams was all we had. Seemed like a body got holt of a dream or a dream got holt of a body and wouldn't turn you loose. My dreams what got me through so many days of nothin, specially when it seemed like the only thing the future had to give was more of the same nothin, day after day."

She stopped abruptly and stared into space. I kept wondering what kind of dream would have forced her to try to kill somebody.

"Ain't nothin wrong with cleanin other folks' homes to make a livin. Nothin wrong with it at all. My mama had to do it and her mama had to do it at one time or nuther, so it didn't bother me none when it turned out I was gonna hafta do it too, least for a while. But my dream told me I wasn't gonna wash and scrub and shine behind other folks the rest of my life. Jobs like that was just temporary, you know what I mean?"

I nodded my head.

"Look at my hands. You never woulda knowed I danced in one of them fancy colored nightclubs and wore silk evenin gloves. Was in a sorority. Went to Xavier University."

As she reminisced, I looked at her hands. They looked rough and wide, like hands that had seen hard labor. I wondered if prison had caused them to look that way.

Oya's eyes pierced into mine. She seemed to know what I was thinking. She cackled.

"Daughter, they'd hafta put more than a prison on me to break my spirit. Don't you know it takes more than bars and beefy guards to break a fightin woman's spirit?"

She cackled some more.

"Un Un. Wouldn't never break me, and they damn sure tried. I spent fifteen years in that hellhole. Fifteen years of my precious life, all for a dreamkiller."

I looked at her and asked, "But what did you do? What did they try to do to your dreams?"

Oya leaned over to me and whispered, "I was gonna get into the space program. I was gonna be a astronaut and fly out into the universe, past all them stars. I was gonna meet up with some folks none of us never seen before, and be ambassador of goodwill; not like the fools bein sent out there now thinkin they own the universe. I was gonna be a real ambassador of goodwill and then that woman I scrubbed floors for had the nerve to tell me no black maid was ever gonna be no astronaut. Well, I could feel all the broken dreams of my mama and my grandmama and her mama swell up and start pulsin in my blood memory. I hauled off and beat that fool over the head with the mop I had in my hands till I couldn't raise up my arms no more. The chantin of my people's broken dreams died down and I looked and there was that dreamkiller in a mess of blood all over the clean floor I'd just scrubbed. And they turned round and put me in jail and never did say nothin bout that old dreamkiller. Just like my dreams never mattered. Like I didn't have no dreams. Like all I could ever think bout doin was cleanin up after nasty white folks for the rest of my life.

"Humph!" She snorted, and I almost eased to my feet so I could run if I had the cause to.

"You got any dreams, daughter?" Oya asked with a gleam in her eye.

I knew I better tell her yes, so I did.

"Well I don't care if you is from up here, you better fight for your dreams!"

Slowly, I reached out and held one of her rough hands. Then I asked, "But was your dream worth going to prison for all them years?"

Oya looked at me for a long, long time.

"I'm still gonna make it past all them stars," she said as she freed her hand and motioned for me to get to getting.

"Right now, this street b'longs to me and don't *nobody* mess with me or my dreams!" She was still shouting as I walked toward Pine Street.

Wanda Coleman

Croon

*I*t was long and black and he drove it with the rhythmic strokes of self-pleasure. It served as a reminder; he wanted nothing in life save love.

And here he was, drunk and alone in a strange town, albeit the dark part frequented by those whose skins were in tone with his own. A city reputed for its glitter and tinsel, this section was grim and subdued. He traveled the street called motel row, fabled for the intersecting of sex, dope and violence. Too, the blocks were unusually long and ill-lit, corners coming up sharp and unexpected causing the car to swerve slightly to the left when taking one and the tires on the right rear to kiss the curb.

From time-to-time he digressed so as to not overlook some hide-a-way or unsuspected source of amusement. But the dimmer side streets housed only low-class wooden A-frames and drab stucco boxes perched on dismal little patches of ground; pleasant as slums went. He suspected that beneath the tropical palms and wistful evergreens there seethed an urban fierceness par to none.

It's the wrong town it's the wrong time but it's all right with me.

Then, too, it was Mr. Johnny Walker reddening his blues, licking at his cerebellum, easing down around his thigh bone. And then he was aching to empty his passion into the illusive thrust of Ms. Girl who'd joined him after a jaunt through the nasal septum. It made for an ecstasy, almost but not quite, a

First published in *The Unforgetting Heart,* edited by Asha Kanwar. San Francisco: Aunt Lute Books, 1993

flirtatious lullaby. He could sense the rawness of her influence at the back of his throat and vaguely regretted leaving the party so soon. But he had to *do that* as well.

Arlene had shown up with Mel James on her arm. The two-timing nerve of the harlot. She was still his wife and it surprised him. The depth of pain stirred as he coolly watched her beneath his tinted lens; her marvelous bronze thighs moving suggestively beneath silver satin, the bold vee neckline betraying her splendid breasts, not long ago his alone and nursed as if he were a newborn, her full broad nose with its partly curled nares; her quick startled fox-eyes seducing at a glance; her pressed and scented brown hair impishly crowning her the fine Mrs. Dalvon Terry III second-to-no-woman in the room if not in the world. And she was there to bring him down a peg or three before their whole crowd including his manager and the label big-boys. Too much.

He drove to the music which kept him from driving too slowly or too fast and which street-wisdom said would keep him from attracting the unwelcomed attention of the police. And in this town they were known for maddoggish behavior/their disrespect for a colored man even if he were a gent and wore a three piece suit, even if he drove a luxury car priced beyond the means of most men Black or White, even if he were a world-famous celebrity crooner whose last long-playing gold platter graced their own personal high-fidelity turntables—on these streets he was just another anonymous troublesome spook suspected of and therefore guilty.

He couldn't say he hadn't been warned, rather lectured to: Why marry a woman nearly a decade your senior? A divorcee with a manchild half your age. You're too fresh with a dynamite career ahead of you they love you in Harlem they love you in Paris they love you in Vegas. You can't afford the emotional strain. She'll hang you by the toes run you into the ground nail you to the cross. There's no such thing as being faithful when you're married to the Music Business. Be good to yourself give yourself a chance. Stay away from the witch.

He listened but not to his friends. They were drowned out by the rush of blood to his head. He married the ex-Mrs. Arlene Troy, ebony model originally from Richmond, California who left home at sixteen to make it big in NYC. But after knocking around on the periphery designed for chocolate starlets who failed to score White Patronage, and therefore success, she opted for the next best thang: Marriage and Family Life. Not that many women of any persuasion who'd survived beyond twenty-five had many options. And while her trustworthy mother nurtured Leroy David Troy Junior, Arlene engaged in the search for Mr. Do-Right-By-Her.

Their stroll down the aisle made national news. The baby-faced twenty-two-year-old Negro crooner married an out-to-pasture indigo ingenue of thirty. And her resentment behind the bad press grew geometrically in proportion to his accelerated success which branched into cameo on-screen film and television appearances and a renegotiated contract which made him the highest paid Black man in American history at the time. Not to mention that his mother, Mrs. Jazmine Terry III, rebuffed his bride reflecting the communal embarrassment of her very staid Protestant peers. In her good book it was written that no man could have two mothers.

Not only that. The Prize Bitch had the nerve to show with Mel James. He had just signed on with the label and Dalvon suspected that the even younger "velvet Mel" was being groomed to replace him. More than once he'd be warned about Losing Control. Dalvon's consumption of alcohol did, as he knew, threaten his kingdom. He had recently pulled his first no-show. And by the time the label watchdogs caught up to him he had been liquored-up and dry-screwed by a prostitute whose attributes he could not recall. She had removed the gaudy five-thousand dollar diamond and gold pinky ring from his finger, lifted his keys and his wallet choked with Ben Franks, and had driven off in his alternative red-on-red roadster. What was left of the roadster had been recovered, but that was all. And so Mel glowered in the background, waiting to be brought forward in that inevitable moment when Dalvon, the King-of-Croon, was at last dethroned.

The cold part was losing Arlene to him as prelude to his fall-down.

Papa told me, "Son don't evah get so lonely you give your precious love to the street. Find yoself a right kind of a woman, tender good and sweet. Find yoself the right kind of woman and make her yo right kind of wife. Remember, son, the right kind of woman will nevah do you dirt. Remember son, the wrong kind of woman will always cause you hurt. So find yourself the nice kind of woman and hold onto her tight. You'll know her by her true true lovin'. She always do you right.

His misfortune had been magnified by his failure to appear at Lance Hank's club, Hussy's. It was rumored that Hank's underworld connexions were more than a little disenchanted. His long-time manager and business buddy, Sol Hoffman, convinced them it was an Ideal Opportunity to hastily debut Mel James in Dalvon's place. Lucky for everyone Mel's satiny falsetto was nearly as hypnotic as Dalvon's even with considerably less range. This won over the angry mobsters and saved Dalvon's biscuits from being burnt.

The next afternoon Dalvon read the raves. Angry at himself he took the punishment Sol Meted as well-earned, and considering the possibilities, lucky. An item planted at the bottom of an industry gossip column reported Dalvon under a great deal of Personal Stress and having earned an ulcer somewhere along his abusive Climb To The Top; had checked himself into an unnamed hospital for Tender Loving recouperation. He laughed when Sol showed him the clipping, but Sol had nothing in his mouth but admonishment and youbetterwatchit chum or you'll be singing out your asshole.

I covered you this time, Dahl but whattayah want? To blow the fuckin' game? Do you know what you are and who you are? You're a Representative of Your Race, forrrkrristssake. Have I gotta spell it out? You've got repect the kinda respect most apes Black or White would kill for. And women—any size shape and color yah want. As long as you're cool with your shit, Dahl. As long as you're cool.

The big finger danced on his chest, lit cigarillo ash curling the tips of his semi-kinky chest hairs. He knew Sol spoke the Absolute Truth and had no retort.

Even me, Dahl, I'd kill for what you got. But I try to be satisfied with the percentage I'm gettin', understand? Listen to me Dahl Babee it's never gonna be sweeter than you've got it—never, No Way!

Sol was the one friend Dalvon could trust, the only decent pinstripe he knew. As much as he loved her, he needed Sol more than he needed Arlene; hence, he was more faithful to Sol. He had to have insurance, meaning steady heavy-paying gigs, especially now that Arlene was makin' leaving noises. Alimony would take a sizeable bite out of his future. Caution if not discretion was required. Besides, he wanted her back.

But in the very nasty meantime, the loins of Dalvon Terry III exhibited a fierce and dizzying hunger. There was this roar inside synchronized to the automatic transmissional flow of his rented black luxury sedan through street after street to the crude modulations of Funk Radio. All the passion inside him raged to get out. He kept seeing Arlene's eyes dancing in the lights refracted on the windshield. He could smell her expensive perfume. He could taste her thick, irresistible, cinnamon lips. He could feel himself sinking into her dark giving softness. Holding on For Life, dearly oozing painfully sweetly out of him into her.

Ghhhhooodddddamn I really love you.

Miss Thing turned towards the sound of his wheels bumping the curb. She was on the verge of popping out of a skin-tight lime-green sateen sheath with capelet sleeves and abbreviated slit skirt. Her dyed auburn wig-hat fell forward in a monster puff, cupping her ears in sexy giant swirls as she tilted her head to stare him to a standstill. He pocketed his shades and honked.

She was all sultry High-Yellow and slid into the seat beside him soundlessly. She turned toward him mascara flashing, blood-red lips and two-inch nails. She had a distinctly Asian cast.

Damn, baby—what are you?

Ever hear of World War II?

Yeah.

Well, my black Daddy was in Japan after Nagasaki and brought back my Mom. End of happy story.

Oh.

So what are you?

Baby, I'm every woman's dream come true.

Dreams can be expensive.

How much?

One bill.

Sounds good to me. Where to?

First stop was the LIQ for a refresher course in Mr. Johnny Walker, red. He gave her the cash then watched her seductive sashay draw starved eyes as she slinked from and to the car. As they zipped forward he rested his hand on her knee and let it ride back and forth, enjoying the teasing static tingle of her flesh.

The night window at The Blue Blazes Motel was reinforced with bullet-proof glass and steel. The night manager at the window was a cafe-au-lait hoot-owl, a heavy-jowled matronly woman in a plaid flannel shirt and slacks. Her deliberately dykish manner was calculatedly brusque to challenge any man inclined to take advantage. A double-ought shotgun could be clearly spotted resting in the corner of her cubbyhole, propped against a stack of phone books. Dalvon flashed his sizable was of green to impress the impervious Miss Thing, peeled off another couple of bills and told her to keep the change. Smiling, she paid, took the key, then snaked herself around Dalvon's arm to offset his tipsy stagger.

You come here often.

How'd you know?

She didn't tell you how to find the room.

A girl's got to have a place to work, now don't she?

Just one place?

I try to be modest.

The room came with black & white television, piped-in jazz, and queen-size bed. The room was clean enough but faintly stained by the aromatic drippings of its variegated clientele. Out by sunrise if not sooner.

Thus Dalvon Terry III began to woozily unload. He took off his coat jacket first revealing his taste in burnished gold one-of-a-kind medallions, diamond cuff-links and designer-label silk shirts. Miss Thing put her arms around him and gave him a cold, routinely mouthy buss.

You got a pimp?

No.

You just free lance.

Why not.

You cut her in?

Let's talk about you.

I'm here for a couple of gigs, then on a plane out of here. This is a strange town. Everything's ass backwards. Even the way poor folk live.

It's home.

She found two little mouth-wash glasses and poured a toast.

Here's to the east.

Here's to the west.

Here's to the very one I love the best.

Dalvon stretched out fully dressed on the bed, letting the jazz and hooch flow through him, the bottle in one hand, glass in the other. Miss Thing propped him up with the available pillows, kicked off her heels, and eeled out of her petite sheath. She was small-boned but meaty in black bra, black girdle with garter belts, and black nylons. She curled up twixt his knees and chest. They clinked glasses. She took a sip. He guzzled his and poured an immediate refill. She reached for her purse and took out a pack of cigarettes.

Put that away.

Huh?

No smoking.

Are you religious or something?

No. I make my living with my voice. I'm a singer, a crooner.

For real? Are you famous?

I might be.

What's your name?

Dalvon Terry.

She broke into a smile, threw her cigarettes back into her purse, snapped it shut.

You're *the* Dalvon Terry.

In the flesh.

What! Geewhiz!

She bounced around on the bed and squealed. He watched her, delighted and amused.

Baby, I must can't lose with the stuff I use.

I've got all your singles, believe it or not.

Do tell.

Starting with *Sha-boom-la Baby.* I bought *Papa Told Me* just the other day.

Come here and sock one to me.

She smelled cheap but good. She snuggled up to him, worked her mouth then leaned in to meet his. He took in her impishly round face, studying the points at which her Negroid features merged flawlessly with the Nippon. He pulled her hard to him, squeezing tight, forcing his tongue toward her throat. He could taste what he wanted beneath the alcohol, feelings. They broke for air then she leaned forward and kissed him again, took a sip from her glass, kissed him and took another sip. Dalvon could feel his nature rising.

Take off your bra.

She unsnapped it from the front, pulled it back off her shoulders, dropped it on the floor. She shimmied slightly and her breasts jiggled fleshily.

They look like apples.

Apples?

Big old golden delicious apples. As big as apples get.

Take a bite.

Undress me first.

Breasts to his chest, Miss Thing slithered down his body, put her glass on the bedside stand, then eased slowly towards the floor, feeling the hardness beneath his trousers, unbuckling his belt as she went. Going into a kneel at the side of the bed, she removed first one shoe and sock then the other. Dalvon recapped the bottle, set it and the glass aside and raised himself with his elbows to watch. She took his bare feet and began licking around his toes. He pulled them away.

Don't you like that?

I'm not a freak. Come back up here.

She slid upwards, along his legs, brushing into him, climbing on top of him, undulating. She could feel him throbbing and ready through his serge. She unzipped his fly and parted her lips.

Uh-uh.

Huh?

Too much teeth. Bring it on up here. And take off the rest of that stuff.

Okay. But before I do....

She strutted around the bed, snatched up her bag again. She fished out a tiny square tin, popped the lid and shook three red capsules into her palm. He watched as she snapped the lid, returned it to her purse, and turned toward him with a daring adventuresome smile.

What's that shit?

Somethin' terrif! I don't normally do this, but you're so special. I want to share with you. This gets you real high and makes sex ten times better.

Ten times better? Is that that Spanish fly I heard about?

No, no. That stuff's for sickos. This is real nice.

I ain't into pills. You take one first and lemme see what happens.

Nothin' happens, honest. It just makes it better when you do it.

You take one first.

Better. I'll take two.

She reached across him, retrieved the bottle, uncapped it, tilted her head back slightly, sat two of the capsules on her tongue then took a sizable swig from the bottle. He kissed her, turned to lumber over her, kneading her breasts, pausing to suck and bite at a nipple, watching her eyes for any sign of change. He didn't see any.

How do you feel.

Ready like Freddy.

I did some Girl earlier. Wish'd I'd saved some for you.

No worry.

All right. Gimme one.

Stick it out.

Miss Thing opened her palm, took the last capsule and placed it on his tongue with a giggle. She handed him the bottle. He turned it up and swallowed three-quarters of it. He stared at her for a minute, felt little except an enhanced systemic radiance starting at his throat easing toward his crotch. Enthusiastic, she peeled him out of his white silk shirt, ribbed red nylon T-shirt, trousers and matching red nylon boxers and laid them neatly at the foot of the bed. He slipped off his medallion and wrist watch and tucked them into his left shoe. Then he crawled toward her. She leaned back into the pillows and spread her legs, easing towards him. He climbed toward her, acutely aware of the texture of the chenille quilt between his fingers like soft grass, like pubic hair. He looked down at his hands and then up again.

Goddamn baby, what'd you give me?

It was Arlene laid out before him. Arlene, her big full thighs spread apart in the welcome he hurt for. It was Arlene he mounted, lowered himself into. Arlene who satisfied his Crying Need.

Dalvon came to consciousness naked and alone. The room was dark and slightly chilly. There was something swimming over his head. It took a minute to realize it was the ceiling. When it stopped moving he sat up, explored the dimness and tried to remember who he was and where. The weight of his body against the mattress caused the empty bottle to roll against his thigh. He picked it up, glanced at it and knocked it aside. Dried expelled semen was crusting between his thighs. He knew himself well enough to know he'd achieved this level of stupidity at least once before.

He groped through the dark towards the bathroom door, opened it, flicked on the light and stumbled into the mirror, bracing himself against the sink. Glazed, inflamed eyes were set symmetrically in his baby-smooth handsome, honey-brown face.

A conga drum played panic between his ears.

Man, what have you gone and one now?

The answer came flooding in, sudden images of wide avenues, the black leather interior, the tight green dress, its seductively revealing slit, the glaring ugly yellow light at the entry of the liquor store, the envious eyes of men following Miss Thing back to the car, the red capsules perched on her tongue, the glee dancing in her eyes.

Oh shit, man! Oh shit! You've been put in a trick.

He rushed back to the other room and found the master light switch at the door. It illuminated and confirmed his dread. She'd taken everything, jewelry, clothes and shoes, leaving him slightly more naked than a jaybird. The onset of rage was so immediate he reeled. He ran back to the bathroom, yanked up the toilet seat and vomited forth his anger. He stumbled back to the room looking for the telephone. There was none. He flung open the door and ran toward the parking lot. The black sedan was gone. He dropped to his knees and hissed.

That bitch, that goddamn funky-ass whore!

Son don't give your love to the streets....

He could hear Sol's I-told-you-so blistering his ears. But Sol's room was the only number he knew, if he could remember the name of the hotel. He had to get to a phone. He had to call Sol. He bee-lined for the night window. The manager was gone. He puzzled it out. She had probably gone to bed. She probably had a room right behind this one. There must be a buzzer he can push. He looked for and found it, pressed it repeatedly. He strained to listen and thought he could hear her moving about. She was taking forever to come out. And it was cold as a muthafucka.

He could hear the faint strains of music. And then it hit him. She knew it was him out here and she knew why. She'd been in on it. She and that High-Yellow Trash had set him up.

He rushed to the side of the building and found the door leading to her apartment. Outraged, he beat heavily against the cheap wood, feeling it give, sensing it was hollow inside, knowing that with enough pressure he could work his fists through it.

Open up. Open up, goddamn it!

The door swung inward. The manager stood there, fully dressed, her pressed sandy hair set in giant rollers. He could hear the music clearly. She was listening to his Best-Of LP released last month. She stood there gaping at him, eyes registering fear. But Dalvon could see only deception and amusement and barged in, pushing her to the floor.

You schemin' bitches! What've you done with my clothes!

A hasty scan of the room revealed it was tiny but tidy in every respect. There was no sign of Miss Thing or his missing belongings. It was only then he remembered the shotgun and became instantly sober. A loud catch and click drew his attention and told him his senses had returned minutes too late. Even if the manager had been in on it, how could he prove it? Standing bare-assed in the middle of her living room?

Stammering, he turned his head reluctantly and looked into the barrel of the double-ought.

Above the blast he could hear the whisper of his own voice coming through the agonizing realization that half his side was blown away. He clutched himself bolting past the horrified woman, falling and stumbling again. He slipped in his own blood and fell to the cement, feeling the redness gush out of him and into the night. He tought her name but could not say it.

He heard voices stirring around him, the harmonies of choirs and hordes, a multitude of songs coming at him out of the ultra-marine, pierced by the hysterical shrieks of the night manager; the voices of men, devils and angels. But none were as mellow as that honeyed lilting falsetto reverberating in the tropical effluvium, rising to cascade above all the others, that marvelous croon which had, Coast-to-Coast, made Dalvon Terry a household name.

Author Biographies

Toni Cade Bambara
(1939–   )
Fiction writer, screenwriter, activist, lecturer, organizer.

Toni Cade Bambara was born in New York City. She received her bachelor's degree in 1959 from Queens College and earned her master's degree in 1964 from City University of New York. She has received many awards for her work, including the American Book Award in 1981 for her novel *The Salt Eaters*.

Toni Cade Bambara is a well known and respected civil rights activist, professor of English and of African-American studies, editor of two anthologies of Black literature, and author of short stories and a novel. According to Alice A. Deck in the *Dictionary of Literary Biography*, "in many ways Toni Cade Bambara is one of the best representatives of the group of Afro-American writers who, during the 1960's, became directly involved in the cultural and sociopolitical activities in urban communities across the country." However, Deck points out that "Bambara is one of the few who continued to work within the Black urban communities (filming, lecturing, organizing, and reading from her works at rallies and conferences), producing imaginative reenactments of these experiences in her fiction. In addition, Bambara established herself over the years as an educator, teaching in colleges and independent community schools in various cities on the East Coast." (*Contemporary Authors, New Revision Series*, Vol. 24, ed. Deborah A. Straub. Detroit: Gale Research, Inc., 1988, p. 42–44.)

Becky Birtha
(1948–   )
Fiction writer, teacher.

Becky Birtha was born in 1948 in Hampton, Virginia and grew up in Philadelphia, Pennsylvania where she now lives and teaches. Her stories and poetry have appeared in several anthologies and feminist periodicals.

Alice Childress
(1920–   )
Writer, actress, director.

Alice Childress was born in Charleston, South Carolina on October 12, 1920 to a poor and uneducated family. Unable to finish high school, Childress worked as an actor and director with the American Negro Theatre from 1940 to 1952. Her play *Trouble in Mind* won the Obie Award in 1956 for the best off-Broadway play. Another controversial play by Childress entitled *Wedding Band: A Love/Hate Story in Black and White* was produced at the University of Michigan, Ann Arbor. Her much-acclaimed novel *A Hero Ain't Nothing But a Sandwich* (1973) was named one of the Outstanding Books of the Year by the *New York Times Book Review*.

Childress was educated at Fisk University and the Radcliffe Institute for Independent Study in Cambridge, Massachusetts. She lives in New York with her second husband Nathan Woodard. She has a daughter Ila from her first marriage. The hallmarks of her craft, according to John O. Killens, are "Love, struggle, humor."[1] Childress believes that "No matter how many celebrities we may accrue, they cannot substitute for the masses of human beings. My writings attempt to interpret the 'ordinary' because they are not ordinary."[2]

NOTES
1. "The Literary Genius," in *Black Women Writers (1950–1980)* edited by Mari Evans. New York: Doubleday, 1984, p. 129
2. "A Candle in a Gale Wind" ibid, p. 112

Wanda Coleman
(1946–   )
Poet, fiction writer, scriptwriter, editor.

Wanda Coleman writes her own biographical note: "Once upon a scream a Black Woman child was born in South Central Los Angeles. Her growth to maturity was a difficult one because, by law, her parents had to give her over to the city. The city did not want her and so abused the child with its diet of rejection and hate. The internalization of these destructive elements stunted her growth, eventually crippling her, making her quite ugly. Yet there was a peculiar power in her bones and it provided her with an unusual strength. While she is yet to overcome her social limitations, she has become famous within the walls of her city. Some consult her as an oracle. Others dread her as a monster. She is all of both."

Having written more than 500 poems, Coleman is the recipient of the National Endowment for the Arts Award for Poetry, 1981–82; the Guggenheim Fellowship for poetry (1984), the California Arts Council Fellowship grant (fiction, 1989) and the 1990 Henrietta Simpson Arnow Prize for fiction by *The American Voice*. In addition to her literary output, Wanda Coleman has also given spoken word performances on cassette and compact disc.

J. California Cooper
Short story/fiction writer, playwright.

J. California Cooper was born in Oakland, California and attended various colleges. She has written four story collections: *A Piece of Mine*, 1984; *Homemade Love*, 1986; *Some Soul to Keep*, 1987; and *Some Good Friend*, 1990. She has also written a novel, *Family*, and seventeen plays, anthologized in *Center Stage*. In 1978 she was named Black Playwright of the year for *Strangers*. Among the many awards she has received are the James Baldwin Writing Award (1988) and the Literary Lion Award (1988) from the American Library Association. J. California Cooper lives in Oakland, the mother of daughter Paris Williams.

Rita Dove
(1952–   )
Poet, fiction writer, professor.

Born in Akron, Ohio in 1952, Rita Dove was educated at Miami University (Oxford, Ohio), the Universitat Tubingen (West Germany) and has received a Master's in Fine Art from the Writers Workshop at the University of Iowa. She is the recipient of several scholarships and awards including the Fulbright/Hays Scholarship, the National Endowment for the Arts Fellowship, the John Simon Guggenheim Memorial Foundation Award as well as a Portia Pittman Fellowship as writer-in-residence at Tuskegee Institute.

Rita Dove won the prestigious Pulitzer Prize for Poetry in 1987. In her prize-winning collection *Thomas and Beulah*, the title characters are modelled on the poet's grandparents.

Rita Dove lives with her husband, novelist Fred Viebahn, and daughter, Aviva, in Charlottesville.

Alice Ruth Moore Dunbar (later Dunbar-Nelson)
(1875–1935)
Fiction writer, essayist, poet, journalist, educator, suffragist, social and political activist.

Alice Dunbar-Nelson was born and received her basic education in New Orleans, a place she has immortalized in her stories and poems. She then studied at Straight University, University of Pennsylvania, Cornell and the School of Industrial Art. A teacher, historian and a sought-after lecturer, Dunbar-Nelson also contributed to several newspapers and magazines, among them *Crisis* and *Opportunity*. She helped Victoria Earle Matthews establish the White Rose Mission in New York. Her romance and marriage to celebrated poet Paul Laurence in 1898 was hailed as an Elizabeth Barrett–Robert Browning love story. However, the couple separated in

1902 and in 1916 she married journalist Robert J. Nelson. She began her *Diary* in 1921 which she continued to write until the end of 1931.

The Goodness of St. Rogue and Other Stories (1898) is the first collection of short stories to be published by an African-American woman. Her earlier book *Violets and Other Tales* (1895) contained not just fiction but poems and essays as well. The reviewers of *The Goodness of St. Rogue* hailed her use of Creole dialect, the colorful New Orleans background and the romance of simple ordinary lives. Nevertheless, the starkly realistic "Tony's Wife" appeared in this collection and plays out an observation Dunbar made in her *Diary* that "Men do like to keep women's personalities swallowed."

Jessie Redmon Fauset
(1882–1961)
Fiction writer, poet, essayist, translator, literary editor, teacher, lecturer.

After a brilliant record at Philadelphia High School for girls, Jessie Fauset became one of the first Black women to receive a scholarship to Cornell from 1901–1905. W.E.B. DuBois, whom she admired, got her a summer teaching position at Fisk University in 1904. After teaching in different high schools, Fauset got her master's degree from the University of Pennsylvania (1918–19) and became literary editor of *Crisis* in New York. Fauset wrote short stories, essays, poems, translations and reviews for *Crisis* and along with Augustus Granville Dill brought out *The Brownies Book: A Monthly Magazine for the Children of the Sun* for children between the ages of six to sixteen. In addition to her writing, Fauset lectured and travelled abroad, spending a year studying at the Sorbonne and the Alliance Francaise in Paris (1924). After she resigned from *Crisis* (1926), she resumed teaching. Married at the age of 47, Fauset lived with her husband until he died in 1958. She herself died of heart failure three years later.

Nikki Giovanni
(1943–   )
Poet, writer, activist, educator, publisher.

Born in Knoxville, Tennessee on June 7, 1943, Nikki Giovanni graduated from Fisk University in 1967. She did graduate work at the University of Pennsylvania School of Social Work in 1967 and also attended the Columbia University of Fine Arts in 1968. She began her writing career in the sixties as a revolutionary poet along with contemporaries Sonia Sanchez and Don L. Lee (Later Haki Madhubuti). As a student at Fisk, she helped found the University's Student Nonviolent Coordinating Committee (SNCC) chapter. Always proud of her Black heritage, she wanted to celebrate and affirm the positive aspects of the Black experience and established her own publishing company Nikton, Limited.

Nikki Giovanni has earned a permanent place in American literary history. She has received honorary degrees from several universities, including Fisk, Wilberforce and Ripon. Her teaching assignments have been, among others, at Rutgers, Ohio State University, and Virginia Polytechnic Institute and State University. She is a popular lecturer and the extent of her prominence can be gaged from the fact that two awards were instituted in her name in 1988: McDonald's Literary Achievement Award for poetry and the Nikki Giovanni Award for young African-American storytellers. She herself has been the recipient of several awards from the Ford Foundation (1967), National Endowment for the Arts (1968) and National Council of the Arts (1970). She has also been named Woman of the Year by *Ebony* (1970), *Mademoiselle* (1971) and *Ladies Home Journal* (1972).

Her development over the decades has been aptly summed up by Arlene Cliff-Pellow: "In the sixties, militancy characterizes her writing, in the seventies, greater introspection and attention to personal relationships: in the eighties a global outlook with a greater concern for humanity in general."[1]

NOTES

1. "Nikki Giovanni," In *Notable Black American Women*, ed. Jessie Carney Smith. Detroit: Gale Research Inc., 1992, p. 404

Maude K. Griffin
Fiction writer.
(Unable to find biographical information in the usual sources)

Angelina Weld Grimké
(1880–1958)
Poet, fiction writer, dramatist.

Born to a biracial couple, the light-skinned Angelina was named after her white great-aunt, the rebellious daughter of a wealthy slaveholder. In spite of her privileged upbringing she was aware of the problems pertaining to her race. Like Jessie Fauset, Angelina taught at the Dunbar High School, Washington D.C. Most of her poems were published in *Crisis* and *Opportunity* and her short stories in the *Colored American Magazine*. Gloria T. Hull has demonstrated in recent studies that her unpublished poems were lesbian in nature. While her poems deal with the themes of love, life, nature and death, her fiction and drama take on issues of racial oppression and social injustice, lynching in particular. When her first play *Rachel* was produced in March 1916, the program hailed it as "the first attempt to use the stage for race propaganda in order to enlighten the American people relative to the lamentable condition of ten million of colored citizens in this free Republic."[1]

In her "Remarks on Literature," Grimké sets the agenda for future generations of Black writers:

"I believe there must be among us a stronger and a growing feeling of race consciousness, race solidarity, race pride. It means a training of the youth of today and of tomorrow in the recognition of the sanctity of all these things. Then perhaps, some day, somewhere Black youth, will come forth, see us clearly, intelligently, sympathetically, and will write about us and then come into his own."[2]

NOTES
1. Jessie Carney Smith, ed. *Epic Lives*. Washington D.C.: Visible Ink Press, 1993, p. 222.
2. Carolivia Herron, ed. *Selected Works of Angelina Weld Grimké*. New York: Oxford University Press, 1991, p. 20

Frances Ellen Watkins Harper
(1825–1911)
Poet, fiction writer, abolitionist, suffragist, orator, social and moral reformer.

Frances Harper's "The Two Offers" is said to be the first short story to be published by an African-American woman. It was published in two installments in the September and October 1859 issues of the *Anglo-African*, a New York City-based journal, started as an organ for Black writing by Thomas Hamilton in January of the same year. The story deals with the theme that marriage is not the sole destiny of a woman of intelligence who can carve out several options for herself. When this story appeared, Frances Harper was already a published writer; she had a privately printed volume of prose entitled *Forest Leaves* (1845) (also known as *Autumn Leaves*, but now lost) and her *Poems on Miscellaneous Subjects* (1854), which launched her literary career. Educated in a school for free Black children, Harper had to work as a housekeeper at the age of thirteen. However, she continued to read in her spare time and was able to write an article when she was fourteen. She worked as a teacher and lecturer and married Fenton Harper, a widower, on November 22, 1860. The couple settled down on a small farm near Columbus. A daughter, Mary, was born to them. After her husband's death in 1866, Harper began a rigorous schedule of lecture tours, speaking on the subjects of slavery, racial uplift, gender equality and the evils of alcohol. Though she had written in various genres, the novel *Iola Leroy or Shadows Uplifted* is generally considered Frances Harper's most memorable work. She believed literature that could not be used "to represent, reprimand, and to revise was frivolous and useless."[1] A dedicated activist and a woman ahead of her time, Frances Harper was full of vision when she wrote:

> We may sigh o'er the heavy burdens
> of the black, the brown and white,
> But if we all clasped hands together
> The burdens would be more light.[2]

NOTES
1. Frances Smith Foster, "Frances E.W. Harper" in *African-American Writers*, ed. Valerie Smith, Lea Beachler & A. Walton Litz. New York: Charles Scribner, 1991, p. 174.
2. "The Burdens of All," in *Poems*, Philadelphia: 1900.

Pauline Elizabeth Hopkins (Sarah A. Allen)
(1859–1930)
Playwright, novelist, editor, writer, singer.

Born in Portland, Maine, Pauline Elizabeth Hopkins graduated from the Boston Girls High School. She began her writing career, composing a four-act musical play, *Peculiar Sam, or, the Underground Railroad* (1879) which was presented as *Slaves Escape, or the Underground Railroad* by the Hopkins Colored Troubadours as a member of which Hopkins received accolades for her singing. She worked as a stenographer and lectured on Black history before being hired as the literary editor of the *Colored American Magazine* which seems to be the primary vehicle for her writing. She protested against the accommodationist philosophy of Booker T. Washington and when he took over the *Colored American* in 1904, Hopkins was eased out. However, she continued to write and contribute to Black magazines and became editor of the *New Era* in 1916. Women's issues and race relations featured prominently in her fiction, plays and articles. "A Dash for Liberty" is based on a male slave narrative. In her tales of adventure, action and suspense, "she seems to combine elements of popular fiction with a more didactic intent to create stories of political and social critique."[1]

NOTES
1. Hazel V. Carby, *Reconstructing Womanhood: The Emergence of the African-American Woman Novelist*, New York: Oxford University Press, 1987, p. 145.

Kristin Hunter
(1931–   )
Fiction writer, professor.

Kristin Hunter was born in Philadelphia in 1931. She began writing as a columnist at age fourteen for *The Pittsburgh Courier*. She is married to John Lattany and tries to "integrate living as a wife and woman, as a person and a teacher with writing."[1] She has written adult novels as well as books for a young audience including the collection of short stories entitled *Guests in the Promised Land* from which "Mom Luby and the Social Worker" is taken. In an interview with Claudia Tate, Kristin Hunter says that "humor and satire are more effective techniques for expressing social statements than direct comment,"[2] as exemplified in "Mom Luby."

Kristin Hunter has taught in the English Department at her alma mater, the University of Pennsylvania, and currently lives and works in California. In addition to her teaching, Hunter contributes regularly to *Philadelphia Magazine* and other periodicals.

NOTES
1. Claudia Tate, *Black Women Writers at Work*. New York: Continuum, 1983, p. 82
2. Ibid, p. 85

Zora Neale Hurston
(1891–1960)
Fiction writer, folklorist, autobiographer, playwright, anthropologist.

After the death of her mother, Zora left her home in Eatonville, Florida at age fourteen and moved North where she worked as a maid and received her high school diploma in 1918. She attended Howard University in Washington, D.C. There she met one of her mentors, philosopher Alain Locke, who published her first short story "John Redding Goes to Sea" in *Stylus* (1921). Sociologist Charles S. Johnson, editor of *Opportunity: A Journal of Negro Life* also published her story "Spunk" in 1925. The penniless but dynamic Zora arrived in New York during the heydey of the Harlem Renaissance and became secretary and chauffeur to white novelist Fannie Hurst. During this time, she collaborated with Langston Hughes and other poets to publish the one-issue journal *Fire!*

Under the guidance of the famous anthropologist Franz Boas at Columbia University, where she continued her graduate study, Zora left for Florida to collect Black folklore which was subsequently published as *Mules and Men*. This was the first collection to be published by a Black American woman. Zora's benefactress, New York socialite Mrs. Osgood Mason helped finance the project. Even though she was now an established writer, Zora had to struggle continually to write. She died penniless and obscure in 1960, an inmate of the St. Lucie County Welfare Home in Florida. It was Alice Walker who placed a tombstone on her grave in 1973, claiming her own and other contemporary Black women writers' descent.

Nella Marian Larsen
(1891–1964)
Fiction writer, nurse.

Born to a Danish mother and a Danish West Indian father, Nella Larsen attended a small private school in California as a child and went to Fisk University in 1907–1908. After leaving Fisk, she attended the University of Copenhagen for three years. Back in the States, she completed a three year program from the Lincoln School for Nurses in the Bronx, New York and served as head nurse from 1915 to 1916 at the John A. Andrew Hospital and Nurse Training School at Tuskegee, Alabama. After serving for a year at Lincoln Hospital as an assistant superintendent of nurses, she left the field to join the New York Public Library in September, 1921 (the Countee Cullen Regional Branch) where she was in charge of the children's room in 1924. After she resigned in January 1926, she wrote *Quicksand* while recuperating from a spell of ill health. She sold the novel to Alfred A. Knopf and it subsequently won the Harmon Foundation literary award of a bronze medal and a hundred dollars. This autobiographical novel was hailed by W.E.B. DuBois as "The best piece of fiction that Negro America has produced since the heyday of Chesnutt."[1] A year later, *Passing* (1929) was published. These were the only novels Nella Larsen was to publish. She married Dr. Elmer Samuel Imes, a Black physicist in 1919. The stormy marriage ended in 1933 while Imes was teaching at Fisk. She received a Guggenheim Fellowship in 1930 which enabled her to travel in Europe to work on a novel. When she returned, the Harlem Renaissance was fading out and she had to take up nursing at Bethel Hospital to make a living. Thus she lived anonymously till her death on March 30, 1964 in New York.

"Sanctuary" was published in the January 1930 issue of *Forum*. She was charged with plagiarizing this story from Sheila Kaye-Smith's "Mrs. Adis" published in the *Century* eight years before. Defending herself, Nella Larsen wrote a letter to the editor of *Forum* saying that the story had been told to her by an old Black woman at Lincoln Hospital and Home between 1912 and 1915.

NOTES
1. "Two Novels" *Crisis* 35 (June 1928): p. 202

Paule Burke Marshall (Paule Marshall)
(1929–   )
Novelist, fiction writer, professor.

Paule Marshall was born on April 9, 1929 in Brooklyn, New York to Barbadian immigrants. She graduated from high school in 1949 and majored in English literature, earning her bachelor's degree in 1953 from Brooklyn College. Two years later she entered graduate school at Hunter College and continued to write for *Our World* magazine where she had been hired a couple of years before. While still a student she began to write her autobiographical novel *Brown Girl, Brownstones* which was completed in Barbados following her marriage in 1957 to Kenneth E. Marshall. A Guggenheim Fellowship in 1960 enabled her to complete a collection of novellas *Soul Clap Hands and Sing* which she dedicated to her only child Eran-Keith. She married Nourry Menard, a Haitian businessman, in 1970.

Paule Marshall has received several awards, including a Ford Foundation grant (1964–65), National Endowment for the Arts grant (1967–68) and the Before Columbus American Book Award for her novel *Praisesong for the Widow* (1984). Marshall has been involved with the Association of Artists for Freedom in the sixties and is also a member of the Harlem Writers Guild. In addition to being a free-lance writer, she has taught at the Universities of Columbia and Cornell, among others. She is currently on the faculty at Virginia Commonwealth University in Richmond, Virginia.

Victoria Earle Matthews
(1861–1907)
Fiction writer, journalist, social reformer, club woman, women's organizer.

Unlike Frances Ellen Watkins Harper, who was born free, Victoria Earle was born to slave parents. The opportunity to attend school presented itself only when her mother, who had escaped slavery, returned south eight years later for her children. An illness in the family forced Victoria to leave school and work as a domestic, but her voracious reading habits ensured her future success as a journalist and writer. She wrote for the *Times* and *Herald* as well as Black newspapers such as the *Boston Advocate* and *A.M.E. Church Review*. In fact, I. Garland Penn records in *The Afro-American Press and its Editors* (1969) that "No other Afro-American woman was so eagerly sought after for stories and articles of a general news character, by the magazines and papers of the whites...."[1]

President of the Women's Loyal Union, Victoria Earle Matthews was also actively involved with the National Federation of Afro-American Women (NFAAW). She organized the White Rose Mission Industrial Association in New York to protect and provide accommodation to young women seeking employment in the city. This home had a rare collection of books by and about Blacks, a unique library predating the Schomburg Center for Research in Black Culture.

NOTES
1. qtd. in Ann Allen Shockley, ed. *Afro-American Women Writers 1746–1933*. New York: Meridian, 1989, p. 182.

Annie McCary
(Unable to find biographical information in the usual sources)

Terry McMillan
(1951–   )
Fiction writer.

Born in Port Huron, Michigan, the oldest of five children, Terry McMillan moved to California in 1968 to study journalism at the University of California, Berkeley. It was there, in a workshop led by Ishmael Reed, that she discovered her writing talents.

After receiving her bachelor's degree, McMillan began graduate work in film at Columbia University. However, the desire to concentrate on her writing led her to quit the master's program and join the Harlem Writer's Guild. With encouragement from this group, she began her first novel, *Mama*.

Her three novels, *Mama* (1987), *Disappearing Acts* (1989) and the popular *Waiting to Exhale* (1992), which made the New York Times bestseller list in its first month, have all met with enthusiastic praise from a diverse reading public. Critics and reviewers have praised the novels for their realistic detail and powerful characterization. McMillan has received a number of grants and fellowships, including those from Yaddo and MacDowell writing colonies, PEN American Center, the Authors' League, the Carnegie Fund, the New York Foundation for the Arts and the National Endowment for the Arts. She now lives in the San Francisco Bay Area with her son Solomon.

Louise Meriwether
(1923–   )
Writer, social activist.

On May 8, 1923, Louise Meriwether was born in Haverstaw, New York. After graduating from Central Commercial High School in Manhattan, she received her bachelor's degree in English from New York University. She married Angelo Meriwether with whom she moved to Los Angeles where she began graduate study at UCLA, receiving a master's degree in journalism in 1965. Her marriage to Meriwether ended in divorce as also did her second marriage to Earle Howe. As a member of the Watts Writers Workshop, she began to submit her work to the *Antioch Review*, where she published her first two short stories "Daddy was a Number Runner" and "A Happening in Barbados."

Louise Meriwether has been an activist with the Congress of Racial Equality (CORE) as well as co-founder of the Black Anti-Defamation Association. She is the recipient of a National Endowment for the Arts grant and a Creative Art Service program grant for her writing. After moving to New York in 1970, she turned her attention to writing biographies of famous African-Americans for children. In addition, Meriwether has taught fiction at Sarah Lawrence College and the Frederick Douglass Creative Arts Center, New York.

In her writings, Meriwether's concern is with themes of racial oppression and the effects of poverty on a Black family—something she knew about first hand; her own father became a number runner to support his family in Harlem during the years of the Depression.

Gloria Naylor
(1950–   )
Novelist, essayist.

Gloria Naylor was born in New York City on January 25, 1950. After high school, she was a Jehovah's Witness missionary for seven years (1968–76). Returning to New York, she briefly studied nursing before joining Brooklyn College from where she received her bachelor's degree in English (1981). Two years later she earned a master's degree from Yale. For the next five years she lectured at several universities: Princeton, Boston, Brandeis, Cornell, among others. Naylor has won the American Book Award for first fiction for *Brewster Place* (1983), a National Endowment for the Arts Fellowship (1985), the Candace Award of the National Coalition of One Hundred Black Women (1986) and a Guggenheim Fellowship (1988).

While Naylor has written essays and screenplays, she is best known for her novels. Summing up her work, Eric L. Haralson says "what we sense, in other words, is an organic correlation between the values of tolerance, mutuality and self empowerment celebrated in Naylor's work, and the values of restraint and respect that inform her practice as an artist."[1]

NOTES

1. Valerie Smith, Lea Baechler & A. Walton Litz, eds. *African-American Writers.* New York: Charles Scribner's Sons, 1991, p. 345

Ann Petry

(1912–   )

Writer, professor, pharmacist.

Ann Lane Petry was born on October 11, 1922 in Old Saybrook, Connecticut. In high school she wrote poetry and one-act plays, but following family tradition entered the Connecticut College of Pharmacy. After graduating in 1931 she worked as a pharmacist until 1938 when she married George David Petry and moved to New York. She then worked for *Amsterdam News* (1938–194 ?) and *People's Voice* (1941–1944).

Ann Petry published her first short story "On Saturday the Siren Sounds at Noon" in the December, 1943 issue of *Crisis.* In the November, 1945 issue of *Crisis* her story "Like a Winding Sheet" appeared and was named the best American short story of 1946. Her first published story caught the attention of an editor at Houghton Mifflin. This led to her winning their Literary Fellowship of $2,400 (1945) which enabled her to complete her first novel *The Street* (1946). Like Louise Meriwether, Petry turned to writing books for young children after she had written her three novels.

In addition to her writing, Petry has been Professor of English at the University of Hawaii (1974–75). She has received honorary degrees from the Universities of Suffolk and Connecticut as well as from Mount Holyoke College. She has been a member of PEN, the Authors Guild and Authors League.

Adeline Ries

(Unable to find biographical information in the usual sources)

Sonia Sanchez

(1934–   )

Poet, playwright, activist, lecturer, professor.

Sonia Sanchez was born Wilsonia Benita Driver in Birmingham, Alabama on September 9, 1934. She received her education at Hunter College (1955) and New York University (1958). An honorary doctorate was conferred upon her by Wilberforce University (1973). Former wife of poet Etheridge Knight and mother of three children, Sonia Sanchez is now married and lives in Philadelphia where she is currently professor of English and poet-in-residence at Temple University.

Sonia Sanchez began her writing career in the militant sixties when, along with Nikki Giovanni, Don L. Lee and Etheridge Knight, she formed the Broadside Quartet of young revolutionary poets. She is known for her use of the language of the people and has used this in innovative ways to speak out against the oppression of her people. Her poems are well known for new forms and new insights. She writes ballads, letters and haikus.

She has taught in several universities, including Rutgers, University of Pittsburgh, City University of New York as well as at Amherst and Spelman colleges. She has received several awards, including a PEN Writing Award (1972) of $1000, to continue writing. She received a National Education Association Award (1977–78) and was named Honorary Citizen of Atlanta (1982) and the same year received the Tribute to Black Womanhood Award by Black students of Smith College. Other honors include a Patricia Lucretia Mott Award from Women's Way and a National Endowment for the Arts Award in 1984, the Outstanding Arts Award and the 1985 American Book Award for her book *Homegirls and Handgrenades*. She is a sponsor of the Women's International League for Peace and Freedom.

Her writing is marked by a deep sense of commitment to her people:

> I keep writing because I realize that until Black people's social reality is free of oppression and exploitation, I will not be free to write as one who's not oppressed or exploited. That is the goal. That is the struggle and the dream.[1]

NOTES

1. "Ruminations/Reflections," *Black Women Writers 1950–1980*, ed. Mari Evans. New York: Doubleday, 1984, p. 417

Charlotte Watson Sherman
(1958–   )
Poet, fiction writer, counselor.

A native of Seattle, Charlotte Watson Sherman received her bachelor's degree in social sciences from Seattle University. She has worked as a sexual abuse counselor as well as Outreach Coordinator for Seattle Rape Relief and is currently a Mental Health Specialist in Seattle. Sherman has been writing poetry and prose for several years and was selected for the King County Arts Commission Fiction Award in 1989. The Seattle Arts Commission Individual Artists Fiction Grant for 1989 was awarded to her.

Ann Allen Shockley
(1927–   )
Fiction writer, essayist, critic, compiler, newspaper columnist, librarian.

Born on June 21, 1927, Ann Allen Shockley has been an avid reader and writer since her school days at Madison Junior High School. As an undergraduate at Fisk University (1944–1948), she was a regular contributor to the *Fisk University Herald*. In

1949, she wrote a weekly Black related column in the white *Federalsburg Times*. After her marriage to William Shockley, a teacher in Delaware in 1953, she wrote a similar column in the white *Bridgeville News*. However, there was a lull in her prolific writing between 1954–1961 during which period she raised two children, got a master's in library science at the Case Western Reserve University and worked as Assistant Librarian at Delaware State College.

Shockley has received several awards for her writings—the National Short Story Award by the American Association of University Women (1962), the Atsheput Award for Literature (1981), the Martin Luther King Award (1982) for literature and the American Library Association Black Caucus Award for her work as editor on *Black Caucus Newsletter*. Her essays on librarianship are based on her extensive experience as curator of Black collections at Delaware State College (1959–1960) then at the University of Maryland, Eastern Shore Branch (1960–1969) and then at Fisk University from 1969. She was the first to write biographical sketches of relatively unknown writers, among them Pauline Elizabeth Hopkins.

Effie Waller Smith
(Unable to find biographical information in the usual sources)

Katherine Davis Chapman Tillman
(1870–?)
Fiction writer, poet dramatist, essayist, feminist.

Born in Mound City, Illinois, Katherine Davis Chapman Tillman was contributing poems, short stories and articles to periodicals while still in high school. She attended the State University of Louisville in Kentucky and Wilberforce University in Ohio and wrote prolifically on a range of subjects. Among her works were literary essays ("Afro-American Poets and their Verse," 1898), literary biographies (*Alexander Dumas Pere*, 1907), and works of special interest to women ("Afro-American Women and Their Work," 1895). Most of these were published in the *A.M.E. Church Review*, a quarterly that focused on Black culture.

Ruth D. Todd
(1878–?)
Fiction writer

Biographical information on Ruth D. Todd does not accompany "The Octoroon's Revenge" which was published in *Colored American Magazine* 4 (March 1902) nor is it available in the usual bibliographical sources. However, Elizabeth Ammons in her introduction to *Short Fiction by Black Women 1900–1920* has said that the 1900 Census identifies Ruth D. Todd as "a black servant working in the home of George M. Cooper in Philadelphia."[1] Todd was born in September, 1878 in Virginia. Her stories "The Taming of a Modern Shrew" and "The Octoroon's Revenge" are both anthologized in *Short Fiction by Black Women 1900–1920.*

NOTES

1. New York: Oxford University Press, 1991, p.10

Alice Walker

(1944–   )

Poet, fiction writer, essayist, biographer, editor, lecturer, activist.

The youngest of eight children, Alice Malsenior Walker was born in Eatonton, Georgia to Willie Lee and Minnie Tallulah (Grant) Walker who were sharecroppers and dairy farmers. Alice's brother blinded her in the right eye with a b.b. gun when she was eight. The child retreated into solitude, but the salutary effect of this mishap was that she developed an "inner" vision and sensitivity to beauty and human relationships. She first attended Spelman College, Atlanta (1961–63) and subsequently graduated from Sarah Lawrence College, New York (1965). As a Civil Rights activist, Alice met and married a Jewish lawyer Melvyn Rosenman Leventhal in 1967 and a daughter Rebecca was born to them. The couple divorced in 1977.

A versatile writer, Alice Walker has written novels, short stories and essays. It was Walker who in 1973 placed a tombstone on the unmarked grave of Zora Neale Hurston, thereby rescuing a brilliant foremother from obscurity. Her continuing commitment to the "survival and wholeness of entire people, male *and* female,"[1] make her a "womanist," a term she has coined and popularized. Her commitment as a serious writer can be surmised from a 1973 interview in which she said:

> I am preoccupied with the spiritual survival,
> the survival *whole* of my people. But beyond
> that I am committed to exploring the
> insanities, the loyalties, and the triumphs
> of black women...For me, black women are
> the most fascinating creations in the world.[2]

Alice Walker has won several awards and honors for her fiction and poetry: the National Endowment for the Arts Fellowship (1979), the Guggenheim Fellowship (1978), the prestigious Pulitzer Prize (1983) and National Book Award for her novel *The Color Purple* which was made into a successful film that brought her international renown. Walker continues to write and lives on a forty-acre farm in California.

NOTES

1. *In Search of Our Mothers' Gardens: Womanist Prose,* xi.
2. In *African American Writers,* ed. Valerie Smith, Lea Baechler & A. Walton Litz. N.Y.: Charles Scribner's Sons, 1991), p. 441.

Fannie Barrier Williams
(1855–1944)

Fannie Barrier Williams was born a free Black in New York on February 12, 1855. After graduating from school she went down south to teach, where she discovered that "life was divided into white and black lines…and that to be a colored woman is to be discredited, mistrusted and often meanly hated."[1] When she returned to New York after a few years, she married S. Laing Williams, a law graduate and the couple moved to Chicago. There she first came into the public eye with her speech on "The Intellectual Progress of Colored Women of the United States since the Emancipation Proclamation" before the World's Congress of Representative Women's Club. She became a sought-after lecturer. She had studied music at the New England Conservatory of Music in Boston and the School of Fine Arts in Washington D.C. As she had no children, Fannie Williams was able to devote much of her time to social work. She helped found the Provident Hospital with its Training School for Nurses (1891) and the Frederick Douglass Center (1905) which was a settlement project. She was a race woman who specifically took up women's issues, especially in areas of education, housing, child welfare, family and employment. She was a supporter of Booker T. Washington but felt that the scope of "industrial education" could be enlarged by including science and arts education.

Three years after her husband's death, Mrs. Williams became the first woman to serve on the Chicago Library Board in 1924. In 1926 she moved to her family home in Brockport, where she died at the age of eighty-nine.

NOTES
1. "A Northern Negro's Autobiography," (1904) In *Bearing Witness*, ed. Henry Louis Gates, Jr. New York: Pantheon Books, 1991, p. 13–14

Bibliographical Information

The Two Offers by Frances Ellen Watkins Harper (pseudonym Ellie Afton). First pub. in *Anglo-African Magazine* 9 (Vol. 1, No. 9: Sept. 1859–Vol. 1, No. 10: Oct. 1859). Reprinted in *Old Maids: Short Stories by US Women Writers*, ed. Susan Koppelman. Boston: Pandora Press, 1984. Reprinted in *Afro-American Writers, 1746–1933*, ed. Ann Allen Shockley. Boston: G.K. Hall & Co., 1988.

Aunt Lindy: A Story Founded on Real Life by Victoria Earle Matthews (pseudonym Mrs. W.E. Matthews). First pub. in *Aunt Lindy: A Story Founded on Real Life* by Victoria Earle. New York: J.J. Little & Co., 1893.

Tony's Wife by Alice Ruth Moore Dunbar-Nelson. First pub. in *The Goodness of St. Rogue and Other Stories*, New York: Dodd Mead and Co., 1899. Reprinted by College Park: McGrath Publishing Co., 1969.

A Dash for Liberty, by Pauline E. Hopkins (pseudonym Sarah Allen). First pub. in *Colored American Magazine* 3 (August 1901): 243–47. Reprinted in *Short Fiction by Black Women, 1900–1920*, intro. Elizabeth Ammons. The Schomburg Library of Nineteenth Century Black Women Writers, New York: Oxford, 1991.

The Octoroon's Revenge, by Ruth D. Todd. First pub. in *Colored American Magazine* 4 (March 1902): 291–95. Reprinted in *Short Fiction by Black Women 1900–1920*.

After Many Days: A Christmas Story by Fannie Barrier Williams. First pub. in *Colored American Magazine* 5 (Dec. 1902): 140–53. Reprinted in *Short Fiction by Black Women 1900–1920*.

The Preacher at Hill Station by Katherine Davis Chapman Tillman. First pub. in *A.M.E. Church Review* 19 (Jan. 1903): 634–43. Reprinted in *The Works of Katherine Davis Chapman Tillman,* ed. Claudia Tate. The Schomburg Library of Nineteenth Century Black Women Writers, New York: Oxford, 1991.

Guests Unexpected: A Thanksgiving Story by Maude K. Griffin. First pub. in *Colored American Magazine* 14 (Nov. 1908) 614–16. Reprinted in *Short Fiction by Black Women 1900–1920*.

The Judgment of Roxenie by Effie Waller Smith. First pub. in *Putnam's Monthly* 6 (June 1909): 309–17. Reprinted in *The Collected Works of Effie Waller Smith*, intro. David Deskins. The Schomburg Library of Nineteenth Century Black Women Writers, New York: Oxford, 1991.

Breaking the Color-line by Annie McCary. First pub. in *Crisis* 9 (Feb. 1915). Reprinted in *Short Fiction by Black Women 1900–1920*.

Mammy: A Story by Adeline F. Ries. First pub. in *Crisis* 13 (Jan. 1917): 117–18. Reprinted in *Short Fiction by Black Women 1900–1920*.

Mary Elizabeth: A Story by Jessie Fauset. First pub. in *Crisis* 19 (Dec. 1919): 51–56. Reprinted in *Short Fiction by Black Women 1900–1920*.

Goldie by Angelina Weld Grimké. First pub. in *Birth Control Review* 4 (Nov.–Dec. 1920). Reprinted in *Selected Works of Angelina Weld Grimké*, ed. Carolivia Herron. The Schomburg Library of Nineteenth Century Black Women Writers, New York: Oxford, 1991.

Isis by Zora Neale Hurston. First pub. in *Opportunity Magazine* (Dec. 1924) under the original title "Drenched in Light." Reprinted in *Spunk, Selected Stories by Zora Neale Hurston*. Berkeley: Turtle Island Foundation, 1985.

Sanctuary by Nella Larsen. First pub. in *The Forum* (Vol. LXXXIII, No. 1: Jan. 1930). Reprinted in *An Intimation of Things Distant: The Collected Fiction of Nella Larsen*, ed. Charles R. Larson. New York: Anchor Books, 1992.

Doby's Gone by Ann Petry. First pub. in *Phylon* V (1944): 361–66. Reprinted in *Miss Muriel and Other Stories* by Ann Petry. Boston: Houghton Mifflin, 1971. Reprinted by Boston: Beacon, 1989.

In the Laundry Room by Alice Childress. First pub. in *Like One of the Family: Conversations from a Domestic's Life* by Alice Childress. Reprinted by Boston: Beacon, 1986. Reprinted in *Women's Friendships*, ed. Susan Koppelman. Norman & London: Oklahoma Univ. Press, 1991.

Brooklyn by Paule Marshall. First pub. in *Soul Clap Hands and Sing* by Paule Marshall. Chatham, NJ: The Chatham Bookseller, 1961. Reprinted in *Reena and Other Stories* by Paule Marshall. New York: Feminist Press, 1983.

The Funeral by Ann Allen Shockley. First pub. in *Phylon 28* (Vol. 1: Spring 1967). Reprinted in *Out of Our Lives*, ed. Quandra Prettyman Stadler. Washington, D.C.: Howard Univ. Press, 1975.

A Happening in Barbados by Louise M. Meriwether. First pub. in *The Antioch Review* (Vol. 27, No. 3: 1968). Reprinted in *Out of Our Lives*.

Mom Luby and the Social Worker by Kristin Hunter. First pub. in *Guests in the Promised Land* by Kristin Hunter. New York: Charles Scribner's Sons, 1968.

The Library by Nikki Giovanni. First pub. in *Brothers and Sisters*, ed. A. Adoff. New York: Macmillan, 1970.

After Saturday Night Comes Sunday by Sonia Sanchez. First pub. in *Black World 20* (Vol. 5: March 1971). Reprinted in *What We Must See*, ed. Orde Coombs. New York: Dodd & Mead and Co., 1971.

Nineteen Fifty-Five by Alice Walker. First pub. in *Ms.* 9 (March 1981). Reprinted in *You Can't Keep a Good Woman Down* by Alice Walker. New York: Harcourt, Brace & Co., 1981.

The Lesson by Toni Cade Bambara. First pub. in *Gorilla, My Love and Other Stories* by Toni Cade Bambara. New York: Random House, 1972.

Kiswana Browne by Gloria Naylor. First pub. in *The Women of Brewster Place* by Gloria Naylor. New York: Viking, Penguin, 1980.

Johnnieruth by Becky Birtha. First pub. in *Lover's Choice* by Becky Birtha. Seattle: Seal Press, 1987. Reprinted in *Breaking Ice: An Anthology of Contemporary African-American Fiction*, ed. Terry McMillan. New York: Penguin, 1990.

Fifth Sunday by Rita Dove. First pub. in *Fifth Sunday: Stories by Rita Dove*. Callaloo Fiction Series (Vol. 1). Lexington, KY: Univ. of Kentucky Press, 1985. Reprinted by Charlottesville: Univ. Of Virginia Press, 1990.

The Life You Live (May Not Be Your Own) by J. California Cooper. First pub. in *Some Soul to Keep* by J. California Cooper. New York: St. Martin's Press, 1987. Reprinted in *Breaking Ice: An Anthology of Contemporary African-American Fiction*, ed. Terry McMillan. New York: Penguin, 1990.

Ma'Dear by Terry McMillan. First pub. in *Callaloo* (Vol. 10, No. 1: 1987): 71–78. Reprinted in *Breaking Ice: An Anthology of Contemporary African-American Fiction*, ed. Terry McMillan. New York: Penguin, 1990.

Emerald City: Third and Pike by Charlotte Watson Sherman. First pub. in *Killing Color* by Charlotte Watson Sherman. Corvallis: Calyx Books, 1992.

Croon by Wanda Coleman. First pub. in 1993. From work in progress *Jazz & Twelve O'Clock Tales,* to be published by Black Sparrow Press.

Editor's Biography

*A*sha S. Kanwar is an Indian woman who lives in New Delhi where she is a Professor of English at the Indira Gandhi National Open University. After a traditionally arranged marriage at eighteen, she continued her education mainly supported by various scholarships. A British Council grant enabled her to obtain her Doctor of Philosophy at the University of Sussex, England where she wrote her doctoral thesis on British Marxism and the nineteenth century novel. Asha received a Fulbright fellowship in 1992 for research on fiction by African-American women writers which she conducted during her tenure at the English department, Iowa State University, Ames, Iowa.

Asha is the author of two critical books entitled *The Novels of Virginia Woolf and Anita Desai* (New Delhi: Prestige, 1989) and *Fictional Theories and Three Great Novels* (New Delhi: Prestige, 1990). She has translated Ngugi wa Thiong'o's novel *Matigari* into Hindi (New Delhi: Atma Ram, 1991). She plans to translate stories from *The Unforgetting Heart* into Hindi so that readers in India, especially Dalits, will have access to the expressions of a people whose resistance is similar to their own.

Being part of an open university, Asha teaches literature in English through the print, audio and video media. Her video on the Victorian Age has recently won a national award.

aunt lute books is a multicultural women's press that has been committed to publishing high quality, culturally diverse literature since 1982. In 1990, the Aunt Lute Foundation was formed as a non-profit corporation to publish and distribute books that reflect the complex truths of women's lives and the possibilities for personal and social change. We seek work that explores the specificities of the very different histories from which we come, and that examines the intersections between the borders we all inhabit.

Please write or phone for a free catalogue of our other books or if you wish to be on our mailing list for future titles. You may buy books directly from us by phoning in a credit card order or mailing a check with the catalogue order form.

Aunt Lute Books
P.O. Box 410687
San Francisco, CA 94141
(415) 558-8116